THE FAE KING'S CURSE

JAMIE SCHLOSSER

The Fae King's Curse
Copyright © 2020 Jamie Schlosser
All rights reserved.

This novel is for your enjoyment only and may not be reproduced, distributed, or transmitted without permission from the author except for brief quotations in a book review. Please do not participate in or encourage piracy of copyrighted materials in violation of the author's rights. Purchase only authorized editions.

This novel is a work of fiction. All names, characters, places, and events are a product of the author's imagination. Any resemblance to actual people, living or dead, or to locations or incidents are coincidental.

Due to language and sexual content, this book is intended for readers 18 and older.

Cover design: Book Cover Kingdom
Formatting: Champagne Book Design
Editing: Amy Q Editing
Proofreading: Deaton Author Services

DEDICATION

To Amy Q. You're an amazing alpha reader and editor, and a great friend. I couldn't have done this without you.

Kirian and I were just twelve years old when I pulled him from the icy waters of the creek behind my house. As he looked in my direction with unseeing lavender eyes, I quickly realized our age was just about the only thing we had in common. He spoke with an accent, he had pointy ears, and he was so beautiful it made my heart ache. Oh, and he claimed to be a fae prince cursed by witches who stole his sight.

I thought he was crazy from hypothermia. Turns out, he wasn't, and for some reason he keeps coming back. But a day in my world is a year in his. Every time I see him, he's older. Wiser. Hotter.

Over the past six years, I've tried not to fall in love with him because the terms of the curse are clear: If he doesn't wait for his fated mate in all ways, including an innocent (or not-so-innocent) kiss, he'll be blind forever.

So when Kirian kisses me and pulls me through the portal to his realm, I make it my mission to do some damage control. It'd be a whole lot easier if he wasn't determined to marry me... And if someone wasn't trying to murder me every step of the way.

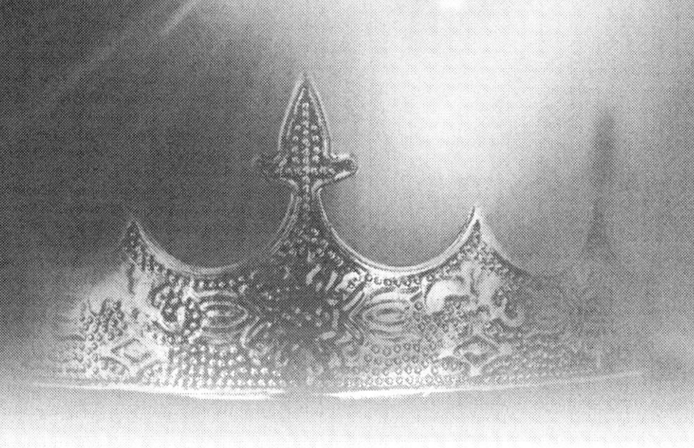

CHAPTER 1

Quinn
12 Years Old

I SIGH OUT A FRUSTRATED HUFF AS I PLOP DOWN ON THE dock. No fishing today. My pole sits pointlessly at my side, and I prop my head in my hands as I look out at the dripping branches and wet mud.

The big snow from last week has been melting, flooding the creek. Peeking through the wooden slats beneath me, I watch the rushing water that's just a few inches away from my face. Any higher and I'd be sitting in it right now.

Oh, well. I've got about a dozen other things I can do out here.

Tilting my face toward the shining sun, I close my eyes and take the pair of marbles out of my overalls pocket. They're smooth as I turn them in my palm. Round and round they go, occasionally clacking as they knock against each other.

It's a soothing habit. The kids at school don't understand why I do it. Then again, they don't seem to understand me at all. Even when I try to fit in—wear the popular clothes, say the right things—they still make fun of me.

So I don't try anymore.

Just as I open my eyes, I hear a shout. Frowning, I glance out at the woods on the other side of the creek. Left, right, behind me.

Nothing. I'm alone. Like always.

People say these woods are haunted. No one else is brave enough to come here. Rumors in town tell tales of ghosts, mysterious flashes of light, and strange sounds.

And yelling, like what I thought I heard.

I'm about to write it off as a bird when I see movement in the water.

I shoot up to my feet when I realize it's a person. A kid. Caught in the powerful current, he's coming straight for me.

"Oh, shit." The cuss word slips from my mouth without thought. It's exactly what my mom says when she realizes she forgot to switch the wet laundry to the dryer before it got musty.

When I see he's going to miss the dock by a few feet, I think fast and grab my fishing pole. Lying flat on my stomach, I extend it out to the water. "Grab on!"

His hands grope wildly, and I think he's going to miss it, but just as he's about to rush past, his fingers close around the end.

"Don't let go," I say, holding tight to the plastic while scooting away from the edge.

If I get pulled in with him, we're both toast. My parents have warned me many times about not getting in the creek when I'm alone, no matter how shallow it is. The only reason I'm allowed to come out here by myself is because I promised I wouldn't. That, and the fact that they know they can't keep me away. But seriously, what would be the point of owning twenty acres of nature if you're never going to enjoy it?

The boy is close enough to the dock to reach it, but he doesn't. I wonder if he's in shock. It's March in Wisconsin. The temperature of the water has to be forty degrees or lower.

"There's a ladder in front of you. Right there, on the side,"

I tell him, then nod encouragingly when his hand lands on the weathered wood. "Yeah. Climb up."

I shed my jacket and my hat, ready to give it to the soaked kid. But as he rolls onto his back, panting and exhausted, I realize he's not a little boy. He's probably my age.

And so freaking beautiful.

It's like time stops as I look at him.

His light brown hair is plastered to his forehead and cheeks, and his dark eyelashes glisten in the sunlight. His skin is perfection, not a freckle or a blemish on his gorgeous face. Lips the color of my mom's prized pink roses are parted as he breathes.

The thin button-up shirt is molded to his body, and although most pre-teen boys don't have much muscle definition, he does. He's wearing loose-fitting khaki pants, and I wonder if he was at church earlier. I doubt it, though. There's only one church in this small town, and there's no way I would've missed him. New people stick out like a sore thumb around here, especially if they look like movie stars.

Maybe his family just moved to Ivesdale.

His eyes flutter open, and I swallow hard. I've never seen such a color on a person before—they're lavender. It's gotta be contacts.

I think of my own appearance, and self-consciousness makes me want to run away.

But I can't.

I can't allow this guy to get hypothermia.

"Take off your shirt," I blurt out, and heat bursts over my cheeks as I shake my pink jacket and hat in his direction. "I mean, I won't look or anything. You need to get into something dry."

"Thank you, peasant." He sits up. "But that's not necessary."

Did he just call me a … peasant? No. That couldn't have been right.

"This water is—" Leaning his head to the side, he closes his eyes before opening them again. "About ten meters wide, yes?"

"About." I nod. "Why?"

"The portal needs to be twenty feet to the east," he mutters to himself. "Strike it all."

"Huh? Strike… what?" Is he speaking the same language as me? His voice has a bit of an accent, but I can't place it. It's not quite British. He just hits his T's a little hard and some of his vowels sound off.

Suddenly, I get a prickly sensation on my arm, then I feel a static shock on my wrist.

"Ow." I rub the tingling spot.

"My apologies. I shouldn't use such foul language in front of a lady. I didn't think it would affect you here."

"Affect me?" What the heck is he talking about?

"Yes. I shocked you." It's the first thing he's said that makes sense.

"I'll say. Finding you in my creek is the surprise of my life."

"Well, I'm sorry for the inconveniences I've caused you." Standing, he shakes his hair, spraying droplets all around him like a dog after a bath.

Confused, I dry my face with the sleeve of my sweatshirt. "It's no problem."

Wringing out his shirt, he faces me. "You saved me, peasant. I owe you a boon."

My jaw pops open. He seriously did call me a peasant. Rude. The pretty melodic lilt of his voice isn't so cute when he's calling me names. "Stop saying that."

"What?" He seems clueless.

"Peasant."

"Why? Are you royalty? Nobility?"

"No."

"Then you're a peasant."

I've been called worse. Much worse.

But being bullied by kids at school isn't the same as being insulted by the most perfect person I've ever seen.

"Stop." I stomp my foot.

He sniffs. "I won't take orders from a child."

I sputter. "I'm almost thirteen, and you're a kid, too. Whatever. We need to get you to the house so you can warm up. How long were you in there?" I point at the creek. "The closest neighbor isn't for half a mile, and I'm pretty sure you didn't come from the Hunts' house."

"What's a hunts house?"

"Exactly." If he doesn't know the Hunt family, then he definitely isn't from around here. "Where did you come from?"

"The Night Realm."

"Oookay." Maybe he's worse off than I thought. Are hallucinations a symptom of freezing to death? "Follow me. My mom's got hot chocolate."

"Wait."

The command stops me mid-turn, and I glance back at him. The sun shines down on his head, creating a halo effect. Geez. Could anyone be more gorgeous? It seriously isn't fair how some people get genes like that. "What?"

He extends an arm. "Guide me to land."

That's when I realize he isn't looking directly at my face. In fact, he doesn't seem to be focusing on anything in particular.

I wave a hand. His eyes don't follow. Just to be sure, I flip him the middle finger. No response.

"You can't see?" I ask, my voice soft.

His lips press together, and he grits out, "Yes, I'm blind."

"Oh." Suddenly his rudeness doesn't sting as much. "What's your name?"

"Kirian."

"I'm Quinn. Not peasant. Okay?"

"Okay. Since we're requesting titles, you can call me 'Your Majesty.'"

I bark out a laugh. "Uh, not happening."

I pace over to him and stare at the hand waiting for me. I've never held hands with a boy, and the fact that I get to touch Kirian has me giddy inside. He gets to be my first hand-holding experience, even if it is just to help him get across the dock.

The second my skin grazes his, I gasp. Because he's warm.

He's not shivering. His lips aren't blue.

That shouldn't be possible.

Once our fingers link, sliding into place like two perfectly matched pieces, my heart goes wild.

Nothing has ever felt this right, and for a selfish second, I'm glad he's blind. He can't see how plain I am. For all he knows, I'm as pretty as Savanah Welch, the most popular girl in my seventh-grade class.

It gives me a boost of confidence.

But as soon as our feet get to the dirt path, he lets go. "Please direct me to the honeysuckle field, and I'll be on my way."

Still concerned for his health, I tilt my head. "Huh?"

I didn't think anyone knew about the meadow but me. It's smackdab in the middle of the forest in a large clearing. I like going there during the summer when the flowers are in full bloom.

"That's why I'm here," Kirian replies. "My mother likes honeysuckle wine. We don't have those flowers in the Night Realm."

There are too many things wrong with his statement. "First of all, I don't know what a night realm is. Is that like a Dungeons and Dragons thing? Because I'd totally be into that. Also, it's too early in the year. The field is dried up and dead right now. And this is private property. You can't just go stealing other people's flowers."

Kirian frowns, and the surly expression only makes him more handsome. "I would've gone there by myself, but the scent took me here." Leaning forward, he sniffs me. "It's you. You smell good."

Did I think my pulse was crazy before? Now it's so fast I'm afraid I might pass out. My knees go weak, and my jacket and hat fall from my fingers.

"Thanks." My voice cracks. I clear my throat, because apparently, I have difficulty accepting a compliment. "Are you sure you don't want to go warm up at my house?"

"There's no need."

Against my better judgment, I nod. "Okay. If you really wanna go to the field, I can take you." I smile when an idea comes to me. "But I haven't cleared the trail from winter. There's a lot of sticks and stuff. You'll have to hold my hand again."

Without hesitation, Kirian reaches for me. "Onward, tour guide."

The arrogant order makes me roll my eyes.

"It's Quinn," I correct. "So, Kirian, the bridge is about two hundred feet ahead—"

"Your Majesty."

"Not calling you that."

"But it's my title. I realize you're an earthling, and this is America, which is a democracy. However, I'm still a prince in my world."

"The Night Realm," I deadpan, not sure if I want to strangle him or kiss him.

"That's right."

"You're pulling my leg."

"No, I'm not." He holds up our intertwined hands. "I'm not touching your leg."

"Not literally," I grumble, amused. "I mean, you're kidding. Making things up."

"Check out my ears as proof."

We stop, and I face him. His shoulder-length hair covers

the sides of his head, and my fingers itch to move the strands out of the way.

"Go ahead," he says, as if reading my mind.

With my free hand, I reach up and lift his damp locks, and I see what looks like an elf ear.

"It's pointy." I rub my finger over the tip.

A sudden laugh bubbles up from him, and I'm so startled by it I jump back, severing all physical contact.

He shrugs. "Tickles."

He's still smiling, and I have no words for the beauty in front of me. The grin on his face reveals straight white teeth and a dimple in his right cheek. Even half-drowned, he looks better than me on my best day.

Life really isn't fair.

"Let's go." I can't look at him anymore. It's too much. I loop my arm through his and resume our walk.

"Quinn?"

"Yeah?"

"Tell me what you see?" It's a request, not a demand.

My already-mushy heart softens even more. I can't imagine losing my sight, and a wave of sympathy makes my chest ache.

"This forest is old, so the trees are really tall. The new leaves are just starting to grow for spring. It's not all filled in yet, so I can see the sky when I look up. It's bright blue today. No clouds." As I'm describing our surroundings, I dig in my pocket and get my marbles. "There's a wild strawberry patch on the other side of the creek. In a couple months when they get ripe, they'll be scattered everywhere."

"What do you look like?"

I don't answer right away. Chewing the inside of my cheek, I think about embellishing a bit. I could tell him I have beautiful raven hair, sky-blue eyes, and peachy skin with rosy cheeks.

But I don't.

"I'm not very pretty," I admit with a sigh. "My eyes are brown, the color of mud. My hair is long, but also just plain brown. And… and my face…" I pause, because this is the worst part. "I have freckles. Not cute freckles. It's called hyperpigmentation. Basically, it's a bunch of little light-brown speckles all over my cheeks, forehead, chin, nose, and a few on my neck. I've tried everything to treat it—lotions, aloe, even prescription stuff. Nothing works. The kids at school make fun of me a lot. I don't have any friends."

Geez. All he asked for was a physical description and I treated him like my own personal therapist.

"Why don't you have friends?" he asks. "Are you contagious with some sort of disease?"

I laugh.

"No. I've just always felt different, like I don't fit in. It doesn't help that my parents don't like technology. Almost everyone I know has a cell phone, but my parents think that stuff rots your brain. We don't have cable. Sometimes I sneak movies home from the library and watch them in my room after everyone's gone to sleep," I admit, hoping Kirian doesn't tell on me. "We have one computer to share, and I'm only allowed to use it for studying. My mom offered to homeschool me, but I said no because if I do that, I'll be even more socially awkward and out of touch than I already am."

"Do you have trouble speaking to people? You seem to be doing just fine."

I give him a playful nudge. "I guess you're just easy to talk to. It's not like that with other kids my age. When someone walks by in the hallway and says *Hey, how's it going*, I'm not sure if it's a rhetorical question or if they really want me to answer. If I'm having a bad day, should I be honest? I might end up boring them with problems they didn't want to know about in the first place."

"You think very deeply."

"Yeah. People just don't understand me. Not even my own family. I'd rather be out here in the woods than at the mall, and apparently, that's not right."

"What's the mall?"

I give him a confused look. Maybe he's just as strange as I am. I might've met my match, and I'm absolutely thrilled. I think about what it would be like to show up to school tomorrow with the new boy in town as *my friend*. Mine. Everyone would be so jealous.

"You know, there's like a bunch of shops," I explain. "Clothes, jewelry, makeup. That sort of stuff."

"Oh. So, it's a bazaar."

I hike a shoulder. "Sure."

"Can I—would it be okay if I—" Kirian's stammering is adorable. It's the first hint of nervousness he's shown, and it makes me like him even more. "May I feel your face?"

"Oh." I feel like a jerk for not offering sooner. Mental note: research how to have a blind friend. "Yeah, sure."

Our hands separate, and our footsteps slow.

My lungs freeze up as I watch his hand find my shoulder. His fingers flit to my collarbone, then they move up. First, he touches my chin and my jaw. Next, my cheeks and nose. My eyebrows. I'm glad when he feels how long and thick my eyelashes are. They're my best asset.

He finishes his exploration by tracing my lips.

I think I could die happy right now.

A smirk quirks up on Kirian's face. "You should probably breathe."

Stepping back, I gulp at the air. "I don't know why I was holding my breath. That was silly."

"It's because you're in awe of my magnificence."

I can't tell if he's being serious. No one can be that full of themselves, but he does have a point. I was literally so mesmerized by him, I'd forgotten I needed oxygen to live.

"For the record," he starts, "you have very nice features. Your face is symmetrical, and your nose is close to perfection."

Blushing, I touch my nose, feeling the straight bridge and the rounded tip. "That's the nicest thing anyone's ever said to me."

It's true that, structurally, my face is great. I have full lips, a nicely shaped chin, and good cheekbones. It's my skin that's the problem.

"What's that noise?" Kirian asks, turning his ear toward me.

I glance down at my palm and stop clicking the glass balls together. "My marbles?"

"No. It sounds like someone's ringing a bell."

"Oh. My mom." Now that I'm paying attention, I hear the far-off tinkling. "I'm supposed to go home now."

"So soon?" He almost sounds disappointed.

"Come to my house with me." I grip his elbow and tug on his arm.

"I can't."

Frowning, I let go. "That sucks."

"I like it here, though," he continues, his nose wrinkling in the cutest way as he sniffs the air. "I think I'll be back."

"Tomorrow?"

He nods, but sudden panic strikes me. I don't know where he lives. What if he's homeschooled? I might never see him again, and my only chance at a friend would be gone. Sure, he's conceited and bossy, but he hasn't been mean.

"Promise?" I ask, not doing a very good job of hiding my desperation.

"If you give me something of yours—something that's important to you—I have to come back." He states it like it's an unbendable rule, and I'm crazy enough to buy into it.

Uncurling my fist, I look at the marbles. There's an identical blue swirl running through each one. I've had them for two years. I carry them at all times, and they calm me when I'm feeling stressed. I guess you could say they're pretty important to me.

I take a deep breath before handing him one. "These two are a pair. They're always together. I'd be devastated if I lost it."

"I'll return with it tomorrow. Meet me here."

"Okay." I start to turn away, but then I remember he can't see where he's going. "How are you going to get home?"

He smiles. "Magic."

The bell is ringing louder now, and I can picture my mom getting all red in the face as she frantically waves it harder. She gets worried when I don't come back right away.

Giving Kirian one last lingering look, I start jogging back to the dock. I'm almost there when I glance over my shoulder.

I stumble. Because he's not standing where I left him. Not on the trail, not in the trees, not in the creek.

"Kirian?" Hopping on the balls of my feet, I roll my eyes when I say, "Your Majesty?"

No answer. Just silence, except for the sound of the rushing water.

He's just… gone.

CHAPTER 2

Kirian

THE SWEET SMELL IS ABSENT TODAY. SHE ISN'T HERE. Quinn. The girl I haven't been able to stop thinking about.

As I stand just inside the portal, the loud commotion on the other side stops me from crossing through. I hear shouts from both men and women. They're calling my name.

Strike my misfortune. I want to kick myself.

This is my fault. I should've explained who I am a little better. I get the feeling Quinn didn't believe most of the things I said, and why would she? As a general rule, humans are oblivious to the existence of faeries.

It was pure coincidence that I crossed paths with her in the first place. I'd thought I was following the honeysuckle flowers when I went through the portal, but my nose led me to Quinn instead. Icy water was an unexpected shock, and I was disoriented from being in an unfamiliar place.

Frustrated with my inability to see, I let out a growl.

My mom says I shouldn't be so hard on myself while I'm relearning how to navigate my surroundings. Besides, it was only my second time using a portal—not to mention, my first time since losing my sight.

The rustling of leaves is loud as someone walks nearby. Too close.

Disappointed, I back away from the wasted portal. My gateway to Earth. If I could see, there'd be a watery film between the two worlds. Like looking through distorted glass.

I roll the marble between my thumb and forefinger, remembering the way it was warm from Quinn's body heat when she gave it to me.

I can feel its importance. A certain heaviness lingers inside the sphere, and it reminds me of the beautiful melancholy Quinn carries with her.

I didn't think anyone could be sadder than me. But Quinn… a longing in her heart tugged at mine. There was an endearing desperation about her, and I was drawn to her transparency. Her honesty. Her compassion.

Her nervous rambling was cute, and she accepted my handicap without a hint of disdain or judgment. Just being around her made me feel normal again.

Drawing in a breath through my nose, I strain to find a stronger hint of her scent woven in with dirt and decaying leaves. But, other than that, I come up with nothing but motor exhaust, sweat, and a hint of gun powder.

Earth is an interesting mix of beauty and stench.

Suddenly, loud barking comes from right in front of me. Startled, I fall back, and the hound continues with the obnoxious sounds. Damn dogs and their sixth sense.

I have to leave, and I hate that I won't be able to see Quinn today.

I heave out a deep sigh.

Not much I can do about it. Except wait.

CHAPTER 3

Quinn

TELLING MY PARENTS ABOUT A BLIND BOY I SAW IN the woods was one of the worst decisions I've ever made.

After explaining how I met my new friend, they called the sheriff. Then the sheriff sent out a search party. No one could survive the cold, they'd said. Especially not a disabled person who was lost in the wilderness.

I'd gotten the scolding of my life for leaving a helpless person out there to die, for being so irresponsible and inconsiderate.

Yesterday, when I was supposed to be meeting up with Kirian, our land was being scoured by police who were on the hunt for a mysterious—and possibly dead—kid. They didn't find him, and no matter how many times I'd argued that Kirian seemed totally fine when I left him there, they wouldn't listen.

I finally had to tell everyone I must've fallen asleep on the dock and dreamed the whole thing.

And maybe I did. Maybe none of it was real. Or maybe the woods really are haunted.

Of course, this doesn't do anything to help my reputation of being a weirdo. The whispers at school today were off the charts.

Oh, and my nickname has been upgraded from Freckle Face to Ghost Girl. So, that's fun.

Laughs and taunts make their way to my ears as I hop off the bus at the end of our lane. I don't turn around—ignoring them is the best tactic.

Instead, I glare at the woods.

If Kirian was a hallucination or a dream, then where the heck is my other marble?

I decide to go look for it. I can retrace my steps, and possibly get some answers. Hoisting up my backpack, I trek through the trees.

I spy my fishing pole. It's still on the dock where I left it. I kick around some leaves and rocks, in search of a blue swirl.

Maybe it fell into the creek.

The old wood of the dock creaks under my sneakers as I peer into the water. The level is a little lower than it was the other day, but the current is still fast. It makes the water muddy. There's no way I'll be able to see my marble at the bottom.

"Why the shenanigans yesterday?" The voice comes from behind me.

Kirian.

Smiling, I pivot toward him, but I yelp when I see a guy at least six inches taller than the boy I met. He's wearing similar clothing, but his shoulders are broader, filling out the shirt in an attractive way. His hair is longer too, falling several inches past his shoulders.

"Where's Kirian?"

He spreads his arms. "I am he."

"Nope. Your voice is deeper than his. You're obviously older." I have to admit he looks just like him, though. "Are you his brother?"

"A day in your world is a year in mine." He holds something up in his fingers. My marble. "I've kept this safe for you for a long time. I wanted to give it back last year, but there were people and—" He wrinkles his nose and his tone is distasteful when he adds, "—hounds."

Okay, so either he's who he says he is, or I'm insane.

"Cadaver dogs," I tell him, putting a hand on my hip. "They were looking for your body."

"Apologies." He gives me a slight bow. "If our conversation hadn't gotten cut short, I would've told you I'm not human. I'm fae. And before you ask me if that's real—yes, it is. I also should've instructed you not to tell anyone about me. I was a little out of sorts that day. I'd just lost my sight the year before, and I wasn't coping very well."

I scrape the toe of my sneaker over the wood. "I'd convinced myself you weren't real."

"I am."

Just to test it again, I flip him the bird.

He tilts one of his pointy ears in my direction. "Why are you showing me your finger?"

I drop my arm. "You can see?"

He laughs. "Unfortunately, no. Still blind. Just guessing, based on how you're waving at me and how a single finger sounds when it cuts through the air. I've learned a lot about gauging movement and distance by sound and smell. For example, the way the wind glides over the closest branch." He points up. "If you were to measure it, you would find it to be about one hundred and sixty-nine centimeters from the tip of my finger. And you. Judging by the potency of your smell, you're eight and a half feet away."

Well, he's certainly honed his other senses. I discreetly sniff my shoulder. "I smell?"

He nods. "Still sweet."

I try not to let the compliment go to my head, but it does anyway. "Thanks."

"I've come a long way since we met," he boasts. "Faeries already have heightened senses, but without my sight, I can hear better than anyone in all the realms. If I'm listening for it, I can even tell facial expressions, like a smirk or when someone rolls their eyes at me."

Happy for him, I smile. Responding to me, he grins back, and I get hit with the same emotions I felt the other day—compassion, giddiness, and excitement.

Only one person has ever made me feel that way, and it's Kirian. If this guy's telling the truth, then he's still him, just older.

"Wait. So, a day here equals a year in your world?" Thinking, I look to the trees above. "That means the last time you saw me was... two years ago?"

"That's correct."

"According to time here, you were born, like, two weeks ago, but now you're older than me?"

"Right again."

"That's so weird."

Slipping my marble back into his pocket, he rocks on his heels. "Are you still willing to be my guide?"

"As long as you don't call me peasant."

"Deal." He offers me his elbow.

Closing the distance between us, I notice how much more attractive he's gotten. His cheekbones are higher, his jaw a little wider, and I feel a muscular forearm when I hook my hand around it.

We start walking in the direction of the field.

"How did you go blind?" As soon as the question flies from my mouth, I regret it. Freaking nerves. Being around Kirian very easily turns me into a bumbling idiot. "Sorry. I shouldn't have asked. It's just, you said it wasn't that long ago, and if you weren't born that way, I'm just wondering."

Much to my surprise, Kirian chuckles at my rambling. "It was a witch's curse. A whole coven of them, actually."

"Well, that's the last thing I was expecting you to say," I tell him honestly.

He pats my hand, and the gesture is a bit patronizing. His fingers are warm again, even though he isn't wearing a coat.

"There's been turmoil in my world for generations. The rival kingdoms constantly fight," he explains. "Day Realm soldiers are particularly cruel. Some of them came upon a witch's village, and the soldiers wanted retribution for a plague they caused years ago. Instead of slaughtering them, the soldiers cut out their eyes to teach them a lesson."

I gasp. The thought of an act so terrible is hard to comprehend. I don't even want to imagine it.

"That's seriously awful. How could any king allow that to happen?" I glance at Kirian's face to find a haunted expression.

"All the kingdoms regret what happened. See, the witches were more powerful than anyone knew. They retaliated, and it wasn't just the Day Realm they went after—they cursed us all. Every king and queen's firstborn child went blind, and I've been living in darkness ever since."

"How do you reverse the curse? Can it be broken? Is that a thing?"

"Yes, that's a thing, young one."

"Young one?" I don't point out that just two days ago, he was my age. Because if I'm being honest, I kind of like the nickname. "So, you have to break the curse," I conclude. "You'll get your sight back if you do."

"It's not that easy. The only way I'll ever see again is if I find my fated mate."

"What's a faded mate?"

"Fated. Meaning, soul mate. If I so much as kiss someone else, the spell will be permanent. Forever." He shrugs. "And so I wait."

"How do you know when you've found her?"

"That's the kicker. The clue the coven gave me doesn't help much. *She is marked by the sky at night, you'll know her by love at first sight,*" he recites the lines as if he's said them many times. "*Sight*. A tricky loophole. The eyes are the window to the soul. When recognizing one's fated mate, eye contact is required. I can't see her until I get my sight back, but I can't be free of the curse until I can see. It's impossible."

"Maybe when you meet her, it'll just happen."

"It's not enough to meet her. I have to consummate the bond."

"Consummate…? Ohh. Sex."

Awkward. My parents gave me 'the talk' a year ago, and it was seriously uncomfortable. My dad got all red, and my mom stuttered a whole bunch. I'm glad they told me, though. It's not like I have any friends to talk about it with.

"Yeah," Kirian sighs. "So I need to be *really* sure it's her."

"I'd say," I agree with an uncomfortable laugh. "But you haven't lost hope. There's a chance."

"Yes, there's a chance."

I'm quiet as I process his story. If he's telling the truth—and at this point, I'm just going with it—then he shouldn't be here with me. He should be out searching for his soul mate every waking minute.

A selfish part of me doesn't want that. I'm too young to be thinking about marriage and babies, but the thought of Kirian having that with someone else makes me want to hurl.

And that's just nuts. I've spent less than an hour with the guy. I should probably get to know him better before I go all *Fatal Attraction* on his ass.

"What do you miss most about being able to see?" I ask as we pass my treehouse, thinking I should see if Kirian wants to hang out up there sometime. The place is pretty awesome. It's about twenty feet up, built onto an old maple.

"I miss the stars," he replies, pausing to let out a wistful sigh. "The sky in the Night Realm is beautiful. According to our astrologists, there are eight times more constellations than what you have here, and we have three moons."

"That does sound pretty great. I'm sorry you don't get to see it anymore."

"It's not all bad. Some good came from it, at least. For the first time in thousands of years, Night and Day are actually working together. Well, sort of. We've joined forces to hunt down the witches."

"To kill them?" I squeak out.

He shakes his head. "To offer them riches—anything they want, if they'll reverse the curse. But so far, there's no trace of them. We're pretty sure they're hiding somewhere between Dawn and Dusk."

I nod like I understand, even though sometimes the things he says don't make sense.

When we get to the bridge, I guide us to the right.

"There's a small step here. That's it," I encourage as Kirian's boot lands on the wood. "Once we get to the other side, the clearing isn't far. So, the kingdoms… what do they fight over?"

"Lots of things. Most recently, grudges over past wrongs and political disagreements. Historically, the land of Dawn and Dusk has been a great source of contention."

"Dawn and Dusk. What is that, exactly?"

"It's unclaimed territory. An enchanted strip of land between Night and Day."

He's talking about time as if it's a location.

I glance at the sky and try to imagine what a place like that would look like. "I don't understand."

Kirian shrugs. "My world isn't like yours. Here, science rules. There's an explanation for everything. It's not the way of things where I'm from. Some things just are."

"Weird." I shake my head. "What's so great about this place? People are willing to kill each other over it, so I assume it's special."

"Indeed, it is. It's a sacred place where ceremonies are performed, like weddings and coronations. It's where we bury all our dead. Certain plants grow there. Flowers and vines that can't be found anywhere else. They make healing tonics, magical potions, and wine."

"Like honeysuckle wine?"

He makes a sound of confirmation. "Yes, but the honeysuckle doesn't belong to the Night Realm, so I look for it elsewhere."

"Speaking of that, we're here." The big field is dried up from the winter. "Like I said before, it's not the right time of year for..." I trail off because Kirian steps forward.

Bending down, his fingers trail over the yellow brush. "These will work just fine."

There's a smile in his voice, and when he straightens, he holds out his arms with his palms facing the ground.

At first, nothing happens. Then I feel it. A shift in the air. A vibration under my feet.

Leaves, twigs, and stems around Kirian begin to move. They grow and twist, before turning green.

All I can do is watch, speechless, with my mouth hanging open while Kirian literally brings life to the area around us. Honeysuckle trumpets bloom, turning toward him as if they can't help but be drawn to him.

I understand how they feel.

When he's done, he drops his arms and grins.

I kind of want to fall down. Propping my shoulder against a small tree, I steady myself.

"You weren't lying about any of it," I say, dumbfounded.

"Of course I wasn't. I don't lie."

"I just wasn't sure until now."

"I inherited two powers," Kirian states proudly. "I can control the weather and nature."

Beyond impressed, I pluck a red wild strawberry near my feet and pop it into my mouth. It's sweet and perfect. The air feels warmer, and it looks like it could be the middle of June around here.

Kirian takes a small burlap bag out of his pocket. At least, it appears small until he unfolds it. And unfolds it again. And again. It gets bigger and bigger. He finally stops when it's about the size of a pillowcase.

"Entertain me while I work." Kirian gathers the honeysuckle, finding it by smell and feel before tossing it into the sack. "Do you sing?"

I scoff. "That would be a big no."

"Are you a poet?"

"No again. Oh, but I have a book. I just got it from the library."

"Read to me, please."

It's the *please* that gets me.

"Well, since you were polite about it..." Smiling, I rummage around in my backpack until my fingers close around The Lion, the Witch, and the Wardrobe by C.S. Lewis.

I'm already on the third chapter, but I remove the bookmark and start reading out loud from the beginning. As I tell a story of a magical world, I can't help but notice the parallels between fiction and fact.

The words spill from me, and Kirian and I fall into a comfortable companionship. I earn laughs when I increase the inflection of my voice with the characters' dialogue. Every now and then, Kirian tosses me a strawberry, and it tastes better, just because it came from him.

At some point, I shed my coat. As the afternoon turns into evening, the temperature rises as if we're inside a greenhouse.

The sun is setting when Kirian stops and announces, "All done."

He shuffles over to sit next to me and drops the bag between his legs. It doesn't look very full, and that must be magic, too. He cleared a lot of flowers, probably enough to fill five trash bags.

Well, he got what he came for. "You're leaving, aren't you?"

"I have to before the portal closes," he says, sounding regretful. "It's getting smaller."

"How do you know it's closing up?"

"I can hear it. Portals use a lot of magic. For one, they freeze time for me, so when I go back it'll be like I never left. But they can't stay open for long. It shrinks as the sun goes down. If I miss it, I'll be stuck here overnight until someone can come retrieve me."

"That wouldn't be a bad thing. We could spend the night in my treehouse."

"And I'd miss a year in my world." He taps the side of his head. "I don't want to lose my pointy ears."

"That would happen?"

"Probably not in a day, but eventually, if I stayed here long enough. The body adapts. Anyway, it wouldn't look good for the future King of Valora, ruler of the Night Realm of the South, to disappear for so long." He proudly thumps his chest.

"That's one heck of a title. Why not the north, too?"

"My uncle rules there. He controls the Dream Realm. Before I was born, he challenged my father for it. They almost killed each other." The way he says it is so nonchalant. "They decided instead of fighting, they'd just divide up the territory." His eyebrows furrow with a thought. "I bet my uncle regrets it, though. Since he's a king now, his son Damon was affected by the curse as well."

"It's a shame your dad and his brother don't get along."

He lifts a shoulder. "It's not any better on my mother's side.

Her brother is king of the Day Realm, but obviously, we don't have warm feelings toward him either. He has a son as well, so I have two cousins I've never met."

"Someday, when you're king, you could change it. You could make everyone get along."

He gives me a cocky smirk. "I like the way you think, young one."

"Do you have time for a snack before you go? I have pudding cups in my backpack." Snatching the bag behind me, I grope around for the two desserts and plastic spoons leftover from lunch.

I always bring extras. Not for me—for anyone who might want to share. It's sad that I go to school armed with treats, hoping to convince someone I'd be worth sitting next to in the cafeteria. Maybe I should stop doing that. I'll save all my pudding cups for Kirian.

Peeling back the film, I stick the spoon inside and hand it to him. He takes a tentative bite.

His face brightens as he makes a satisfied sound. "What flavor is this?"

"Butterscotch."

"It's really good."

"Right?" I smile before digging into my own.

We sit together among the sounds of nature while we eat our snack. Birds chirp happily as they bask in the warm clearing. A few rabbits come out to nibble on the strawberries and dandelions, and I hear the buzzing of a few insects.

Kirian's scraping up the last bit of pudding when I muster up the courage to ask, "Will you come back again?"

"Of course. I need to find out what happens next." He reaches for the book, but his hand lands on mine instead. He doesn't move it, and a thrill runs through me. "Thank you, Quinn."

Suddenly, dozens of tiny butterflies float up from the ground. They flutter around me before landing on my shoulders, my head, my arms. One even pauses at my nose, seeming to give me the lightest kiss.

I giggle.

Somehow, I know Kirian's not thanking me for the flowers. Maybe his people don't treat him as an equal because of his disability, but I couldn't care less. I think… I think it's safe to say we're friends now.

"Anytime." I flip my hand and squeeze his fingers. "I'll see you tomorrow?"

He sends me a grin. "See you next year."

CHAPTER 4

Quinn
15 Years Old

TEARS TRICKLE DOWN MY CHEEKS AS I STOMP through the woods. I wipe them away, but new hot tracks take their place. I've spent the last hour trying to get my emotions under control, but I can't wait any longer. As it is, Kirian might already be gone. Not getting to see him at all would make this day ten times shittier.

My spirits lift when I hear a twig snap to my left.

"Why are you crying?" The voice is deep, familiar, and soothing.

I sniffle. "I'm not."

"Liar." He steps closer. "You're sad. I can feel it. Besides, the grasshoppers already told me you're upset, so you might as well let me know what it's about."

"Can we just… not?" I really don't want to replay the devastating events. Plus, if Kirian finds out what happened, he'll be pissed off, too. Then we'll both be in a bad mood. So I change the subject. "I brought a book."

I hold up the hardback, but when I see the title and cover, I sheepishly set it on a nearby tree stump. I was in such a hurry to leave the house, I'd grabbed a random book off the shelf, but it's one of my mom's racy romance novels.

I'm not making that mistake again. Been there, done that. A few months ago during the summer, I didn't feel like running to the library, so I borrowed something from my mom's collection. It was—uh—educational for both Kirian and me.

"I don't feel like reading." Thoughtfully tapping his chin, Kirian circles me. "I'd rather talk."

I shake my head.

When he wants something, he's relentless. I guess that's what makes him worthy of leading an entire kingdom.

He's only a foot away from me now, and I can feel the warmth radiating from his large body. I'm used to his size now, even if standing next to him does make me feel like a little shrimp.

Within the first week of knowing each other, Kirian's childhood slipped away right before my eyes. In a matter of days, he became a strong formidable man, while I stayed the same awkward girl I'd always been.

I'll never forget the first time I saw him with a full beard. It made him look so much older. More rugged.

Today, his face is covered in short stubble. His muscles are bulky and defined, and his hair is almost waist-length. The long strands are formed into dreadlocks and decorated with shiny black beads.

Adult Kirian is breathtaking. No surprise there. Apparently, the fae stop aging at their physical peak, which is about twenty-five years. Kirian grew to a towering six and a half feet. I'm just under 5' 6", so he's an entire foot taller than me.

Putting his arms out, he goes to hug me.

I dart away. "Don't."

His lips turn down. "Since when do you hate hugs?"

"Since... now. Starting today." That's a big fat lie. I want nothing more than to melt into him, but then he'd know how ugly I am.

He pauses, listening to a sound I can't hear. "The grasshoppers tell me you're full of shit."

I almost smile.

Kirian's become a fan of human swear words.

Apparently, that first day when he said the word 'strike,' the shock I felt wasn't a coincidence. Thousands of years ago in his world, a fae wizard put a spell on the profanity. Since then, whenever someone says it out loud, it causes a rise of static electricity, leading to an unpleasant spark for anyone nearby.

Luckily, 'strike' is easily interchangeable with the F-word. Like a good friend, I've taught Kirian all about the versatile use of 'fuck.' However, sometimes when he's really pissed, he reverts back to the fae way of saying it and I end up getting shocked.

"Well, if you won't tell me what's going on, then I guess I won't tell you my news." Kirian paces in front of me, his boots rustling the fall leaves with every measured step. "Don't you want to know what it is?"

I roll my eyes. Sensing the silent movement, he smirks.

"Is it good news?" I ask hopefully. "I'd love to hear something happy."

"Ah, ah. Only if we make a deal."

Tricky fae. He knows I can't resist. Not when it comes to information about him. By now, he knows my mannerisms, my habits, and my weakness when it comes to secrets.

"You're this close to caving." Pinching his fingers together, he stops a few feet to my left.

Sometimes his ability to read me freaks me out.

"Fine," I agree with a huff. "You first, though."

A grin splits his face when he says, "I've earned my spot on the throne. I'll be crowned king within the next fortnight."

My stomach drops. "You found her? Your mate?"

I rarely ask about that anymore. In the past, curiosity has gotten the best of me. I used to question him constantly about his soul mate. Then I realized I don't want to know the answer.

Someday, he'll stop coming here.

Maybe today is the last time I'll ever see him.

I'm about to start crying again when he replies, "No."

I can't stop the whoosh of air leaving my lungs.

I shouldn't be relieved. Kirian didn't just end up being my friend—he became my *best* friend. Best friends are supposed to wish good things for each other. I should want him to fall in love and get his eyesight back.

I'm a selfish jerk. "They'll let you be king without a queen? I thought that was frowned upon."

"Frowned upon, but not illegal. The curse has made things difficult, but we can't let the kingdom suffer for it. My father is tired, and he needs a successor. I'll be a great ruler, with or without a queen."

"I know you will." Forgetting to feel sorry for myself, I smile along with him. "I'm proud of you. Congratulations."

Kirian lifts his arms again, inviting me in, and I can't resist anymore. I go to him, wrapping my arms around his torso while pressing my head to his sternum. His steady heartbeat is loud under my ear, and it's a comforting sound.

"What's this?" When he tries to stroke my hair, he finds exactly what I was wanting to hide.

"This morning—" Sniff "—on the bus, the kids behind me took turns spitting gum in my hair. I had to go home so my mom could try to get it out, but there was so much of it. The only solution was to chop my hair off. My hair was one of the only pretty things about me, and now it's gone. I'm hideous."

I burst into sobs, and my tears soak Kirian's shirt while he pets my head. The stylist tried to keep it as long as possible, but I still look like a boy.

"Those striking bastards," Kirian cusses.

Since we're so close, the strong spark from the forbidden word ignites against my cheek.

"Ouch." My hand goes up to the spot.

"Sorry, sorry, sorry." Backing up to cup my jaw, he frantically rubs my face with his thumb to take away the sting. "Tell me who these criminals are," he demands, his tone hard. "Fae hair is very precious. Damaging or stealing it is a punishable offense in my kingdom."

His rage and threats pull a genuine laugh from me. "I'm not a fae, but thanks anyway. That's not how it works here. My mom is going to talk to their moms. They might wish for an execution by the time she's done with them, though."

Kirian grunts out a dissatisfied sound as his fingers flit down to the straps of my dress. "And what are you wearing?"

"Tonight is the homecoming dance at school," I answer, miserable as I look down at the pink glitter and tulle. "I was planning to go, but I can't with my hair looking like this."

I only put on the gown to appease my mom. She spent a lot of money on it and she'd convinced herself she could talk me into going to the dance if I felt pretty.

Well, wearing a two-hundred-dollar dress only enhances how out of place my head looks on my body.

Hard pass.

Kirian clears his throat. "You were supposed to go to this ball with a... suitor?"

"A suitor?" I glance up at Kirian's pinched expression. "Oh, you mean like a date. No. No one asked me. I was just gonna show up by myself. I don't want to miss out on the fun high school stuff just because people don't like me." A fresh wave of wetness fills my eyes when I think of tonight. "I just wanted to be normal. For one night, I wanted to feel like I fit in. That's obviously not happening. Not now. Not ever. I give up. I've already got plans to ask my mom if her homeschooling offer still stands."

Kirian pulls me in for another hug. "Quinn, you won't ever be normal. You're too kind, too smart, and too beautiful to ever be lumped in with those imbeciles."

"Thanks," I say. It's the acceptable response, even if I don't agree with him.

"Milady, I would be so honored if you would allow me this dance." When he backs away and offers me his hand, his shirt sleeve rides up.

I gasp when I see a one-inch band of red blisters on his skin. "What happened to your wrist?"

He shrugs. "Iron shackle. Gia challenged me for the crown."

"Again?"

"And I won." He grins. "Again, and for the final time."

Disgusted by the cruelty of Kirian's own family, I bite the inside of my cheek to keep myself from saying something awful.

After knowing him for two and a half years, I still don't understand the way of the fae. Bloodshed is just a description of a regular Tuesday to them. They're often violent and ruthless.

I mean, his own sister used iron on him during a fight. You'd think that'd be a big no-no, considering it instantly burns them.

From the sounds of it, Gia's power hungry. She's been salivating over the possibility of taking over, but she's second in line. Kirian's the rightful heir, by birth and by strength. He's spent centuries honing his fighting skills. He's undefeated, despite having only four senses to rely on.

To sum it up, he's a badass of epic proportions.

My brother and I aren't close—that's what happens when there's a fifteen-year age gap—but I know he loves me. My parents only wanted one child. They planned it, achieved it, and thought they were done. I was the "surprise" my mother never expected at age forty-seven. She didn't even know she was pregnant with me. She just thought she'd gained weight, then one day she got some cramps and gave birth to me in the bathtub.

Sometimes I wonder if that's why she's so lenient with me. Not gonna lie, I get away with a lot. She's just too tired to stop me from running off to the woods every day.

"Gia hurt you." Pressing my lips together, I inspect the injury, careful not to touch the raw area. "This isn't right. She's your family."

"In her own way, she believes she's doing me a favor. She thinks taking my place would make it easier for me."

"Bet it really chaps her ass to get beat by a blind dude," I quip.

Kirian chuckles. "And one-handed, no less. Don't worry about me. It'll be healed by the time we're done with our dance."

I sigh. As much as I want to baby him, he's right. The big, scary fae king doesn't need me to fix anything for him.

"Okay." Awkwardly placing my hand in his, I put my other hand on his shoulder.

I don't know how to dance, and there's no music. But it doesn't matter. This is way better than any homecoming at school could ever be.

Kirian closes his eyes, and I feel his power rise. The hair on my arms stand up, and there's a prickly sensation on my scalp.

Suddenly, hundreds of fireflies blink around us, twinkling as the crickets start to chirp. Those chirps change and merge until it blends into a haunting melody.

Kirian's ability to persuade nature is an impressive power, and it never ceases to amaze me.

Now I get misty-eyed for a different reason. "It's so pretty."

"Only the best for you, young one."

I didn't think it was possible for my crush on him to get stronger, but I was wrong. Because the way he makes me feel—beautiful and worthy—is like an addicting drug I'll never get enough of.

In a soft voice I suspect he only saves for me, he teaches me the dance steps of the fae. It isn't too dissimilar from a waltz, and I catch on quickly.

Before I know it, we're moving together seamlessly. Aside from where our hands are placed, there isn't much physical contact. I'm a little disappointed about that, but it's probably for the best. Kirian doesn't need a pathetic fifteen-year-old perving on him.

Even if I totally want to.

As we sway together, I think about how much Kirian and I have learned from each other, how close we've gotten. I read books to him, we hang out in my treehouse, and he often collects the honeysuckle from the field. We eat pudding and sometimes he lets me play with his hair.

Many times, I've confided in him about the bullying at school—to which he promptly threatens to behead someone. And he's told me about the hardships in his kingdom, from the poverty-stricken peasants to the constant disputes with the Day Realm.

The peace treaty is still in place, but it's on shaky ground. Kirian hasn't gone into details, but something sketchy is happening in the Day Realm.

They still have a reason to get along, though—the curse is very much alive since none of the men have found their soul mates.

Kirian twirls me in a circle before lowering my body in a dip.

"You're my best friend," I say softly as I hover parallel with the ground.

His hand flexes on my back. I've never told him that before. I assumed he knew, but it's always nice to hear it.

He doesn't respond for several seconds, and my heart sinks because I don't think he's going to say it back.

But then he lifts me up and smiles. "And you're mine." Bowing, he ends the dance. "The portal calls. I have to go, young one."

"Take me with you." It's an impulsive request. One I haven't quite thought through. But in this moment, I mean it.

"I can't do that," Kirian replies, stroking my pixie cut. "I can only open one portal a year. That means you'd have to spend an entire twelve months in my world before you could come back to yours."

"You only get one portal a year?" That's new information. I was under the impression he could hop around to wherever he wanted. "And you use it to come here? To see me?"

"There's nowhere else I'd rather go," he says, certain.

And just like that, I forget about my hair.

CHAPTER 5

Kirian

Anxiety swarms my mind as I plunge through the portal, but calm blankets me when I catch the distinct sweet scent that only belongs to one person. Quinn is near.

Every time I visit her, I'm afraid she won't show up—that circumstances beyond my control will keep us apart. It's happened before. I can't explain why this bothers me as much as it does. I just know she makes me happy, and when I can't see her, I'm beyond disappointed.

As her footsteps come closer, the branches above tremble with excitement.

Nature loves her. The trees, the insects, the grass.

They wait for her just as I do.

I've never known a purer heart than hers. The only time I know true contentment is when I'm here.

Smiling, I reach into my pocket and close my hand around the gift I brought for Quinn. The smooth bottle is small—about the length of my palm—but it holds a powerful potion inside.

I wasn't kidding when I told her fae hair is precious, and I traded mine for hers. It took me eight months to track down the wizard who gave me my portals. In exchange for a tonic that will make Quinn's hair grow back six times as fast, I had to give him six inches of my own locks. Not that it made much of a difference to me. My hair was getting too long anyway.

"Hi," she greets me, sounding much more cheerful than yesterday.

I'm glad. I hate it when she cries. When she weeps, I get an unnerving ache in my bones. My mind fogs with bloodlust, and I crave vengeance on all who've wronged her.

"Remember when I said I owed you a boon?" I ask when she's a few feet away.

"You mean the day we met?"

"Yes."

"Yeah," she replies slowly. "But that was a long time ago. I never expected anything in return. I would've helped you anyway."

"That's not the point. I've been in your debt since then, and I finally have a way to repay you." Turning my hand over, I reveal the bottle in my palm. "This will make your hair grow back. Not right away, but fast enough that people might have questions. You have shops in your town that sell beauty tonics, yes? Maybe at the mall you speak of?"

"Yeah."

"Good. Just say you got it from there. Explain that it's made from the coconut oil humans seem to love so much."

Accepting it, she shakes the milky liquid as she inspects it. "How do you know coconut oil is popular here?"

"Damon." My cousin's knowledge of Quinn's world is more extensive than mine. "Massage it into your scalp once a day until it runs out."

"And it'll just make it longer? Like magic?"

I nod. "Exactly like magic."

She squeals. "Ohmigod, I can't believe this! This is so great. I promise I'll love you forever."

Her words make my heart jump with a delighted flutter.

She doesn't mean it. It's one of those things humans say

without thought about future consequences, but the fae take oaths very seriously.

"Quinn, what have I told you about making promises you can't keep?"

"That I shouldn't do it, especially with a fae?"

"That's right. Don't say something you can't follow through with."

I've been selective with how much I tell Quinn about my world. Rules and customs are fine, but there are aspects of Valora she's too innocent to hear about. Like the fact that Day Realm men kidnap females—both human and fae—for breeding purposes.

I also haven't told Quinn I called off the search for the witches a few years ago. It was just too dangerous. During our hunts, we kept running into bandits, rogue Day soldiers, and wild animals. It created unnecessary fights, injuries, and lives lost. The last straw was when one of my best men died in the Shadowlands. His head was severed by an unknown beast, and his family still mourns him.

"But I mean it, Kirian." Quinn's arms go around my torso as she squeezes me tight. "I'll love you forever and ever and ever."

I feel the truth to her vow, even if it the root of it is based on deep friendship. It settles in my abdomen like a warm gulp of tea.

I want to say it back, but I'm scared. Funny how a child could terrify me as much as Quinn does. And that's what she is—a kid.

Young people are impulsive and fickle. They change their minds as quickly as the wind changes course. One day, she'll grow up and see me differently. How differently, I don't know.

I just know eventually, our relationship will either progress to something more or fade away to nothing.

It's the thought of *nothing* that makes me hug her a little tighter.

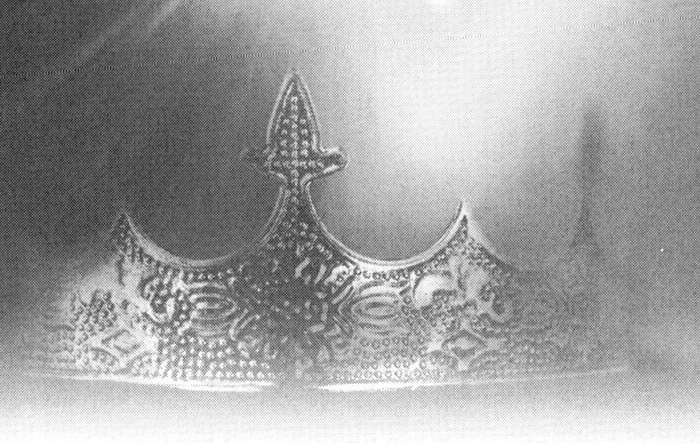

CHAPTER 6

Quinn

18 Years Old

I'M ALREADY SWEATING AS I TRUDGE TO OUR SPOT, AND it's not because of the summer heat. As I roll the marble around my palm at a rapid speed, I question myself for the hundredth time today.

Can I really go through with this?

My heart feels like it's going to break into pieces, just like the twigs snapping under my feet.

When I see Kirian standing in the honeysuckle field, I stop for a second to admire him.

His white cotton shirt stretches over his muscular back and shoulders. The pearlescent beads he had in his hair yesterday are gone, and the long locks flow freely in the breeze. The trousers he wears hug his narrow hips. And damn, that man has a great ass.

I'm going to miss it.

I'm going to miss him.

Over the years, our friendship has become so much more than I ever thought it would be. Kirian's the first thing I think about when I wake up. He's on my mind all day, and I'm not content until I'm with him. He's my last wish before I fall asleep.

He's my world.

And that's a problem.

I can't let my life revolve around someone who doesn't belong to me.

"I know you're there," he calls, grinning as he turns.

"The grasshoppers?" My throat gets tight while I close the distance between us. "Did they tell on me again?"

Shaking his head, he answers, "The scent in the breeze. Nothing in all of the realms smells as sweet as you."

Oh, he's going to make this so much harder.

Dread fills me with every step I take, and my lungs feel like they're being crushed by an invisible weight.

When I'm just a couple feet away, I straighten my spine with steely resolve. "I have something to tell you."

"What's that, young one?" He cocks his head to the side. "Your heart beats so fast."

Reaching out, he toys with a strand of my hair, which, thanks to him, still grows faster than it should, even though I ran out of the magic oil he gave me within two months.

Remembering little gestures like that sends sharp pains through my chest. Heartbreak hurts. Literally.

Swallowing hard, I rub at my sternum. "I won't be here tomorrow."

Kirian's smile falls. "Where will you be?"

"Or the day after that," I continue. "Or the day after that."

His face darkens. "What are you saying?"

"I'm leaving for college tomorrow. I waited until the last minute to tell you because I know it means we won't see each other for a long time."

"How long?"

"Well, I'll be back for Thanksgiving, which is in, like, a hundred days."

"A hundred days?" he thunders out. "That's a century for me!"

"I know, but—"

"No. I forbid it." With his firm tone, he sounds very much like the king he is. "You're not going."

I gape at him. "Excuse me, you can't do that. I'm not one of your subjects."

"Yes, I can and I am. I won't go that long without seeing you. I can't." His voice cracks. "Remember the time you had the flu a couple years ago? You were gone for eight days. I waited eight agonizing years to see you. And that bad snowstorm when you couldn't leave the house? Three years."

As much as I've tried to be here every day, it wasn't always possible. There were times when I had to miss a day or eight, and it seemed like the longer Kirian went without our meetings, the crankier he was.

"I think we both need this time apart," I reason, looking down at the ground, because I can't handle seeing his sad face. "We're holding each other back."

"Holding each other back from what?"

"From everything!" I throw my hands up. "I've spent my teenage years mooning over you instead of making friends, being in sports, and going to dances—real dances."

"You moon over me?" A half-smile appears on his face.

"I'm being serious here, Kirian."

"So am I. Don't do this to us."

I don't want to. The last thing I want is for our friendship to end. The truth is, I'd give up a lifetime of "normal" if I could be with him.

But I can't. That's not how this works. We're worlds apart.

"I love you, Kirian. I'm *in love* with you." My eyes sting. Damn it. I promised myself I wouldn't cry. "Every day, when you come back to me, I'm terrified you're going to tell me you found her—your mate. And it's going to break my heart, because it's not me. It'll happen eventually, and I know when that time comes, I'll never see you again. If you really care about me, you'll leave right now and never come ba—"

Without warning, Kirian steps forward, cradles my face in his hands, and bends down. It seems like time is in slow motion as he comes closer.

I'm frozen in place when his breath ghosts across my mouth, right before his lips press to mine.

For a glorious second, all my dreams come true.

Kirian's mouth is just as soft as I'd imagined it would be, and this isn't just a single peck. His lips massage and nip at mine as he kisses me over and over again.

Kiss.

The curse.

No.

Pushing at his chest, I separate from him with a gasp. "What did you do? Kirian, if you so much as kiss someone else..."

I don't have to finish that sentence. He knows the terms of the curse just as well as I do.

Permanent.

He'll never see again because he kissed me.

"Why?" I demand, panting. "Why would you do that?"

Gripping my shoulders, he leans down until we're nose to nose. "Because I can live without my sight, but I cannot live without you."

Oh, those words. Those beautiful, wonderful, perfect words. I want to ask him to say it again. I want to beg for another kiss.

But it's wrong. I can't let him give up something so precious for me.

I shake my head violently. "Maybe it doesn't count because it happened here."

"It counts," he says, final. "It's done."

"You can find the witches," I go on irrationally, breaking away from him to pace back and forth. "You guys have been searching for freaking ever, so you've got to run into them soon. You can ask about this situation—"

"Quinn, it's done."

I look up at his unfocused lavender eyes, and another fracture forms on my mangled heart when I think about him never seeing the stars again.

His stars.

His family. Trees, flowers, clouds, and smiling faces. All the things regular people take for granted every day.

"This doesn't change anything." My voice wavers. "I'm still leaving tomorrow."

Kirian's lip curls with a sneer, and I get the feeling he doesn't hear the word *no* very often.

His hands go to his hips and he blows out a breath. "All right."

Huh?

"All right?" I echo. If I'm being honest, I'm a bit insulted he's actually letting me go without more of a fight. "Okay, then." I blink. "I need my marble back."

For some reason, watching Kirian dig into his pocket and drop the round ball into my palm is the most painful part of all. Because it's so final.

The end.

"I'll be back here around the last week of November. Maybe I'll see you then?" My nose burns, and I'm holding back tears as I shove the reunited marbles into my pocket.

"Hug goodbye?" Kirian's face is stoic as he spreads his arms.

My chin quivers as I go to him.

Don't cry, don't cry.

Pressing my face to his chiseled chest, I roam the muscles on his back. My fingers start low, bumping over the dimples right above his seriously great ass. Then I travel up, feeling the sinew encasing his spine. I end at his shoulder blades, splaying my hands out, measuring how broad he is by touch.

Kirian and I both sigh at the same time.

Now that I know what it's like to have his lips on mine, now that I know my feelings for him aren't completely unrequited… this hug feels different than all the others. It's charged.

I don't want to let him go, and I'm rethinking my life decisions.

Would it be so bad to just stay in this town, keep my job at the ice cream shop, and spend my days waiting for a few hours with Kirian?

Yes. Yes, it would be bad. Maybe not right away, but someday. When he leaves me.

I'm pulling away from him when he says, "If a kiss doesn't count here, then it won't matter if we do it again."

The man has a point.

And I'm weak.

I don't protest as he fits a knuckle under my chin and lifts my face. I barely breathe as he moves forward. I close my eyes when our lips connect again.

His tongue darts out, parting my lips. Surprised by his pleasant taste, I gasp into his mouth. When he does it a second time, I'm ready for it. My tongue meets his, sliding and stroking.

Groaning, he deepens the kiss, slanting his mouth over mine. My hands slide up his chest and I dig my fingernails into his pecs.

He growls, the rumbling sound vibrating against my lips.

When his hands slide down my body, they stop at my ass. He cups me there, groping the soft flesh. I automatically arch my back and it makes my nipples rub against his stomach. Pleasure zings through my belly.

I'm dizzy.

I feel like I'm falling.

Then I open my eyes and realize I *am* falling. Kirian's entire body is tilting backward, and he's taking me down with him.

"Wha—" I get cut off when cool, humid air coats my skin. Light suddenly turns to dark. "Ooof." The air is knocked out of me when we both land on the ground, even though Kirian's hulking body breaks my fall.

I look to my left. To my right. Down at Kirian's grinning face.

"Welcome to your kingdom, my queen."

Speechless, my only response is a few incoherent sounds. This isn't my woods. This isn't like any world I know, and it's then that I realize what he did.

"You took me through the portal?" I rasp, pushing myself to my feet.

Disoriented, I sway as I get my bearings.

I see a night sky with the brightest stars and three moons. *Three*. One is so luminous it reminds me of a dimmed-down sun, and the light casts a silver glow over the landscape. There are rolling hills covered in perfect green grass—not a weed in sight. Mountains line the horizon in the distance, and right behind me is a deserted cobblestone road.

"Kirian," I scold. "Take me back."

"I'm afraid that isn't possible." Standing, he plants his hands on my waist and orders, "Arms around my neck."

That's all the warning I get before I hear a ripping sound and two giant shadows loom up behind him.

"Wings," I squeak out. Maybe that's why his back is so massive. He's got big ole flappers in there. They're not translucent like insect wings or feathered like a bird. They're grayish-brown and leathery, reminding me of a gargoyle or a dragon. "You can freaking fly? Why didn't you ever tell me that?"

"They don't work in realms outside of Valora," Kirian says

casually, as if we're talking about the weather. "What good would it do to tell you if I couldn't show you?"

Before I can respond, his hold on my waist tightens, and he takes off. I scream as we leave the ground, and my arms practically strangle his neck when he tips to a horizontal position.

I could fall. I might plummet to my death right now.

Shutting my eyes, I blubber a few protests. I'm not even sure what I'm saying. There's just a lot of *please* and *holy crap* and *ohmigod*.

The brute shushes me.

Shushes me. He hasn't been that rude since the day we met when he called me a peasant.

"I have to go home!" I shout in the wind.

"You are home."

Great. Rational, level-headed Kirian is gone. In his place is an oaf who literally kidnapped me.

Ever wonder what it's like to witness a fae king having a mental breakdown?

Well, this is it.

CHAPTER 7

Kirian

I'VE MADE THIS TRIP THOUSANDS OF TIMES, BUT NEVER while carrying someone. A very wiggly someone.

"Stop kicking. I don't want to drop you." I would never do such a thing, but Quinn doesn't know that.

She shrieks and squeezes my neck to the point of painful. Her legs wrap around my waist, and the warm place between her thighs rubs against my cock.

I groan. My wings falter and we dip, but I quickly right us as I flap harder.

I've been erect ever since we kissed, and I just know my cock won't be satisfied until I have her.

Over the years, I've been so careful with Quinn.

After that first week of knowing each other, we never held hands again. It seemed inappropriate, given the vast age difference.

We were affectionate in other ways. Occasional hugs were fine. Comforting pats on the back were necessary. Dancing was fun. She let me touch her face whenever I wanted, since it was the only way I could see her.

But as she got older and matured, our relationship

developed into something I'd desperately hoped for since I was a boy. Our interactions turned flirtatious. Our hugs lasted longer. Our hearts beat a little faster.

The past hundred years or so were particularly rough for me. It became difficult to hold back. I often found myself reaching for her when we were together. Not for comfort.

Just because I wanted to touch her.

Then today, she revealed her true feelings, without filter. I knew she cared for me, but I didn't realize the extent of it.

She loves me.

I have the ability to break her heart, such a fragile thing.

I refuse to be the reason for her pain, even when she's been the cause of mine. I've lived through hundreds of battles. Been gravely wounded. And even though waiting to see her every year was agony, nothing ever hurt as much as today.

When Quinn told me she was leaving, that she'd be gone for such a long time, I couldn't handle it.

I snapped.

When I kissed her, I damned myself to this curse forever.

It was worth it.

Quinn has expressed her wishes to join me in Valora for quite some time, and it feels right to have her here with me.

I don't know why it took me this long to give in, but I can recognize an ultimatum when I hear one. She pretended to be upset about her sudden departure from her home, but this is what she's wanted in the past.

I meant it when I told her I didn't need my eyes. I've been thriving without my sight for over two millennia. Blindness hasn't prevented me from becoming one of the fiercest fighters our realm has ever seen.

It won't stop me from taking Quinn as my chosen mate.

Having her by my side will only make me stronger. She can complete our kingdom.

She's silent and still now. She's hiding her face against my neck, and her warm breath puffs over my skin.

Too bad she's missing the sights.

It's been a long time since I saw the landscape, but I still remember the way the starlight glittered on the ponds, the waddling of the gnomes as they worked in the gardens, and the purple trees that seem to glow from within.

No matter. Quinn will have plenty of time to memorize my realm.

Soaring over familiar terrain, I listen for the sounds that guide me. The low humming lets me know I'm gliding over the sprite forest. The squeaking marks the windmill in a small village. A bell tower chimes as I near the palace in Delaveria.

I fly past the flapping Night Realm flag.

By the time we go over the castle gates, I'm exhausted from carrying the extra weight and Quinn is trembling.

"Be brave, young one," I say as my feet touch the stone bridge right outside the large entrance. "Come meet my family."

As soon as she's on solid ground, Quinn lets go of me and shoves my chest. "What the hell, Kirian? Seriously. What. The. Hell."

Dozens of footsteps hurry our way.

"You dare to speak to the king in such a manner?" That's Torius, the head of my guard. He's almost as big as I am. And from what I've been told, a scary-looking motherfucker, with dark dreadlocks and tattoos all over his face.

Gasping, Quinn backs up until she bumps into me.

I wrap my arms around her and set my chin on her head. "Torius, stand down. This is your future queen. Meet Quinn Prescott."

I hear the distinctive scrape of their weapons as they lay them at their feet and kneel.

"Hail, Queen Quinn."

"Oh, no." Quinn violently shakes her head. "No, no. Nope. So much nope. Queen Quinn? That just sounds ridiculous. A whole mountain of nope right there."

"Your Majesty?" Torius still speaks with his head bowed. "I don't understand all of her phrases, but we're overjoyed that you've found your fated mate. This is amazing news for the kingdom."

Quinn elbows me in the ribs, and it prompts me to say, "Fated or not, she is to be my wife." I receive another elbow jab, but she's smart enough not to contradict me in front of my soldiers. "Where would I find my parents?"

"In the dining hall, my king."

"Thank you." My shirt's shredded. Too bad, considering it's one of the few formal outfits I own. I've always wanted to look good for Quinn, but the button up isn't what I wear on a daily basis. Normally before flying, I'd take the time to remove it so it doesn't get ruined, but I was in a hurry. I tear the scraps off and toss it to Torius. "Dispose of this."

"Will do." He reaches up to press my axe and my crown into my hand as I pass him.

I set the simple band of gold on my head. It isn't flashy or overly opulent. No jewels. Just a few intricate designs carved into the precious metal, with seven dull spikes on top. I don't wear it often—just around the palace.

My axe, however, is like an extension of me. Except for my visits to Quinn and when I'm sleeping, I always have it hooked onto my belt, and it feels good to have my weapon holstered at my side once again.

"Oh, great," Quinn exclaims as I loop an arm around her shoulders and shuffle her forward. "As if I wasn't already attracted to you. Now you look like a royal version of Thor with an axe."

"Who's Thor?"

"Remember the comic books we read? The hot guy with the hammer?"

When she says another man is hot, my blood boils with jealousy. I scoff. "Yes, I remember, but I'm way better looking than him."

"How would you know?"

Her jab about my lack of visual knowledge doesn't bother me—in fact, I appreciate it. She's the only person who doesn't tiptoe around it.

I shrug. "You be the judge. Who's better looking?"

"That's not fair. I'm biased."

I stop right outside the tall palace entrance. Two men stand guard, opening the double doors for us. Before we go in, I turn to Quinn.

Running my fingers under her denim overall straps, I lower my face next to hers. "Tell me. Which one of us would you choose?"

Her breath hitches when my nose grazes her cute rounded ear.

I want her to say it. To tell me how much she wants me. Her praise is all that matters.

Vanity isn't a luxury I've had in a long time, but Quinn could make me a very arrogant man.

When I grab the metal hooks on her overalls and circle the buttons with my thumbs, my knuckles brush against her chest. I feel her nipples harden under the tank top.

Now I'm just toying with her, while also torturing myself. My shaft stiffens to the point of painful, and I fear I might erupt in my pants.

"You're both dismissed," I bark at the guards.

They don't question my order. Quick footsteps scurry away, and then Quinn and I are alone.

We've both spent so much time and energy denying our

attraction to each other, but now our feelings are unleashed. As I caress her tight buds again, I feel a crackle in the air. It isn't a palpable thing—it's more like the hair-raising sensation someone experiences when they're about to get struck by lightning.

"You," she whispers the answer. "You know I'll always choose you."

I smirk. "Likewise. And that's why you're here." Tugging her by the hand, I pull her through the doorway into the foyer. She isn't coming along easily. "Why do you drag your feet? Are you shy?"

"Kirian, we need to talk about this."

"What's there to talk about?"

"Uh, for starters—your *wife*? Are you insane?"

"When it comes to you? Apparently."

"And I can't meet your family right now."

"Why not?"

"I look like shit."

"Nonsense." I wave off her concern.

Quinn huffs as she glances around, her head shifting from left to right as she takes in the floor-to-ceiling marble in the grand entrance. Having memorized every square inch of this place, my footsteps are confident as we stride past the main staircase and turn left into the dining room.

I hear four different sets of knives and forks against the china. Good. They're all here.

As we approach, Quinn moves closer to me, angles her head toward my chest, and covers her face with her hands. I want to tell her to stand tall. If she shows signs of timidity, Gia's likely to chew her up and spit her back out.

"Father, Mother, Gia, Farrel," I address my family by their assigned seats at the end of the long table. "This is Quinn Prescott."

My mother drops her silverware with loud clatter. "A human? What have you done?"

Ignoring her panic, I go on, "Quinn, this is my father, Keryth, and my mother, Zella. My sister, Gia and her mate, Farrel."

"You know our laws," Mother scolds. "You can't steal a human. This isn't the Day Realm."

"She has asked to come before." I graze my thumb down Quinn's forearm. "She was willing." A half-truth. I try not to think about her request to return her to Earth. Clearly, she couldn't have meant it.

"I'm sure," Gia says flatly, feigning boredom. "That's why she looks like she was just chased by a pack of lycans."

"Is she all right?" Father asks, ever the gentleman.

"She's fine." I give Quinn a hardy pat on the shoulder, but she doesn't stop cowering.

"You hide your face from us." Mother again. "Why?"

Quinn lets out a shuddering breath. When she turns toward them and lowers her hands, they all gasp. Even the two servants who are refilling goblets suck in a breath. Dramatic as ever, Gia spits out her drink.

I frown at their reaction. Quinn is gorgeous. I know her, inside and out. She has the softest heart I've ever encountered, and her delicate bone structure is one to be envied.

"I've never seen such skin," Gia exclaims, losing her bored façade. "So many speckles. Are they battle scars? Did someone toss a potion on your face? What caused it?"

"I was born like this," Quinn says, her voice hard. I sense a shift in her mood as she straightens her spine. I feel anger, resentment, and strength. "Gia—can I call you that? You might want to get a napkin. You have a little something dribbling down your chin."

Gia makes a sound of outrage as she dries her face. "Kirian, she can't speak to me that way."

"She can." My statement is filled with authority and an edge of warning. "She's my betrothed."

Gia's shocked into silence—a very rare occasion. Farrel is wise to stay quiet as well.

"Is she your fated mate?" The hope in my father's question is obvious.

"Does it matter?" I spread my arms. "Am I not whole, just as I am? Why does everyone else care so much about my blindness? Haven't I proven myself?"

"Kirian," Mother sighs heavily, and I can hear her lifting her hand to pinch the bridge of her nose. "This isn't about you. A human as queen… it isn't right."

"Why not? How could you, of all people, say that? After everything you've done to fight for equality—"

"For the good of our people. To better our kingdom. Strength starts at the foundation."

It's the same line I've heard from her many times.

We learned that lesson the hard way. After an uprising about fifteen hundred years ago, when my father was still king, our livelihood was threatened. We'd been dumping so much time and energy into hunting the coven, we unknowingly neglected our people. Naturally, they fought back. Our family was almost taken out by the lower-class citizens. That's what happens when forces are joined. A million peasants were no match for our army of fifty thousand. And they didn't even have to fight. No, they just quit working. Supplies stopped coming in. We ran low on coal, wood, herbs, and food.

Starving wouldn't have killed us, but it was a miserable existence.

Together, the people of our realm showed us we need to value them more, and we were able to reach an agreement. Lower taxes on the poor. School for all children, no matter their social status. Two festivals within the palace walls every year, and everyone is invited.

"Exactly," I agree with her. "No one would do a better job of maintaining unity in our realm than Quinn."

"The foundation belongs at the bottom, not the top." Gia's snobby opinion is unwelcomed.

She's lumping Quinn in with the miners and the mill workers, when the truth is, my bride-to-be is in a class all her own.

Mother makes a noise of frustration. "It's not about station either. Look at what my brother has done to the Day Realm. Do you really want them to think we're okay with their customs? Lead by example, Kirian."

I can't refute my mother's concern. King Zarid himself took an unwilling earthling as a bride. Kidnapping is a practice we condemn, so being with a human would raise questions for our people.

I'm confident that'll change once everyone sees how much Quinn and I care for one another. They'll know she's here because she loves me, not because I plucked up some random person against their will.

"Then there's the matter of the curse," Father chimes in, clearing his throat. "We realize you've been very patient—"

"Patient." I bark out a laugh, though it holds no humor. "Patient is a child waiting for the solstice. I've lived a solitary existence for over two thousand years. I've been a good ruler, I've defended our lands, and I've brought joy to our people. All while living in darkness. Don't you think I've earned the right to choose my mate?"

"What about producing an heir?"

I don't have much of an answer for that. It's uncommon for fae to be able to reproduce with someone who isn't their fated mate. That's why Gia and Farrel haven't had kids yet. It wasn't a fate match, plus Gia was too old by the time they got together. I don't know for sure, but I suspect Gia became so desperate to be queen she pursued Farrel in hopes that her chance to gain the crown would be better if she was married.

"I suppose I'll just have to live forever," I joke wryly. No one laughs, so I get serious. "It wouldn't be impossible for us to conceive."

Quinn makes a sound of protest. "Could we *not* talk about me having a baby?"

"Is it true you wanted to come to Valora?" Mother directs the question at her, gracefully changing the subject.

"I've asked Kirian to bring me a few times," she replies diplomatically.

I bite back a grin. Quinn's learned a few tricks from me. She speaks the truth without revealing my lie. She might be mad at me for bringing her here so abruptly, but she doesn't want to get me in trouble. Yes, she'll be a great queen and an even better wife.

"How old are you, dear?" Mother continues her interrogation.

"Eighteen."

"So young."

Frustrated, I grunt. "Humans mature faster than fae. Quinn's an adult."

My mother lets out a resigned sigh. "I'm aware."

"And," I go on. "I've known her since I was twelve. It's not like I just met her today."

"So, Earth is where you run off to every birthday?"

"It's your birthday?" Quinn asks sharply.

I might be in trouble. "I suppose I never mentioned that the portals were a birthday gift from a wizard."

"Nope, you left that out."

"Birthdays don't hold as much importance here. Since we live so long, it'd be silly to celebrate every single year," I tell her, even if my own annual party says differently.

Gia snickers. "Seems like she doesn't know you that well, Kirian."

"She knows me better than anyone in all of Valora." And that's the truth. In Quinn's world, I don't have to overcompensate.

Be tougher or smarter than anyone else. I can just be me, a man who likes fantasy books and board games. A faerie who carries a marble in his pocket because it belongs to a certain human girl. "You'd all do well to remember that I am your king."

I hate to play that card, but I'll do what I must. Once a king and queen abdicate the throne, they're moved to the royal council. My parents' opinion is taken into consideration, but my word is law. Whether Mother and Father agree with this union is irrelevant.

"Of course she'd want to snag the throne," Gia sneers. "But she doesn't know our ways. Our customs. Our traditions."

"She knows more than you think," I tell her.

"What are you drinking?" Quinn pipes up.

"Honeysuckle wine," Gia replies.

My woman lets out a knowing hum. "Is it good?"

"Yes."

"You're welcome."

"Excuse me?"

"I said, you're welcome. The flowers come from my field," Quinn announces, and I smile because I know where she's going with this. "I've supplied your honeysuckle for—how long did you say, Kirian?"

"Over two thousand years."

"That's right. I've never asked for anything in return, but I believe the fae custom says you owe me."

I cover my laugh with a cough. Of all the times Quinn decides to be done with people's shit, she does it in front of the royal family.

I'm proud of her.

According to the fae, if you accept a gift from someone who isn't a family member, you have to give something back in return.

Gia turns her nose up haughtily. "There's an expiration date on those gifts."

"A decade," Quinn agrees, and I know Gia can feel the weight of her debt.

I've collected honeysuckle eight out of the last ten visits to Quinn's field. Gia won't feel right until she's repaid them. Of course, my mother has consumed the wine as well. She can split the cost with my sister. Four favors apiece isn't so bad.

"The ball starts in two hours," Mother reminds me, going back to her roasted duck and potatoes.

"Fantastic." I find Quinn's hand and interlock our fingers. "Alert the staff of the event change. This is no longer a birthday gala. It's an engagement party."

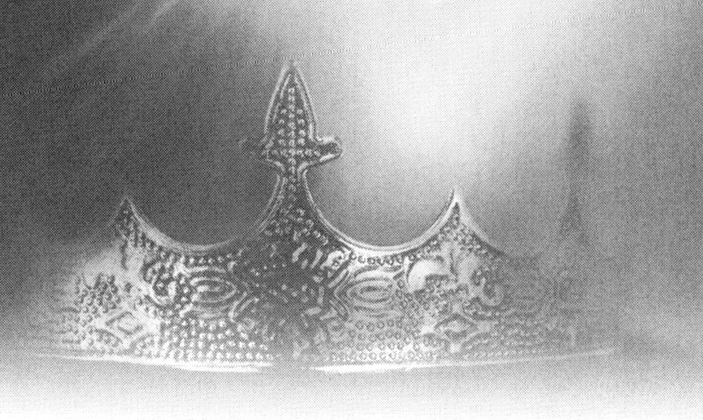

CHAPTER 8

Quinn

He's serious about this. He really thinks we're getting married.

"I didn't realize when I asked for my marble back, you were actually going to lose your marbles," I whisper-yell as Kirian pulls me down a long corridor on the second floor. "I don't know how it works here, but where I come from, you can't just caveman your way into a marriage."

Yeah, I just used caveman as a verb.

"Why not?" Kirian sounds absolutely clueless, and I'm reminded that he has zero experience when it comes to romance.

Neither do I, but as a woman, I feel like I have a general concept of how it's supposed to work.

Kirian's still shirtless, which isn't doing my brain any favors. Thankfully, he pulls a small square out of his back pocket and starts unfolding it. The dark blue material multiplies in size until it's big enough for him to tug it over his head.

Enchanted clothing. Of course. This shirt is a little different than all the ones I've seen him wear. A little more revealing. It's like a loose tank top, but the back shape is an X, exposing his muscular shoulder blades.

For his wings. The wings I didn't even know about until today.

The men who first greeted us wore similar clothing. I bet it's so they're ready to fly at any moment.

I thought I was self-conscious in my world.

Now, I realize I didn't know the meaning of the word.

Everyone here is so beautiful. Even the tough guy with the tattooed face could be in a magazine.

My appearance isn't something I worry about when I'm with Kirian.

But here I am, with the same overalls I've had since I was a preteen. I grew out of them a long time ago. In order to make them fit, I adjusted the straps and cut the legs off to make shorts. They're ratty and stained. My faded pink tank top isn't much better.

Don't even get me started on my hair. Before Kirian took me, it was pulled into a neat ponytail. Now it's a wind-blown mess.

To make matters worse, Gia actually thought my face was the result of some tragic injury. I'm still pissed about that.

"Listen," I start, trying to reel in my temper. "A little warning about this visit would've been nice. I could've presented myself a little better."

"You handled yourself fine. Really put Gia in her place."

"I don't mean that, and you know it. I look like a bum."

And his family... they were all so elegant. His father was dressed in a dark blue jacket with gold trim. His mother was in a matching gown, and it looked like something straight out of the Renaissance. Gia and Farrel were both wearing cream colors, but they were just as formal.

Kirian's face gets serious as we stop at the end of the hall. "If I'd asked you to come with me today, would you have said yes?" While he waits for my answer, he touches his hand to the doorknob. The lock must be enchanted too, because it just clicks open.

"No. Probably not," I reply. "I was trying really hard to stick to my guns."

"Then I'm glad I did what I did," he says, stubborn and unapologetic.

With a light shove to my ass—seriously, he did that on purpose—Kirian shuffles me inside. "Our bedchambers."

Using the word 'our' already? How presumptuous.

When I see the two huge rooms, a part of me thinks it wouldn't be so bad to call this place mine.

There's a fireplace to my left. It's a rustic style, with round stones going all the way up to the cathedral ceilings. The walls are exposed brick, but they've been painted white. It brightens up the room, which is much needed with the darkness outside.

Since walking into the castle, I've noticed their preference for lighter shades. Creamy marble. White walls. Lots of chandeliers.

Six wall sconces light the room, and when I look closer, I realize they're actually hanging lanterns. I wonder where the electricity comes from. There's no fire inside, but they don't appear to be plugged into the wall either. It can't be solar power, since they don't have a sun here. Star power, maybe? Is that a thing?

A dark-blue velvet couch and chairs sit in the middle of the room. There's a huge round rug with various shades of blue and yellow spun through the fibers. A stained-glass window is straight ahead, and it has the same royal blue and gold in the shape of a long, triangular flag.

The Night Realm colors.

I walk forward when I see a painting of a young Kirian mounted in a gold frame.

"I remember when you looked like that." Nostalgia sweeps

over me as I step closer to examine the picture. He's probably about fifteen here.

"I've never seen it," Kirian says from behind me. "But I've been told the artist did a good job of catching my likeness. Someday you could have one right next to mine. Or, even better, we could have one of us together."

Enough of this silliness. Playtime is over.

I face Kirian. "We need to talk."

Dread forms in my stomach for two conflicting reasons. One, I don't want to leave, but I have to. Two, I'm not sure I can get back to my world.

"Valora isn't so different from the human realm," Kirian goes on optimistically. "I think you'll like it here. The fae have adopted many of your customs. Your metric system and your calendar year, for example. English is the primary language, although figures of speech and sarcasm are still lost on many. We've taken animals from your world, so we have species you're familiar with. Like kittens. Would you like a kitten?"

"No." He's so not getting the point.

"A marriage ceremony isn't necessary—a verbal agreement is binding—but we do it anyway. The people like to see the union, and they love to celebrate after. Weddings are a big deal." He flashes me a wolfish grin before continuing, "Unfortunately, we're behind on technology. I don't think that'll bother you too much, since your parents were so against it. You won't find cars, internet, or cell phones here. There are certain citizens who can't withstand the fumes or the electronic radiofrequencies. The sprites are very delicate creatures. We do have indoor plumbing, though."

"That all sounds great, but I have a life somewhere else."

"How can that be true when I'm not there with you?" Kirian comes closer, and I can feel the heat coming off his body. "I'm your life, Quinn."

He's not trying to be cruel, but the truth of it stings. All my hobbies revolve around Kirian. Since becoming homeschooled, he's been my main source of social interaction.

My memories are so tangled up with him, I'm not sure I know how to be on my own. My college major is still undecided, and I'll probably hate living in a dorm.

But, damn it, I'm determined to try. "I'm supposed to be leaving for school tomorrow. I have plans."

"We have a university here in Delaveria." Kirian's eyebrows furrow with frustration because I'm not backing down. "You can study whatever you want. Philosophy, history, literature, art."

"The way your family looked at me." I touch my face. "They were disgusted. I don't belong here."

I can't stop picturing the way Gia wrinkled her nose. Or her perfectly perfect face, her porcelain skin, her long light-brown hair, and lavender eyes. Physically, she's like the female version of Kirian.

It's been a long time since I cared about anyone calling out my freckles. But seeing all that blinding beauty made the insult a hundred times worse than being teased by a jock who eats his own boogers.

Kirian's mom and dad are just as stunning, and they're total opposites. Zella is light, with blond hair and vibrant violet eyes. Keryth has darker features, with crystal-blue eyes, tan skin, and coal-colored hair. I have no idea how old they are, since fae take a crap ton of years to show age.

I hate to admit it, but Kirian's family is right to be concerned. He could do so much better than me.

"You... really want to be free of me?" he rasps. The pain in his voice is so heavy, it makes my chest hurt.

"You don't want to be stuck with me when you have a soul mate out there somewhere," I remind him softly, touching his arm. "What happens when you find her?"

That's my real fear. Sure, he says he wants me now, but I'm all he knows.

"I'll never love another the way I love you." He drops to a knee. Grasping my hands, he bows his head and presses my knuckles to his brow. "The first day I met you, you did so much more than pull me out of the water. You gave me something to look forward to. You didn't judge me. You became my sanctuary, my happy place. I crave your company and your attention, and I feel like I might die if I had to go the rest of my life without you."

Whoa. Talk about intense. "Why didn't you tell me how you feel sooner?"

"I didn't know you love me. I've always sensed your affection, even known you desired me, but I thought your feelings might fade with time. But after what you said earlier, I know you want to be my mate."

I chew my lip. "I've honestly never considered the possibly. In my mind, you're already spoken for."

"Fuck that, Quinn," he responds gruffly, lifting his face. "The only person who owns me is you."

Kirian's still kneeling in front of me, and the scene is surreal. I'm in a castle with the man of my dreams. He looks good enough to lick and knowing what his lips taste like only makes me want him more.

When I remember the way his tongue stroked mine, I get all tingly. My lips buzz with anticipation and I grow hot between my thighs.

Abruptly, Kirian stands, and when he picks me up, I let out a surprised squeak.

"We're not flying again, right? You gotta give a girl some warning first."

"No more flying today." Smirking, Kirian walks into the second room where I see a gigantic four-poster bed made from dark wood. The same blue velvet from the couch is draped over the top, and the mattress is covered by a white comforter and furry white pillows.

And we're headed straight for it.

Kirian dumps me on the soft surface. My butt sinks in before I feel it firm up while conforming to my shape. Like it's alive.

"What kind of mattress is this?"

"It's made from the feathers of a goose that lays golden eggs."

"You're not serious."

"I am. No pulling of your leg," he teases, grabbing my foot to unlace my sneakers. One by one, they hit the floor. His boots join them before he climbs on the bed, stretching out next to me.

Lying on his side, he props his head up with one hand. It makes his bicep bulge, and the shirt is so loose it falls down far enough for me to see his nipple.

We've never been in a bed together before. We've shared the same blanket in my treehouse, but that's not the same.

This feels intimate.

Real.

Kirian's scent is stronger here. After all, it's where he sleeps—maybe even naked. Leaning down, I discreetly sniff the pillow.

Ah. Fresh fallen leaves and crisp autumn air mixed with a hint of pine. The best smell in the world.

Kirian's fingers touch my knee, and the rough callouses on his hand tickle my skin. Holding my breath, I watch those thick digits skim up my thigh. He idly fiddles with the frayed hem of my shorts, seemingly unaware of what he's doing to me.

God, he turns me on so much.

"In the past thousand years or so, I think the only time I've missed my sight was earlier today when you got the best of Gia. To see her face…" He chuckles. "The rule about gift giving—I told you that so long ago. How did you remember it?"

My voice is quiet when I confess, "Don't you know I hang on your every word?"

Kirian's face gets serious as he hooks an arm around my waist and pulls me closer. "Marry me, Quinn."

"I can't say yes to that." Like he said—a verbal agreement is binding.

"Then don't right away. Think about it. Stay with me for a year."

I make a grumbling noise. "Do I have much of a choice?"

"It would be difficult to find a way back now," he admits. "Another portal won't be available until my next birthday."

"How will I explain that to my parents?"

"You're forgetting something very important." He gently bops me on the nose with his finger. "A day in your world is a year in mine. Mere seconds have passed there since you've been here. You'll age at the same rate you would on Earth, which means you won't look older when you go back. As far as your parents are concerned, you'll only have been gone for a night."

If being in Valora causes me to age more slowly, then that means... "You mean to tell me I could live here for, like, twenty-five thousand years before I die?"

"Probably longer. Thirty thousand years is the full lifespan of the fae."

"Will my ears get pointy?"

"Eventually, but they'll change back if you go home."

"*When* I go home."

"Whatever," Kirian huffs, sounding very human. "Come on, Quinn. What do you have to lose?"

He's right. What do I have to lose? A day. Literally. I can spend twelve months here and my family would be none the wiser. My resolve is crumbling.

Then he adds, "Please. Please, Quinn."

I can't resist when he begs, and he knows it.

"Okay, I'll stay on one condition." Kirian's eyebrows raise, and I continue, "We try to find the witches or any witch that can give you some answers."

"Fine."

He agreed way too quickly. I feel like he knows something I don't. So I tack on, "And we can't get married until we find some information of use."

A few foreign swear words burst from him. Although I don't know what he just said, I know it's in the old fae language and it isn't about rainbows.

"Don't be rude." Laughing, I push his shoulder. "When was the last time anyone searched for the witches?"

His lips twist as he thinks. "About seven hundred years ago."

"What?!" I yell, and he winces.

"I called off the mission. It was a pointless waste of resources. My men were getting injured or losing their lives venturing into dangerous lands. It wasn't worth it."

"You can't just give up." I stick a finger in his face. "Agree."

"Let me get this straight," he says. "We have to find a witch and ask about the curse. It doesn't have to be the coven that cursed me, but they have to tell me something about the curse that I didn't know before."

"Yes."

"What if they can't?"

"We need to at least try."

"And then you'll marry me." He states it like an order.

"No. Maybe. I don't know." For all I know, once he gets some new facts, he won't want me anymore. "But I'll stay with you. I mean, it's not like I have a portal laying around, so what am I gonna do?"

Kirian rubs his bottom lip with his thumb before he says, "Deal."

I get a flutter in my chest, almost like a heart palpitation.

Pressing a hand to my rib cage, I gasp, "What was that?"

"The agreement."

"We've made deals and promises before. How come it never felt like that?"

"Because you weren't here. You'll see—all kinds of magic can happen in my realm."

Oh, I bet.

His fingers move up on my thigh, slipping underneath the denim. Kirian's so close to my panties, and I want to know what it would feel like to have him tug the cotton material to the side and touch me.

But that would definitely make the curse permanent.

I clear my throat. "Speaking of magic, we probably shouldn't kiss again, just in case the other kisses didn't affect the curse."

"They did." Kirian scoots toward me, eliminating the few inches between us.

Our bodies press together, and my mind suddenly feels foggy. My nipples tighten, and my panties get damp.

"How can you be sure?" I ask, struggling to keep a rational train of thought. "Did the witches say anything else about other realms?"

Frowning, his hand travels higher, dangerously close to my ass. "No. The details are vague, just the way they meant for it to be."

"So you can't be sure."

"I'm sure I want to kiss you again."

"Kirian," I warn. "Don't."

He runs his nose over mine while massaging my hip. His fingers are so long, they wrap around to my backside, digging into the flesh. My eyelids grow heavy, my heart starts pounding, and the throbbing in my center becomes painful.

Sniffing the air, Kirian smiles wide. "I know you want me."

"Can you—can you smell—" I can't bring myself to say it.

"Your arousal? Yes."

And I'm horrified. "Is that a fae thing? Can anyone else—"

"They better not," he interrupts gruffly, like the idea of someone catching a hint of my scent is appalling to him. "Other fae don't have senses as good as mine." He breathes through his nose again and shudders. "It's times like this when I wonder if the witches did me a favor. Because you smell delicious."

Oh.

Kirian nuzzles my neck, causing goose bumps to skitter over my skin. My toes brush against his legs, my nipples graze his chest, and his stomach is warm against mine. Lifting his head, his stubble scrapes over my cheek, and the tip of his nose nudges my chin.

Inhaling sharply, he lines up our mouths.

Our lips are just an inch apart, and my suggestion that we don't kiss again is just a far-off whisper in my mind.

I'm about to say to hell with the curse when loud knocking interrupts us.

I jerk back, and the look of extreme disappointment on Kirian's face is seriously funny. My effort to keep my giggle in fails, and I snort.

"What are you laughing about?" He scowls.

I laugh again. "You're just really cute when you're sexually frustrated."

"I'm not cute." He sounds genuinely offended. "Kings aren't cute."

The rapping continues, and he heaves out a sigh before leaping off the bed. Feeling shy, I stay put. I'm not sure I'm ready for a run-in with another gorgeous fae right now.

When I hear a female voice, curiosity gets the best of me. My bare feet pad over the cold floor as I hide just inside the bedroom. Peeking around the doorframe, I try to see who it is, but Kirian's so big, he's blocking my line of sight.

"I have a dress for Quinn," the woman says. "She'll be the beauty of the ball."

"Thank you, Mother. Just leave it with me."

"She's going to need my help."

"I appreciate the offer, but it's not necessary."

"There are thirty-two buttons along the back and corsets on the sides. Not to mention her hair. Are you really up for the task of dressing a woman?"

Kirian pauses.

Although I don't love the idea of being left alone with his mom, it seems like she has good intentions while he has no clue how to work female clothing.

"It's okay." I step out of my hiding place and hope I sound brave. "I'd like to look good tonight. It'll be like the homecoming I never went to."

"Wonderful." Kirian's mom bustles in, brushing past him. He purses his lips at the intrusion, but he doesn't kick her out. "I'll just be in the bathroom getting a few things ready."

She disappears through a door at the other end of the room, and I catch a glimpse of a big white tub surrounded by four marble columns.

Kirian steps over to me. "Are you okay with this?"

"Sure, as long as she's not going to strangle me or anything." I add a forced laugh because I'm kinda joking, kinda not.

Shaking his head, Kirian chuckles. "My mother is one of the kindest souls I know. She was taken by surprise earlier when I introduced you. Don't hold it against her if she seemed cold."

He's talking like I have the power to hold anything against the former queen. Yeah, right. She intimidates the crap out of me, but I won't say that.

"We'll be fine," I tell him. "Where will you be?"

"I suppose I should be getting ready as well." He touches my face, running his fingertips over my forehead, my nose, my cheek. "I'll see you soon."

He saunters away, and then I'm alone.

Well, not alone. I'm with his mother. The woman he thinks is my future mother-in-law.

Despite grilling Kirian about his family in the past, I don't know a lot about them. Dodging questions has always been his specialty. I assumed it was because he liked staying present in the moment with me.

Now I wonder if he was keeping secrets.

I swallow hard as I enter the bathroom.

"Queen Zella." I give her a weird, uncoordinated bow. I've never curtsied in my life, and I probably look like a camel trying to hold in a fart. "It's nice of you to offer your assistance. Thank you."

"You're welcome. And you can just call me Zella." She smiles, her hands resting on the back of the ivory chair that's waiting for me.

It's in front of a mirrored vanity with brushes, combs, and barrettes lined up. There's a floor-length gown hanging from a hook on the marble-tiled wall. The silky lavender material is the same color as Kirian's eyes. It has cap sleeves and an empire waist.

"That's the most beautiful dress I've ever seen," I say honestly.

"It was Gia's. She's hoping you'll accept it as a partial payment for the honeysuckle."

"She doesn't have to give me anything." Shaking my head, I admit, "I only said what I said earlier because she hurt my feelings."

"It's our way to settle a debt. And don't let Gia's comments get to you. She's always been a bit abrasive."

As I take a seat, I look at Zella's reflection. "With all due respect, if you've come to tell me what a bad idea this is, I don't need to hear it. I already know."

She makes a sound, and I'm not sure if she's agreeing with me. From the subtle rise of her eyebrows and the incline of her head, I'd say yes. "We'll do your hair first, then we'll put on the dress."

"Sounds like a plan." I pull the hair tie out, hoping she can fix the mess on my head.

Parting my hair down the middle with a glass comb, she gently works through a few tangles I acquired during my flight with Kirian. "You have a very nice mane. It's thick and shiny. I'll definitely have enough to work with."

I warm at her compliment. "Thanks."

She lifts a chunk away from my face and peeks at my ear. "I can do braids on each side of your head to cover these. News of Kirian's betrothal will be a shock to many. It might be better to let them get used to the idea before they know you're a human."

"Won't it be obvious?"

"Not if you're dressed like a royal. The only reason I knew you're not from here is because of your interesting outfit."

I nod, suddenly grateful she's here. I'm not sure what to say about the whole engagement thing. Kirian's already announced it to several people, and I have no doubt rumors are spreading this very second. It wouldn't look good for him if it seems like I'm opposed to the marriage.

So I decide it's best to just go along with it for now.

"Did Kirian tell you about how I fell in love with his father?" Zella asks, and her friendly tone puts me at ease.

"Kinda." I don't know all the details, but Zella was originally a princess of the Day Realm, while Keryth was king here. Naturally, I can conclude it was messy.

"Our relationship was a bit of a Romeo and Juliet situation, minus the dying."

"You're familiar with Shakespeare?" My eyebrows go up.

"Oh, yes, I know your literature. We have all kinds of books in our library. Kirian seems to know a lot of stories, too. I've often wondered if he convinced the librarians to read to him, but now I suspect that's your doing?"

"Yeah. I read to him a lot. I offered to learn Braille and teach him, but he said he'd rather hear my voice instead."

Zella's eyes get misty. "You've been good to my son. I keep thinking back on all the times he came home happy after using his portal. Sometimes over the course of the year, he'd grow darker. Colder. Grumpier. But most of the time on his birthday, the shadows around him seemed to lift. Now I know that was because of you."

"He's not the only one who's benefited from our friendship. I need him just as much as he needs me. Without him, my life would've been really lonely."

"I'm glad you two have each other," she says sincerely.

I'm not sure if it's a stamp of approval, but it's something positive, so I'll take it.

Zella's fingers work at a rapid pace, and the intricate braids are done in less than five minutes. She clips them at the nape of my neck with a pearl barrette, then gets to work on the rest with what looks like a curling iron. Only, it isn't plugged in. Once my locks are wrapped tightly around the metal wand, she covers it with her hand. I feel heat on my neck, and when she releases it, there's a bouncy curl.

"That's amazing," I say, impressed.

"My special ability is fire."

Excited that I'm not completely unknowledgeable about Kirian's family, I nod. "And Gia can manipulate nature and Keryth can control the weather."

"That's right. What else did Kirian tell you?"

"Nothing huge. He didn't like to talk about violence much, so a lot of information was off-limits. I know you have a thing for sweets. Kirian says we have that in common."

"We do." Smiling, she moves on to the next curl. She does two more before she says, "I understand what it means to feel out of place here. Ending up mated to my father's enemy was unexpected, and I wasn't exactly welcomed with open arms."

"That must've been tough," I say, hoping she'll keep spilling new details.

"I'm afraid Night and Day have never gotten along. Trade deals are necessary, but it's difficult to manage when there's no trust. In order to ensure a smooth transaction, a member of each royal family was required to go along to Dawn and Dusk. Since I was the youngest of three, I was always chosen." She laughs, but there's a bitter note to the sound. "Third in line. It wouldn't matter if I was killed or captured during a trade gone wrong."

I'm not sure how to respond. That's kind of terrible. I'd be pretty pissed if my parents turned me into a sacrificial lamb.

"But the joke was on my father, because he never predicted I'd fall in love with Keryth." As Zella sighs, she smiles a little. "The second I saw him I knew he was my fated mate, and he knew I was his. That's just how it works, and you can't change destiny."

Love at first sight. It reminds me of the curse and how devious the witches were when they cast the spell. They made Kirian blind so he wouldn't be able to recognize his soul mate. So freaking cruel.

"Keryth had no children to send in his place," she continues. "Not that he would've done that. I guess he could've had his brother do it, but Keryth's the kind of ruler who leads by example. He's strong and he has a good heart."

"So you ran away with him?"

"Not right away, no. I was only seventeen when we met. Fae females don't reach maturity until twenty-one, and Keryth wanted to go about it the right way. After four years of stolen moments during trade deals, he and his men came back to my palace with me. He asked my father to agree to the mating. My father refused. After that, I was no longer allowed to go to Dawn and Dusk. In fact, I wasn't even permitted to leave my bedroom."

"What did you do?"

"*I* didn't do anything." She chuckles before her face gets serious. "Well, I cried a lot, but that's to be expected. Keryth, however, formed a plan to help me escape."

"So romantic," I say wistfully.

She nods. "Trying to keep fated mates apart is dangerous. Keryth was desperate, and desperate men don't think about consequences. He flew to my room to retrieve me and I left with him. It almost caused a war between the kingdoms. It would have if..."

The pause is heavy and long.

Swiveling in my chair, I give her a look. "You can't just stop there. I need to know how it ends."

She blinks with her unbelievably long eyelashes. "It doesn't end. It only continues. What I was about to say is—if my brother, Zarid, hadn't killed my father, I wouldn't be alive today. There'd be no Kirian or Gia."

No wonder Kirian was vague about this story. "I'm so sorry. That's terrible about your dad."

"As bad as it sounds, it was for the best. When my mother died, my father lost his fated mate and he was drowning in misery." She shrugs like it doesn't matter, but I can see the pain on her face. "Zarid still rules today. Although we don't see eye-to-eye on how to run our kingdoms, we have a mostly functional treaty."

I turn back around as she finishes the last curl, and I have to admit I look pretty, freckles and all. "Thank you for helping me. You did a great job on my hair."

"The truth is," Zella starts, "I have ulterior motives in coming here. There are things I want to say to you in private."

Oh, boy. Here it is. I knew this female bonding sesh was too good to be true.

Feeling like a kid in the principal's office, I swallow hard as Zella puts herself in front of me.

She takes a seat on the edge of the vanity, but what she says next surprises me. "I don't want you to think I'm not proud of my son. It's not Kirian's blindness that bothers us—it's the guilt. *Our* guilt. The soldiers who maimed the witches might not have belonged to the Night Realm, but the fault falls on all of us." She takes a deep breath. "Our desire to break the curse is for our own benefit, really. We just wanted to set things right and lift the burden of our blame. Kirian is beyond amazing. He's overcome so much, and we love him just the way he is."

So this meeting is because of mom guilt, not because she disapproves of me.

Relieved, I ask, "Does Kirian know how you feel?"

She looks away. "I've never told him in those exact words."

"I think you should. He'd love to hear it."

Smiling at me, she lifts my chin. She turns my face this way and that as she studies my skin. I want to squirm under her scrutiny, but I force myself to stay still.

"Freckles are rare among the fae, but I have a powder that can cover them, if you like."

I perk up. "Really? That would be great."

"This is makeup made from stardust and a few other minerals." Zella opens a compact, and I see a white iridescent substance under a fluffy ball. "It's mined from the mountains in the Dream Realm."

"Super cool." Closing my eyes, I picture myself with porcelain skin as she blots my cheeks and nose. "Is it true what Keryth said about not being able to have children?" I ask as Zella swipes the puff over my forehead. "I mean, Kirian and me?"

"Faeries aren't very fertile. Females don't start ovulating until their twenties and they stop around age forty-five. It's not impossible for a woman to get pregnant beyond that age—just very rare. It's probably for the best. We live so long, if we were able to reproduce through our entire lives, Valora would be severely overpopulated. It is possible for a chosen pair to have a child," she adds optimistically. "It's just not as common. My brother—he has a son with his chosen mate."

"That would be Kirian's cousin Zander?"

"Correct." Zella pauses her motions and makes a humming sound.

I peek at her through one eye. "What?"

"The powder isn't working."

I glance in the mirror and see she's right. There's a shimmer to my skin now, but no matter how much of the stuff she applied to my face, my freckles are still distinct as ever.

Sighing, I shrug. "At least you tried."

"Well, let's get you into your gown." She grins as she clasps her hands. "You wouldn't want to be late for your own party."

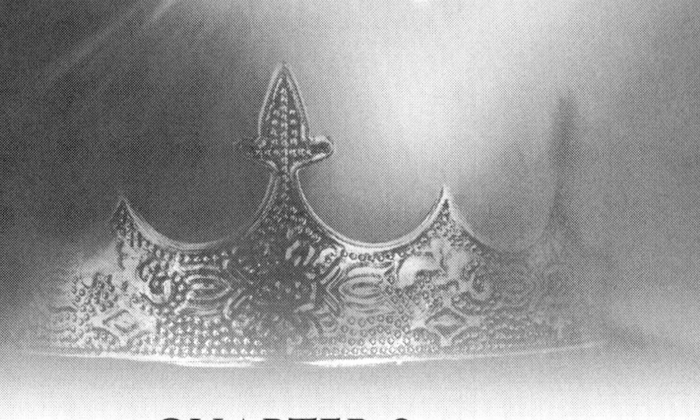

CHAPTER 9

Kirian

I feel her approaching before she enters the grand hall. Such an odd sensation. It's like there's a thousand water spiders darting about in my veins, and it's both unnerving and thrilling. Quinn's presence has always affected me, but not like this.

This is new.

The buzzing intensifies, and somehow I know she's twenty feet from the entryway on the second floor. She's passing by the hallway of portraits, probably looking at all the paintings of past and current royals.

Now she's ten feet away, approaching the pearlescent double doors. They open to a platform with a balcony overlooking the ballroom. The curved staircase is unoccupied as it waits for our next guest.

My special guest.

Five feet.

She's here.

The room goes quiet, then I hear gasps and whispers.

Who is that?

She smells like a human.

What's wrong with her face?

"Silence." My command bounces off the high ceiling as I stand from the throne.

Everyone freezes. You could hear a pin drop in here. Good.

I give a nod to the announcer standing at the balcony. His fingers are trembling, the paper crinkling in his hand as he reads what I ordered him to write.

"His Majesty presents to you, Quinn Prescott, his mate and future queen of Valora."

The ballroom erupts. Everyone's talking at once. There are some guffaws of outrage, and a few are reluctantly clapping while muttering behind their hands.

Really, though. What happened to her face?

Does it matter? He's blind. He doesn't have to look at it.

But what if she's his fated mate? Once they consummate the bond, he'll get his sight back. Then he'll be stuck with that.

She's not his soul mate. Destiny wouldn't be that cruel.

Quinn can't hear the rude murmurs, but I can.

"Enough!" The uproar dies down. "You will treat your future queen as you treat me—with the utmost respect. Anything less, and you'll be banished to the Shadowlands."

Several partygoers gulp.

I'm known as a kind and fair ruler. It's been ages since I made such a threat against my own people, but I won't tolerate less than the best for Quinn. I couldn't protect her in her world, but sure as hell can do it here.

The Shadowlands isn't a place anyone wants to end up. It's unclaimed territory—a vast enchanted cavern in the mountains on the way to the Dream Realm—and it's pitch black. Lights don't work there. My cousin Damon and myself are the only ones who can navigate it without injury or death. After all, complete darkness is what we're accustomed to.

The announcer clears his throat. "Next, I present, Her Majesty Queen Zella."

Applause helps diffuse the tension in the air.

"Well, dear," my mother whispers to Quinn as she comes to her side. "I haven't seen an entrance like this since my own introduction to the Night Realm."

"Really?" Quinn sounds hopeful.

"At least you won't light the royal gardens on fire."

"Huh?"

"Oh, nothing." Mother laughs lightly. "Long story. Let's just say I didn't make any friends that night."

They start descending the stairs together, and I'm glad Quinn has an ally. Their time together must've gone well.

Father stands next to me as we wait for our women.

"The curse is final, isn't it?" he asks low, barely even a whisper.

I give him a curt nod.

I know Quinn holds out hope that I won't be blind for eternity because of our kiss, but I've come to terms with it. I've chosen my fate.

"I'm happy for you," Father tells me. "I'm actually… relieved."

That surprises me. "Yeah?"

He lets out a long exhale. "Yes. It's time for you to live."

"Thank you." I reach out and grasp his shoulder, feeling the midnight-blue velvet under my fingers. He's wearing the same outfit I am. The suit is customary for special events, and I'm glad Quinn will get to see me in something formal for once.

As Quinn and my mother walk toward us, my father quietly gives me the rundown of what my bride-to-be looks like tonight. He's used to being my eyes when I need a description, and from the sounds of it, Quinn is breathtaking.

When she gets close, I hold my hand out to her. "May I have this dance?"

"Of course." I can hear the smile in her voice as she fits her fingers against mine, just like all the other times we've done this in her field. It's familiar and comforting for us both.

Spinning her, I tuck her against my side, keeping our fingers intertwined as we make our way to the middle of the vacant dance floor. I flex my hand over hers, digging into the softness of her waist. I love the way her body feels pressed against mine, and nothing can stop me from touching her like this ever again.

"You look beautiful." I lean down to murmur the compliment in her ear. "My father tells me so, and he doesn't lie."

"I don't think everyone else shares his opinion." Insecurity bleeds through her words as we come to a stop.

Unwilling to let go of her hand, I turn her again until she's facing me. Like a proper king, I bow, though I have reasons other than manners. When I lower my head, I let the tips of our noses brush. Quinn sucks in a breath at my nearness, but she doesn't move away.

While I'm down there, I slide my cheek against hers and whisper, "Ask me how much I care about what other people think?"

She sways slightly, and I don't miss the way she sniffs my hair. "H-how much?"

"Frankly, they can all go fuck themselves."

She loves it when I use the humans' dirty language, and it makes her snicker. The puff of her warm breath against my jaw is almost too much to bear. I've gone my entire life—my very long life—without intimacy. Now that I'm getting a taste of it, I want more.

So much more.

Overwhelmed by the sexual tension crackling between us, I straighten and clear my throat.

I'm resisting the urge to adjust the front of my pants when Quinn observes, "You said there's no electricity." The slippers on her feet make quiet scuffling sounds against the floor as she shifts around to marvel at the wall sconces and the over-sized crystal chandeliers. "How do the lights work?"

"Stardust. About twenty thousand years ago there was a meteor shower. Some of the stars fell and landed in the mountains surrounding the Dream Realm. When the rocks are ground to a fine powder and mixed with water from the Day Realm, it can glow for years."

"Star power," she whispers, chuckling. "You've been holding out on me. I thought I had a good idea of what your home is like, but it's unlike anything I've ever imagined."

Music starts up, and her hand spasms in mine, showing her nerves.

"It'll be fine," I reassure her.

"What dance are we supposed to do?"

She has nothing to worry about. She could do these steps in her sleep. "Remember the second one I taught you?"

"You mean the one with all the elbow touching and circling each other?"

I laugh. "Exactly."

"Well." She shrugs. "I guess this is my chance to impress everyone with my skills. If there's one thing I know, it's how to cut up a fae dance floor."

A harpist plucks out the beginning of the song, and a flute joins in. As we begin to move, I can feel the anxious energy running off Quinn, but I couldn't be more content.

Gracefully orbiting around each other, I murmur, "Tonight will be the first time I ever actually enjoy one of these ridiculous events."

"Yeah, what's up with that? Earlier, you said you don't celebrate birthdays, but this sure looks like a party to me."

I grunt. "Since the curse, every evening of my birthday we've had a ball under the guise that it's an annual celebration. Really, it's a ploy my parents put together. An attempt to find my mate. They invite all the nobles, thinking surely my destined partner will be amongst the females."

I've always despised it. The women who dance with me either pity me or want me for the crown. Enduring their tittering, fawning, and fake laughs is torture. I'd rather be getting poked with iron needles.

But with Quinn here to claim me, I won't have to go through that.

Thank the constellations.

"Oh, I see." Quinn's mood suddenly takes a dive. "I'm getting some pretty dirty looks right now. I don't think the women are very happy that I'm stealing you."

"Are you jealous, young one?"

"Yes," she says, straightforward and a little sad. "Every day, when you left me, you got to have your own dance. Without me. It shouldn't bother me, but it does. After hanging out with me, you came here and searched for your mate."

"You're wrong about two things—first, yes, it should bother you. If you were okay with me being with someone else, I'd be insulted. I'm yours and you're mine. Period. Second, I didn't search for anyone. The only reason I went along with it was to appease my parents and make the people happy. Look around. Do you see the smiling faces? The laughter? They're not here for me. They never were. They come for the drinks and the music."

"I can't believe that's true. I know it's been a long time since you were able to look in a mirror, but, Kirian... you're so handsome it hurts."

Male pride swells within me. I don't know if what she says is true, but her opinion is all that matters. "Fae females are extremely vain. They don't want to be with someone who can't appreciate their outer beauty."

"They are gorgeous," Quinn agrees, smoothly moving through a twirl. "I mean, all of them could be models. It's intimidating for someone like me."

"Quinn, your heart is a thousand times more beautiful than they could ever be."

"In the human world, that's exactly the kind of thing someone says when you're ugly," she says wryly. "But thank you."

I halt, messing up the steps of the dance to press her hand to my chest. "I hope to own your beautiful heart, your sweet lips, your perfect face, your soft hair, and your body."

She blushes so violently warmth emanates from her face. "People heard you."

"Good. I'm not giving up until I have every part of you, and after tonight, everyone will know it."

Stepping close, she grabs the lapels of my jacket to tug me down so she can whisper, "Wanna hear a secret?" Her sweet scent makes me dizzy, and I sway forward until my nose is buried in her hair. "I don't think I could ever belong with someone else, even if I tried."

Her unwavering feelings for me are a welcome reminder. She's never been touched by another man, just as I've never experienced physical intimacy with another woman.

When it comes to Quinn, I'm selfish. I want her all to myself. It's why I kept her a secret for so long.

A single slow clap interrupts the end of the song, and the musicians go quiet. The women of the room suddenly giggle and sigh—even the mated ones are reacting like smitten schoolgirls.

Several whisper, "Pretty boy."

They're not talking about me.

There's only one person who could elicit that kind of reaction in my kingdom.

Separating from Quinn, I turn to the source of excitement. "King Damon. I wasn't sure if you'd show up."

"Well, I wasn't going to, but I had a visit with a witch a few days ago, and she told me I'd want to be here for your party." He saunters toward us, his footsteps a distinct lazy drag. "She was right."

He holds out his arm. I accept the handshake, gripping his forearm while he squeezes mine.

"I've missed you, cousin," I say, pulling him in for a manly hug, complete with a few slaps on the back.

Our fathers might not get along, but Damon is one of my closest friends, even if we don't see each other often.

"Congratulations are in order," he says. "When I heard you'd be taking a mate, I didn't believe it."

"Hang on," Quinn cuts in. "A witch told you the future?"

"In exchange for a few secrets," Damon responds slyly.

"That's perfect timing." Excited, Quinn yanks on my arm as she bounces. "Can you take us to her?"

Oh, my relentless mate. For someone who despises the idea of me with another woman, she sure is determined to follow through with this pointless mission.

I put an arm around her shoulders. "Why don't we forget about witches tonight. Let's just have fun."

"But if she can tell the future, maybe she could help us."

"Are you staying tonight?" Changing the subject, I direct the question to Damon.

"I'd planned on it. The wine's calling my name. Although, before I get shnockered, I'd like to speak with you in private."

There's an edge to his voice that has me concerned. Damon's a happy-go-lucky kind of guy. It takes a lot to upset him, and even more to scare him.

"Quinn, why don't you join my mother at the buffet table? There's butterscotch pudding. You won't want to miss it."

She sighs, getting the hint that she's not invited to this discussion. "You know I can't turn down a good pudding. See you soon?"

Every other time she's asked me that question, I've had to wait a year to be with her again. Not now.

I grin. "Very soon."

As Damon and I walk to a door underneath the staircase, we're careful not to say anything beyond basic pleasantries. Other faeries can't hear as well as we can, but I don't want to risk anyone eavesdropping. Which is why we're headed to a secret office.

If I were to take a right, it would lead to one of the kitchens. We go left, slipping through a door camouflaged in the stone pattern on the walls.

"Your chosen mate is beautiful, by the way," Damon says as we walk side by side. "Don't listen to the uppity nobles. Their standards are skewed."

"Chosen mate? How do you know Quinn's not my fated?"

"A human, Kirian?" he deadpans. "Really?"

He has a point. "And how do you know what she looks like?"

"I may or may not have followed you to the portal one year."

"What?" I bark.

"Don't throw a hissy fit. I didn't cross over to her world."

"You spied on me."

"Not on you, per say. I was just curious about where you always went." He pauses guiltily. "But I did go into Quinn's dreams once."

"How were you able to do that," I demand, "when you didn't have an object that belongs to her?"

"She was putting flowers in your hair that day. You two are really cute together, by the way." When I growl, he rushes to explain, "When you got back and flew away, a couple of the flowers fell off your head. What was I supposed to do? *Not* use them?"

"Yes," I grit out. "Does privacy mean nothing to you?"

He just shrugs.

Damon's ability is one I'd trade mine for a thousand times over. He's a dream walker. As long as he possesses something a person used to own, he can enter their dream and see what they see. He's a silent observer, undetected by the dreamer themselves. Although he can't interfere or manipulate the outcome, he can find out personal information. Secrets and the inner workings of their minds.

Most importantly, he can *see* anytime he wants.

It's good for him, though.

He wasn't born yet when the curse happened. My uncle Silas thought they were in the clear because his mate got pregnant after shit went down, but Damon was born blind. At least I had almost eleven years of getting to know the world before my sight was taken away. Darkness is all Damon knows, except through someone else's perspective.

"What was she dreaming about?" I ask, hating how Damon might know something about Quinn that I don't.

He shakes his head. "It was one of those frustrating looping dreams. She was trying to finish a school assignment, but every time she was almost done, the paper would go blank. Her parents were there, though. Did you ever meet her family?"

"No," I respond grumpily.

On days when Quinn didn't show up for our meetings, I usually lingered in the woods, listening to whatever was going on inside her house. Sometimes I heard her parents' voices, but I always kept my distance.

Even though he can't see it, I flip Damon the middle finger Quinn's so fond of. "Stay out of Quinn's head from now on. She's mine."

"Whoa, there. Calm down. You know I'm saving myself for my soul mate."

I'm well aware of his feelings on the subject. Damon isn't like me—he isn't okay with being blind forever. His clues aren't any better than mine, though, and he's never come close to finding his mate.

When we get to the office, I shut the heavy wooden door behind us. Circling the room, I trail my fingertips over the built-in bookcases, the window, and the fireplace. I sniff as I go, wanting to make sure we're alone. I smell nothing but the wood polish the maid uses and the scent of old books.

"What's going on?" I lean my ass against the windowsill.

"Although I'm happy to meet your mate, there's another reason I'm here." Damon paces around the desk before coming to a stop in front of me. "I came to warn you."

"About?"

"Something the witch said about Quinn."

My heart starts to pound. "I'm listening."

"She's in danger here. Someone you trust will betray you."

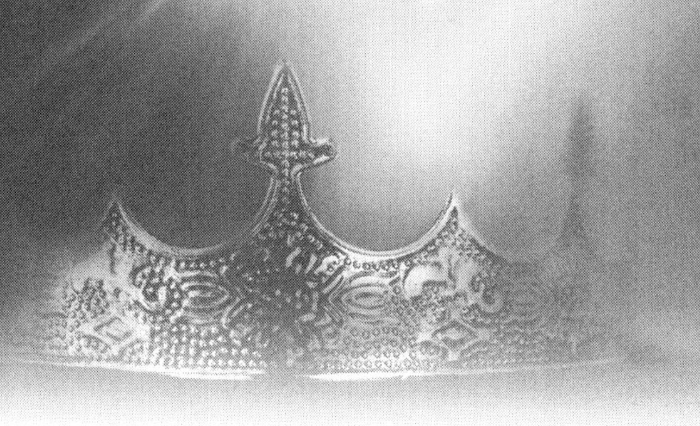

CHAPTER 10

Quinn

Since coming back from chatting with Damon, Kirian's been quiet, serious, and broody.

It's making me nervous.

"Are you sure you're okay?" I ask for the tenth time.

He nods as we waltz, but it's almost like he's not completely here with me. He's distracted.

Turning his head, he listens to the crowd around us as we finish the last dance of the evening. The tip of his ear twitches. Normally, that'd be adorable, but I'm concerned about how weird he's being.

When he rejoined me by the food earlier, he told me he wouldn't be leaving my side again. I didn't realize he meant that literally. He even followed me to the bathroom when I had to pee. Yeah, okay, so he couldn't see me, but he obviously heard the tinkle. We're not at that comfort level yet. I wanted to die of embarrassment.

The music comes to an end, and the swaying bodies on the dance floor stop to clap for the musicians.

... hideous.

Yes, tragic.

She must have cast a spell on him.

As much as I've tried to tune out the snide comments, I can't. They're not even trying to be quiet about it. Maybe that's why Kirian's in such a bad mood. His people are acting like obnoxious children.

At least Kirian's family has been nice. Whenever he's gotten pulled into 'kingdom talk' with his father or other council members, Zella's drawn me into conversations filled with pleasantries about the food, saving me from standing there all silent and awkward.

If there's one subject I can discuss for long periods of time, it's dessert. Apparently, the butterscotch pudding is a recipe Kirian insisted the cooks create when he was fourteen. I couldn't help smiling when she told me that. He must've done it after the first pudding cups we shared together.

Even Gia's been making an effort to be kind—or at least repay her debt. She let me drink juice from her favorite enchanted goblet. It was a birthday gift from the same wizard who gave Kirian his portals. All I had to do was think about the flavor I wanted while holding it, and the liquid inside would match whatever I wanted to taste.

If it weren't for all the judgmental fae surrounding us, tonight would've been one of the best nights of my life.

In my wildest dreams, I couldn't have cooked up a room as beautiful as this one.

It's light, airy, and dripping with elegance. The second-story balcony goes all the way around the oval shape. Round pillars made from marble with gold swirls hold it up. There are three chandeliers overhead, and the stardust lights flicker through hundreds of dangling crystals.

There's a mural on the ceiling, and it reminds me of the Sistine Chapel. Except this scene depicts a bloody battle. I see Kirian among the animated soldiers, axe in hand, his hair flying wildly around his handsome face.

Windows line the entire perimeter of the second level. Down here on the first floor, French doors are open to the night. We haven't gone out there, but I spied a balcony overlooking a garden.

I want to see it.

I'm about to ask Kirian if I can go take a look when he turns away from me and holds a silencing hand up to the crowd of still-gawking fae. A pair of girls about my age giggle behind their hands as they stare at my face.

Shifting closer to Kirian, I let my gaze fall to the floor.

I wonder if their assessment of my physical appearance is making him have second thoughts. If I were a king, I'd value the opinion of my subjects.

Kirian's warm fingers trail down my spine before his palm flattens over my bare skin. A sudden hot flash ripples through my body, while goose bumps spread over my arms.

One thing I didn't notice about the dress when it was on the hanger is how low it dips in the back. All the fae dresses are designed this way, and it's not just a fashion statement. It's for wings. Wings I don't have. At least the skin on my back is something to be proud of. It's smooth, creamy, and unblemished. Not even one mole.

"Thank you all for coming tonight." Kirian's booming voice echoes off the walls. "I expect I can count on your allegiance to Quinn. An enemy of hers is an enemy of mine, and my enemies won't live to regret their betrayal. It's been a long time since we've held a public execution here, but you all know the punishment for treason."

His stern warning earns worried expressions and obligated murmurs of loyalty.

Well, I guess we're not ending the evening on a happy note.

Without another word, Kirian takes my hand and walks me to one of the exits. I'm not sure if I should wave or bow or say goodbye, but I don't get the chance before we're walking down a stone hallway.

This castle is like a maze. There are so many doors, staircases, and secret rooms. It makes me feel disoriented.

It doesn't help that it's always nighttime here. I have no idea what time it is or how many hours have passed since Kirian dragged me through the portal.

However, I do know that I'm tired.

I yawn, and Kirian gives my hand a squeeze.

"These events can be draining. Fortunately, they don't happen very often." He seems a little more at ease now, but there's still a stiffness in his shoulders.

"Now that we're alone, are you going to tell me who put the stick up your ass?"

The corner of his mouth twitches. "I just want you to be safe."

"Am I not safe?"

"I want everyone to respect you," he says, avoiding my question. "Or else."

"Or else," I mutter deeply, mocking him. At least it gets his lips to tilt up a little more. "Seriously, though. What's wrong? I've never seen you like this before."

"Like what?"

"I don't know." We climb the stairs to his wing of the castle. "All, king-mode."

Shrugging, he sends me a forced grin. "That's because I am in king mode."

I shake my head. Obviously, he's not going to give me a straight answer. Whatever. I'm too exhausted to pry it out of him.

"So, Damon knows a witch," I say. "That's good news, right?"

Kirian hums, seeming distracted again, and a bad feeling comes over me. Maybe he learned something about his mate?

Suddenly, I'm not so tired anymore. The energy I need to interrogate him comes pouring in.

"Well?" I prod. "What did Damon say?"

"He's willing to take us to see the witch."

"And?"

"We leave tomorrow."

"That soon? Wow."

I should be glad.

I'm not.

Earlier, when I forced Kirian into that promise, I didn't consider one awful possibility: he might find his true mate and then I'd be stuck here for a year watching them together.

I honestly don't think I could handle that.

"We should get some sleep," Kirian says, stopping in front of his bedroom. "We'll start planning the trip in the morning." He points to a room down the hall. "The guest suite has been prepared for you, but I'd prefer it if you slept in my room."

I'm torn. How many times have I begged Kirian to stay the night with me in my treehouse? A lot. I would've given anything to have a sleepover with the big hunky fae.

But things are different now. We've kissed. Feelings and truths are out in the open.

If we're in the same bed, I'm not sure I can resist mauling him. I might not even do it on purpose. It might happen in my sleep.

And then the curse would be permanent for sure, all because I couldn't keep my lips to myself.

"I don't think that's a good idea." I want to question him more. I want him to tell me there's a zero percent chance he'll be matched with his mate when we go see the witch.

But he seems determined to keep the information to himself. We've played this game before. No matter how much I pester him, he'll give me half-truths and riddles until I give up.

"I'll take the guest suite." My reply is quiet and sad.

Kirian frowns. "Are you sure?"

No. "Yes."

Displeased, he purses his lips and raises an eyebrow.

Gah, he's so cute when he doesn't get his way.

"All right." Cupping my face, he leans down, like he's going to kiss me. But he stops halfway and straightens. "Torius will be standing guard outside your door, so don't be surprised if you find him there in the morning."

"Is that necessary?" Just as I ask, I see the tattooed fae approaching us. He's got at least three swords strapped to his belt, and the hilt of a dagger is sticking out of his right boot.

"Just a precaution," Kirian tells me, escorting me to the suite.

Although it's only one room with an attached bathroom, the décor is similar to Kirian's room. Even the bed looks the same.

Walking around to each lantern, Kirian turns a knob at the bottom to dim the light. I stand in the middle of the room, watching his prowling movements. His tailored pants fit his behind perfectly. With each stride, his glutes flex and shift under the blue material.

When he's done, he comes over to me. "You'll need help getting out of your dress."

"Is your mom coming up?"

"No." His fingers spasm at his sides.

Oh. So he plans to undo the trillion buttons down my backside himself. Swallowing, I turn around.

Kirian gently sweeps my hair to the side, draping it over my shoulder. His callouses scrape over my skin as he finds the first pearl mid-back. It easily slides through the loop, then he moves down to the next one.

Cool air wafts over my exposed spine as the material slowly parts. With every inch, my insides burn a little hotter. My lower belly clenches. Wetness pools in my center.

Everything is quiet, except for our breathing.

My lungs suck in air with shallow puffs, and my breasts strain against the low-cut top with every inhale. Heaving bosoms, anyone?

This is the sexiest moment of my life.

Unfortunately, it's over too soon.

Kirian makes it down to the last button. It's just above my butt crack, and I swear his touch lingers there longer than necessary.

Holding the dress to my chest, I pivot toward him. "Thank you."

"You're welcome." Pressing his nose to the top of my head, he murmurs, "Goodnight, young one."

"Goodnight." I grip his forearm, and I'm so close to begging him to take me back to his bed with him.

But I don't.

Instead, I watch him leave.

As he shuts the door, I hear him exchange a few terse words with my "precaution."

And all I can think is… a precaution for what?

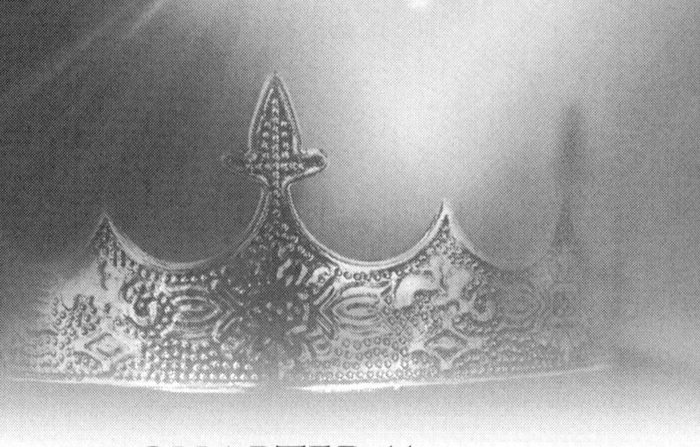

CHAPTER 11

Quinn

I HATE BEING ALONE HERE. IT'S DARK AND UNFAMILIAR.

As I stare up at the dark canopy, I think about the predicament I'm in. I'm engaged. Sort of. But probably not for long, thanks to my meddling.

At least the bed is comfortable. The mattress must be made with the golden goose feathers, because it conforms to my backside in the most perfect way. It's like being on a cloud.

Maybe the feathers are enchanted, lulling me into a false sense of security.

Although my eyes sting with threatening tears, it doesn't take me long to fall asleep. Thoughts of snooty nobles and Kirian's fated mate slip away as my lids droop.

In my dream, I'm flying. I have wings of my own and Kirian's by my side. We laugh as we soar over the palace together. The night sky above us shines bright with the three moons and thousands of twinkling stars. I've never been happier.

But now I'm waking up. It takes me a second to figure out why—I'm cold.

The nightgown that was hanging up for me in the

bathroom is long and old-fashioned, but the material is light. Not enough to keep me warm in a drafty room.

When I open my eyes, I reach for the covers to pull them up.

But my heart nearly stops when I see a shadow looming over me.

It's not the canopy. There's a distinct outline of wings, long hair, and the glint of something metal.

Something sharp.

I scream. Crab-walking backward, my shoulders hit the solid wooden headboard.

Within a split second, Torius bursts in, a lantern in one hand and a long sword in the other.

I'm still screaming, but when I look back at where the dark figure was, there's nothing.

"Milady?" Torius briefly glances at me before scanning the room with his light-green eyes.

"I—I thought I saw something. I'm sorry." Hugging my knees to my chest, I try to calm my racing heart.

I'm shaken up, panting. I can't seem to get enough air.

Kirian comes barreling in next, his white pants hung loosely on his hips like he just tugged them on and didn't have time to tie the drawstring. His wings are out, and he's carrying his axe. He almost runs into Torius, who jumps out of the way, just in time to miss a blade to the face.

"What happened?" Kirian demands. "Quinn!"

"I'm right here." My voice trembles. I want to go to him, but I'm too scared to move.

He staggers over to the bed and gropes around until his hand lands on my ankle. "Are you hurt?"

Man, he must be more terrified than I am. Kirian's always so aware of his surroundings. He doesn't trip or bump into people. He never has trouble finding me.

I cover his fingers with mine. "I'm okay. I just woke up and I could've sworn I saw…"

"Saw what?" he presses.

"There was someone standing over me with a sword or a knife. At least, I thought there was, but no one's here. Maybe it was just a nightmare."

Kirian growls, deep and menacing. "You're not wrong. Someone used magic." He sniffs the air. "I smell a portal."

The blood drains from my face. "Someone really was here?"

Instead of answering me, Kirian pushes away from the bed to pace the room.

"They came into my castle and tried to hurt my mate," he mutters, his voice gravelly with emotion. "*Mine.*"

"What did he look like, my queen?" Torius looks even more intimidating with the light from the lantern casting shadows over his face.

"A faerie?" That's not very helpful. "All I saw was wings and hair. I'm not even sure if it was a man or a woman."

"Your Majesty." Torius turns his attention to the king. "Should I order a search of the palace?"

In answer, Kirian lets out a rageful, animalistic roar.

Holy shit, it's loud.

I'm reminded again that he isn't human. No one I've ever known could make that kind of sound. The deafening noise shakes the bed, and dust crumbles off the stone walls. A glass vase falls from the mantel over the fireplace. The distinct shatter of glass joins Kirian's ungodly howl.

It hurts my head. Covering my ears, I tip over on the mattress and curl into the fetal position.

As I hear a few more muffled shouts, the light fades away when Torius quickly leaves the room.

I don't like the darkness.

I squeeze my eyes shut, because maybe I can pretend all this didn't happen. Maybe it was just a bad dream.

"Quinn. Quinn, love. I'm sorry." Kirian's soft pleas are barely audible, so I take my hands away from my head and open my eyes. He's kneeling on the bed next to me, and I've never seen him look so remorseful. "Please don't be scared of me."

"I'm not scared of *you*. I'm just... scared."

He pets my head, running his hands over my face like he's done so many times before. "I never should've left you alone."

Something he said a few seconds ago sticks out in my mind. "Did you call me love?"

"Yeah, I guess I did."

"I like it."

"Then I'll do it more often." Scooping his arms under me, he picks me up, cradling my body against his. "Come on. You're sleeping in my bed from now on."

This time I don't argue.

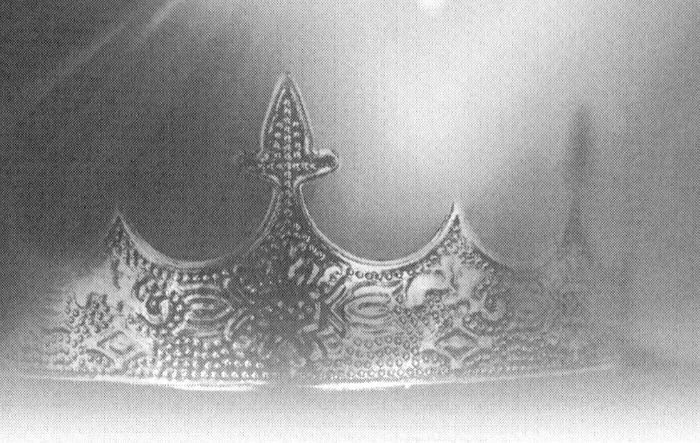

CHAPTER 12

Kirian

My impulsive decision to bring Quinn into my life will have consequences. As it is, damage has already been done. I hate how scared she was last night. The fact that she was in danger for even a second is unacceptable. In hindsight, it would've been better to order her to sleep with me instead of giving her a choice.

No one can protect her like I can, so she'll stay with me always. I'm not unhappy about that. Keeping her close will be a benefit to our unfortunate predicament.

Even with the unknown hanging over my head, I still don't regret pulling her through the portal.

Because she's here with me, in my bed. It's a hell of a lot better than waking up alone.

Making a noise, she jerks as if she's having a bad dream. Her sleep has been fretful, and I tighten my arms around her body, hoping she can feel that I'm here.

I could almost be content to just hold her like this.

If I didn't know what it was like to kiss her, maybe it would be enough. But it's not. My need for her has multiplied since yesterday.

Her nightgown has ridden up, exposing her smooth legs and her cotton panties. My hard cock presses against her back, and when she squirms, I groan.

She wakes with a start.

"Shh. You're safe," I tell her, and she relaxes, her warm body melting into mine.

Her softness is intriguing. My hand splays out on her hip, and I move it up, tracing the dip of her waist. The curve of her ass molds perfectly to my crotch. That sweet scent she carries is so strong it feels like it's imbedded in my pores.

I love it.

I love her.

"What's that light coming through the window?" Quinn rolls onto her back and turns her face to me.

"Dawn," I reply.

"The sun?" Sitting up, she throws the covers off and leaps out of bed. "I thought you said you don't get daylight here."

"We don't." I smile at her excitement. Pushing up on an elbow, I explain, "The sun won't actually rise. Two suns orbit the Day Realm. Twice a day, they cross paths on the eastern border. The merging is so bright, the light travels all the way over Dawn and Dusk to here."

"Dawn and Dusk… Can you tell me more about it?"

"I've been there many times, but I've only *seen* it once."

"How old were you?"

"Ten. It was my first time using a portal. I wanted to see the mystical land my mother spoke so fondly of." I smirk. "It was one of the places she forbade me to go."

"So, naturally, that's where you went," Quinn says, amused. "And? Was it amazing?"

"Yes. I remember the rainbows. There were so many of them, dividing a sky that was both day and night. Stars twinkled faintly near the Night Realm border, and bright blue with fluffy clouds lined the Day Realm. It was the best of both worlds. There are these fruit trees. The leaves look like orange fur. A round blue ball can be found in the fuzz. Under the peel, there's a pink citrus fruit with juice that tastes somewhere between a tangerine and a cherry. It's called a gozzel. I must've eaten at least fifteen that day."

"Sounds yummy. Do you import them here?"

"That particular item is owned by the Day Realm. Part of the treaty. But don't worry, love. We claimed the waterfall mist."

"What's so special about that?"

"It's the most refreshing drink I've ever had. It's great for long days of travel, since it has extreme hydrating properties." My heart feels a rare twinge because of the unending darkness stealing my vision. Quinn is still standing at the window, her fingers making soft sounds on the velvet curtains, and I wish I could see what she sees. "Describe the horizon for me. Please."

She likes it when I'm polite. I don't say please to anyone but her, and I'm not sure she realizes that. She doesn't know how special she is to me, and that's no one's fault but my own.

I've spent so much time fighting this pull between us, but instead of trying to keep my distance, I should've been telling her how much I love her. How much she means to me.

The day she reached adulthood, I should've confessed my growing feelings.

Letting out a wistful sigh, she lifts the curtain a little more. "It's like the sun is right there, below the mountains in the distance. If it were any higher, I think I'd be able to see a sliver of it. The clouds—they're so bright, Kirian. They're wispy and pink. They fade to purple as they get higher in the sky. The stars are still bright as ever, though. It's like they won't be outdone by daylight."

Her vivid description triggers so many memories from my youth. I recall how beautiful the sky was during early morning sparring sessions with my father and other young soldiers in training.

"We'll get about an hour of that twice a day," I tell her. "You missed dusk last night because you were busy getting ready for the ball."

Her mood sinks at the mention of yesterday, and some of her happiness drains away. She's still peering out the glass when she says, "I need to know what happened."

I scrub a hand down my face. "I never should've left you alone."

She approaches the bed, stopping just a foot away from the mattress. "I want you to keep me in the loop. I know you, Kirian. Don't you think I can tell when you're keeping something from me?"

Sighing, I sit up and turn away, draping my legs over the side of the bed. I plant my feet on the floor as I hang my head.

I can't get anything past Quinn. It's been like that since she was a kid. But I don't want to tell her the rest of the information Damon gave me—the witch said I would lose her.

When, where, or how is a mystery.

Witches like to leave out vital details. It's what keeps us coming back, making deals, offering valuable possessions in return for snippets of information.

It's one of the reasons I stopped dealing with them all those centuries ago. Even the kind-hearted ones love to play tricks. It's just in their nature.

But this time, I can't let my pride or my opinion get in the way. I need help. I can't gamble with Quinn's well-being. If Damon's witch has answers, I'll give her anything she requests.

A feather-light touch on my back makes me startle.

"Sorry," Quinn quickly rushes out the apology when I jerk.

Fuck. I didn't even hear her come up behind me on the bed, didn't feel the mattress dip. I was so deep in thought I wasn't paying attention.

Since Quinn's been here, I've been off. Distracted.

In the best way, of course. All my senses are overloaded with her scent, the memory of our kiss, the way she makes my cock so hard it hurts.

I can't let that keep happening. Being alert could save her life.

"I told you, you can touch me anytime you want." I grunt, before honestly admitting, "Sometimes it just feels too good. You make me crazy, Quinn."

Tentatively, she brushes her fingertips over my shoulder blades again, right over the invisible slit to one of my wings.

I hold in a shudder.

Just like a faerie's ears, it's a hypersensitive spot on the body. Touching me there is basically foreplay.

"It's so impressive that those big wings are all tucked away in here," Quinn whispers. Her breath tickles the back of my neck as she continues to caress my skin. "Do you just bring them out whenever you want?"

Nodding, I try to ignore the throbbing erection in my pants. "When I want to fly. Sometimes they'll come out during a time of aggression, anger, or fear."

"Like last night when you thought I was hurt."

"Yes." I dip my head again, and Quinn's arms snake around me as she hugs me from behind.

"Talk to me, Kirian. Please."

I can't deny her. Even if what I say will be frightening, I have to give in.

"Damon told me something bad would happen to you," I tell her, my voice gruff with emotion.

"Like what?"

"The fortune was vague, so I have no idea."

She heaves out a sigh. "So, that's why you've been a grumpy butt? Because you're worried about me?"

She sounds relieved, which is odd, considering the unsettling information I just passed on.

I turn my head her way. "Yes. Why else would I be a grumpy butt?"

She giggles at my use of her words. "No reason."

"Don't lie to me. I can tell when you're being secretive as well." Reaching behind me with both hands, I tickle her ribs.

She laughs and wiggles, but I don't let up until she says, "Fine, fine. Geez."

Huffing, she presses the side of her face to mine as she bashfully explains her suspicions that I'd found something out about my fated mate.

"No." Dropping my hand to her thigh, I rub her reassuringly. "And even if I did, it wouldn't change how I feel about you." Quinn lets out a skeptical sound, but she nods. Because she trusts me. "Try not to worry about what the witch said. I won't allow you to be hurt. You'll stay near me at all times. No exceptions."

Twirling a lock of my hair around her finger, she grins. "I guess that means you'll get to hear me pee a lot more, huh?"

Despite the seriousness of the situation, her humor pulls a chuckle from me. "I have a feeling we're going to learn a lot more about each other in a very short amount of time."

CHAPTER 13

Kirian

As with any morning after a big party, the great hall has been transformed into a grand breakfast. The thirty-foot dining table is covered in trays full of pastries, cured meats, five different types of eggs, and fruit juice from the palace orchards.

The chairs are filled with the highest nobles. The ones who get the privilege of staying in the guest wing the night after a big event. Some are old friends. Some are trusted and revered council members.

Every single one of them are suspects to me.

Pacing behind the chairs, I sniff the air.

I can sense the confusion and nerves from the occupants. Most of them don't understand why I'm acting so strangely. Only the perpetrator knows I'm hunting for a hint of the portal smell. It's similar to the way earth smells right before it rains, and it coats the skin. Sometimes the scent lingers for a day or so afterward.

But I come up with nothing.

"Several hours ago, someone tried to harm my mate," I tell the room. The clink of silverware on plates stops as everyone gives me their full attention. "I guess the threat of banishment and execution wasn't enough. If I find out who did it, the punishment will be worse. I'm thinking an iron spike to the heart."

Everyone, including my parents, gasps.

The iron spike is one of the cruelest deaths. Agonizing. Slow and painful.

See, getting run through the heart with iron will kill a faerie, but not right away. It can take as long as five days.

Once the iron gets into the heart of the impaled fae, it pumps the infected blood to the entire body, causing twitching, seizures, organ failure, and internal bleeding. Eventually, the fingers and other extremities turn black and shrivel before falling off. All of this happens before death relieves the suffering.

I've witnessed men cry and writhe and beg for the end.

I, myself, have doled out this particular punishment three times. They were all Day Realm males who dared to steal a female from the Night Realm. But it wasn't just the forced breeding they inflicted on my people that triggered my temper. No, it was the fact that the girls were children—fifteen or younger. Not even old enough to procreate. When I heard the cries of the girls who'd been rescued too late, all I could think about was Quinn. How angry I'd be if someone did something like that to her.

In the Night Realm, torture is seen as barbaric, but I don't fuck around with that shit.

And I'm not fucking around now.

I stop behind Quinn's chair and reach out to lovingly caress her face. "Are you well, love?"

"Yep. Gia gave me another dress, and she let me have the last gooseberry tart."

"That's four gifts or favors," my sister interjects happily, brushing her hands together as if she's physically ridding herself of the honeysuckle debt.

It's amusing. Gia never did like owing anyone anything.

"I need a word with King Damon before our departure," I say toward the chair my cousin occupies next to my father. Then I lower my mouth to Quinn's ear. "I'll be where you can see me. Don't go anywhere."

My lips brush against her flesh with every syllable. It's not a kiss, but it affects her. Heat bursts from her skin and her pulse skyrockets.

I love what I can do to her with just a simple touch.

A chair scoots back, and Damon follows me to the other end of the room.

Once we're away from nosy ears, I quietly ask, "Will you travel with us to the Dream Realm? I don't know your witch. She might be more willing to do business with me if you're present."

"I figured you'd say that. That's why I asked Torius to prepare a caravan. I'm ready to go whenever you are."

"Thank you," I sigh, relieved.

If there's one person I trust with my life—with Quinn's life, for that matter—it's Torius. We've known each other since we were children. We trained together, fought together, won battles side by side. I know he'll choose a good crew to travel with us.

"There's just one problem," Damon says, rocking back on his heels.

"What's that?"

"Astrid isn't in the Dream Realm. She lives in the Shadowlands."

CHAPTER 14

Quinn

Good news: Kirian isn't gung-ho about finding his true mate.

Bad news: Someone's trying to murder me.

Speaking of murder, Kirian really knows how to kill a mood.

Before he made his morbid announcement, everyone was cheerfully eating, and several fae were actually talking to me. One woman had heard the famous honeysuckle wine was from my field and she told me the gooseberries from the tart I liked so much were harvested from her estate.

That was as far as the conversation got before Buzz Killington spoke up.

Now I'm getting the silent treatment. Everyone's eyes are downcast, as if their plates suddenly became the most interesting thing they've ever seen. It's like they're too afraid to even look at me.

As I nibble on a biscuit, everyone eats quickly and makes a polite exit. One by one the table clears out.

I glance over at Kirian. He's still talking to Damon, and they both look so serious.

"I owe you an apology."

I follow the voice to Gia, and for a second, I'm so shocked at what she said, I look around to see if she's talking to someone else. But she's staring right at me with those lavender eyes.

"Oh, um, thanks?" It comes out sounding like a question.

She sips from her golden goblet—the same one she let me drink from last night. "I'm sorry I was rude to you yesterday. I'm afraid I've been... jealous—" She makes a face, like the word tasted bad coming out "—of Kirian my whole life. I was just a baby when he went blind. Most of my early memories are of him getting all the attention. My parents were absent a lot of the time, searching for the witches."

"It's true," Zella interjects sadly. "Kirian wasn't the only one affected. We all suffered, and Gia was too young to understand what was happening."

I know what it's like to be lonely. I think of how my brother always got to do everything first and how he got my parents to himself for most of his childhood—he'd had one hell of a head start by the time I came along.

And for the first time since Gia started challenging Kirian for the throne years ago, I actually feel sorry for her.

"It's not fun to be left out," I tell her sympathetically. "I know that more than most. Apology accepted."

Frowning, she opens her mouth, but no words come out. She looks almost... disappointed. Like she expected me to lash out or argue with her. Maybe the fae aren't as forgiving as humans. Maybe she wanted a fight.

I'm not the right person for that. I've never been good at confrontation, especially when it comes to people I find intimidating.

"No hard feelings," I add. "I'd love it if we could be friends."

Pleased with the interaction, Zella smiles and Keryth raises his glass. "To new friends."

The few left at the table follow his lead, doing the same and repeating the toast.

I don't know why I thought we were going to fly again for our travel. If I had wings, I'd use them every chance I got. But I guess this is a five-day trip. Apparently, while flying is faster, it's physically draining.

My one regret from this morning is keeping Gia's dress on. I should've asked for pants instead. Although I'm seated comfortably in the carriage, the bodice is restrictive. The corset makes my breasts bulge in the most ridiculous way, and when I'm sitting, it's a little hard to breathe.

I'm not sure how I'll get the damn thing off tonight. With Kirian's help, probably, since he refused to let any of his female staff ride along with us. He said he wants to keep our traveling crew small, and after what I learned this morning, I have to agree.

Seriously, though. Corsets suck.

When we go over a bump in the road, I bounce up in the seat. I come back down hard, the stiff rods inside the bodice poke my ribs.

Ugh.

Muttering a few obscenities about the female fae fashion trends, I rub my side. All the women here dress like they're at a renaissance fair. It's beautiful, but not practical at all.

The guys, however, are decked out in battle gear. I'm talking black leather pants, heavy boots, and special shirts that let their wings out, should the need arise. They all have some kind of weapon strapped to their belt.

Like a medieval biker gang.

I'm a little sad I can't see Kirian from here, because leather is a good look on him.

The carriage is nice, though. I'm definitely getting the royal treatment in here. The padded cushions are upholstered in dark blue fabric and gold buttons, and there are a few pillows if I want to get comfy. There's a basket full of snacks—cheese, bread, and fruit.

But this ride, man. My ass can only take so much.

As the wheel thumps over a rock, I groan.

Maybe the fae should take a lesson from humans and get some shocks installed on their vehicles.

I stick my head out the window, still thrown off by the perpetual night sky. "Um, guys? Do you think I could walk for a bit?"

Slowly, we all come to a stop, and Kirian leaves his place behind Torius, trotting over to me on his horse. "What's wrong?"

"Nothing. I'm just having trouble getting comfortable. Plus, I'm bored. I feel like I need to move my legs."

Frowning, he faces the front of the line where Torius leads. Then he turns to me, before tilting an ear toward the rear where another Night Realm soldier rides.

I glance back at the warrior.

Kai is a terrifying motherfucker. Even more so than Torius. There's something cold and distant in his gray eyes.

His sandy blond hair is braided in tight cornrows against his scalp and the rest is a tangled mess. He's been burned so severely by iron, it left scars all over his face, neck, and arms. According to Kirian, Kai could've healed himself—since that's his power—but he chose not to because he wanted the marks.

See? Crazy motherfucker. Who does that?

But if Kirian says he's a good man, then he must be.

I was told he and Torius saved Kai from slaughter in the Day Realm. He was seconds away from getting an axe to the neck. Rumor has it, he was such a good fighter he made King Zarid jealous. Instead of utilizing his skills, the Day King just wanted him gone.

And that's the main reason Kirian trusts the guy. Kai owes him his life.

"It's been less than an hour since we left," Kirian says to me, pursing his lips. "Are you always this impatient when you travel?"

I think of the road trip my parents and I took to Florida when I was ten. It was the first and last time we went anywhere far away. Apparently, I asked *are we there yet* way too many times.

I shrug and admit, "Yeah."

"You can ride on my horse with me."

"I appreciate the offer, but that's not going to help my ass. I'm taking a serious pounding back here."

Kirian's lips twitch. Kai coughs, and I suspect it's to cover a laugh.

Okay, so I could've worded that better.

"I can walk with her." Damon pops his head around the front of the carriage. He's riding with the driver, Gunther, since he didn't travel here with a horse. He must have some serious wing stamina, because he flew the whole way to Kirian's by himself.

"All right." Kirian nods, hopping off his horse to open the carriage door and help me down. "Thirty minutes only. Stay between the carriage and Kai."

"Got it." Leaning from side to side, I stretch my back and thank my lucky stars I declined Zella's offer to wear her slippers. I still have on the sneakers I came here with yesterday, and I don't care if they seem out of place with my outfit. Arch support is important.

Here, women's shoes are almost like socks—soft and not great for hiking. I should know. I danced in a borrowed pair for hours last night.

"Protect her." Kirian barks the order at Damon as he mounts up again.

Damon gives a mock salute before joining me in the road. "I'll protect her as if she were my own mate."

"She's not your mate." A possessive growl rumbles in Kirian's chest and he looks like he's about two seconds away from jumping back down to the ground.

Someone's sensitive. I wave him on.

"It's fine. We'll just be right here." I motion to the place behind the carriage.

He bites his lip as he hesitates, and it's seriously sexy. His straight white teeth dig into the pink flesh of his bottom lip, and I remember the way they scraped against my tongue when we kissed.

Shuffling my feet, I try not to get turned on. Kirian said other fae don't have heightened senses like he does, but I'd bet Damon's ability to smell is just as good as Kirian's.

From the way Kirian's acting, I'm not sure if he'd let me walk with his cousin if Damon caught a hint of my 'arousal.' The undergarments Zella brought me this morning are thin. Basically see-through mesh. Don't get me wrong, I'm grateful for clean underwear, but it's almost as if the fae don't like panties. I'm all for a breathable crotch, but I might as well not be wearing anything down there.

Reluctantly, Kirian goes back to his place behind Torius, and we get moving again. The pace is faster than I thought, but it's preferable to sitting still. My muscles feel better already.

Plus, it's nice being out in the open. There's a sweet essence in the breeze and I'm not sure where it's coming from. White wildflowers grow in the grass on either side of us. Maybe they're just super fragrant.

Breathing in the fresh air, I look up at the sky. So many bright orbs glow against the dark-blue background. It's like the Milky Way took over the entire sky. I can see why Kirian loves it so much. It's stunning.

"It's said that the stars are our ancestors shining down on us," Damon drawls, pulling my attention to his bright green eyes. They're unfocused, blankly staring ahead.

"Oh? Do you believe that?"

"I don't know. I guess I'll find out when I die." His response is nonchalant, like the idea of death doesn't bother him.

"Guess so." The wind picks up a little, and it cools me off. Not that it's hot. The temperature is actually perfect. "Is the weather always so nice in Valora?"

"Depends on what your definition of nice is. Here in the Night Realm, it's a push and pull between autumn and spring. The harvest turnover is quicker, and I think it's to make up for the lack of solar exposure. The Day Realm is warmer, like summer. And the Dream Realm is so far north, it's cold most of the time."

"Do you like that?"

With a half-smile, he shrugs. "We've cornered the ice market and we have all the stardust. It's not a bad deal."

"So, what's your story?" I ask, a little breathy from exertion.

My yellow skirt swishes violently around my ankles with every rapid step I take. Since Gia's taller than me, the dress is almost too long, and the hem is dragging in the dirt. Gathering fistfuls of the silky material, I lift it a little to keep it clean.

"My story? What do you mean?" Damon hasn't even broken a sweat, and I'm guessing just like all the other fae, he's in way better shape than I am.

"Your curse," I elaborate. "It's the same as Kirian, but you got different clues about your mate, right?"

He grins, and I can see why all the women swooned when he made his entrance last night. The pretty boy image isn't really my thing—I can't imagine wanting anyone but Kirian—but the reason Damon got that nickname is obvious.

"She's surrounded with buttons and strings. You'll find her in someone else's dreams." As he recites the rhyme, there's a sad undertone to his words. His laidback attitude slips for a second, and I suspect I just found Damon's weakness.

I make a thoughtful sound. Kirian's already told me about Damon's ability to dream walk, which is pretty freaking cool. It eliminates the issue of not being able to see his mate, but he has to find her first.

"A seamstress, maybe?" I suggest.

He shakes his head. "I've already invaded the minds of every seamstress in Valora. Their family and friends, too. I've never felt anything of significance."

"That sucks."

"It does," he agrees, serious.

Yep, Damon's sight and solitude are definitely his Achilles heel.

It makes me wonder if Kirian's sure about all this. About me. If I had to go over two thousand years without ever having sex, I might settle, too.

"I think Kirian's making a mistake," I whisper. "With me."

"How so?"

I definitely don't want to explain that Kirian might be thinking with the wrong head, so I take a different approach. "Wouldn't you give anything to break the curse?"

"Yes," Damon replies, certain. "I'll wait for my mate forever, if that's what it takes. Being able to see through someone else's eyes is a blessing and a tease. My only view of the world isn't up to me. When I go into someone's dreams, I don't get to choose what I see. I want control." He places a hand on his chest, as if his heart literally aches. "For once, I want my own outlook."

"That's understandable. And that's why I'm afraid Kirian will regret this."

"Listen, Kirian and I aren't the same person. Living in darkness doesn't bother him the way it does me. If he says he chooses you, then he means it."

That does make me feel a little better. "Thanks. I needed to hear tha—"

"Shh." He cuts me off, coming to a halt.

The caravan keeps moving ahead, but Kai's horse knickers behind us as he stomps an impatient hoof.

"What?" I ask quietly.

"I smell something burning." Inhaling deeply, Damon wrinkles his nose. "Does anyone else smell that? Something's wrong—"

He's barely finished the warning when a loud pop comes from inside the carriage. There's a flash of light, then all of the sudden, the entire thing is engulfed in flames.

I don't even have time to scream.

Right as an explosion detonates, Damon tackles me to the ground, covering my body with his.

Boom.

The sound of the blast is deafening. Splintering wood. Groaning metal. Shattering glass.

I close my eyes against the blinding brightness, but I can feel the heat on my face like I'm right next to a bonfire. My hair blows back with the force of it. Tucking my chin to my chest and keeping my arms folded to my stomach, I try to make myself as small as possible under Damon.

When the worst of it is over, I hear shouts and the sound of hooves beating on the ground.

And suddenly, my concern isn't for myself.

Kirian. The horses. Torius and Kai.

Wiggling, I try to get up, but I can't budge an inch with Damon's weight pinning me to the ground.

Frustrated, I cry out. I squint as I look around, but the hot flames make my eyes water. All I see through blurry vision is fire and smoke. A tear glides down my temple, and I can't even move my arms to wipe it away.

I don't know if everyone's okay, and I'm trapped under Damon. He's not moving at all, and this dude is heavy.

Oh, God. What if he's dead?

"Damon?" My voice is shaky.

"Stay still," he orders, strained, as if he's in pain.

A wet drop lands on my forehead and my worry increases. "Are you crying? Are you hurt that bad?"

Damon huffs out a laugh. "That's rain. Your boyfriend's putting out the fire."

Raindrops come down faster now, and the cool water is a relief for my heated skin.

Craning my neck, I peek over Damon's shoulder. Sure enough, Kirian's standing in the grass on the side of the road, his hands lifted into the air. Storm clouds gather over us, and the downpour gets serious.

Blinking through the drops pelting my face, I watch as all the flames disappear. Thick clouds of smoke take their place, billowing out of the carriage. Or, what's left of it. The windows, doors, and the top are gone. No more pretty blue cushions. The gold trim is charred. Our luggage, which was being stored in a rear compartment, is blown to unrecognizable bits on the road.

Once Kirian's mission is accomplished, he lowers his arms and the storm recedes. I'm officially soaked and probably traumatized.

Before I have a chance to shove Damon off me, Kirian runs over to us and tosses his cousin to the side of the road.

"Ow," Damon grunts as he rolls onto his stomach on the grass. "That's the thanks I get for becoming a fae rotisserie?"

I gasp when I see his charred shirt and the reddened skin on his back. He blocked the majority of the heat with his body. He protected me. Thanks to him, I don't have a burn on me.

"Damon's hurt," I say to Kirian, but he's too busy patting me down as he searches for injuries.

"Quinn, Quinn, Quinn. Are you okay?"

"I'm fine." I rub my butt where I landed on a small rock. The worst it'll do is turn into a bruise. My hand skates over several rips in my damp skirt, and now it seems silly that I was worried about getting it dirty.

A ruined dress and a sore rear end are nothing compared to the rest of the crew.

Kai is limping and his horse is nowhere to be seen. He probably got thrown from the saddle. Kirian's right hand is burnt and blistered, like he'd turned around and tried to reach for me when the explosion happened. I don't see Torius anywhere, and I wonder if he's chasing the missing horses down.

There's a steaming lump on the road about fifteen feet away, and I swallow hard when I realize it's Gunther, the driver. He was the closest when it happened.

"Kirian, I'm not the one who needs help." I lightly push his hands away. "Please. Gunther..."

The older fae is face down on the ground. His back rises with a ragged breath, but it looks like that side of him took the brunt of the blast. His shirt is practically disintegrated, and the moonlight's bright enough to see big blisters forming on his skin.

After pulling me up, Kirian walks over to Gunther and helps him stand. "You're the worst off. Your blood and burnt flesh are strong in the air."

"He's the worst off?" Damon cuts in incredulously, getting to his feet. "My hair got singed! How am I supposed to face the kingdom looking like this?"

Turning, he points to the back where, yeah, about ten inches got fried. The shoulder-length ends are uneven, and he's going to need a trim to straighten it out.

Although he can't see it, I give him a *really?* look. How can he possibly be thinking of his hair right now?

Ignoring Damon's vanity-filled rant, Kirian stays focused on Gunther. "Can you fly? We'll need to get word back to my family."

"My wing." A hiss of pain escapes as he lets his wings unfold and expand. On the right side, an area near the top is patchy. Little holes and wrinkles decorate what was once a smooth iridescent surface. "I'm afraid I'm no good like this."

I resist the urge to hug him.

Not only would that be inappropriate, but it'd also hurt like hell. Gunther's not a soldier like the other guys. Just a faithful servant of the royal family. He's shorter, thinner, and I'm not sure how long he's been around, but he must be old. All the faeries I've seen don't have gray hair or wrinkles. While I wouldn't classify Gunther as elderly, his sandy hair is white near his temples, and he's got crow's feet around his eyes.

"Kai." Kirian motions the burly, angry-looking man over.

Mr. Frowny Face doesn't have any visible wounds, and his limp is already gone.

I'm still worried about the horses. Squinting, I look out at the dark landscape around us, searching for movement.

Then I see Kai reach for Gunther out of my peripheral vision.

At first, I'm not sure what he's going to do. His large hands are open, and it seems like he's aiming for Gunther's neck.

Is he—is he going to strangle him? Rip his head off to put him out of his misery? I can't let that happen.

"Don't hurt him!" I jump between the two men, and Kai flinches back like I just slapped him.

Chuckling, Kirian places his hands on my shoulders and gently guides me out of the way. "He won't harm him, love. He's going to fix him. Kai's a healer, remember?"

"Oh, yeah." Now I feel dumb.

My face heats again, but this time, it's from humiliation.

I watch as Kai brings his hands to Gunther's chest, and there's a faint glow under his palms. Right before my eyes, the damaged skin and tissues mend back together.

The sound is somewhat nauseating. There's a lot of wet crackling and quiet popping. Fortunately, it doesn't take long.

Letting out a sigh, Gunther rolls his shoulders and stretches his wings. "Better."

"That's amazing," I say, dumbfounded, as Kai turns his attention to Kirian's hand.

"Kai's a good man to have around." Healed, Kirian makes a fist and grins at his friend.

"And you're a lady I want in my corner," Gunther says, laugh lines deepening when he smiles at me. "You were willing to take on this ogre for me?"

Still embarrassed, I kick a tattered remnant of some white mesh panties on the road. "I thought he was going to snap your neck."

All the men laugh, and I give a shrug. At least my awkwardness is good for one thing—comic relief. I'm happy to provide the lighthearted moment, even if it's at my expense.

"How can you all find this funny?" Torius's expression is downright murderous as he leads five horses out of the thick purple trees.

Kai responds with an uncharacteristic grin, and it's slightly more disturbing than seeing him serious. "Our future queen isn't one you want to go toe-to-toe with."

Not included in the joke, Torius grunts. With reins in each hand, he tilts his head to the animals on his right. "Lady and Mosby are hurt. Their rear ends are burnt to a crisp."

The healer rubs his hands together before getting to work on their injuries. Torius passes the three unharmed steeds to Gunther's care and goes to inspect the carriage.

As Kirian joins him, I stand a good distance away while they take inventory of what's left—which is nothing but some warped metal on broken wheels. Another ruined pair of panties gets tossed over Torius's shoulder.

I sigh. No clean undies for me.

"What happened?" I slowly come up behind them, afraid to get too close to the wreckage.

"A bomb of sorts, made from strong magic," Torius replies, peering down at the most blackened area at the center of the blast. "I can't identify it, though. Can you, my lord?"

"No." Kirian lets out a frustrated growl. "The smell is unfamiliar. A potion of some kind. I don't recognize it."

As he backs away, he reaches for me with shaking hands.

I don't know how, but I can actually *feel* his rage. It's like indigestion, simmering in my stomach and coating my throat.

I let him hold me—comfort for us both—and he takes measured breaths to control himself.

He's pushing his anger down. For me. He doesn't want to scare me like he did last night.

"It was probably stowed in the food compartment," Torius observes. "The fuse must've been timed, making sure we were far away from the palace by the time it went off."

"Who has that kind of power?" Kai asks, his eyebrows furrowed as he pets the side of Lady's face.

"The former Night Realm Queen," Damon pipes up, finger-combing his destroyed locks.

"Zella?" I don't want to believe that.

Damon shrugs. "I'm not saying I think she did it. She's just the only person I know who can light a fuse from so far away with that level of precision."

"My mother wouldn't do this," Kirian states, his voice hard. "There's no way."

"Whoever did it, they wanted to make sure the damage was localized to the carriage." Torius's conclusion is troubled, and all attention turns my way.

Everyone's silent, but I know what they're thinking. I was supposed to be in there.

That bomb was meant for me.

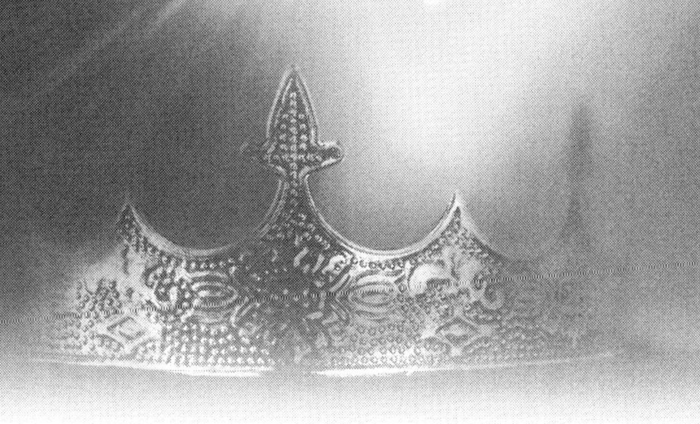

CHAPTER 15

Quinn

I GET MY OWN HORSE. THE ONE NAMED LADY. SINCE there's five of them and five of us, it's necessary. But I wish I could ride with Kirian. I feel too exposed, even if I am sandwiched between him and Damon. Torius is in the lead again, and Kai is in the back. They're all surrounding me like the Secret Service.

The saddle is hard, but my concern over the welfare of my ass and the length of our travel is gone. Those things seem trivial now.

I feel guilty. And terrified.

Someone wants me dead, and people got hurt today because of it.

I take a deep inhale, and my lungs expand easily with the motion. As luck would have it, when I fell, one of the side seams of my dress busted. I can breathe. Silver linings, and all that.

"Quinn? You good?" Kirian is concerned.

He has every right to be, but the fact that he's worried doesn't do anything to calm my nerves. If the unshakable king is scared… well, the outlook isn't good for me.

Within less than twenty-four hours, I've almost died twice.

It was pure coincidence that I wasn't in the carriage when the bomb went off.

Just thinking about the incident causes a wave of anxiety.

"Yeah," I lie, wishing we could stop to rest.

I want to get out of this tattered gown. It smells like a campfire, which just reminds me of my brush with death. More than anything, I wish I could have a few minutes to myself. I predict a minor—or major—breakdown in my near future, and I'd prefer to do it in private.

It feels like we've been traveling for hours and hours. And maybe we have. It's hard to tell when there's no sun to give away the time.

I will not ask how much longer it'll take until we get there. I will not.

"How's your ass?" Damon asks lightly.

I roll my eyes, but I'm glad for his cheeky attitude. It's definitely needed right now.

"Don't talk about her ass," Kirian snaps. "Don't even think about her ass."

"Seriously? I just sacrificed my golden locks for your mate. You'd think you could be a little more grateful."

"I'll be grateful when I talk to your witch. She'll tell me who's doing this. Whoever's going after Quinn will pay with their life. I won't be satisfied until their head is on a pike in my courtyard." As the morbid promise rolls from him like thunder, the wildflowers on either side of the road flatten to the ground. The wispy trees sway away, and birds scatter.

His bare shoulders ripple in the moonlight as he tenses, strangling the reins in his white-knuckled hands. My nipples pucker, and heat blooms between my thighs.

Why's he so hot when he's bloodthirsty?

It doesn't help that he's naked from the waist up. He literally gave Gunther the shirt off his back so the driver could maintain some dignity when he flew back to the castle to report the news.

Obviously, Kirian values his workers. Treats them like friends. Family, even. Which is why it's so puzzling to me that he has a traitor lurking somewhere. Who would go against such a respectable leader?

Just thinking about it gives me the willies. Digging into the pocket of my dress, I find my marbles. At least I still have these. I circle them in my palm, concentrating on the way they clack against each other.

I close my eyes, and for a second, I'm able to clear my mind.

Suddenly, Kirian reaches over and snatches one before pushing it into his own pocket. "That belongs to me, thank you very much."

My lips twist as I slide a glance his way, but I can't disagree. I've been making do with one marble for years. Honestly, it doesn't feel right to have them both.

Torius whistles loudly, and my entire body locks up.

"What?" I gasp, my grip tightening on the reins. "What does that mean?"

Kirian reaches over to graze my cheek with his thumb. "Calm, my love, and look ahead."

I do as he says. Straining to see in the darkness, I perk up when I catch a glimpse of a faint light in the distance.

I never thought I'd be so happy to see a lamppost. "A town?"

"A small village called Ailee," Kirian confirms. "It'll do for supplies and a place to sleep."

"Oh, good." I release a relieved breath.

As we get closer, I see rows of little houses. They're adorable, with stone walls and straw roofs. Unfortunately, I don't think we'll fit inside. When we pass them, I realize they didn't look small because we were far away—they're actually tiny, not even as tall as my horse.

"Um—" Throwing a questioning glance at the guys, I point at the nearest cottage.

"This is the gnome district," Kirian informs me. "The farther we get from the castle, the more you'll see all kinds of citizens, not just fae."

"Did you say gnomes?" My eyes get wide.

"The king! The king is here!"

I look over just in time to see a stout little man running to each door, knocking as he announces Kirian's arrival. His voice is higher, like he just sucked in helium from a balloon.

I bite my lip to keep from laughing, because that would be rude.

But he's just so dang cute. Even with the pointy hat, he's barely two feet tall. As others join in on the quest to alert the neighborhood, more gnomes start running from door to door. Entire families pour out into the road, and children chase each other around.

It's wonderful chaos, and for a second, I forget all the bad shit that's happened.

Torius throws up a hand signal, and I recognize it as the one he uses when we're stopping. The horses slow, and then we're just standing in the street among the excitement.

Soon, all the residents are surrounding us as they kneel. They're fair-skinned and most have light hair. Both males and females wear regular clothes—a variety of pants and button-up shirts—and they all have the same red hats on.

My mom had garden gnome statues. She used to tell me tales about how they tended to her garden at night when no one was looking. I used to think her stories were so silly, but maybe those myths came from something real.

Collectively, all the villagers get to their feet and face the king.

"What do you need, Your Majesty?" a woman asks, tilting her head far back so she can look up at Kirian.

She's older and plump, and there's a red apron around her waist.

"Nothing," Kirian replies kindly, using a warm tone as he smiles. He's fond of these people. "We're just passing through, but I want you all to meet my mate, Quinn."

Oh, here we go again with the mate business. Sometimes I feel like he should just say it like it is—*here's the human I settled for.*

At least the gnomes' reaction is a lot different than the fae nobles. There's no sneering or whispering about my appearance. None of them look upset. No one even comments on the dirt and destruction I'm literally wearing on my dress.

No, it's the opposite—unbridled joy follows.

There's cheering and jumping. Some of the children start running around again and watching them waddle might be the best part of my visit to Valora so far. Aside from sleeping next to Kirian, of course. That was unbelievably awesome, and I'm looking forward to a repeat.

As if reading my mind, Kirian says, "We need to find lodging for the night. Carry on with your evening."

"Hail, Queen Quinn!" It's a united shout from everyone around us, and for the first time since coming here, I feel welcomed. Valued. Appreciated and respected.

I want to thank each and every one of them for being so accepting, but they start disappearing back into their homes. The enthusiastic murmuring fades away as the crowd disperses.

A family of four stays on their front stoop, waving. They have two daughters, and I smile as I wave back. The kids giggle and hop, gaping at their parents in shock, like they can't believe I acknowledged them. A third girl scurries out from behind the mom, and she's got something in her hand as she runs to the other side of Kirian's horse.

"Wait! For the queen. I already took the thorns off." She holds up a dark-blue rose. She's so short I can't see her face, but she waves the flower until Kirian takes it.

He gives it a sniff before handing it to me. "It's a Midnight Rose from their garden. It takes decades to cultivate these flowers, and receiving one is the highest honor."

"It'll stay alive for at least a year!" the child shouts, darting under Kirian's horse to approach me. She's got blond shoulder-length hair, rosy cheeks, and the cutest button nose.

"Thank you," I breathe out, truly touched. "I wish I had something to give you, too."

"A hug will do." Reaching up for me, she spreads her tiny arms wide.

"Fiona," her mother reprimands, coming over to drag her daughter back to their house. "Don't be ridiculous. The royals don't hug us."

Fiona's lip wobbles as she's taken farther away, and my heart breaks for her a little. She gifted me with more than just a rose. She offered acceptance, which is worth more to me than any object.

And let's face it—after the day I've had, I could use a hug or a hundred.

"Technically, I'm not a royal yet," I say, impulsively deciding to grant her request.

Swinging my leg over the saddle, I wait for Kirian's protest when my foot touches the ground, but it doesn't come. He doesn't make a peep as I follow the family to their stoop.

Kneeling, I put myself at eye level with Fiona. Her big blue eyes dart from me to her mom, as if she's asking permission.

Slack-jawed, her mother seems too shocked to respond, so I scoop the little girl into my arms. She's heavier than she looks. I end up setting her on my thigh, and she hugs me back with fervor, giggling in my ear.

"No fair," the other kids complain. "We want a hug, too."

Pulling back, I wave the flower. "You're in luck because this seems to have given me an unlimited hug supply."

They don't need to be told twice. Barreling toward me so fast they almost knock me over, they latch onto my neck.

"Girls!" their parents scold, standing off to the side, fretting as they wring their hands.

I can't talk because I'm being squeezed too hard—these kids have a surprising amount of strength—so I send them a thumbs up.

With a confused tilt of their heads, the man and woman look at the lone digit pointing up in the air, and it occurs to me that they've probably never seen that hand gesture before.

"It's a good thing," I manage to say, though my air supply is limited.

Before I know it, the other families are piling out of their houses again, and I'm surrounded by two dozen gnome children. They take turns climbing onto my lap and wrapping their chubby little arms around me; the smallest boy of the neighborhood has had three turns already. They smell like flowers and grass, and they all exude innocence and happiness.

I'm not sure I've ever smiled this hard.

"That's enough," an older gnome says gently, patting each kid on the head before sending them away. "Let the queen breathe."

"Please, call me Quinn," I tell him.

He smiles behind his long white beard while leaning heavily on a cane made from a knotted tree branch. When the last of the kids toddles away, he turns his blue eyes on me. "You're going to make a wonderful mother someday, Quinn."

"Thank you." My grin fades.

As nice as the compliment is, it reminds me if Kirian and I go through with this mating business, I'm the hope of a kingdom. That my ability to have children—with Kirian—is what will ensure the royal bloodline continues.

But there are two problems. I'm not his fated mate and I'm human. I'm not even sure if it's possible for us to reproduce. I've always wanted to be a mom. When I've thought about my future, the career path was always unclear, but a family was definitely in my vision.

As I say goodbye to the gnomes, I try to hold onto their contagious cheerfulness.

Once we're on our way again, I can't help glancing behind us. A laugh bursts from me when I see all of them standing in the road giving me the thumbs up sign.

Like it's my own personal salute.

I smile over at Kirian. "That was really fun."

Pleased, he grins. "The gnomes are a friendly, peaceful bunch. We'll pass through here again on the way back. I'll be sure to bring them something special for making you happy."

I nod, already looking forward to it. "That's a good idea."

"You made them happy, too." Approval is strong in Kirian's tone. "You have no idea what your affection means to them. They have a long history of being subjected to mistreatment and discrimination, so to be treated as equals by you… well, they'll never forget it. You have their loyalty for life. They're probably breaking out the sugar beet vodka to celebrate right now."

"Is that safe?" I imagine the little people staggering around drunk. "They're so small."

Kirian barks out a laugh.

"Don't let their size fool you. One thing I can say about gnomes is that they can handle their alcohol. They could drink all four of us under the table." He gestures to Damon, Torius, and Kai.

"It's true," Kai says. "I challenged one to a contest once. I'll never do that again. The next day I woke up naked in a sprite forest seven miles away. I still don't know what happened that night."

That sounds like some of the stories the high school seniors used to brag about after a weekend party. The longer I'm here, the more I'm noticing the similarities between their world and mine. Last night at the ball was especially tough for me. Being surrounded by all those fae nobles made me feel like I was fifteen again.

I realize that's why I had an instant connection with the gnomes. Like me, they're not given a fair chance.

"How could anyone possibly dislike them?" I ask Kirian. "They're so nice and cute."

"It's not about like or dislike. By some, they're viewed as lesser beings. They don't live as long as fae. They can't fight. They don't have powers. In the past, they've been used for hard labor in the mountains because they're small and they can fit into tight spaces. That's illegal now. In the Night Realm, anyway."

After we pass some trees, another neighborhood looms ahead. The farther we go into the village, the bigger the homes get. Through lit windows, I can see people milling about their kitchens.

Like a good tour guide, Kirian explains we're going by the troll dwellings. Apparently, their average height is about four feet tall and they're a versatile species. Some possess minor powers. A few dabble in witchcraft, but witchcraft isn't exclusive to one type of person. Anyone can be born with the ability to cast spells and see the future, though it's rare. To sum it up, not all witches are trolls, but some trolls are witches.

The two-story buildings on either side of us are full-size now. Inside, fae families are gathering around dining tables.

I can smell the food.

My stomach growls. I haven't eaten since breakfast. We had canteen-like things the guys kept calling waterskins, and Kirian's had the waterfall mist in it. Somehow, it stayed ice cold all day. He was right—very refreshing. So at least I'm not dehydrated, but I'd give just about anything for a sandwich right now.

"The inn is right here," Kirian announces, coming to a stop next to a post to tie up our horses.

I look at the Tudor-style house. The roof is steep in several places, and the exterior is covered in a combination of wood planks and light-colored stone. There's no sign out front to indicate it's a business. If Kirian hadn't said so, I wouldn't have known it's a hotel.

Although he doesn't need to, Kirian helps me down from the horse. It's flattering that he wants to touch me every chance he gets. As my feet land on the ground, he combs his fingers through my hair.

"Are you okay?"

"Yeah," I answer. It's the same response I've been giving him all day whenever he asks.

It's not exactly the truth, and we both know it. But what else can I say? I don't want to unload on him in front of all his big, tough friends. They probably already think I'm fragile and weak. Unfit for the title of queen. Not right for Kirian.

And they wouldn't be wrong.

Bumping his forehead against mine, Kirian's hands linger at my waist. "You have no idea how glad I am that you weren't hurt today. It's only by your own stubbornness you weren't harmed. If you hadn't been so ridiculously, unbelievably, infuriatingly impatient during our travel—"

Insulted, I interrupt him by clearing my throat.

He grins wickedly, but his smile disappears when he solemnly finishes, "You would've been in there. You'd be gone, Quinn. I've never felt this distraught before. It's like I'm too devastated to be angry. I feel powerless, and I don't like it."

As his hands frame my face, I grip his muscular forearms. "You'll keep me safe."

Even with all the shit that's happened, I still believe that. Today wasn't his fault.

"What if I can't?" His question is husky with emotion. "If I lose you, I'll die. I can't face the rest of my life without you. I live for you now. I—I think I always have, if I'm being honest."

Wow, he's intense. But I dig it. When he says things like

that, it makes it really hard for me to stick to the plan of not jumping his bones.

I wrap my arms around his middle and press the side of my face to his bare chest.

Hugging is okay. At least the curse never said anything about that.

Kirian's skin is warm, and his heart thumps loudly beneath my ear. There's a small spasm inside my chest, and I swear our pulses sync up. Something about being near this man calms me. When we touch, it's like all my problems fade into the background.

I'm aware of the guys waiting for us by the front entrance of the inn, though they talk quietly amongst themselves, giving us the illusion of privacy.

The streets are empty. All the fae families must be too busy eating to notice our arrival. Or they don't care. Either way, I'm glad we have a minute to ourselves. I'm used to being alone with Kirian. Having him all to myself.

This is the first quiet moment we've had since we woke up this morning. I know it won't last, but I want to keep it for a little while longer.

Unfortunately, my stomach chooses to let out an angry rumble.

"Come." Kirian steps back and holds out a hand. "You're hungry."

Sighing, I go with him. When we get inside, the smell of food makes my mouth water. It reminds me of Thanksgiving dinner—roasted meat, fresh-baked bread, herbs and spices.

There's a bar along the right wall with a female bartender serving frothy liquid in a clear mug to the one customer they have.

The man—a thin fae with long stringy hair—does a double take when Kirian walks through the door.

"Your Majesty," he slurs, before dropping to the floor.

And I don't mean he's kneeling. No, he fell over. He's struggling to get back up when Torius gives him a hand.

The bartender's reaction isn't much different. She has absolutely no chill. Her eyes are wide with shock at the sight of Kirian and Damon, and she sways unsteadily on her feet while giving a curtsy to both kings. Losing her balance, she tries to straighten herself by grabbing onto something under the bar, but a clatter of falling dishes follows.

Ignoring the mess, she stands and sends the men a too-wide smile. "Your Majesties, what a pleasant surprise."

Kirian gives a nod of acknowledgement before escorting me to a vacant table on the other side of the room.

Sore for a variety of reasons, I wince when I sink to the hard seat. The benches are made from halved logs. There's exposed bark on some areas, and the dark wood is a contrast to the bright white walls. The floor is covered in some kind of lighter stone, and stardust lanterns hang over each table, restaurant style.

Charming. Rustic. I like it, but I wish I had a pillow to sit on.

"I'll go put in our order at the bar." Kirian leans down, placing his mouth by my ear. Some of his long hair tickles my nose, and I have the urge to spear my fingers through it. "Just a warning—there's probably only one meal on the menu. That's typical with these places."

"Good thing I'm not picky." Whatever they're cooking, it smells delicious.

"I'll see if they have anything for dessert. If you haven't noticed, butterscotch pudding has become a staple in the Night Realm, thanks to you."

As he pulls back, he runs his nose along my jawline. His crisp smell engulfs me, and I can't help letting out a dreamy sigh.

I'm dazed as Kirian struts away, and I watch the way his glutes flex with every step in his leather pants.

Damn.

Such. A. Great. Ass.

What? The curse never said anything about *admiring* either.

The guys look like giants towering over the lone drunken fae as they order drinks for themselves. Motioning to his mug, Kirian asks me if I want one, but I'm guessing it's beer. I'm not a fan. I've sampled my dad's favorite dark ale before. Yuck.

"Just water for me," I say with a shrug.

A waitress comes bustling through a swinging door on my left, and she's got a metal cup in her hand. "I'm already on it."

She places the beverage in front of me, and I give her a smile. "Thanks."

"No prob," she responds, and there's something different about her. Something familiar.

I study her face. Her high cheekbones, straight nose, and brown eyes. "Have we met before?"

She shakes her head, and her long brown ponytail swishes with the movement. "I don't think so."

"What's your name?"

"Brittney."

"That's a very… human name." And that's when it clicks. She's not fae. I lower my voice. "You're a human, too?"

Snickering, she takes a seat next to me.

"Well, not anymore." She tucks a flyaway piece of hair behind her ear. Her pointy ear. Which means she's been here for a while. "And you don't have to whisper. It's not a secret. Half of the women in this village are originally from the human realm."

My jaw drops. "Seriously? How?"

Her amusement slowly drains away as seriousness takes over. "The Day Realm. One night, I was taken from my home and put up for auction there."

I gape at her. "Auction?"

"Yep. Like cattle. I was being sold as a mate."

"That's—that's terrible."

A memory from yesterday flashes through my mind—when Zella said something about how the Night Realm doesn't steal humans.

Then the realization hits me like a ton of bricks—the Day Realm does. They're human traffickers. Whenever Kirian's told me the kingdoms don't see eye-to-eye, that's what he was referring to.

Holy shit.

Brittney toys with a string on her dark-blue apron. "It would've been awful if Toby hadn't found me. He's a toymaker from here. He just happened to be there that day selling his puppets. He bought me, and the rest is history."

She doesn't sound upset, and I'm baffled. "How can you be happy with someone who *paid* for you?"

Wide-eyed, she shakes her head. "He's my fated mate. We both knew it as soon as we saw each other."

I blink. "But you're human."

Hiking a shoulder, she smiles again while rubbing her slightly swollen belly. "I didn't know it at the time but getting kidnapped was the best thing that ever happened to me."

Very rudely, I stare at her rounded stomach. Either she's packing one hell of a food baby, or she's pregnant.

Then I think about all the families I saw here. There were a lot of children at those dinner tables. If what Brittney says is true, then the women who used to be human aren't having any trouble with fertility.

Obnoxious giggling draws my attention to the other side of the room, and jealousy spikes when I see the bartender flirting with the men. More specifically, Kirian. She's looking right at him as she twirls her white-blond hair around a perfect finger. I can tell she's fae. The unnaturally bright green eyes give it away.

"Don't worry about her," Brittney drawls, keeping her voice so low I almost don't hear it. "Adina's unmated, and she hits on everyone. I mean, literally everyone. Even me sometimes, and I'm as taken as can be."

Brittney's right, because two seconds later, Adina turns her attention to Damon. Raising a pair of scissors, she offers to even out his hair for him. Begrudgingly, he agrees.

"Speaking of mates," Brittney starts, "I hear you're engaged to the king."

Surprised, I glance back at her. "News travels fast."

"Yep. A messenger sprite flew here this morning to tell us."

"Brittney," Adina calls. "We need meals for five, and then their horses need to be moved to the stables for the night."

My new acquaintance sends the bartender a brittle smile before whispering through gritted teeth, "And she thinks she's my boss, even though she's not."

Before she can walk away, I impulsively grab her arm. "Thanks for talking to me like, well, like a person. It was really great meeting you."

Her eyes soften with understanding. "You, too."

My eyes drop to her stomach. "You gave me hope. The other human women—" I nervously fidget, because I'm not used to prying into someone's private business.

Thankfully, Brittney saves me from my own awkwardness.

"Yes," she answers. "Some of them have kids. Most aren't fated matches. The snatchers choose us based on how much we'll be missed on Earth, which isn't much. They go after women who don't have families, who live in poverty, or who just have a sucky life in general. After being rescued, a lot of girls decide to stay here because it's better than going back."

Wow, that's really sad.

"I'm glad you found happiness," I tell her honestly.

She beams. "This world takes some getting used to, but it's

awesome once you settle in. And I can't tell you how happy I am to have someone representing us."

Us.

She's talking about humans. She's talking about me. Having a human queen—it could be a game changer for the people of the Night Realm.

And suddenly, I feel a spark of confidence.

I'm needed here.

Regardless of almost being killed, this trip has had some positive moments. First the gnomes, now—

"Brittney! What's the hold up?"

Adina's rude. Can't she see we're having a moment here? I cut her a cold glance, and she shuts her mouth so fast I can hear her teeth clack from twenty feet away.

Kirian's lips curl up with a discreet smirk as he takes a sip of his drink.

A strange satisfaction flows through me. Being queen might not be so bad. Not if I can put someone in their place with just one look.

Sending me one last smile, Brittney heaves out a sigh and walks away.

"Bye." I wave at her back as she disappears into the kitchen, and the guys join me at the table.

When Brittney returns, she's balancing heaping plates of food. Each one has a steaming pile of sliced white meat, a mountain of mashed potatoes, and a variety of mixed green vegetables.

I'm practically hopping in my seat by the time my food is placed in front of me.

Ever the faithful servants, Torius and Kai don't pick up their forks until Kirian does. It's like they're waiting for his permission to eat.

Screw that. I'm starving.

Using my hands, I dig in. First, I bite off a piece of the juicy meat, and I hum out a content sound. It tastes like turkey. I want to ask if they have turkey here, but my mouth is full.

Grabbing a utensil, I ungracefully scoop up the mashed potatoes. I notice it has a chunkier texture than what I'm used to. There might be parsnips or other root vegetables in it. Or maybe they just grow weird potatoes here. I don't care, because it's perfectly seasoned and it has a pleasant nutty aftertaste.

It isn't until I've made it around to the leafy greens that I realize I'm getting sly looks from Kirian's friends.

"What?"

"You might want to ask Zella to set you up with some etiquette classes," Damon says with a laugh. "I haven't heard chewing like that since I came upon a pack of wild boars attacking a centaur."

I wrinkle my nose. "That doesn't help my appetite."

"Good. Maybe you'll slow down so the rest of us can enjoy our fine dining experience," he teases.

"Don't be a snob," I say through a lump of what I think is spinach.

"I'm a king. It's my job to put on airs."

Kirian clears his throat. "If you two are done flirting, I'd like to finish my dinner so I can go to bed."

Well, well.

I guess I'm not the only one having trouble controlling my jealousy.

"Sourpuss," Damon whispers under his breath.

Lowering his hand beneath the table, Kirian squeezes my thigh. It's possessive and sexy. Just that little gesture makes me want to lick him from head to toe.

Tonight's gonna be rough.

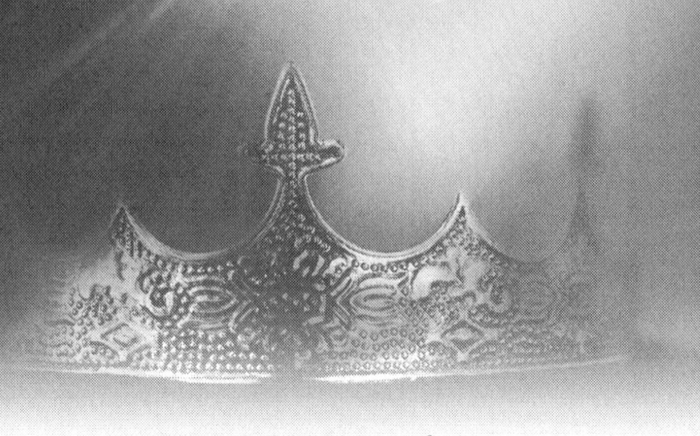

CHAPTER 16

Kirian

My need for Quinn has reached a tipping point. We've never spent this many consecutive hours together. Maybe that's why my cock is throbbing and my balls feel heavy.

Now that we've retired to our room, I have nothing to distract me from the sexual energy in the air.

It vibrates over my skin and makes the hairs on my arms stand.

And it isn't just coming from me.

Although Quinn seems determined to keep her distance for the sake of the curse, she can't hide her desire. Her sweet scent is driving me wild, and I've never been so compelled to claim something. To take it.

To take her.

All I can think about is getting her naked. I want to bury my face between her thighs, lick her juices, and suck on her clit until she comes.

As Quinn's feet pad over the wooden floor, I can smell her arousal getting stronger. She just took a bath, but she can't wash away the pheromones. After she hangs up her ruined dress, she puts her underthings back on.

I smile.

"What are you grinning about?" She sounds suspicious as she approaches the bed, and she has every reason to be.

Before my own bath, the innkeeper asked me if we wanted spare clothing. I declined. I'm nude under the covers, and I stretch my arms, knowing Quinn likes to look.

After all the time we've known each other, she still underestimates my abilities. I can tell when she's staring at me, and she does it a lot. I notice every shift of her head, the fluttering of her eyelashes when she blinks, and every breath aimed my way.

It's probably wrong of me to seduce her.

I don't care.

She wants me and I want her. Simple.

When she lifts the blanket to get in, she gasps and drops it. "Kirian."

"You're sexy when you scold me." I clasp my hands behind my head.

"Put some clothes on."

"No."

"Do it."

"Or what?"

"Or… Or I'll sleep on the floor."

"You'll do no such thing. You had no problem sleeping in my bed last night." Snatching her hand, I pull her down next to me.

She grunts as she lands on the soft bedding. "This is different."

"How so?"

"Um, I was terrified, and you had pants on?"

I gesture to my body. "I usually sleep naked. Covering myself was a courtesy."

"Oh, and now you've suddenly lost your manners?"

"Let's not lie to ourselves, love." I wrap my arms around her, pulling her close and nuzzling her neck. "We both know I've never been very good at manners."

She whimpers as I run my nose from her collarbone to her ear, and the sound is like a sledgehammer to my pulse. My heart has never raced like this, not even in the thick of battle.

Quinn's still on top of the covers, the quilt separating us, but I can feel her body heat. Putting my hand on her thigh, I move up to her hip. Her skin is so warm and smooth.

My fingers start to tremble. To keep them still, I fist a handful of her panties. The thin material stretches with the movement, and I want nothing more than to rip them in two.

I don't know what's happening to me, but I'm losing control.

"Why didn't you let me undo your dress?" The question comes out rougher than I intend, but I didn't like the human-fae touching my woman.

"Brittney was happy to help. Plus, you know why."

My hand slides up to the dip of her waist, discovering bare skin. Traveling along her spine, I stop when my fingers bump over elastic and a clasp. I feel the mechanism, realizing how easy it would be to unhook the bra with one dexterous flick.

"Don't you think we should be getting rest?" Quinn's breathing is shallow. "We need to be alert tomorrow. Just in case…"

Ah. Appealing to my fear about her safety. Smart girl.

But she doesn't realize she just made me want her more. When I think about losing her, my need multiplies.

My fingers flex against her back, pressing her closer. "I can't think of anything else I'd rather be doing right now."

I roll us slightly, so she's on top of me. Her leg falls to one side, and I hook a hand under her knee to spread her wider until she's basically straddling my hard-on.

"Your weight feels good on my cock," I rasp, my lips ghosting over her pounding pulse point.

"Oh, God," she moans, her exhale tickling my ear. "I'm not gonna make it."

"What?" Now I'm alarmed. "You can't say things like that. Don't talk about dying."

"I'm not talking about dying. It's this." Lifting her head, she waves a hand between us. "You and me. I can't *not* kiss you."

"Then kiss me."

"I'm so selfish." She tries to roll away from me, but I don't let her.

"If you're selfish, then so am I. I want this just as badly as you do."

Her palm flattens on my chest, and for a second, I think she's going to push me away.

But she doesn't. She slides it from one pec to the other, her fingertips scraping through the dusting of coarse hair on my body. When her pinky nail catches one of my nipples, I groan.

"Quinn."

The torture continues. As her hand glides up to the back of my neck, her mouth hovers less than an inch from my face.

I'd trade all the stars in the sky for her kiss.

She's so close. I can feel her breath teasing me. I lick my lips, wanting just a hint of her taste.

It feels like minutes go by as we stay like this. We're separated by fabric, but our bodies are plastered together. Quinn shifts, and it makes her hot center rub against my length.

If a kiss can solidify the curse, then I'm pretty sure dry humping is against the rules. I'm about to argue that point when Quinn sucks in a quick breath.

"I'm sorry, Kirian," she whispers, her voice breaking, right before her lips connect with mine.

Her mouth is soft as she kisses me slowly. Once, twice, three times she pecks me with closed-mouth nips and sucks. We both moan when she changes the angle and slips her tongue out.

Bliss. Peace. Happiness.

These are all the things she gives me in this moment.

But I can feel her emotions as if they're mine. Lust, pleasure, remorse, guilt. They clash together like a thunderclap.

"I'm sorry," she says between kisses. "I'm so sorry. So sorry."

"Stop apologizing."

"I can't." Kiss. "I've doomed you." Kiss. Kiss.

"You haven't," I disagree, my lips brushing against hers with every syllable. "My life is exactly how I want it to be, and this is the best moment, thus far. Don't ruin it with regret."

She makes a sound of frustration. "Sorry."

I chuckle into her mouth, sweeping my tongue inside. "No more talking."

Making a sound of agreement, she licks my bottom lip. Her body relaxes, letting go of the tension and shame. And I'm glad. I don't want our relationship to be needlessly tainted.

Quinn is everything to me. I'll choose her. Always.

Time seems to stop as our mouths meld in a dance. Sucking, nibbling, stroking. We go slow, exploring each other. Learning each other.

Quinn's tongue pushes mine. I push back.

Cupping her delicate face, I roll so I'm on top of her. That striking blanket's still in the way, but when she parts her legs, my cock nestles against the apex of her thighs.

Growling, I buck my hips.

Quinn cries out, and I freeze. "I'm sorry. I didn't mean to do that."

And that's the truth. It was an involuntary action. I feel disoriented, like I'm submerged in the depths of Issika Lake, and I don't know which way is up. I'm drowning in Quinn, and the only way to keep breathing, to stay alive, is to have more of her.

She laughs breathlessly. "Now who's the one apologizing?" Her kiss turns shy. "I liked it."

"In that case, I'll do it again."

Rocking against her—slowly, at first—I trail my lips down the column of her neck and suckle her sweet skin.

She gasps, and it's such an encouraging sound.

I palm her breast through the lacy material of her bra. I find her nipple and circle it with my thumb. Pinching the stiffened peak, I marvel at the way it tightens until it feels like a pebble.

All the while, I grind my shaft against Quinn in short strokes.

I wish there wasn't anything between us.

I want to rut so deep inside her that she'll feel it for days. I want to spill my seed in her womb over and over again, and every time she gets a twinge of soreness, she'll remember who she belongs to.

Chills race through me, and I'm shaking. It's odd. I don't get cold. Unlike this fragile human, my body adjusts to temperature changes.

But I'm hot, too. Burning from the inside out. I feel like I could combust at any moment. Sweat trickles down my temple, my skin flushes, and a sizzle infuses my veins.

"I need you. I've never wanted anything this much," I say, going for her mouth again.

She responds to my kiss, sucking on my tongue. "I'm not ready for everything, but..."

"But what?" I'm tense as I wait for her answer.

"We've already gone this far." She swallows audibly.

"What are you saying?"

"It wouldn't be the worst thing if we did a little more."

I didn't think tonight could get better, but this... this is better. "How much more?"

"I want to touch you," she says boldly, lightly scraping her fingernails down my spine.

"My body is yours. Do as you please." Flopping onto my back, I sprawl out.

I tuck my hands behind my head, attempting a casual pose when I feel anything but relaxed.

Seconds go by. All I hear is Quinn's rapid breathing and the quiet thumping of her heart.

Just when I think she's changed her mind, she tugs the blanket down. My cock bobs up and lightly slaps me on my lower stomach.

"Holy shit," she whispers.

Taking that as a compliment, I smirk. "That good, huh?"

"I knew it was big, but wow. That's a lot of dick."

I laugh. "Thank you."

When the tip of her finger grazes my slit, I nearly jump off the bed.

"It's so soft," she observes innocently. "Silky. Remember the time you helped me with my anatomy homework?"

I do. Sex Education is what she called it. Although I couldn't see the pictures, Quinn had me quiz her on the reproductive system of both males and females.

Such classes aren't needed here. Many young fae figure it out for themselves through experience. Not everyone waits for their soul mate, and I can't blame them. The instances of fated matches are rare. At some point, we all have to make a choice.

I don't regret mine.

Realizing Quinn's waiting for my answer, I grunt out an affirmative response as her touch trails down the underside of my erection. She stops just above my sac before tracing a vein back up to the tip.

"I remember thinking all dicks probably looked the same," she says quietly. "But there's no way anyone could compare to you. Yours has to be way, way above average."

Wrapping her fingers around my girth, she lightly squeezes. She pumps me a few times, and my back arches. I ball my hands into tight fists. My heels dig into the mattress.

I'm trying really hard not to explode.

With heightened senses, I feel everything. The scratchy linens under my body. The ridges and lines of Quinn's fingerprints massaging my velvety skin with every movement. The way she shifts her weight to hover over me.

Her body heat. Her scent.

Swiping her thumb over the swollen head of my cock, she smears the bead of precum leaking from the tip.

I'm panting like I just got done winning a challenge for the throne.

"If I keep doing this, will you come?" Quinn asks, and her naivety only ramps up my desire.

"Yes," I rasp. "It feels good. It's almost too much."

Her motions cease. "Do you want me to stop?"

"No!" I burst out, and my extreme reaction draws a giggle from her.

"Well, I was just asking because I want you to be in my mouth when you finish."

I barely have time to process her statement before my cock is engulfed in warmth. Wet, smooth warmth. The roof of Quinn's mouth has ridges, and the texture is exquisite against my sensitive skin.

She doesn't go down very far, but it's enough to make me groan. My husky, strained sound echoes off the walls as I hit the resistance of her closed throat.

Quinn backs off, circling the head with her tongue before taking me deeper. The light suction from her mouth tempts me to grab the back of her head, fist her hair, and shove my cock all the way in.

But I don't want to scare her. Instead, I grip the pillow and wait to see what she'll do next.

Popping off, she spreads her saliva around with her fingers before licking me from base to tip. Then she touches my balls, testing the weight of each one in her hand.

She puts me back in her mouth, bobbing up and down with more vigor than before.

I can't believe I've gone my whole life without this sensation, but at the same time, I'm glad for it. There's no one else I'd rather have for my first time—my first everything.

From here on out, Quinn is mine. Until the end of time. Forever.

"My mate," I sigh reverently, threading my fingers through her hair.

I gently fist the strands at the back of her scalp to help guide her. Up and down. Up and down. The rhythmic suckling sounds are erotic.

When she grabs the base of my shaft, I moan. "Yes. Use your hand, too. Just like that—in time with your head. Oh, fuck. Faster. Please."

Encouraged, Quinn does exactly as I say.

Pressure builds, and my toes curl. My muscles seize.

Completion approaches so quickly, I'm not prepared for the intensity of it. I erupt with a shout, and I come so hard I see stars.

See.

I actually see for a second. It's just a few bright bursts behind my eyelids, but it's the first light I've witnessed since I was a child.

It's gone just as fast as it flashed by, and I don't have time to think about it, because my cock is still lodged in Quinn's mouth. I groan as my hips buck up, and my seed continues to spill out in hot spurts.

Quinn swallows as much as she can, but some of it leaks down her chin, dripping onto my balls.

When I'm finally finished, she sits up and wipes her face. "You have no idea how many times I've thought about doing that."

I have no idea? I'd laugh it if wasn't so false. It's just a human saying. She doesn't mean it literally, but if she knew how many fantasies I'd had about this very scenario, she'd probably be frightened.

Now that my awareness is coming back, I sniff the air to find it saturated with Quinn's desire. Pleasuring me turned her on.

My mate needs me. I sit up so suddenly it startles her.

"It's your turn."

CHAPTER 17

Quinn

I think I've awoken something in Kirian. A side of him I've never seen before emerges as he roughly pulls me down next to him.

His unseeing eyes are wild as he tugs at my underwear. Worried he might rip the only panties I have, I wiggle them down my legs and toss them to the floor.

My bra is next, and I'm reminded again of how skilled his hands are. His fingers easily release the clasp at my back.

Flattening his palm in the valley between my breasts, he pins me in place as he positions himself on the mattress, my legs on either side of him.

"Kirian?" I question, unsure of what he's planning to do.

His erection hasn't gone down. If anything, it looks even harder than before. How's that possible?

I bite my lip when I think about what it would feel like to have that inside me. I pretty much told him sex was off the table tonight, but I might've been lying. I'm soaked between my legs, my inner thighs sticky with my wetness.

Who knew giving a blow job could be so hot?

Kirian was totally at my mercy. I was in control of everything he felt. I got to decide how and when he came.

And now he's determined to return the favor.

His hand slides down my abdomen, dipping into my belly button before roaming over my trimmed patch of hair.

"Quinn?"

"Yeah?"

"I love you." That's all he says before he dives in face first.

I let out a moan when his tongue spears my opening. He licks inside me a few times before going up to my clit. Latching on, he sucks. Hard.

Grasping the pillow under my head, I spread my legs wider. A loud whimper escapes me as I close my eyes.

His lips and tongue trace every inch of me, memorizing my flesh by feel. Everything gets explored. This is his way of looking at me and, somehow, it's more intimate than if he could see it.

Even though I was expecting Kirian's enthusiasm—because, come on, the guy's waited his entire life to touch a woman—I'm surprised by his gusto.

He eats me out like I'm the last thing he'll ever taste.

When I peek through my heavy eyelids and look down, I almost can't believe what I'm seeing.

The Night Realm king is kneeling before me. Worshipping me. His broad shoulders keep my thighs far apart, and his strong hands slide under my ass. He squeezes my butt and a sound of pure ecstasy escapes him when he licks my entire slit.

Stiffening his tongue, Kirian focuses on my clit, strumming the swollen bud. Something inside my lower belly clenches, and I'm resisting the urge to move my hips.

Humping his face would be weird, right?

Apparently, my body doesn't care.

I start rocking, rubbing my clit against his mouth.

"Mmm." Kirian makes a satisfied noise. "Fuck my face, Quinn."

Oh. My. God.

The heat from his breath and the movement of his lips while talking make me feel warm and puffy down there. Swollen. Aching.

His thick finger prods at my opening, pushing inside up to the second knuckle. When he adds another finger, there's a stretching sensation, but it doesn't hurt.

There's a different kind of pain throbbing in my core.

The pain of needing to be filled by him.

I'm thinking about asking him to just fuck me already, but the thought of his cock sliding into me, the image of him thrusting over me—it's too good.

My inner walls start to flutter.

I'm close.

Bringing one of my hands to the top of Kirian's head, I swivel my hips as my core tightens. My pussy rubs against his chin, his nose, his mouth.

I'm losing control.

From the sounds he's making, he likes it. Grunts and growls vibrate against my most sensitive parts.

Heat tingles all over my body. I'm sweating and shaking. Whines and whimpers fill the room, and I'm vaguely aware the sounds are coming from my throat.

I don't know what's coming over me.

It's almost like a force is driving me to keep going. I'm not sure if I could stop, even if my life depended on it.

Kirian adds a third finger as he latches onto my clit, and my body winds up until it feels like something inside of me is going to snap.

And then it does.

Arching my back, I wail as my pussy spasms. My inner walls clamp around Kirian's fingers and my clit pulses in his mouth.

He doesn't let up.

He keeps sucking, rubbing, and pumping into me, drawing the orgasm out for as long as possible.

When it's over, my body goes limp, and the hand that was in his hair falls lifelessly to my side.

As Kirian raises his head, I'm gulping for air while admiring how disheveled he is. His long brown hair is in total disarray, reminding me of a windblown Tarzan. Certainly not the put-together king I've known.

His lips glisten with my juices.

Instead of wiping my wetness off, he licks it. He laps at his face, his tongue stretching farther than I thought possible to get as much as he can.

Like a fucking animal.

Only after he's sure he's tasted every bit of me does he dry his mouth with the back of his hand.

"Nothing, Quinn," he sighs, falling down next to me. "Nothing, in all the realms, tastes as sweet as you."

"Thanks," I say, my face heating from the compliment. "I like the way you taste, too."

I never thought I'd actually enjoy having jizz in my mouth, but Kirian was the perfect combination of salty and sweet. I wouldn't mind doing that again. Soon.

But first, we need to talk, and this conversation isn't going to be sexy. Nothing like politics to kill the mood.

I wait a minute, allowing us both to come down from the high we're riding.

When our breathing finally slows to normal, I snuggle close and request, "Tell me about the Day Realm. They steal humans?"

Kirian stiffens slightly, his arms tightening around me. I can tell he tries to hide the reaction by playing it off like he's just shifting to get comfortable, but I noticed.

For several seconds, he doesn't respond. He kisses my forehead while running a finger down my arm.

"I was wondering when you were going to ask me about it," he says, resigned. "It's something I've shielded you from, but you're part of this world now. I can't keep it from you any longer."

"A long time ago, you told me your world doesn't do the changeling thing." That was something I'd asked Kirian about after doing some research on fae folklore. Not gonna lie, when I read about fae exchanging their sick babies for healthy human ones, I was freaked out.

"We don't—not anymore. The humans who eventually turn fae could be considered changelings, but that word has negative connotations stemming from a shameful past, so we avoid using that term. Long before I was born, the realms unanimously decided children were off-limits. It's strictly forbidden to abduct a child."

"Brittney was kidnapped."

"As an adult, yes."

"That's not much better."

"I agree with you. The truth is, the Day Realm doesn't just take humans. They go after fae women, too—any female of breeding age."

"Why?"

"There's a bit of history to explain first." He rolls toward me until we're facing each other. His erection prods my thigh, but I try to ignore it because I want to hear this. "During the time when my mother was an infant, my father's parents were assassinated by Day Realm soldiers. Although he couldn't prove it was the king and queen who ordered the ambush, he knew. As a form of retaliation, he cut off trade with them for many years."

Yikes. "It doesn't sound like enough. I mean, I respect him for not going ape shit on everyone, but damn."

"Well, someone did go ape shit—my uncle. Silas hired a coven of witches to inflict a terrible plague on the Day Realm."

I gasp. "The witches. The ones who cursed you."

Kirian nods. "You know faeries don't get sick, right? At least, not by natural causes, like viruses or bacteria. We're immune."

"Yeah."

"Then you can see why it would be so mysterious for a plague to sweep through an entire realm. It only affected reproductively mature women. Within a year, ninety-five percent of them had died."

"Almost all of them?" I can't hide the horror I feel at the brutality of it.

Pressing his lips together, Kirian pauses. "This is too much for you."

"No. I mean, yeah, it's a lot. But I need to know."

He blows out a breath. "My mother was too young to catch it, but her mother and oldest sister weren't so lucky."

"They both died?"

"Her sister recovered. Her mother did not."

"Poor Zella."

"Things only got worse from there. Many men lost their wives, including my grandfather Zed, who was king at the time. The thing you have to understand about fated mates is they'll go crazy without each other. Being separated is unbearable."

All the pieces are coming together now, from what I know about the curse to what Zella told me in the bathroom. "Your mother mentioned that."

"She would know from experience. In his madness, King Zed tried to keep her from my father. He'd already promised her to one of his council members. The Day Realm was suffering a great shortage of females and Keryth, King of the Night Realm, was his rival. He wasn't about to let his youngest daughter get swept away. But, enemy or not, you can't keep soul mates apart."

"Where was his compassion?" The ruthless nature of this culture is mind-blowing. "If King Zed knew how awful it felt, why would he want to inflict that pain on his own daughter?"

Kirian idly twirls a lock of my hair around his finger as he continues, "His mind wasn't right. From what I've heard, mourning a mate is so consuming, there's no room for rational thought. For a halfway-insane king to try to rule his lands while coping with a grief that never eases… it's a recipe for disaster."

"So he was crazy from sadness." It's not an excuse, but I've never lost anyone close to me. I don't know what grief feels like. I try to imagine what watching Kirian die would do to me. Just the thought of it makes my heart hurt.

I scoot a little closer, resting my head on his bicep as he adds, "In order to replenish their female population, King Zed ordered the unthinkable—abduct humans to fill their place."

And just when I was starting to feel sorry for the guy. "Where I come from, that's called sex slavery."

"And it's wrong. Here, there, anywhere."

"But King Zarid allowed the human trafficking to continue after he took over?"

Kirian gives a noncommittal tilt of his head. "Although he created a law against it some years later, rebels still went on with the abductions, and Zarid pretended not to notice. I think he feared an uprising would happen if he cut the people off. By the time the younger surviving generation of females were old enough to marry, the auctions were already common practice. Even thousands of years later, the Day Realm hasn't recovered from the plague. The male to female ratio there is five to one."

"That's a lot of horny, unmated men."

"We've tried to be fair. We allow Day Realm men to move here if they're willing to go through a process to prove their loyalty. Many have done it, because their chance of meeting someone here is better. But some of them don't want to do things our way—they want a female on their terms."

"I've always wondered why you fight. With the treaty in place, I didn't understand why there were battles. But now…"

"Yes. Now you understand." He caresses my cheek. "We've fought for the Night Realm females who were taken. If someone went missing, we made it our mission to get them back. Physical force was often necessary."

I don't like the idea of Kirian fighting. Now that I'm here, I can't imagine sitting around the castle, knowing he's out there potentially getting hurt.

"Will it ever end?" I ask, worried.

"My cousin Zander is next in line. He's not like his father. He's good and fair. I hope his day comes soon, because I have faith he'll do the right thing." Kirian pauses. "There's something else you should know about King Zarid. Desperate to produce an heir, he took a mate. When I say took, I mean an unwilling woman."

Why am I not surprised? "It'd be hard to enforce a law when you don't lead by example."

"Exactly. But that's not all. I know it's possible for a human who isn't a fated match to get pregnant because Queen Rowan is from your world."

Shocked, I sit up. "You mean to tell me the queen of the Day Realm is human?"

"Not anymore. Her body has acclimated. She's fae now, but once upon a time, yes, she was like you."

"That's why your mom seemed to disapprove of me at first," I conclude. "Not simply because I'm human, but because she thought our situation was like her brother's. She thought you went off the deep end and kidnapped me."

"Yes."

Scooting closer, I place my head on his chest. "You're wrong, Kirian. Queen Rowan's not like me. I'm not unwilling. Yeah, I was pissed when you first took me here without my permission, but I'm not mad anymore. Regardless of how I ended up here, I'm happy I'm with you."

Tears prick my eyes when I think about the possibility that he'll find his true mate someday. Would it change everything? Would years of friendship, trust, and love be overshadowed by a mystical bond?

"And—" Sniffle. "—And I don't want you to be with anyone else. Ever. Be with me. Only me." God, I sound so pathetic. I'm begging, but I can't help it.

Kirian gives me a squeeze. "Love, look at me."

I lift my gaze to his face, knowing the unfocused lavender eyes I love so much will never see my face. They'll never see our children, if we have any.

Selfishly, I'm okay with that if it means he's mine.

My mindset has changed since yesterday. Falling through the portal and flying with Kirian feels like it was ages ago. So much has happened in the last twenty-four hours.

"You're all I've ever wanted," he says, certain. "I promise."

"I promise you back." The magic of this world must recognize our words as an oath, because I get the telltale flutter in my chest.

I rise up and kiss Kirian's lips, just because I can.

Moving down on the bed, he aligns our faces, making it easier for our mouths to caress. Lazily. Softly.

I lightly touch his face. He absentmindedly runs his fingers through my hair.

Silence falls between us as we continue to get to know each other in a new way. It's familiar and natural, yet different at the same time. It's like all those afternoons we spent in my field and treehouse. We don't have to fill the space with conversation. It's easy to just be together. Only now, I can touch him the way I want to.

Of course, it's hard not to let my mind wander to sex. Sex makes me think of babies. When I think of babies, I remember Brittney's belly and everything Kirian just told me. From the sounds of it, humans have a better chance at getting pregnant than faeries.

That's the best news, and I feel like I'm exactly where I'm meant to be.

"When I'm queen, I'm going to do something about the women in the Day Realm," I tell Kirian, pulling back.

His hand comes to a halt in my hair. "*When* you're queen? You want that? To rule at my side?" He sucks in a breath. "To marry me?"

"Well, yeah." Propping my head on my hand, I smirk at him. "That's the plan, isn't it?"

Kirian grins, and in all the years I've known him, I've never seen him smile like this. His happiness is breathtaking.

"Yeah, that's the plan."

CHAPTER 18

Quinn

"NOT MUCH FARTHER," KIRIAN TELLS ME. "WE'LL reach the Shadowlands by tomorrow."

I'm a little surprised to feel a stab of disappointment.

I've enjoyed our road trip, and I don't want it to end. Honestly, it's been the most fun I've ever had.

Over the last several days, we've traveled across the Night Realm. We've spent hours on our horses before passing through quaint villages and small towns. I've come across three more gnome neighborhoods, all of which included a lot of hugs and ended with a thumbs-up salute.

I think I started a trend. Thumbs up is totally a thing now in Valora.

Kirian was sure to pick up something special for me from each place. Pants and a shirt, given to us from one of the innkeepers—which I've refused to take off, except to wash and dry them. Men's underwear, a gift from a clothing maker, which thankfully are more like shorts instead of a freaking fishing net. A necklace with river rocks chiseled into stars, bought from a peddler on the street.

In the last village, he got me a brown suede jacket because it's starting to get chilly as we go farther north.

The lights up ahead guide us to the biggest city yet. Kirian says our bedroom accommodations should be much nicer, but I didn't mind the taverns and inns where we've stayed so far.

It's hard to be displeased with a room when I have Kirian naked in the bed.

For the past four nights, Kirian and I have learned so much about each other. Physically, that is. Not a lot of talking has been done. There's not much to say, especially when we already know each other so well and we could be doing other activities to occupy our mouths.

I discovered Kirian has a ticklish spot behind his knees, kissing him is enough to give him an erection, and if I tug on his ball sac while I'm sucking him off, he'll come in less than a minute. He knows I love it when he kisses my neck, my nipples are automatic turn-on buttons, and the other night we discovered my g-spot.

We've done everything but sex.

But tonight, that'll change.

Tonight's the night.

I'm ready. Like, *now*.

Just thinking about all the ways Kirian's touched me makes me wet.

Squirming on my saddle, I slide a glance his way. A knowing smirk tilts up on his face.

When I remember the noises he makes, it gets worse. Kirian might be a stoic leader on the outside, but behind closed doors, he's wild. All the grunts, groans, and growls.

"Do you hear that?" Damon asks me.

"What?" I jump like a kid who just got caught stealing from the cookie jar. "Nothing. I didn't say anything." Did I?

"They're expecting us." He nods to the looming city ahead. "Aelustria awaits."

In the distance, a Night Realm flag waves in the breeze, flapping from the top of a tall pole. I see cottage-like houses, some taller four-story buildings, and one bell tower.

But I don't hear anything, except for the occasional chirp of an insect and the trickling water of the creek to our right.

When we get closer to the city, I catch a faint melody, and by the time we're riding past the welcome banner someone strung above the road, I realize there's a full-on party in the streets. A celebration for our arrival.

Colorful tents are set up, with vendors displaying their goods like a bazaar.

Fae and gnomes alike are belting out a song I don't know. The lyrics aren't in any language I recognize, but the words remind me of a really thick Irish accent.

"Old Fae language," Kirian explains. "It was the kingdom anthem before English became popular."

As we go down the street, more people gather on the sidewalks. We enter what looks like a business district, with shops and restaurants. But the part I love the most? How bright it is.

"Aelustria is so beautiful," I breathe out. "All the lights..."

"Tell me what you see," Kirian requests, like he's done so many times before.

"The road is paved with white bricks. There're lampposts about every fifteen feet on both sides of the street, and strings of lights connect each one." I look behind us. "It seems like they've got an endless supply of them."

He nods. "They were a gift to the city during one of the annual festivals long ago. They line this entire street all the way through. What else?"

"The storefront windows are lit up, and there's a toy store on our right and a bakery to the left."

He hums. "I can smell the pastries and cakes."

Now that he mentions it, so can I. The sweet smell of bread

and sugar lingers in the air. "And now there's a clothing store with three dresses on display. They're not on mannequins, but just hung up by hangers."

"Mannequins?"

"Yeah, you know, like fake headless bodies people use to show what it would look like on?"

"A fake headless body," he deadpans. "Is that a human thing? It seems so morbid."

I laugh. It's not often a new topic of conversation gets brought up between us, but then again, we've never been shopping together.

"I guess it would be a little off-putting in a world where people get beheaded as punishment," I surmise.

"We haven't beheaded anyone on purpose in hundreds of years." He sounds offended, and I just shake my head.

On purpose, he said. As if it's a regular occurrence for people to get their heads chopped off on accident.

"Ooh, there's a Maypole up ahead in the center of town," I add, trying to look around Torius. "The road splits into a big circle, like a town square. I see a gazebo."

"There's a park there. For the children. That was also a gift during one of the festivals."

In awe of the man beside me, I study his handsome profile. "I love how much you care about your people."

"Our people," he corrects, and it's still hard for me to believe that I get to be a part of this world.

I look out at all the faces on either side of the street. Everyone's packed so closely together they fight for space, nudging and pushing each other in their quest to see me. "They're waving at me. Am I supposed to wave back?"

"Only if you feel like it."

Being the center of attention is completely out of my comfort zone, but it's something I'll need to get used to. Deciding to play nice, I smile as I raise a hand in greeting. I try to make eye contact with as many people as I can, but we're moving at a brisk pace.

"Be alert." Kirian squares his shoulders as he addresses my entourage. "The large crowds make me nervous."

Just as he mutters the words, I see someone toss something out of the corner of my eye. A blur of blue comes flying at my head. I don't even have time to react.

Kirian reaches out, intercepting it mid-air, just a few inches from my face.

Yanking the reins, he pulls his ride to a halt, and all the other horses stop, too. It's so sudden, I get a bit dizzy. Ready to take on the threat, Torius and Kai both draw their swords with a metallic clink.

"Who dares to throw objects at the future queen?" Kirian roars, silencing the onlookers.

All the smiles around us drop immediately.

A male troll steps forward. His nose is long and his ears are large, and if I had to guess his height, I'd say he's about four and a half feet tall.

"My apologies, Your Majesty." He drops to his knees and puts his face to the ground, causing his brown hat to fall off his balding head. His next words come out muffled. "It's a scarf made from my silk spiders. It would be such an honor to have it worn by royalty."

Crushing the fabric in his fist, Kirian feels the length of it, inspecting it as though it might turn into a snake and bite me.

And shit, I dunno. Maybe that's totally possible.

But it just looks like an ordinary scarf to me, and it's beautiful. The blue is a lighter shade than the kingdom color, and there are gold stars spun throughout the fibers.

"Please," the man begs, trembling. "I meant no harm. I became too ambitious, my lord. I wanted to be able to brag about the queen wearing my scarf."

A shiver races up my spine, and I don't know how, but I can feel the truth of what he says. He's not lying.

I reach over and pat the uptight fae king's muscular arm.

"Kirian, it's just a present. And to be honest, I really want it." I project my volume a little, hoping the poor guy hears I'm happy with the gift.

Relinquishing his strangling hold on the silk, Kirian passes it to me. It's softer than I thought it would be. I rub it against my cheek before wrapping it around my neck.

"Thank you," I say down to the still-kneeling troll. His face is pressed so hard against the ground, he's probably eating dirt.

"Stand up," Kirian orders, and the troll scrambles to his feet. "What's your name?"

"Fallon, Your Majesty." Wringing his hat in his hands, he won't even look at us.

Kirian's temper isn't usually this short, but I can sense his tension as if it's mine. We've always been able to read each other. Our friendship has been easy because it seems like we're on the same page most of the time.

When Kirian's mood is darker, so is mine. When he's happy, so am I. That's only become more apparent since I've been here. We're closer than we've ever been.

"If my mate is pleased, then I am as well," Kirian says, his voice losing the off-with-his-head tone. "We're grateful for your generosity."

"Yeah," I add. "This is beautiful, Fallon. I'll wear it every chance I get."

Fallon finally raises his head, and when he grins, I see several missing teeth. "You've made me a very happy troll today, milady."

I give him a genuine smile, and Kirian clicks his tongue, indicating we should get moving. The horses obey the signal and start walking again.

Crisis averted. Now that the drama has passed, people chatter and cheer—a little more subdued than before.

I glance at Kirian. "What's wrong?"

"Too many people here." His jaw clenches. "It's making me nervous."

I frown. "Just try to relax."

"I'll relax when I know who's trying to kill you."

There it is. The unpleasant reminder. Since the explosion, there haven't been anymore murder attempts.

It's been easy to get caught up in the fun.

He's right, though. We need answers. I don't want to be constantly looking over my shoulder. Living in fear. Waiting for the other shoe to drop.

"Everything will be okay." I inject as much optimism into my voice as I can. "We'll be seeing the witch by tomorrow night. I think we're in the clear."

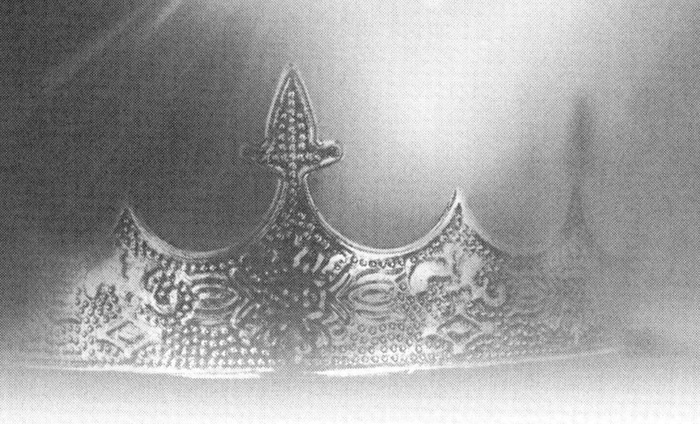

CHAPTER 19

Quinn

I SPOKE TOO SOON. I REALLY DID.

Tears run down my face as I heave, emptying the contents of my stomach for the fifth time.

I've never been a quiet puker. It sucks, but I'm too sick to be mortified. The humiliation of sounding like a dying donkey in front of Kirian will come back to haunt me later, I'm sure.

But right now, I'm just grateful he's with me. Holding my hair back. Rubbing my shoulder. Murmuring concerned words.

"I jinxed myself," I gripe. As Kirian helps me stand, I hold a hand to my roiling stomach. "Of course I'd get the stomach flu at a time like this."

After the scarf incident, Kirian seemed to be in a hurry to find our hotel for the night. He chose the biggest one, and they were already prepared for our arrival. It's a gorgeous three-story building, with a white stucco front and tan shutters framing each window. Like all the other places we've stayed, there's a restaurant and bar downstairs.

Soup was on the menu. That's it. Same meal for everyone. I ate it, even though it had a bitter taste to it. Who was I to judge? Maybe they have some funky-flavored vegetables in

Aelustria. Or maybe I was already coming down with the virus, in which case, nothing would've tasted great anyway.

"Quinn, we don't get the stomach flu in Valora." Eyebrows furrowed, Kirian hands me some toilet paper to wipe my mouth.

I shrug. "Maybe I was exposed to the virus before I came here."

"It wouldn't matter." His frown deepens. "You shouldn't be getting sick. Not in this world."

"Let's just go up to our room." Saliva floods my mouth, and I can tell the worst of it isn't over. "I want to lie down."

"I need to tell Torius to stand guard in the hall, then we can head up." He hooks an arm around my shoulders, and I lean into him.

"You haven't made him do that all the other nights. Is that because you didn't want him to hear us?" I try to inject sexiness into my voice, but it gets ruined when the last word is interrupted by a juicy burp. "I guess it's not like we'll be doing anything tonight."

Such a shame. I had plans, damn it.

"I'm pretty sure half of Valora has heard us, Quinn," Kirian says wryly, leading me down a brightly lit hallway. "But before, we weren't in a big city like this. Security is necessary now. Plus…"

"Plus, what?"

"I've had a bad feeling all day. I don't like that you're sick. Something isn't right."

I'm about to tell him it'll pass and I'll probably be fine by morning, but I don't get the chance.

When we walk back into the dining room, it's mayhem. Several trolls are puking in trash cans, random buckets, and bowls.

A fae woman runs out the front door just in time to vomit

in the bushes. She expels the contents of her stomach with so much force her wings bust out.

I cover my mouth, because watching everyone else hurl isn't doing great things for my queasiness. "I thought it was just me."

"Not just you, love." Kirian's arm tightens around my shoulders.

Most of the room has cleared out, but there are a few fae lingering by the bar as they try to pay their tab. But by the time we make it back over to our table, they start vomiting, too.

Every container in the place must be occupied, because the soupy barf splashes across the floor.

Oh my God.

I barely manage to suppress a gag. Groaning, I shield my eyes and avoid the awful smell by pressing my nose to Kirian's chest.

"What can I do?" Damon gets up from his chair, and his face is flushed and covered in sweat.

He doesn't look so good.

"Are you okay?" I ask, knowing he's going to say he's fine.

"I'm fine." See?

"You're not. You look like you're about two seconds away from barfing back into your bowl."

"Poison." Damon directs the claim at Kirian. "It has to be."

"Yes," Kirian agrees, his voice strained.

Damon lets out a visible shudder as he clutches his middle. "I need to go to my room. I'm not about to regurgitate my dinner in front of everyone. Send a doctor my way when you get a chance."

As he shuffles away, a hard cramp twists in my belly.

Kirian holds me tighter, and he sounds desperate when he pleads, "Kai, please fix her."

"I can heal injuries, not illness." The grumpy fae shakes his head. "You know this."

"Try!"

Pursing his lips, Kai approaches me. As usual, his eyes have an emptiness to them when he brings his palms to my shoulders. Warmth comes from his hands, but other than that, I feel nothing.

"Better?" Kirian asks, so full of hope.

"No." I lick my dry lips as a sickening gurgle rumbles in my gut.

"It's no use." Kai drops his hands. "I can't cure poison."

Kirian growls, but I can see from the resigned look on his face he already knew it wouldn't work. "Torius, I need you stationed in the hallway outside our room. Kai, go find a doctor. They're to treat Quinn first, no exceptions."

"Yes, Your Majesty." Kai jogs outside.

I can hear him shouting. Someone starts ringing a bell, and I'm not sure if it's an emergency warning or part of the festivities still going on in the streets. There's screaming, but I can't tell if it's happy sounds or if people are horrified by all the upchucking.

All I know is the loud sounds are making me feel worse.

"Poison," I repeat, pressing a hand to my pounding head. When I glance up at Kirian, his face is twisted into a grimace of pain. Suddenly, my concern isn't for myself anymore. I've never seen him look so pale before. "What kind of poison?"

"That's what we need to find out."

CHAPTER 20

Kirian

As soon as we get to our room, Quinn runs to the toilet. I follow.

I don't know what to do, and I feel helpless. I've never taken care of someone who suffers from ailments.

My mother got bad morning sickness when she was pregnant with Gia. That was a long time ago. I was young, and all she wanted was privacy.

Just as my father refused to leave her side then, I won't leave Quinn now.

A wave of dizziness hits me as I wet a rag with cold water.

Having zero experience with illness, I don't know how to recognize what my body needs. I feel something happening in my abdomen. My muscles cramp, and my stomach feels heavy, like a cannon ball is lodged inside my body.

"Is it normal for it to be this... violent?" I ask, wondering what's in my immediate future.

Quinn's laugh turns into a gag.

"For me? Yeah." Her response is echoey because her face is hanging down into the toilet bowl. "You've never puked before? Not even once?"

"No. That might change soon, though," I tell her, pressing the cloth to her forehead as I sink to the tiled floor.

I'll hold off for as long as I can. Quinn needs me, so I'll do everything I can to suppress my own urges.

"Poison," she says again, worried. "Are we going to die?"

"No."

Actually, I'm not sure. I'd like to think my body is strong enough to withstand something like this, but I don't even know what *this* is.

There are many poisonous plants in the kingdom that can kill. It had to be in the soup, and there's no way it got put there by accident. Too coincidental.

We were targeted.

My head swims and my throat burns. I feel a spasm in my diaphragm, and I can't put off the inevitable any longer.

"Watch out." I practically shove Quinn aside in my haste to get to the toilet. As I grasp the sides of the porcelain bowl, chunks and bile pass through my mouth. The odor of it makes me get sick all over again, and I heave until it seems like there's nothing left. "Does it always smell this foul?"

"Oh, yeah. It's nasty stuff."

I don't get a reprieve before my body is expelling more of the mysterious substance.

Amidst my vomiting, I realize Quinn is holding my hair back, just like I did for her. She rubs soft circles on my back and whispers soothing words. The wet rag mops the sweat from my forehead.

And I've never loved her more than I do right now.

She's my best friend, my partner, my everything.

Being fated mates couldn't possibly beat what we have.

"I love you," I say, before spitting the bad taste out of my mouth. "I wouldn't let anyone else see me like this."

"I love you, too." Quinn finger-combs my hair, gently

scraping my scalp. "We'll get through this. I already feel better." Her motions stop before she frantically pats my shoulder. "Wait—no, I don't."

And then it's her turn again.

A minute later, there's knocking. "That must be the doctor."

Quinn gropes my leg as I get up. "Don't go without me."

I love how she's so desperate to stay near me. Mentally fighting off my own sickness, I will my guts to stop churning as I pick her up. I kiss her forehead, not caring that it's clammy. She sighs as she lays her head on my shoulder.

After placing her on the bed, I answer the door. I sense a small male troll in front of me. He snaps his suspenders and lifts his glasses up on his nose. I smell antiseptic coming from his leather bag.

"Your Majesty, Doctor Whittle here. I am at your service."

"Thank you." I move so he can pass by me. "Treat my mate first."

"I need that trash can," Quinn says, panicked.

Before I have a chance to retrieve it for her, the doctor is already at the bedside, catching her latest round of vomit.

"That's it, dear," he encourages gently. "Get it all out."

I grab a clean cloth for her from the bathroom and sit on the edge of the bed. While she wipes her mouth, Doctor Whittle opens his bag.

"Do you need to do, like, a blood tessst or s-something?" Quinn slurs and her slow speech has me concerned.

"What's wrong?" I reach out to feel her face, and her skin is hot under my palm.

"I-I think I'm getting a f-fever," she says, shivering.

"No blood test required," Doctor Whittle answers patiently. "Wow, you got a lot out." He actually sounds happy as he holds up the bucket. "I have everything I need right here."

"Oh. You're going to test that?" Quinn sounds disgusted.

He chuckles. "Yes. The proof is in the puke."

The doctor hums a cheerful tune as he digs around in his bag. When he finds what he's looking for, he pops a cork.

A second later, flames erupt from the bucket in a scorching burst. Quinn yelps. Heat kisses my skin, but it's gone just as fast as it came.

Standing, I palm my axe. "What the fuck was that?"

"Aha!" the doctor says, ignoring the fact that I might take a swing at his head. "I suspected this. Singed my eyebrows off, too."

"Suspected what?" I demand, impatient.

"When ingested, stardust can make any creature very ill."

"We were poisoned with stardust? How do you know?"

"I put a drop of distilled Day Realm water in the bucket."

I have no idea what that has to do with anything. "I'm not following."

"Distilled Day water is extremely concentrated and more acidic. What happens when you put normal Day water with stardust? Light," he answers his own question. "Now multiply that reaction by a hundred. When the two are mixed together, things go boom."

"I've never heard of Day water being distilled. Is that some kind of secret they're keeping over in the Day Realm?" Feeling dizzy, I sink to the edge of the mattress.

"Oh, yes. It's a recent discovery, though." He shakes the bottle and the liquid sloshes inside. "They have a new distillery set up and it's a hot commodity. Would you believe it takes ten barrels of regular water just to make this little flask?"

"Why go through all that work? What's the reward? Explosions?"

"Well, that, and..." Pausing, Doctor Whittle adjusts the glasses on his nose. "It has healing properties, when used correctly. But most of all... drinking it amplifies fae abilities."

A magical drink that can be used for warfare, healing, and strength. In the hands of the wrong fae, it could be very dangerous.

If I wasn't already sitting down, I'd probably fall on my ass.

"Someone put stardust in the soup?" Quinn pipes up, missing the significance of what the doctor just revealed. "Are we going to die?"

"No," Doctor Whittle scoffs. "You might feel like you want to, but this should pass by morning. Just don't drink distilled Day water while the stardust is still in your system. Or else—"

"Boom," I interject, wanting to save Quinn from the gory details. "I get it."

Troubled, I wipe the sweat from my brow.

A mystery has been solved. It makes sense now. The bomb in the carriage could've been due to this combination. It wasn't a matter of magic, but of chemistry. Simple science.

A horrifying thought hits me as I cover Quinn's hand. "Did you drink any of your water at dinner?"

She pauses to think. "No. I'd just had the rest of the waterfall mist before we came inside. I was hungry so I went for the soup first. I started to feel sick before I got thirsty. Do you—do you think someone put the distilled water in my cup?"

Yes. Maybe. Probably.

I hate to consider the possibility, but it adds up. If my suspicions are right, whoever we're dealing with is ruthless and clever.

Exploding from the inside out would've been one of the most gruesome deaths I've ever heard of. The thought of such a thing happening to Quinn makes my heart lurch in protest.

Slipping a gold coin to Doctor Whittle, I instruct him to go downstairs to see if Quinn's glass is still on the table. If so, he's to test it.

I pace the room, my guts churning and cramping as I wait for his return.

When he comes back several minutes later, he has no answers for me. The dining room has already been cleaned by local business owners who pitched in to help. Any evidence is gone.

I drop two more coins into his hand. "Thank you. Please check on King Damon across the hall next, then tend to my men."

"Will do. I'm going to leave you with some diluted Grevillea nectar for when you're ready to rehydrate." A few glass bottles clink together as the doctor sets them on the bedside table. "Don't fight the illness. Getting the stardust out is the quickest way to recovery."

Once he's gone, I lean down to feel Quinn's forehead. Still hot and damp.

"My plans are ruined." She pouts, pulling the covers up to her chin as she gets more comfortable.

"What plans, love?"

"I'm ready." She doesn't have to elaborate for me to know what she means. "But sex is *so* not happening tonight."

"We have the rest of our lives for that."

Yawning, she nods. "I'm so tired."

"I need to check on Torius. He might be decorating the hallways right now."

"Are you okay?" Quinn grabs my hand before I can move away.

Am I? No, not really.

I'm striking pissed. Someone poisoned an entire restaurant in order to hurt Quinn. She could've died. And for the first time in my life, I'm sick. It's absolutely awful. How do humans tolerate this?

I don't want to lie to Quinn, so I don't answer her question. "I'll be right back. I'll leave the door open, so if you need me, just yell."

I'm doubled over as I stagger to the door. The stardust is wreaking havoc on my system, but I need to be strong for a few more minutes. It's not good for my men to see me like this. I refuse to appear weak.

Standing as straight as I can, I go out into the hallway. Torius is there, guarding my room like he said he would, despite the fact that he's probably in a world of pain. Duty comes first, and I'm proud of him.

I lean against the wall for support. "We need to narrow down a list of suspects. Interview the staff to see who was in the kitchen earlier."

"I already did." Kai walks over to us. "But the cooks and servants are all down for the count."

"The innkeeper?"

"Incapacitated."

"Did you see anyone suspicious? Anyone who hung around in the dining room but didn't eat?"

"No," Kai answers.

"How are you both feeling?"

There's a heavy pause, before Torius replies, "Fine."

I cock my head to the side. "You're not sick?"

Another pause. "No."

"And you, Kai?"

"Feeling fine."

Confusion and paranoia swirl with the nausea. "You mean to tell me you both ate the soup and you're not sick."

Torius clears his throat. "That's correct, Your Majesty."

"You," I whisper, unable to believe my men would betray me. But the witch did tell Damon it would be someone I trust, and for the past several days, these men have been the only people I'd bet my life on. Quinn's life. Seems I was wrong to do that. "You two conspire against me."

"No, my king," Torius rushes out.

Both men kneel, and a thud resounds on the wooden floorboards.

Stepping back, I sneer. Their fake show of loyalty is pointless.

"It was you in Quinn's room that first night," I say to Kai, before pivoting toward Torius. "And you're the one who secured the carriage."

Torius thumps his chest. "I would never—"

I cut him off with a wave of my hand. "And stardust was perfect, wasn't it, Kai? You knew you couldn't help with poison. Are you disappointed Quinn didn't drink the distilled Day water?"

"Distilled what? I have no idea what you're talking about." Kai must've practiced his denial. Or maybe he's just always been good at lying, because he sounds utterly clueless.

"Why?" I rasp. "You didn't want a human to rule over you? Quinn has been nothing but kind to you both."

Kai sighs, defeat heavy in the sound. "I suppose it won't do any good to try to convince you we had nothing to do with it?"

"No," I answer honestly.

What does a king do when he can't trust his own soldiers?

Eliminate them.

But I don't have proof, and sentimentality with a niggling of doubt is getting in the way. I keep remembering all the times we've covered each other's asses. Saved each other's lives.

My mind is too foggy to think clearly right now.

"You won't be with us on the rest of the journey," I decide. "Go to the citadel on the west side of the Aelustria. Tell them your king has sent you to do an inspection of the fortress. Stay there until I send for you. Swear it."

"I swear," they both say the oath at the same time, and a flutter in my chest solidifies the promise.

"If you disobey me and we cross paths before then… may

the stars be merciful on your souls." I don't wait for them to respond before slamming the door in their faces.

I run a hand over my jaw, and my palm comes away slick with perspiration.

"Kirian." Quinn's tone is sympathetic. "I heard, um, everything." The sheets rustle as she struggles to sit up. "Do you really think it was them?"

I want to answer her, but I can't put my emotions into words.

Torius and Kai were my closest friends. I'm sad. I feel betrayed. I feel vulnerable and weak, and I'm questioning my judgment. My pride is wounded, and my heart is broken.

But before I can say any of that, my stomach revolts, and I'm bolting to the bathroom.

CHAPTER 21

Quinn

KIRIAN'S EYES ARE CLOSED, BUT I KNOW HE'S AWAKE. Dawn glows on the horizon over the expanse of rooftops outside our third-story window. The soft light throws shadows on Kirian's troubled face.

"Do you realize you're frowning right now?" I ask, snuggling closer.

The corners of his lips dip even more. "No. Are you still feeling okay?"

I nod, my cheek rubbing against the hair on his bare chest.

The stardust poisoning set us back a whole day. We'd planned to leave yesterday morning, but we weren't in any shape to travel. The doctor was right, though. By the time lunch rolled around, our appetites were back. Sort of. We were able to nibble on some bread, and the Grevillea nectar helped to curb the dehydration headache.

But although we're physically better, Kirian's mood has never been worse.

My poor king is depressed.

I've seen him come through the portal injured. I've listened to him talk about hard times in his kingdom. Poverty, famine, injustice.

This is different, though. Kirian's never seemed so… human. He's hurt, and it's not the kind of pain that can be healed.

"I just don't get it," I say. "I don't see what they would have to gain from hurting me. And I know it sounds crazy, but I swear I could sense their honesty when they denied it."

"You're not crazy. I think you just want to believe the best in people, and I love that about you."

He's not wrong. I've always given everyone the benefit of the doubt before judging them. "Do you want to talk about it?"

It's not the first time I've asked since he let Torius and Kai go, but every time I bring it up, he turns the subject around to me. I think he's using his concern for my well-being to distract himself, which is fine. I get it. But I want to be here for him.

Seconds pass before he says, "Torius and I were born the same year. His father was my father's best friend and one of our best warriors. When Torius was five, his father was run through the heart with an iron spear." He doesn't have to remind me what that means—the worst kind of death for a fae. "My father made a promise to him before he died. He'd train Torius and I together. Basically raise us as brothers."

"Maybe Torius wasn't lying," I suggest.

"It doesn't matter. At this point, I can't take anymore chances." He lovingly strokes my nose with a finger. "Not when your life is involved."

"You're so good to me." My hand slides down his abdomen, and my clit starts pulsing when my fingers comb over his happy trail. "I can be good to you, too."

Kirian spreads his legs a little, getting comfortable as I squeeze his rock-hard cock. When my other hand cups his sac, he groans.

Biting my lip, I think about my decision to have sex. We got derailed, but I haven't changed my mind. I want Kirian. All of him.

Wetness floods my core as I lick his nipple and pump his cock. A bead of precum gathers at the tip, and I use it to lube up his head with my thumb.

If I keep going like this, I know he'll get off.

Keeping my firm grip on his shaft, I halt my movements. Jerking his hips, Kirian attempts to fuck my hand, but he's not getting enough friction.

"Why'd you stop?" he pants.

"Because I want something else."

His lips part, and he lets out a growl. That's all the warning I get before he flips us over, and suddenly he's on top of me.

Pushing my thighs apart with his strong hands, he sniffs the air. "So fucking sweet."

He lowers himself until our naked chests are touching, and I lightly scrape my nails down his back. As if we're magnets, Kirian's cock is drawn to my soaked center, and the swollen head bumps against my clit.

Bracing himself on one elbow, Kirian reaches between us and starts rubbing the tip along my slit. Each time the thick flesh presses against my entrance, I want nothing more than to thrust up until he sinks inside.

But he keeps teasing me. "You want me to fuck this pussy?"

God. Teaching him dirty words has certainly paid off. "Yes."

"How do you want it? Slow? Hard?"

To be honest, I'm past the point of caring. "I—I don't know. Just give it to me."

He chuckles darkly, lining his cock up perfectly. He's about to push forward when a loud knock raps on the wooden door.

Frustrated, we both blow out a breath.

"That would be breakfast," Kirian says through gritted teeth.

I huff. "Tell them to go away."

"I can't." Reluctantly, he lifts himself off me. "You need your strength today. We'll have to go on foot to the Shadowlands."

"Why can't the horses come?"

"Because it's likely they wouldn't survive the trip."

Yikes. I don't even know how to respond to that.

Kirian tosses a robe to me before pulling on a pair of loose-fitting pants.

When he answers the door, a troll wheels the food cart in, and it's covered in steaming plates and bowls of fresh fruit. The smell of sausages and freshly baked bread wafts through the air.

The innkeeper, a dark-skinned fae with long white hair, trails in after our breakfast. Like all the other times we've eaten here since the soup debacle, Titus insists on testing the food himself. He seems happy to be our guinea pig. The culprit for the poisoning has yet to be found, and I've never seen someone so apologetic about something that wasn't his fault in the first place.

We wait fifteen minutes, and he and Kirian pass the time by chatting about last year's festival and the weather. Snow is expected later today. When Titus shows no signs of illness, we finally get to eat.

I'm not sure I want to. Although I'm better, every now and then I get a wave of nausea when I smell food.

I'm pouring myself a glass of citrus juice from the pitcher when another knock comes at the door.

"It's me," Damon calls through the wood. "Don't make me eat alone again."

Kirian doesn't get up. With a surly expression, his butt stays planted in his seat while he bites into the loaf of bread. Doesn't even slice it. Just mauls it like a barbarian.

I nudge his leg with my toe. "Let him in."

"He's trying to crash all our dates," he grumps, then yells, "Get your own mate!"

"Gladly," Damon shoots back. "Are you offering to help me find her? How kind of you. If you don't open the door in less than five seconds, I'll take that as a yes. Five, four—"

Kirian's out of his chair at lightning speed. He jerks the knob with so much force it shakes the crystals on the chandelier.

He sweeps a hand toward the table. "Please, join us, cousin."

Laid-back as always, Damon snickers and saunters in, already wearing his leather get-up for the day. Only two dining chairs are available, so he pulls an armchair over to the table.

"That's too bad, Kirian. You have a queen. Just think—if I had one too, you and I would be a power couple."

Holding in a laugh, I bite my lip. Thanks to Damon's occasional dream walking in the human world, he's picked up some phrases. It's entertaining when he gets them wrong.

"I have my power couple right here." Kirian gestures back and forth between us.

"Fine," Damon sighs. "I've just had so much fun on our recent adventures."

Kirian makes an exasperated sound. "Are you insane?"

"I'm serious. In the grand scheme of things, the other night was a blip on the radar."

"And the damage to your hair earlier in the week?" Oh, Kirian's hitting below the belt now.

I smile behind a pastry when Damon sniffs. "It'll grow back. And, hey, we learned something new from Doctor Whittle. Distilled Day water is a thing." He shakes his head. "Once word spreads, we might have a new crisis to deal with."

"You're not wrong about that. Speaking of learning something new, how did dream walking go last night?" Kirian asks, changing the subject.

"Uneventful. Torius dreams of battle. Kai, well, let's just say in his dreams he was a lover, not a fighter."

Pressing his lips together, Kirian hums. "Well, I trust your witch will be able to shed some light on things today. After that, Quinn and I plan to go home to Delavaria."

For some reason, the mention of home causes a pang in my

chest. My mom and dad's faces flash through my mind, and I feel a deep sadness. I miss them.

Of course, always attuned to me, Kirian notices.

"Quinn? What's wrong?"

When I think about returning to the palace, I'm not as excited as I should be.

Aside from the mishaps along the way—okay, it's an understatement to refer to nearly dying as that. But if I'm not thinking about the unfortunate events, this road trip has been the best time of my life. The countryside is beyond beautiful. Kirian always points out the sights. Lakes, landmarks, and plants. I like being outside during dusk when the glow lights up the horizon.

That's what Kirian and I are used to—nature. The great outdoors.

"Do we have to go back right away?" I ask.

Kirian's eyebrows knit together. "I thought you'd want to go home."

"It just doesn't feel like home to me," I admit, taking a small nibble of the pastry. It's filled with a fruity jam, and I'm relieved when my stomach doesn't protest.

At least Kirian's not having any trouble with his appetite. He's shoveling the food into his face like it's his last meal.

The creases on his forehead deepen as he swallows a mouthful. "It will in time, especially after we get married. It'll be ours."

"I've enjoyed traveling," I go on, fussing with my napkin. I'm not sure how to explain my feelings without coming across as an ungrateful snot. "The people of Valora are so great. Everyone's welcoming. Most of the villagers have been happy to see me. When I show up, I'm celebrated. No one says anything about my freckles. Plus, I mean, gnome hugs. How can you beat that?"

"You don't like the palace?" Kirian presses, sounding concerned but not insulted.

"It's not the palace that's the issue. The nobles don't like me. I'm not even sure your family likes me." It hurts to say it, but it's true. "And everyone thinks I'm ugly." Kirian opens his mouth to argue, but I hold a hand up. "Don't deny it. Don't lie to me."

His jaw snaps shut.

That's what I thought.

"What if we spent some time away from Delaveria? We could visit the villages. Build maypoles and parks. Give them lights." Getting excited, I wave my hands. "It'd be a tour of happiness."

"It's a nice gesture, Quinn, but I'm the king. If the villagers need something, I have people who take care of it. I'm expected in Delaveria. We both are."

Swallowing hard, I look down at my plate. I don't know why I'm rebelling at the idea of going back. All along, I've known that's where we're headed.

"Lovers' quarrel, amiright?" Damon reaches across the table and casually plucks the last sausage off Kirian's plate. "Maybe I don't want a mate after all."

Kirian snatches it back. "That's mine."

"Mine, mine, everything is mine," Damon mimics with a huff. He gestures to the spread. "You know what I got for breakfast this morning? Porridge. The Dream Realm king doesn't get the same respect here that you do. They didn't give me any sausages. I'm just a poor blind man trying to find something to eat."

"As if playing that card could work with me." Kirian lets out a chuckle at Damon's antics, and I'm glad to see my man smiling again. "But fine."

He tosses the meat at Damon's head.

Damon catches it, but instead of eating it, he places it in front of me. "For you, future queen. You'll need your strength today."

I grimace. "That's the second time I've heard that warning this morning. Is this Shadowlands place really that bad?"

The guys are suddenly serious and silent, and that's all the confirmation I need.

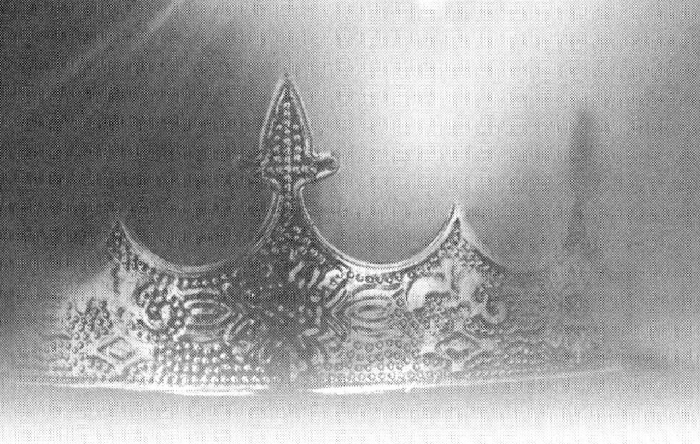

CHAPTER 22

Quinn

Mountains loom ahead. I could see them when we left town, but they looked small in the distance. Now they're huge.

And it's freaking freezing.

Good thing the innkeeper's wife went shopping for me. Apparently, while I was recovering yesterday, she took it upon herself to go to one of the clothing boutiques. She got me pants with a thicker khaki-like fabric, a fur coat, and a matching hat. They're super heavy and warm, and I'm grateful to have them.

Snowflakes have been falling for the last ten minutes, and they're coming down harder with every passing second. The wind gusts, and my face is pelted with icy crystals.

As I huddle under the shelter of Kirian's arm, my footsteps crunch over the dark terrain. I don't like how the clouds hide the moons and the stars. Not only did they give us light, but I've gotten used to seeing them.

We're not even in the Shadowlands yet, and it's all kinds of gloomy around here. The closer we get to our destination, all the living things just shrivel up and die. There are no birds or wild animals in sight. The trees look sad. Wiry, leafless branches wilt toward the ground, like they're depressed to be growing here.

"You're being affected by the area already," Kirian observes, reading my mood. He waves a finger toward the murky sky. "Do you want me to clear all this?"

It's nice of him to offer, but I'm not the only one who needs to conserve energy and strength. "No, just let it be. Maybe talk to me instead."

"If we were traveling to the Dream Realm the conventional way, we'd go on a trail through there." Kirian points to the left where the rocky road splits. "It's a beautiful detour. Lots of great sights to see."

I notice the way the trees and bushes flourish in that direction.

Then I look forward to where we're headed. My feet drag a little when I see the dark crevice leading into the cavern. The opening is about fifteen feet wide at the base, and old wooden signs are posted outside, saying things like *BEWARE* and *DO NOT ENTER*.

That's reassuring.

"Why would anyone choose to go through this place if they don't absolutely have to?" I wonder.

"The safer path through the mountains is winding and long," Kirian replies. "It's about fifteen miles, while going straight through the Shadowlands is less than three. A faerie can fly over if they don't have a wagon or a carriage, but most coming through here have a load of goods for trade. Some people like to take their chances with the short cut."

"And some people don't make it out alive," Damon cracks cheerfully. If he's trying to be funny, it's not working. "Astrid is a badass witch. She's lived in here for years and never had a problem. Going to see her is always dangerous. But as humans say—no risk, no reward."

"Hey, you actually got that one right." I smile at him.

His eyebrows furrow. "Don't I always get the humanisms right?"

I grimace. He's putting his life on the line for me. Now's probably not the best time to tell him he needs to work on it.

Shrugging off his backpack, Kirian digs inside and pulls out a small square about the size of my palm. He does that unfolding trick, and the material multiplies. As it unravels, I notice there are straps coming from each corner. He throws two over his shoulders and ties the others around his waist until it resembles a loose pouch.

Satisfied with the way it fits, he nods and pats it. "You'll be right here the whole time."

I gape at him. "Is that a baby carrier?"

"Technically, yes."

"And you want me to ride in it?"

"It's the best way for me to protect you. You'll be close to me, and my hands will be free to use my weapon."

My heart starts to pound. Oh, God. He'll need to use his axe.

Untying the top straps of the carrier, Kirian motions for me to hop onto him.

Who am I to say no when we're about to enter the pits of hell?

After climbing Kirian like a tree, I get secured in my safety seat. My face is just inches from his neck, our chests are smashed together, and my center is snugly pressed to the hardening bulge in his leather pants.

"Hey, this isn't all that bad," I joke, attempting to lighten the mood.

"Good. Hold onto that attitude. Just keep thinking as many happy thoughts as you can while we're in there." His tone is full of caution, and it only makes me more nervous.

"Why?"

"Because some of the creatures living in there are attracted to fear," Damon answers. "As humans say, you can run, but they can find you if they smell you. Is that correct?"

"No," I whimper. What the fuck am I getting into?

Trying to put on a brave face, I wrap my arms around Kirian's neck. I press my nose to the hollow of his throat, breathing in the comforting scent of crisp air and fallen leaves.

"Close your eyes," Kirian says softly as he walks forward. "You won't be able to see anyway. The darkness might not freak you out as much if you just pretend you're taking a nap. We'll go as quickly as possible."

I do as he says, and my world becomes dark as I slam my eyes shut. The guys draw their weapons, and the sound of metal scraping against metal only adds to my anxiousness.

Happy thoughts. That's what I need.

I picture my treehouse. I remember all the times Kirian and I hung out up there. It was our go-to spot whenever it was raining or snowing. Our shelter. Our safety. He loved to plop down onto my bean bag and drink hot chocolate while I sat next to him on a cushion of blankets. Usually, I'd lean back against his leg and read to him or we'd do my homework.

As soon as we enter the Shadowlands, I can tell. I feel the air change. It becomes impossibly colder, but there's no wind. It's so still.

Too still.

It's like the air itself has no life. I breathe it in, but it feels thin. Unsatisfying.

Kirian's quick steps make me bounce. Although our bodies are rubbing together, for once, I'm not turned on. When I'm around Kirian, I'm in a constant state of horniness. If this place can kill my libido, there must be something really wrong with it.

A couple minutes in, I give into temptation and open my eyes.

And there's nothing. It's the blackest black I've ever seen.

I whip my head to the right. To the left. I'm searching for any glimmer of light, even though I know I won't find it.

I feel trapped. Claustrophobic.

This is what Kirian woke up to the day he went blind, and he's been living in it ever since.

How awful. It's terrifying.

Now I realize the full weight of our decision to be together. This will be his reality. Forever.

Because of me. Because I couldn't leave him alone.

We've done way more than kiss. We've blown the fucking curse. To smithereens.

But what if it's not too late? What if Astrid could pull off something huge—like turning back time?

If I could go back to a week ago, I could stop this chain of events. I could simply not show up at our field that day. Ghosting Kirian would be super harsh, but I'd do it if it was for his own good.

I don't know if there's some kind of magic in the Shadowlands that crushes a person's hopes and dreams, but despair crashes down on me.

I hug Kirian tighter, wishing there was something I could do to fix this.

I have to try. I have to see if there's still a way to break the curse.

Even if that means he won't be with me.

He said witches like deals, and I wonder if there's anything I could offer Astrid as payment for such a large request. There's got to be something I can bargain with.

What would I give up for him? Anything. Everything.

Would I die for him? Yes. That's how much I care about this man.

A lump forms in my throat, and I'm trying not to cry. Can the creatures sense sadness, too? I sure hope not. Because if they can, they'll all be flocking to us soon.

"What's wrong, young one?" Kirian's use of my old nickname only makes my heartache worse.

"Nothing," I squeak out.

"I can feel your melancholy as if it's my own." He rubs my thigh. "I'm sorry."

"For what?"

"For not being open to your suggestions earlier. If you don't want to go back to the palace right away, we don't have to."

I'm glad he can't read my mind. If he knew what was really bothering me, he'd try to convince me I'm wrong.

I clear my throat. "Of course Delaveria is where you want to be. I don't expect you to change your ways for me."

"Well, you should. You're going to be queen. Your opinion matters, and it would be good for the kingdom to see us more. Maybe I could appoint a second in command to take my place while we're gone."

Oh, this sweet man.

"Like who?" I humor him, even though I'm too uncertain of the future to make plans.

"Gia. She'd love it. She's been asking for more responsibility for a long time. Maybe it's her turn."

Kirian's willingness to compromise makes me love him more, and I want to tell him that, but a sudden screech pulls my attention away.

"What was that?" My entire body tenses.

"Hold on tight," Kirian orders before spinning in a circle.

His axe makes a wet sound when it connects with something, and I clamp my lips together to keep myself from screaming.

"It's a pack," Damon calls next to us, but the words get swallowed up into the dark unknown.

A pack? A pack of what?

Tightening my legs and arms, I hold on for dear life as Kirian's body sways back and forth. Yeah, I'm probably not going anywhere when I'm in the pouch, but I feel a bit like I'm on one of those mechanical bulls. His motions are jerky as he turns this way and that, and the lingering queasiness from the stardust poisoning gets stirred up.

Although the fight lasts less than two minutes, it feels like forever before we finally resume walking. I'm assuming the immediate threat is gone, but I don't want it to happen again.

I go back to thinking about the field. Helping Kirian gather honeysuckle and hearing the songs he coaxed from the crickets.

The creek. Teaching Kirian how to catch a fish and watching his face scrunch up when he felt how slimy it was.

Butterscotch pudding. Books. Board games.

We encounter another pack of something. I think this one has wings because I hear frantic flapping above and around us.

Climbing trees. Dancing. Playing with Kirian's hair.

I stay in my happy place, shutting out everything around me, until we make it to our destination.

Patting my butt, Kirian says, "We're here."

I'm shaking as he unties the carrier and I slide down his body, staying as close as possible.

"It's just through here," Damon tells us.

At my back, Kirian molds himself to me, gripping my hips and curling his upper body over mine as he nudges me forward.

All of the sudden, there's light. It's not super bright, but after being in complete darkness, it takes my eyes a few seconds to adjust.

"So, you just walk in here like you own the place now?"

I follow the raspy voice to a small, frail troll. She's sitting in a rocking chair by a fireplace. With her gray dress, silver hair, pale skin, and honey-colored eyes, she almost blends in with the drab surroundings.

When I look around, I see we're in a cave.

The walls, ceiling, and floor are rocky and uneven. Shelves have been chiseled into the stone, and there are several stacks of books. There's a bubbling spring in the far back corner, and the water is steaming like a hot tub.

Three circular rope rugs create designated areas in the open space. One for the dining room, one by the fireplace, and one in front of what looks like a kitchen counter. They're multicolored—a mish mash of black, brown, yellow, and white. There's something strange about the material they're made from. It's glossy, almost like… hair.

A cot with brown blankets sits along the wall to our left.

It's surprisingly cozy in here, considering the location.

"Please forgive me, Astrid." Damon swaggers over to her wooden table and pulls out a chair for himself. "We've been through quite a lot to come see you."

"I know," she responds, still rocking in her chair. "Nice hair style, by the way. I told you to let me cut it last time."

Damon flips his shoulder-length locks. "You just wanted my golden mane for your rugs."

"Better than getting it burnt off, don't you think?" she counters.

Wrinkling my nose, I peer closer at the woven mats. Yeah, they're definitely made out of hair.

Disturbing.

Kirian draws in a measured breath, as if he's calling on his patience. "We need—"

"Two kings in my cave." Astrid rocks forward with so much force, she catapults herself up to a standing position. "Two kings. My, my, my. What luck I have."

"It wasn't luck, and you know it," Kirian deadpans. "You told Damon something important about my future. Something you knew I couldn't resist learning more about. Now I'm here. You have answers I need."

I lightly pinch his arm and whisper yell, "Don't be rude."

"Listen to the lady." Shuffling over to the kitchen area, Astrid picks up an empty ceramic bowl and brings it to the table. "Shoo." She waves Damon away.

With a huff, he joins us by the door.

Humming a random tune, Astrid begins stirring the bowl of nothing with a wooden spoon. "You can't just come in here demanding things. You have to be willing to give something in return."

"I can pay you." Kirian puts his hand in his pocket.

"Your gold will do me no good here." Her eyes shift to me. "And if you want answers, you'll have to ask the right questions."

"I'm prepared for that—"

"Not you," she interrupts Kirian before pointing a crooked finger in my direction. "Her."

"Me?" I ask. "Why me?"

"Because you're the one with the right questions." Her tone is downright condescending. Like, duh.

But there's a knowledge about her. She understands why I'm here.

My heart drops.

This is it.

I'll find out how to get Kirian's sight back. I'll find out who his mate is.

And I'll never be the same. For as long as I live, I'll mourn the loss of the man I almost had.

"You two have to go." Astrid flicks a hand at the men next to me.

Kirian's expression turns hard. "Absolutely not. I refuse to leave Quinn's side."

Astrid shrugs. "Then there's no deal."

Lacing my fingers with Kirian's, I tug on his arm. "You have to let me do this."

"I don't have to do anything. Not when your safety's at risk."

"I'm safe here with Astrid." I turn to her. "Right?"

"Eh." She gives a non-committal nod.

I resist the urge to roll my eyes. Not helpful.

"Kirian, please. We came all this way." I hate to be dishonest with him but appealing to his fear is the only way to get through to him. "I deserve to find out who's after me."

It's not a complete lie. I might explore the whole who's-trying-to-murder-me thing. After I get my answers for Kirian.

If he senses my deceit, he doesn't show it. His face softens, and he presses a kiss to my forehead. "I'll be right outside the door. If you're not out in fifteen minutes, I'm coming back."

"Okay. See you soon." I smile, trying my best to sound confident.

"I love you." He turns to leave.

"I love you, too." More than you'll ever know. "Wait!"

Before he can get too far, I launch myself at him. If this is the last time I'll ever kiss him, I'm going to make it a good one.

Wrapping my legs around his waist, I smash my lips to his. I breathe in his scent through my nose, and revel in the way his silky hair feels between my fingers. When his tongue brushes mine, I try to memorize his taste. My fingers scrape over his sharp jaw and the rough stubble on his face.

I want to tell him how much he means to me. That I don't regret a second of our time together. That he's literally my hero; his friendship saved me in so many ways.

But I can't.

If I do, he'll definitely know something's up.

"You're not doing a very good job of making me want to leave," Kirian rumbles out, rubbing the tip of his nose against mine.

"Sorry." I detach from him and slide down.

Smirking, he tucks some of my hair behind my ear. "What did I say about apologizing for kissing me?"

In answer, I turn my head and kiss his palm, holding his hand to my face for a couple more seconds.

"Go," I tell him softly.

"Fifteen minutes," he says again, and it sounds like a warning.

The doorway where we came in must be enchanted, because I see nothing but rock. As I watch the guys leave, my mouth pops open. They just walked through a solid wall.

"Payment will be needed upfront," Astrid announces, still moving the spoon around in the bowl. I pace over to her, expecting to find something in it, but nope. It's definitely empty.

"What do you want?" I ask warily.

"I'll take your hair."

I grasp my long strands, remembering the bubble gum incident. I was so traumatized by it, I haven't had more than a few trims since then. But I'll let her shave my head if that's what it'll take.

"I won't take off much," Astrid promises, mistaking my silence for hesitation. "Just six inches."

Holding up the length, I estimate it would put the ends right above my nipple. I blow out a breath. "Okay."

A bright smile lights up Astrid's face, revealing a wide gap between her front teeth. "Wonderful. Let me go get my scissors. Then we'll talk about what you want to know."

I swallow hard.

Now's my chance to bargain with a witch.

CHAPTER 23

Quinn

After the last snip, I look down at my new hair. I thought Astrid might do a quick hack job, but she didn't. Instructing me to stand very still, she took her time. She even created some framing layers around my face.

"Well, what do you think?" She holds up a mirror.

The handle is white, and it looks like it's carved from bone. I try not to visibly cringe as I wrap my fingers around it. Turning my head, I peer at my reflection and flip my new style around. It's bouncy and I decide I love it.

"You should've been a hairdresser," I say, admiring Astrid's work.

"A girl can be many things, if she wants." Her footsteps scuffle across the floor as she gets a teacup from the kitchen. Lifting a kettle away from the fireplace, she comes back to the table. "You, for example. You could be a queen, if you choose. Please, sit."

I sink to the chair Damon had occupied a while ago. And now that I think about the passing time, it feels like it's been longer than fifteen minutes.

Glancing back at the rock wall, I wonder if Kirian's okay or if he's freaking out because I'm still in here.

"Now, then. It's time for your questions." The teacup lands in front of me with a soft clatter, and Astrid pours hot liquid into it. "Ginger tea. It will help settle your stomach. Quite the fiasco you went through recently."

"You know about that," I say, surprised.

"I know everything."

"So, you'll tell me?"

"Everything? Oh, no. There's not enough time for that."

"No, I mean about Kirian. To help him. I don't really need to tell you why I'm here, do I?"

"Your blood pumps so fast," Astrid observes, avoiding my question as she peers at my pulse point. "Are you scared?"

"Yes," I answer honestly.

"Of me?"

"Of what you'll tell me."

"Ah. You're afraid to lose the king."

"Well, coming here was my idea in the first place." I sip at the tea. It's actually pretty good; sweetened with honey, just how I like it. "I sort of pushed him into it. I thought I was doing the right thing by helping him find his mate. I want the curse to be broken."

"Such a selfless act. You must care for him greatly."

I nod. "I'd do anything for him."

Astrid hums. "You know, I'm much more interested in you. In your world, people don't understand you."

"It feels that way, yeah."

"You've always been different. Sort of off. Like you can't relate to your fellow humans."

"Yes."

"They rejected you, over and over again, no matter how hard you tried to fit in."

Man, she's really nailing it. At least there's no pity in her voice. It'd be worse if she felt sorry for me. "Until Kirian came along, I really didn't have anyone but my parents."

Astrid squints at my face. "Tell me... what was your first impression of the young prince?"

"Well, he was kind of rude." I laugh, remembering how snooty Kirian had been. "But he was also really beautiful. My poor twelve-year-old heart could barely stand it."

She smiles. "Quite taken with him, were you?"

"Yeah." I blush. "And after we talked for a little while, I knew he wasn't mean. He was sad."

"And how did that make you feel?"

"Sad." I shrug. "Sad for him."

"Empathy is an emotion I lack. You can't have love without empathy."

I tilt my head to the side. "You've never loved anyone?"

We're getting off track, but I feel for the lady. She's obviously lived a long time and she's all alone. In the Shadowlands, no less.

She doesn't answer me. Instead, she reaches into her pocket, then drops a few strands of my hair into the empty bowl before adding some tea. I scrunch up my face because I think she might drink it, but then she sprinkles something on top. The powdery substance is white and a little sparkly. It looks like stardust.

A dim light glows from inside the container, and Astrid motions me forward. "Take a peek in here."

I do as she says, and as I hover over the bowl, I see the sky in the liquid, stars and all.

"Recognize this?" she asks. "This is the solar system of the Night Realm."

"Of course. I've been staring at it for the past six days."

She cackles. "Oh, you've been staring at it for a lot longer than that."

"Huh?" Glancing up at Astrid, I watch as she picks up the mirror again. She puts it in my right hand and begins manipulating my arm. "Hold it out, like so. Angle it this way. Yes, just like that. Don't move."

I'm in an awkward position, bent over the table with the mirror over my head. I look from my reflection to Astrid. "Okay?"

"Keep looking at your face."

Lights coming from the concoction dance over my cheeks. Not wanting to piss Astrid off, I stay focused on the mirror as she rotates the bowl and tilts it slightly upward. She rolls it to the right. Then to the left. Round and round the constellations go, reminding me of a night light I had when I was a kid.

Then Astrid starts to slow. "Yes, here it is. Almost there."

My heart thunders as I watch the glittery lights come to a stop.

When the pattern shifts into place, I gasp so hard I almost choke on my own tonsils.

Every single star in the sky lines up perfectly to my freckles. All the dots on my cheeks. The cluster under my left eye. The blob over the bridge of my nose. A few spots on my chin.

The full moon fits into my right iris, the smaller crescent moon outlines the left side of my nose, and a half moon sits on the curve of my bottom lip.

"She is marked by the sky at night," Astrid sings in an eerie tune.

I almost drop the mirror. Grappling with the bone handle, I manage to catch it right before it hits the ground.

Straightening, I slump back in my chair and whisper, "It's me. It's me?"

Chuckling, Astrid does a funny jig with her feet as she finishes her song. "You'll know her by love at first sight."

Panting from excitement, I shake my head. "But it wasn't. He's never seen me."

"But *you* saw *him*."

"Oh my God!" I exclaim, shooting up from my chair. Raking a hand through my hair, I pace from one end of the room to the other. "I did. I loved him right away."

The curse never specified *who* it would be love at first sight for. Those tricky witches. Kirian's fated mate has been under his nose this entire time.

And it's me. I'm his soul mate.

Coming to a stop, I lean against the counter in the kitchen for support. Because I might pass out from hyperventilation. "No wonder he got so pissy when he didn't get to see me for a long time. He couldn't help it."

Astrid nods. "I'm surprised he lasted as long as he did. When you were a child, the pull wasn't as strong. But after you became an adult, the bond would've been very hard for him to resist."

I rub my temple as my head swims. Obviously, I know it's possible for a fae and a human to be soul mates. After all, it happened for Brittney. I just never thought that was the case for me.

"I figured since I'm human..."

"You are, mostly," Astrid replies, stepping close to me with a magnifying glass. She grabs my arm and pushes up my sleeve before inspecting the veins on my inner wrist. "But you've got some fae blood in you. On your maternal side. Probably a great great grandmother." She pauses at the crease of my elbow. "Nah, add one more great. It's faint, but it's there."

"You're saying one of my ancestors got knocked up by a fae dude?"

"How long has your family owned your land?" She looks up at me.

"Like, five generations."

"A lot of portal access there." Letting go, she walks back to the table. "It's likely she had a tryst with the man, never even knowing he wasn't human."

"Is he still alive?" If so, I've got a distant grandfather here.

Returning to the bowl, she gazes into it with the magnifying glass. "Nope. He was a lowly Day soldier who stole portals from his general. He was caught and executed shortly after his crime."

My sneakers squeak as I begin pacing again. "This changes everything. I have to tell Kirian."

I can't stop smiling.

I don't have to ask Astrid to pull off some impossible task. I don't have to give Kirian up.

Grabbing my coat and hat from the hook next to the sink where Astrid told me to hang them before we played beauty salon, I hastily put them on.

I imagine Kirian's face when I tell him the news.

His brilliant smile.

How happy he'll be.

He'll get his sight back and we'll be together. It's a scenario I've never considered.

But it's real.

"Thank you, Astrid. Thank you so much."

I'm rushing for the doorway when she says, "Are you sure you don't have more questions?"

Well, yeah. I'd have a whole load of them if I could think straight. But as it is, the only thing I want right now is to get to Kirian.

"I'll be back," I call over my shoulder.

I hesitate at the rock wall. It doesn't look penetrable, but I saw Kirian walk through it.

Deciding to risk a few bruises, I surge ahead. I don't feel any kind of barrier, and suddenly, darkness is all around me once again.

"Kirian?"

No answer.

"Kirian? Damon? I'm here."

Nothing.

Seconds tick by, and panic slowly creeps in.

He said he'd be right outside the door.

Oh, God.

What if something happened to him? What if he got attacked by some awful deadly creatures? What if he's hurt?

Despite the cold air, sweat beads on my forehead and my hands get clammy.

I can't see, and even if I could, I have no idea where I'm going. I don't know how to get out of here.

I'm completely helpless and unprotected.

Lost.

Astrid. I should go back. She can help.

But when I turn around, my hands connect with nothing. I swing my arms, but all I get is air.

Shit. I must've gotten turned around.

My fear escalates when I hear a howl somewhere in the pitch-black abyss. I need to calm down and think rationally.

I can't be far from Astrid's. I literally just walked out her door, so it can't be more than a few feet away.

I back up five paces and try to feel behind me. Then I step to the left. To the right. As I go forward, I feel like I'm stuck in a bad line dance.

My hand grazes something, but it's not rock. It feels like feathers.

Not good. Not good at all.

Screaming, I fall backward and land hard on my butt. "Kirian! Help!"

Someone grabs me from behind, and for a second, I'm relieved. I'm saved.

Only, I'm not. I get a whiff of alcohol, sweat, and dirt. Not Kirian's scent.

Before I can cry out, a hand clamps over my mouth and the stranger drags me backward, pulling me deeper into the Shadowlands.

CHAPTER 24

Kirian

It's hard to keep track of time when I'm in so much pain, but I'm estimating it's been about two hours since I left Quinn in Astrid's cave.

The iron chains burn my flesh. It's a net of some sort, and the tangled web is marring my skin from head to toe. Even through my clothes, I can feel the metal affecting me.

Damon lies next to me in the same predicament, occasionally writhing and moaning.

We were set up. As soon as we came out of Astrid's, we were ambushed. Someone was ready for us.

"If I get my hands on that witch, I swear on all the stars..." I grit out, finishing my threat with a hiss.

"It wasn't her doing," Damon insists. "I swear it."

"How would you know? You really trust her that much?"

"Yes."

As if talking about Astrid summons her presence, she appears next to us. I can smell the mixture of soot from her fireplace, ginger, and a hint of Quinn.

"You boys need a hand?"

"That'd be great," Damon rasps. "I'm kinda wondering what took you so long."

"Figured you two could handle yourselves. Big burly kings, and all." Sarcasm is evident in her voice.

"Is she always this cheeky?" I ask Damon, and he sighs as the iron is removed.

"Yes. It's one of the things I love most about her."

Next, the net is slowly peeled away from me, taking a few chunks of skin with it. Damn. Quinn's seen me messed up before, but this is on another level. I just hope my appearance doesn't scare her too badly.

Limping, Damon and I follow Astrid through her door, but when we get inside, I don't sense Quinn. I sniff the air, but her scent is old. Lingering. Stale.

"Where is she?" I demand.

"Who?"

"Don't give me that bullshit. You know who."

Taking her time, Astrid putters to her rocking chair and lowers to the seat. Her fingers get to work on something. She's braiding.

I storm over and swipe the rug out of her hands. Finding the end she's weaving, I feel the smooth texture and take a whiff.

It's Quinn's hair.

"What did you do to her?" My roar is so loud the rocks shake and some dust crumbles from the ceiling.

"Calm down." Damon puts a hand on my shoulder, but I shrug it off. "Quinn gave it to her willingly."

"You don't know that."

"I do. It's Astrid's payment. Why do you think I get haircuts every year? It's not for my pretty boy image."

"Quinn left a while ago," Astrid says coolly, snatching the rug away before going back to work. "She got the answers she wanted."

"And?" This woman is the most frustrating creature in all of Valora. "Where is she now?"

"Ah, ah. I don't give information for free."

I know what she's going to ask for before she says it. "Fine. Take my hair."

A gleeful giggle bubbles up from Astrid as she claps her hands. The metallic click of her shears follows, and she steps toward me. "Just six inches. This time, anyway. Maybe next time I'll get more."

I don't care how much she cuts off, as long as she tells me where I can find Quinn. If she's out in the Shadowlands by herself, she could be dead already. Time isn't on my side.

"Lovely," Astrid coos, picking up a lock of my hair. "Just lovely."

"Don't worry about how it looks," I bark. "Just chop it and tell me."

"Fine, fine." She gathers my hair in her grip and cuts the bunch, then sits in her chair again. "Oh, this will be beautiful. I'll weave your hair with hers. Isn't that nice?"

"I don't give a fuck," I grit out. "Where. Is. Quinn?"

"Somewhere near, somewhere far, where she wished upon a star," she sings. Rocking, rocking, rocking in her damn chair, like she doesn't have a care in the world.

She's toying with me. I never should've left Quinn in here alone. My knuckles crack as my hands form into tight fists.

"Damon. I'm going to kill your witch."

CHAPTER 25

Quinn

"LET GO," I SAY. WELL, I TRY TO SAY IT, BUT MY words get smothered under beefy fingers. It doesn't stop me from begging for my life, though. "Please, don't hurt me. Kai? Torius? Please. Please!"

It could be either of them. Struggling is pointless. Whoever has me is strong.

Kirian was right. His men were plotting against him. They must've followed us instead of going to the citadel.

I could bite him, but that would require getting a taste of his disgusting skin. I want to gag just thinking about it.

Self-defense isn't something I've ever been good at. When it comes to fight or flight, I'm one hundred percent the latter. Although, now I'm wishing I'd paid more attention in P.E. when we studied self-defense one semester my sophomore year.

I recall something about kicking an attacker in the shin and decide it's better than doing nothing.

Blindly flailing, I bring my leg back. The heel of my tennis shoe connects with something, and the person's leg buckles. When their hand slips away from my face, I suck in a breath.

I'm about to start screaming when suddenly, they release me completely. Disoriented, I sway on my feet.

I did it. I got away.

Before I can get too excited about my victory, strong hands push me from behind.

I'm falling.

Expecting to hit rock-hard ground, I instinctively close my eyes and bring my arms up to shield my face.

"Unnfff." I land on a soft bed of weeds, and then there's a light so bright it temporarily blinds me.

Also, it's hot. Suffocating heat gets pulled into my lungs as I gasp for air.

Blinking, I look around through squinted eyelids.

"What the fuck?" I whisper.

I'm back in my field. In my world.

Digging my fingers into the dirt, I push myself up and look around.

I'm alone. The late afternoon sun is still high in the sky, just like it was when Kirian dragged me through the portal.

Disbelief pummels me as I turn in a circle. This can't be. I'm not supposed to be here.

How did I get here?

Suddenly drenched in sweat, I strip off my extra layers. When I get down to the loose white cotton shirt, I unbutton the top so the breeze can get to my neck and chest, but I decide to leave it on. All I have under this is my bra. Not like it matters. No one would see me out here anyway.

But the shirt smells like Kirian, and it's comforting.

Kirian.

Shit.

He's still in Valora. Every minute that goes by here is hours there. He must be going crazy not knowing where I am. That is, if he's okay.

Oh, please, please let him be okay.

I couldn't bear it if something happened to him. If I never saw him again. If he died never knowing I'm the one. Tears well up and spill over my cheeks as I fall to my knees.

I refuse to think that way. I have to be positive.

He's fine.

Forming the sweater, jacket, and fur coat into a pile, I make a comfortable place to sit. I'll wait here. He'll come for me. He always does.

But the seconds keep slipping away. I try to do the math, converting Earth time to Valora time, but it just makes my head hurt.

Picking at some grass, I cry as the sun sinks lower in the sky.

Mosquitos bite and cicadas sing. The breeze does nothing to cool me off in the August heat. Fluffy white clouds float by in the too-blue sky. I miss the stars.

An hour passes.

Then two.

Months. It's been months there now.

Wiping at my damp cheeks, I swipe over the freckles I've hated for so long.

I don't hate them anymore. They're still unattractive, but they're what connects me to Kirian. They're proof that I'm his.

The faint tinkling of my mom's bell signals dinnertime. She stopped doing that a year ago, but in this world, it's still the day before I'm supposed to leave for college. To celebrate, my mom's making my favorite meal. My parents want to give me a special send-off, and I'm going to have to act like everything's fine. Like I didn't just experience the most wonderful and most frightening six days of my life.

Blinking, I try to compose myself.

I don't even know what I'm going to tell them about college. Obviously, I'm not going anymore. I have every intention of going back to Valora with Kirian.

Standing, I decide to leave my extra clothes here. If—no, *when* Kirian comes back, he'll find them and know I was here. They'll be my breadcrumbs.

Glancing back at the empty field, I hesitate, willing my fae king to appear. But he doesn't.

I know how this goes—Kirian gets one portal a year. That's it, and that's all. Knowing he has to wait so long to see me makes me physically ache for him.

Jogging away from our usual meeting spot, I tell myself he found a way out of the Shadowlands. He's probably back in Delaveria scaring the crap out of people with his grumpiness.

And he'll come for me tomorrow when he can.

I take a detour on the way to my house. The treehouse sits about fifteen feet up in an old oak. Splinters stick out of the weathered rungs of the wooden ladder, but I know where to put my hands to avoid them.

When I make it up to the trap door, I pop my head through the hole in the floor. Since the shutters are closed, it's dim, but sunlight beams through the cracks between the wood slats. A little light is a thousand times better than zero after being in the Shadowlands. I suppress a shiver when I think about the endless darkness.

I zero in on what I'm looking for. I keep a change of clothes in here for when I get wet while fishing.

And right now, I'm practically dripping with sweat.

Plus, showing up at my house wearing a Night Realm getup would definitely raise questions. With the high-waisted pants and puffy white shirt, I kind of look like I just stepped off a pirate ship from the 1800s.

Pulling out the drawer of a small dresser, I find some jean shorts and a ratty purple T-shirt I got from a fundraiser at my high school.

After I'm changed, I lay the damp clothes on top of a toy

chest full of blankets. It hurts to see a corner of the blue flannel comforter sticking out. Kirian and I used it in the cold months. Although he didn't need it, sometimes he'd lend his body heat, huddling under there with me while I read him my latest find at the library.

A few stacks of our favorite books sit on a small bookshelf, along with some candles and a bucket of interesting rocks we found in the creek. My fishing pole is propped up in the corner.

Every square inch of this place is saturated with memories of Kirian.

Gah, I'm going to start crying again.

Sighing out a shuddering breath, I climb down and make the trek back to my house.

As I approach the yellow farmhouse, a wave of nostalgia hits me. I thought I wouldn't see this place again for a while. And when my mom waves at me from the porch, I realize how much I missed her.

She's wearing her usual sunflower apron over a T-shirt and jeans, and her gray hair is pulled back into a ponytail with a scrunchie.

My walk turns into a run, and my shoes pound up the wooden steps before I throw my arms around her.

"Oh." She laughs, taken aback. "What's this for?"

"I just need a hug." My voice waivers.

Rubbing my back, she chuckles. "Getting a little homesick already?"

"Something like that."

I don't let go for at least thirty seconds. One thing I've always loved about my mom is how soft she is. I guess you could say she's on the plump side, but it just makes her extra good at cuddles.

When I finally pull back, her eyes go to my hair and she touches the ends. "You got a haircut."

Oh, yeah. Forgot about that.

"Uh huh," I say, not offering any information about where I got it done.

"It looks nice," Dad chimes in from inside the screen door. "A new style for our college girl."

"The spaghetti and meatballs are ready." Mom unties her apron. "You hungry?"

"Starving." I don't know what was in that ginger tea, but it made my appetite come back with a vengeance.

Kicking off my shoes, I stroll past the living room on the right. The dark blue couch is the same shade as the night realm flag, and it hurts my heart a little to look at it.

Going to the farmhouse-style sink in the kitchen, I wash the dirt from under my fingernails as I gaze out the window. I search the woods for a hint of movement, a flash of clothing or skin.

But it's just tall trees, green leaves, and birds.

After drying my hands, I take a left into the dining room, and the smell of dinner makes my mouth water. The plates are already on the table, complete with a bottle of root beer at each place setting.

I smile when I remember the first time I made Kirian try the carbonated beverage. He'd sneezed, then hiccupped for fifteen minutes. Didn't stop him from drinking more, though.

I sprinkle parmesan cheese on my pasta before digging in.

After I've had a few bites, Mom speaks up, "So, you've got some packing to do tonight. You've procrastinated long enough."

"About that." I set my fork down. "I've been doing some thinking. I know this is last minute, but I've had a change of heart about school. I'd like to take some time off. I'd learn more by traveling and working."

It's easy to sound convincing because it's the truth. These past several days in Valora were more educational than all my years of being buried in textbooks.

Mom and Dad share a glance, and I'm afraid they're going to argue with me.

But my dad nods slowly as he scratches his white hair. "I suspected this."

"You did?" I'm surprised. "You're not mad?"

Adjusting his wire-rimmed glasses, he chuckles. "I don't know if you realize it, but you didn't seem very excited about going in the first place."

"Really?"

"Yeah. You sulked the entire time we were there for that tour."

"Oh." That was one of the days I missed being with Kirian because I was busy on the campus at the university an hour away. I'd hated knowing he was here, waiting for me.

"We've never been able to stop you from going your own way," Mom adds, tipping her head toward the window. "You spent half your life out in those woods."

"Have you thought about money?" Dad sounds concerned. "It can be expensive to see the world."

"That's not an issue," I reply. "I've been saving my money from the ice cream shop for two years." Also true. Not that my money will have any value where I'm going. Maybe I could donate it to the animal shelter or something. And here's the big lie I'd thought up on my way back to the house. "I was thinking I could get a job on a cruise ship. Cleaning rooms, washing dishes, maybe scooping ice cream. It'd be a great way to get some income while doing what I want."

Plus, it would explain why I might not be reachable by phone at all times.

"Well, listen, Quinn," Dad starts. "You're an adult. These decisions are yours to make. As long as you come back home every once in a while, we'll be happy."

"I will," I promise. Hell, I could visit every day with Kirian's portals.

Dad smiles. "We'll hold onto your college fund until next year, and we can talk about it then. But if you still don't want it, your mother and I are going on a vacation."

Grinning, I nod. Mom and Dad deserve that.

Now that the conversation is out of the way, I feel lighter.

I shove another forkful of pasta into my mouth, and my response is garbled when I say, "Deal."

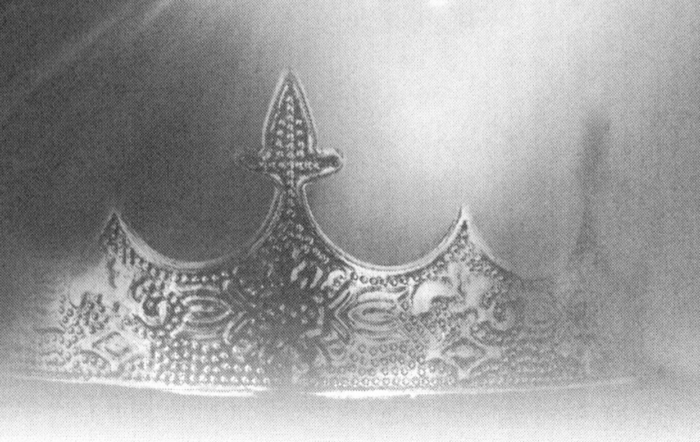

CHAPTER 26

Kirian

Back in the Shadowlands…

"DON'T HAVE A HISSY FIT," ASTRID SAYS LIGHTLY, as if I'm not two seconds away from snapping her neck. "Quinn is fine. She's home."

My eyebrows furrow. "Delaveria?"

"No. Her world."

"How? Why?" My heart feels like it might cave in when I wonder if Quinn asked to be sent home. She wouldn't have left me without a good reason. My fury returns, because there can only be one person to blame for this, and she's rocking in that fucking chair like my world isn't imploding. "What did you tell her to make her want to leave?"

"She didn't want to leave."

"Then why did she?"

"I said she went home, not that she wanted to."

Fucking witches and their riddles. I think Damon can sense I'm about to lose it, because he intervenes.

"How did she get there, Astrid?"

"Ah, ah—"

"No way. Come on," Damon practically whines. "Most of my hair got burnt off in the explosion. Just tell us. Please?"

"Oh, all right. Only because I like you."

"Thank you." There's a smile in my cousin's voice, like he knew she'd give in to his charm.

Astrid directs her next words at me. "Someone sent her back through a portal."

"Who?"

"Someone you trust."

Oh, for fuck's sake. "Did you give them the portal?"

"No," she scoffs. "I like Quinn. I wouldn't do that to her."

"Where would someone get a portal?" I ask, more to myself than anyone else, but surprisingly, Astrid answers without hesitation.

"The same witches who cursed you."

That information only produces more questions. The coven has been untraceable for centuries. Why would they resurface now?

It doesn't matter. I know where Quinn is, and I have to get to her.

"I need a portal. Can you do that for me, Astrid? I'll give you all my hair." I'd give her a lot more than that if she could help me. Gold. Stardust. A position on the royal council.

"I don't just have one on hand. You know how long it takes to grow a portal," she replies, her voice soft and pitying.

I do know. Six months to a year, depending on how powerful the maker is.

That feels like forever.

Groping for the chair near me, I slump into the seat as desperation weighs down on me.

I thought the waiting was over. Quinn and I were going to get to be together, always.

We were so close to getting everything we've ever wanted.

What if she leaves for college like she'd originally planned? What if I go to the field and she's not there?

"No chance of that," Astrid says, clearly reading my mind. "When you go to her, she'll be waiting."

"Thank you." My tone is defeated, but there's a glimmer of hope. Astrid's powerful. Probably the most powerful witch I've ever met in person. I can feel it emanating from her in waves. If anyone can grow a portal in record time, it's her. "What do you need from me to make this happen?"

CHAPTER 27

Quinn

My finger moves over the mouse pad, and I click the last button. It's done. I've canceled my classes. Going all-in with the lie, I even looked up a few cruise ships that are hiring, filled out job applications, and printed the info for my parents.

I scatter the papers out on my white desk and think about what I'd like to take with me to the Night Realm. This time, I'll be prepared.

Closing the laptop, I glance out my bedroom window.

The sun has fully set now. The stars are out, but it's not the same. They're too dim. Too far away.

Not as good as the Night Realm.

My new home.

I wish I could take back everything I said this morning about how I didn't want to go to Delaveria. Honestly, I don't care where I am as long as I'm with Kirian. I'll endure snide remarks and insults. I won't wither under the scrutiny of anyone with my king by my side.

I'll hold my head high.

After digging around in my closet, I find a small duffle bag.

It'll do. My dresser drawers creak as I open them, and I grab handfuls of cotton panties, a few T-shirts, and some skinny jeans. Some socks and a couple bras join the collection, and I zip it up.

If I were down in the kitchen, I'd raid the pantry of all our pudding cups.

But I'm too tired.

Climbing onto my bed, I recline on the pillow. My hair is still wet from my shower and I roll onto my side, gazing at the lavender walls. The color reminds me of Kirian's eyes.

Although he's never been in this house, he's invaded this place.

Everywhere I go, I see him in everything around me. Because it's not the location—he's embedded so far into my soul, I know he'll never leave.

I guess that's what being fated mates is all about. A connection that goes beyond space and time.

I wonder what Kirian's doing. I wonder if he's happy, or if he's losing his mind like I am.

My eyes grow heavy with fatigue, but I don't fight sleep. The faster tomorrow comes, the sooner I can see him again.

I've spent so many nights like this. Lying here alone. Thinking about him. His eyes, his smile, the way he makes my heart flutter.

I'd thought it was a silly crush.

But now I know it's more.

It's destiny.

"I love you," I whisper, sending it up into the universe, hoping it will make it to Kirian's ears.

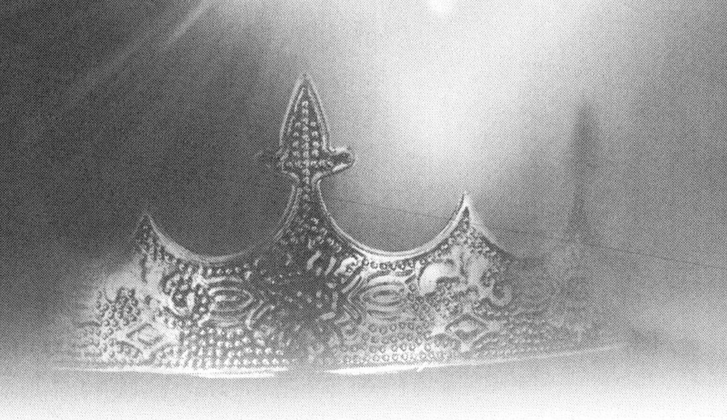

CHAPTER 28

Kirian

Five and a Half Months Later

AGONY. I THOUGHT I KNEW WHAT PAIN WAS, BUT these past several months have been the worst of my existence.

During Quinn's time here, I became addicted to her. That's the only way I can describe it. My sleep is restless. My appetite is gone. I physically ache and itch.

But today I'll get my portal.

I'll be reunited with my love.

The day Quinn disappeared, Damon and I made a pact—we wouldn't tell anyone what happened. I let people make their own assumptions, and a rumor that Quinn had been killed spread like wildfire through the kingdom.

So many mourned her loss.

They still do.

Just last week, a sprite delivered a message to me in the Dream Realm to tell me the gnomes were sculpting a statue in her honor, even though they don't have the resources to do so.

They'll be rewarded for their loyalty.

Since Damon's palace is just on the other side of the

Shadowlands, I decided to stay there until further notice. I sent word to Delaveria saying Gia should take over while I'm gone.

I almost feel bad about letting people believe Quinn died, but I still don't know who the traitor is. Whoever they are, they think I'm hiding out in Damon's castle licking my wounds. Too depressed to face the world.

Never underestimate the power of being underestimated.

In reality, I've been planning my revenge. That's the thing about missing Quinn. To distract myself, I've thought of every cruel and unusual way to punish my enemy.

They will pay.

My body hums with excitement as I make my way through the Shadowlands.

This is a trip I know too well now. Although Astrid said the portal wouldn't be ready for months, I've visited her often. Just in case it developed sooner.

And also because I actually enjoy her company. Damon's right—she grows on you after a while.

As soon as I enter Astrid's cave, I smell the portal. Yeah, this one's got some kick.

"Ready?" I ask, unable to hide the anxiousness in my voice.

"Ah, ah—"

"Right." I pull the band from my hair, and the knot falls free. "Let's get on with business then."

This time, instead of scissors, I hear a tiny crank before a buzzing sound follows.

"Sit here, mighty king."

"Are those sheep shearers?" I go to one of the dining chairs.

"Something like that."

"You're taking it all?"

"Just the sides and the back." She ties up the top section of my hair before getting to work.

The vibrations feel weird on my scalp as at least twelve

inches of my hair rain down to the floor. After she's done, she puts the clippers away and starts to brush what's left on my head.

"Can I go now?" I ask, impatiently.

She clicks her tongue with disapproval. "You can't go to Quinn like this. You look like your hair got into a fight with a meat cleaver and lost."

Pressing my lips together, I let out a hum. "A very apt description of what just happened."

"I'll fix it for you," she says, her fingernails sectioning off rows on my scalp.

Doesn't she know I'm in a hurry? This isn't the time to play hairdresser.

I hold up a hand. "Really, you don't have to do that."

"I work fast."

"Astrid."

"Mighty king."

"Fine," I relent with a grunt, relaxing in the chair.

I'll let her have her fun. She deserves it after helping me get to Quinn.

Besides, she's not wrong about being efficient. In the short time we've been arguing about it, she's already gotten through one braid.

She moves onto the next.

My scalp prickles as her gentle movements weave the strands together. It reminds me of all the times Quinn practiced her braiding skills on my head. At first, she was clumsy, and sometimes she pulled too hard. But eventually, she became an expert. I remember the way she liked to touch it, absentmindedly playing with the ends, twirling them around her delicate fingers.

"I miss her," I rasp out, my eyes burning as my throat gets tight.

Crying isn't something I do. Ever. But I've reached a breaking point.

"There, there, my king," Astrid soothes. "You'll be with Quinn soon enough. I've ticked off all the boxes to make sure of it."

"What boxes?"

The quick motions of Astrid's fingers stop as she finishes the last row. Then she uses my hair band to form the long strands into a small bun.

The clatter of a bowl on the table makes me turn. I hear the pouring of liquid and the scraping of a spoon as she stirs the contents.

"Someone doesn't want you to get to Quinn's world. Not now, not ever. I see a spell. An unsuccessful one. She's been trying to block portal access in Quinn's area. She's casting a pretty wide net."

"She? One of the witches?"

Instead of answering me, Astrid continues, "But you have something that's keeping her from being able to complete it. An object. A promise. It looks like a little glass ball."

"Quinn's marble." My hand goes to the pocket of my leather pants where I feel the small bump. "She let me borrow it years ago. I carry it with me always."

"A borrowed item." She chuckles. "How very clever of you."

The day Quinn let me have her prized possession, I wasn't thinking of the future. Not like this, anyway. I just wanted her to believe I'd return. As long as I had something of hers—something she valued—I had to. And I've been going back to her ever since.

"Well, my work is done here." Astrid places the portal in my palm.

It's small, cold, and almost feels wet.

"Thank you." For the first time since Quinn was taken from me all those months ago, I smile.

It's time to go get my woman.

I throw the portal down right here, and Astrid doesn't try to stop me. That means Quinn and I will end up in this spot when we return. I probably should've at least taken it to the Dream Realm first, but I'm too impatient.

Just as I step through, Astrid's fading voice calls, "When you have children, bring the little ones to me whenever they need a trim."

CHAPTER 29

Kirian

PLINK. *PLINK. TICK.*

Tick. Plink.

As I toss pebbles at Quinn's window, I hope to the stars it's the right bedroom. Although I've never been this close to her house, she's told me of the layout. I can hear three different patterns of breathing inside, and the one nearest to me has to be her.

Plus, I can feel she's close. My veins buzz with awareness. The sensation isn't as strong as it was in my realm, but I recognize it.

I welcome it.

The nighttime air is humid and warm. Anticipation and hope flood my system, giving me energy. Summoning my ability, I call on the cicadas and crickets to merge into a flowing melody.

Come on, Quinn. Where are you?

Tick. Tick. Plink.

The window slides up with a groan.

"Kirian!" Quinn whisper-yells. There's so much happiness in her voice, and everything is right again. My heart is mended just by hearing her say my name.

"Quinn," I choke out, overcome by emotion.

"Stay right there. I'm coming down."

Not more than twenty seconds later, Quinn's flying out the door and running toward me. I open my arms, and she leaps, latching onto my body by strangling my neck and wrapping her legs around my middle.

A canvas bag she carries smacks me on the back, but I barely feel it. What I do feel, however, is that she's not wearing any pants.

Our lips fuse together like magnets. Palming her smooth thighs, I roam her supple flesh as I taste her mouth. Her sweet scent fills my nostrils.

I groan. I could get drunk on her.

"It's three o'clock in the morning," she says without moving her mouth away from mine. "How are you here?"

Stroking my tongue against hers, I deepen the kiss. I don't want to answer her because I'd rather use my mouth for other things. Like making up for lost time.

Standing in the grass, we stay in this spot for several minutes, just holding each other. Soaking up every kiss. Every touch.

When she grinds her center against my hard cock, my patience unravels.

Turning, I start walking us back into the woods. Back to the portal. Back to where Quinn belongs—in my bed.

Twigs snap under my feet as I duck under a low branch, and I squeeze Quinn's luscious ass to keep her anchored to me.

"Missed you," she says between the frantic kisses she peppers onto my face. "So much."

"Missed you more."

She huffs out a laugh before pulling away. "I don't doubt it. Kirian, I have to tell you—"

"Who took you?" I interrupt, needing answers.

Shaking her head, Quinn nips at my jaw. "I don't know. I

tried to find you in the Shadowlands, but it was so scary. So dark. Then the guy grabbed me, and I couldn't see him. He never said anything, so I didn't hear his voice either."

"Shh," I calm her, stroking her hair—which I notice is a bit shorter than I remember it. Astrid's handiwork. "I know the events are fresh for you." To her, this all happened about eleven hours ago. "None of that was your fault."

"You didn't figure out who's behind everything?"

"Not exactly. My life has sort of been on hold ever since you got taken away. Astrid mentioned the witches who cursed me, but I know there's more to it than that."

"Are you okay? It must've been hard for you to wait so long to get to me."

"You have no idea." Nuzzling her cheek, I briefly summarize the hell I've been through. I tell her about the rumors of her death, my absence from Delaveria, and my unexpected friendship with Astrid. "All will be well again once we go back. We can stay at Damon's until we find who's after you. Then we can continue with our plans to marry."

"Wait. Wait, wait." Wiggling until I set her down, Quinn laces our fingers. "We need to go to the treehouse. We need to consummate the bond."

"Now?" Our separation made me yearn for her as well, but I don't know how long the portal will stay open. "What's the hurry? I can wait."

"No, you can't. I'm your mate."

"I know." Striking right, she is.

"No, you don't understand." Her voice takes on a hard edge. "I'm your *mate* mate. Fated, Kirian."

She's forging ahead, dragging me by the hand, but I have to stop to process her words. I plant my feet on the ground. "What?"

Quinn reaches up and links her hands behind my neck. "It's

me, Kirian. My face—my hyperpigmentation—it's the night realm sky. Every star. Every constellation. It's here." Taking my fingers, she presses them to her cheeks. "I'm marked by the night sky, and I've loved you since I laid eyes on you when I pulled you out of the creek."

This is… incomprehensible.

But suddenly, the facts click into place. The way her scent lured me. My inability to resist coming back. How disgruntled I became when I couldn't see her.

Being away from her always felt wrong. If I had to go years at a time without seeing her, I became irritable and sometimes violent.

I didn't realize it at the time, but I was experiencing mate withdrawal.

"How did I not know?" I rasp.

"I don't think you were supposed to," Quinn answers wryly. "Those witches are tricky bitches."

"It makes sense now…"

Every time she's made me come, sparks detonated in my vision. Was it a sign that the curse was being weakened?

Happiness, unlike anything I've ever experienced, rushes from my heart to every extremity in my body.

I lunge for Quinn, scooping her up and spinning her around. "I told you you're mine."

"I think our hearts knew it the whole time." She places a slow, sensual kiss on my lips. "Now make me yours all the way."

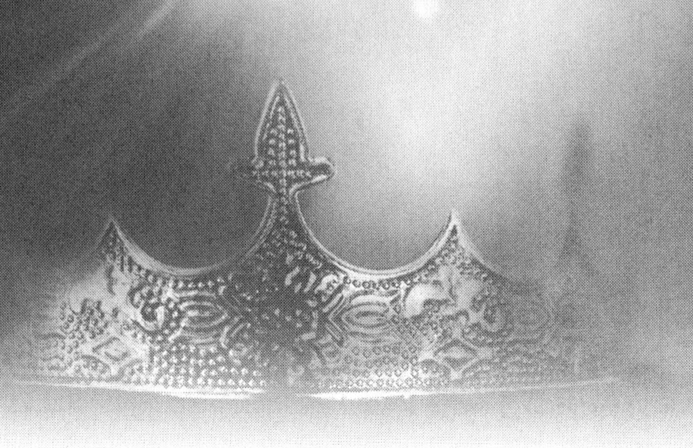

CHAPTER 30

Quinn

HUNDREDS. THAT'S HOW MANY TIMES KIRIAN AND I have climbed this ladder together. But this is completely new.

My pulse hammers as Kirian pushes up on the trap door and lends a hand to help me in.

We haven't even started having sex, but I feel like I could get off any second. Just the thought of Kirian's cock pushing into me makes my clit throb.

I'm shaking as I slide my shoes off, and I realize I'm not wearing much. I'd gone to bed in a tank top and underwear, and I was in such a hurry to get to Kirian, I forgot to put shorts on.

Wanting to set the mood, I light a few votive candles and spread the comforter out on the floor. The air in here is stiflingly hot, so I open the shudders to let the breeze in.

The highest part of the ceiling is just tall enough for Kirian to stand while slightly hunched over. The sound of him undoing his belt is like an electric shock to my libido.

I glance over my shoulder, and I like the way his strong, masculine fingers pull at the leather strap.

I know what it feels like to have those fingers inside me.

I'm about to know what it's like to have a whole lot more inside me, too.

I swallow hard when Kirian pushes his black pants down and his cock springs free. It bobs there, large and swollen. Ready.

Wetness and warmth spreads through my center, and I figure I better get rid of my panties before they get too damp. They join Kirian's pants on the floor.

Next, he peels off his shirt.

All the air whooshes out of me, and I whip my tank top over my head. "I'll never get tired of seeing you naked."

"I can't wait to see you," Kirian responds, his breath hitching, his face serious.

This is a big deal. Not just because we're having sex for the first time, but because our lives are about to change in a drastic way.

We'll be bonded forever, and the curse will be broken.

I lie on my back, getting as comfortable as possible.

"Guess we better get this show on the road." I try to keep the nervous quiver out of my voice, but I fail.

Getting down on his knees, Kirian puts himself between my open legs. "I don't want to rush it too much."

He flattens a hand next to my head and leans down to give me an unhurried kiss. He nips at my top lip, my bottom lip, and scrapes his teeth over my jaw.

Lowering his mouth to my breast, he sucks on my nipple. Pleasure zings up my spine, and my back arches.

He blows on the dampened flesh before going over to the other side. Once Kirian's had his fill of both breasts, his large body covers mine as he braces himself on his elbows.

Pressing another sweet kiss to my lips, he whispers, "From dawn 'til dusk, from dusk 'til dawn, I'll never love another." He lets out a reverent sigh. "That's the vow fated mates say during the ceremony, but I couldn't wait. Now you're mine forever."

Tears blur my vision. It's such a beautiful promise, and I know he's been saving these words for me.

"From dawn 'til dusk, from dusk 'til dawn, I'll never love another," I repeat as a tear slips down my right temple.

We seal it with a scorching kiss. Kirian's tongue plunges into my mouth, and I push back in a stroking rhythm.

His hand slips between us, and he groans when he discovers how soaked I am. His fingers easily glide through my folds, sliding down to my entrance. He inserts two fingers, stretching my tight channel. Making me wetter. Priming me for his cock.

As he massages my g-spot, his thumb draws circles on my clit.

My breathing picks up, my lower belly tightens, and my inner walls spasm, warning us of how close I am to climax.

Kirian withdraws his fingers and replaces them with his erection. I spread my thighs wider, surrendering my body as the large head presses into me.

At first, it's just an intense stretching sensation, but then Kirian thrusts, surging forward.

I cry out when it feels like fire ignites deep inside me. It takes my breath away, and I gasp out a pained sob.

Kirian freezes.

"Quinn, I'm sorry." He kisses me. "So sorry, love. It's not supposed to hurt with fated mates, or so I've heard."

"Does that mean we're not?" I ask, doubt replacing my confidence.

He shakes his head. "I think it's because you're human. You don't heal as quickly as faeries do. Plus, we're in your world—magic isn't as strong here. I'll make it better for you."

Snaking an arm between us, his fingers go to my clit. He rubs me the way I like. Just the right speed, exactly the perfect amount of pressure.

Little by little, my muscles relax, allowing Kirian to work himself into me with shallow strokes.

Once he's buried deep, he rests his sweaty forehead on mine. "You okay?"

Surprisingly, I am. The temporary pain has faded, and the burning from before has morphed into a sensation of urgent need.

"Yeah," I breathe out, wiggling to encourage him to move.

My sigh turns into a gasp when Kirian jerks his hips, driving himself impossibly deeper.

"I can't—I can't stop." His entire body is trembling with the effort to stay still, but it's like he's being driven by a force out of his control. His muscles ripple as he fights against the urge to move. He has a pained expression on his face when he adds, "I'm trying to hold back, Quinn. I really am."

"Don't." I caress his cheek. "I've wanted this for so long. Just let it happen."

Groaning, he gives into a power that's beyond us. His hips begin pumping into me. Our ragged breathing is loud as our bodies slap together. Every time he thrusts, the sensation of being so full makes me whimper, but it doesn't hurt.

In fact, it starts to feel really fucking good.

Kirian's hand goes to my face. "My queen. My mate. You're the best thing I've ever felt."

"Anything yet?" I ask, studying his unfocused lavender eyes. He's not showing any signs of vision.

"Let's not think about that right now. This isn't about the curse. It's just about you and me."

He's right. After everything we've been through, we deserve this moment.

Sliding a hand around his back, I cling to him and moan, "You and me."

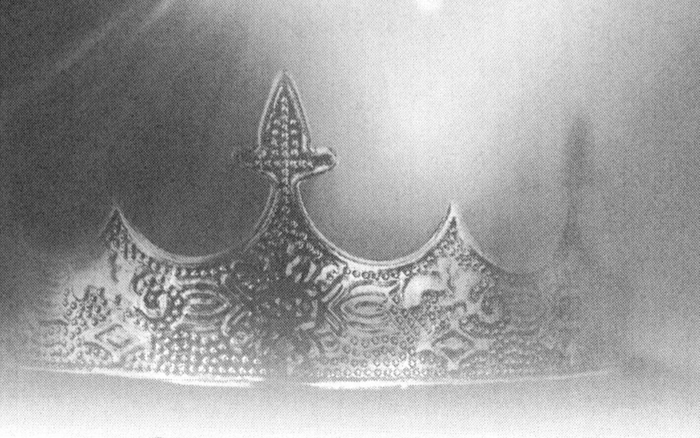

CHAPTER 31

Kirian

I'M SO LOST IN THE PLEASURE, I FORGET ABOUT THE curse. My eyes are closed, because all I can focus on is Quinn's impossibly snug pussy. Her slick walls are like velvet around my cock, and every time I push into her, there's a gush of liquid, making the glide smoother.

I love the feeling of her soft body pinned beneath mine. The sweet scent of her sweat mixed with arousal. The wet sounds coming from where we're joined.

I want to do this every day, all day. I'll take up residence inside Quinn's body. She'll be my palace, my fortress, my home.

I must be insane with lust, because I even consider making her sit on my cock during dinners and meetings.

Opening my eyes, I expect to get nothing but darkness, but there's a faint glow.

I blink. Once. Twice.

My vision is fuzzy, but I can see.

I grunt, unable to stop ramming my cock into Quinn. I can't—it feels too good, and it's like my motions are being driven by something more than just physical need.

Calling on all my willpower, I force my body to slow. The

best I'm able to accomplish is a languid thrust. It's so difficult to do, I'm shaking from exertion, but I want to be able to look at Quinn.

Her face—the one I've memorized by touch—is scrunched up in ecstasy. There's a cute wrinkle on the bridge of her nose. Her pink lips are parted, and her eyes are slammed shut. For a second, I think my sight is spotty because there are a bunch of shadows on her skin.

But what I'm seeing is her freckles. The Night Realm sky. It's all there on her face.

"Why're you stopping?" Keeping her eyes closed, Quinn rolls her hips, pushing me deep. "It's so good."

"It's working. The curse… it's lifting."

"It is?" Peeking through her dark lashes, Quinn gazes up at me.

The second our eyes connect, my view sharpens.

I gasp.

My soul realigns. Before, it was disjointed. Untethered.

But as I see my love's chocolate brown eyes for the first time, I feel my essence click into place. I'm whole now.

Quinn's my purpose. This beautiful, kind-hearted girl is my reason for existing.

"Kirian?" She places a hand on my cheek. "You see me?"

"I do." Grinning, a triumphant laugh bursts from me.

I fight the pull of the bond long enough to go still for a few seconds. I want to admire Quinn. Caressing her face, like I've done so many times before, I trace the dots on her smooth skin.

She watches me as I memorize her. My finger trails over her forehead, down her nose, across her cheek. It's familiar and new at the same time.

I travel down to her neck. Her collarbone.

Pushing up with one arm, I cup her breast in my other hand. I like the way the flesh moves when I squeeze the round globe. Her dusky pink nipple is hardened into a tight bud, and I enjoy watching her back arch when I pinch it.

As much fun as it is to ogle her tits, I can't resist completion much longer. The bond is demanding it, and the visual stimulation is overwhelming.

Against my will, my hips jerk, burying my cock as far as it can go.

Quinn moans, but her face screws up in pleasure, not pain. She already gave me permission to let go.

So I do.

Grasping her waist, I anchor her to the floor as I pound into her pussy. My motions are fast, hard, and frantic.

My balls draw up tight to my body, and I know I won't last much longer. The closer I get to coming, the more I'm driven by instinct.

I've never needed anything this much. Not air, not food, not flight.

This is something primal.

It's a good thing we're so far away from anyone. Every time I sink into Quinn, she cries out. Between her sounds, my grunts, and our bodies smacking together, we're not being quiet.

"Quinn," I say through gritted teeth. "My Quinn."

She looks at me, mouth parted, panting. Candlelight casts a warm glow over her beautiful face, and I love every single mark on her skin.

Our eyes stay locked as I shimmy a hand between us.

Rubbing Quinn's clit with the pad of my middle finger, I wring an orgasm out of her in less than a minute.

Her thighs shake, her head tilts back, and a guttural scream echoes through the night as her inner muscles clench around my cock.

Quinn's heels dig into the blanket, propelling her away from me, but I follow.

I don't let up as I chase my own release. Hooking my arms under her back, I hold onto the top of her shoulders so I can get more leverage.

"Fuck. So good." My eyes are heavy, threatening to close.

Something big is happening. I can feel it in my soul.

As the pressure builds, there's a sizzle and a pop somewhere above us. Sparks burst, causing flashes of bright light over Quinn's surprised face.

Right there is proof that we're meant for each other—it's the bond detonating.

I'd love to watch, but there isn't time to look around to see what's happening.

Because I'm about to come.

Roaring, I bury my face by Quinn's neck.

My cock swells even more, and I come hard, my muscles tensing as my seed shoots into her tight channel. The powerful jets fill her to the brim, and my thrusts make wet sounds as blinding pleasure races through every cell of my body.

Rutting as far into her pussy as I can go, the last of my orgasm tapers off. I'm breathing hard as my hips buck one more time.

Spent, I collapse, bracing myself on my elbows so I don't crush Quinn. I run my nose along her temple, breathing in her sweetness and the scent of our mating.

I wonder if she'll get pregnant.

I wonder when she'll be ready to do it again.

Giddy anticipation overwhelms me at the thought of both.

I imagine Quinn's belly round with my baby, and I want it so badly I physically ache. I wasn't sure I'd ever get to have a child, but the picture of a chubby-cheeked baby with lavender eyes fills my mind. However, I don't mind if it takes us several tries. Or hundreds. We'll keep at it until we've succeeded.

A strange sensation takes up residence inside my chest. The bond, I realize. My heart is so full.

"You missed the fireworks." There's a teasing lilt to Quinn's voice, and I lift my head to see her smile.

Her lips are puffy and red from my kisses, and I love the way the corners of her mouth curl up with a hint of mischief. The way her skin creases with the laugh lines framing that grin. The way her right incisor is slightly crooked compared to the rest of the straight teeth.

I'll never get tired of looking at her.

"I was a little too busy to pay attention to the show." Keeping my eyes open, I kiss her. It's closed-mouthed and gentle, which is a sharp contrast to how rough I'd just been with her.

I'm about to apologize for my lack of self-control when she asks, "Is it always like that? With fated mates and the fireworks, I mean."

The tip of my nose brushes against hers when I nod. "I've heard sparks literally fly when mates make love for the first time."

Something catches her attention to the left, and she gasps. "Kirian, look."

I follow her gaze to the open window. Outside, hundreds of fireflies have gathered around the treehouse. They're swirling in the air, surrounding us. I hear the humming of the cicadas and crickets. They're playing our song—the one I made up for her so long ago.

"Are you doing that on purpose?" Quinn asks, full of awe.

"I hadn't meant to, no." I glance back at her. "Fae abilities tend to increase when mates bond. Now that our souls are fully connected, I'm more powerful. It's about proximity—the closer I am to you, the better." Looking down at our joined bodies, I grin. "And we're about as close as we can get."

"So, you really do need me."

From her light tone, I can tell she means it as a joke, but it's no laughing matter. "More than you know. That's one reason mates can't be separated for long. I'm a more complete person with you than without you."

"That's the sweetest thing I've ever heard. I hope—" Her eyes get misty. "—I hope you always feel that way."

Blinking, Quinn reaches up to wipe a tear away.

I catch her hand midair. "Allow me."

Dragging my fingertip over her dampened skin, I gather the wet drop. I angle my hand toward the flickering candle, watching the way the light dances in the moisture.

Fascinating.

My intrigue quickly turns to concern as I look down at Quinn's leaking eyes. "Are you sad?"

She shakes her head. "No."

Slowly, I pull my cock out of her, noticing the way she winces. "Did I hurt you?"

"No."

"Are you… happy?"

"No. I mean, yes." She sniffles. "But that's not why I'm crying."

Impatient, I frown. "Well, out with it, woman."

She half laughs, half sobs. "You can see me now. I'm afraid you'll change your mind or feel differently."

"Why would I do that?" I'm baffled. How could she think such a thing?

"This doesn't bother you?" She spins a finger around her face. "Not even a little? You got stuck with me."

"Stuck with you?" I ask incredulously. Her freckles are the most adorable thing I've ever seen. "Quinn, you're a gift. A gift from the stars. The Night Realm used to be my favorite sight in the whole kingdom. Now, anytime I want to see it, I can just look at you. I could stare at you for days. In fact, when we get back home, I intend to do just that."

Satisfied with my answer, she grins. "Well, what are we waiting for? Let's go home."

CHAPTER 32

Quinn

"ASTRID!" BEFORE I CAN THINK BETTER OF IT, I RUN over and hug the witch. "I'm so happy to see you."

Chuckling, she awkwardly pats my back before pointing a skinny finger at Kirian. "Your portal's stinking up my house. But it's good to see your sight restored."

Relieving Astrid of the uninvited embrace, I glance behind me to see Kirian shrugging, his eyes firmly glued to my ass. It doesn't seem to matter that I'm wearing the baggy pants, oversized shirt, and the fur coat. He's still attempting x-ray vision. Men.

"And you." Putting her hands on her hips, Astrid raises her eyebrows at me. "You left before I was finished."

I lean into Kirian when he puts an arm around my waist and pulls my back to his front. "Sorry. I was just so excited."

"No matter." Astrid waves a hand. "I knew you would. This is exactly how it's supposed to happen."

"What's happening, exactly?" I ask, sharing a questioning glance with Kirian as I look up at him.

His stare lingers on my face. His eyes soften, and a small smile spreads over his lips. He enjoys looking at me. He likes my appearance. All my worrying was for nothing.

"The darkest day in the history of the Night Realm," Astrid replies solemnly. "At least, since the young princes were cursed."

"That doesn't sound good," I comment needlessly. It's not like I expected a cake walk when we came back, but that's pretty freaking ominous.

I'm a bit pissed Kirian neglected the kingdom while I was gone, but I can't be too hard on him about it. If the situation were reversed, I'd have been just as much of a wreck as he was. Probably worse.

Drawn by the light of the fire, Kirian paces away from me to peer at the low flames around the logs. He straightens and his fingers bump over the rough texture of the rock walls. Studying the grooves and divots, he moves over to the kitchen area and pokes a few dishes around.

It's cute and a little startling. I'm not used to seeing Kirian explore his surroundings with his eyes. As if he can sense me watching, those beautiful irises flit to me.

Despite Astrid's warning hanging over our heads, he smiles. His gaze goes lower, pausing at my chest before moving down to my lower half. My nipples prick and I swallow hard.

Snapping her fingers between us, Astrid makes a slicing motion through the air. "Hello? Did you hear me? Danger. Death. Destruction."

"Yeah." Kirian squares his shoulders as he looks down at the witch who's almost half his height. "I get it."

"No, you don't. Today, you'll choose between right and wrong. You'll choose between your people and your family. There will be a fracture in your kingdom, but whether or not you fix it is up to you." She clicks her tongue as she goes over to her empty bowl. Pouting, she peers inside. "This is one of the rare occasions when I can't see what's coming. I don't like it."

"Explain further." Kirian takes on a softer tone than the last time I heard him talking to Astrid, and the familiarity between them is endearing.

"I wish I could, my king."

"What fracture?" I butt in, because I'm not willing to let her off that easy. "What about his family?"

Her honey-colored eyes dart to me. "If you'd stayed longer, I would've told you who your biggest danger is."

Didn't we already go over this? Yes, I was hasty and made a mistake. No need to rub it in my face, especially when she seems to think destiny wanted it this way in the first place.

I wait several seconds for her to elaborate. When she doesn't, I sputter, "Well, who is it? Torius and Kai?"

"That would be preferable. An easy fix. But unfortunately, no." Dramatic pause. "Princess Gia's the one who wants you gone."

Kirian's body goes rigid as disbelief paints his features. "That can't be."

"It is."

"Are you positive?"

Astrid nods sadly. "Yes."

As we absorb the news, there's a heavy silence. I can feel Kirian's anger building. I remember days ago when I could physically feel his rage. Now that the bond is complete, the sensation is tenfold.

I clutch my burning throat and press a hand to my twisting stomach. I can barely breathe. Wheezing, I struggle to suck in air while Kirian fumes.

"I put her in charge of the kingdom in my absence. I—trusted her." A string of profanity bursts from him as he grabs the back of his neck with both hands. "Why would she want to hurt Quinn?"

"Can you try to calm down?" I whisper, swaying on my feet as I swallow around the painful lump in my esophagus.

The unpleasant feeling recedes a little when Kirian's emotions turn to concern.

He rushes over to me. "What's wrong?"

I open my mouth to respond, but it's difficult for me to talk.

Luckily, Astrid has an answer as she peers at us through her magnifying glass. "Amazing. Your bond is one of the strongest I've ever seen." Her attention shifts to Kirian. "You need to control your temper. It seems to have a physical manifestation in Quinn."

"You mean my anger hurts her?" Cupping my face, he gazes down at me with an apology in his eyes. "Will it always be this way?"

"Maybe," Astrid replies. "Maybe not. She'll probably get used to it after a while."

Kirian pets my hair, soothing himself and me at the same time.

"It was a man who pushed me through the portal," I supply, hoping Gia isn't to blame. "I'm sure of it."

"That just means she has accomplices." Kirian takes a deep breath before asking Astrid, "My men? Gia made them turn from me?"

"Your friends were loyal to you. They still are. Gia set them up so you'd send them away and have less protection."

Well. That information would've been helpful a long time ago. From the tic in Kirian's jaw, I can tell he's thinking the same thing and his rage starts to burn hotter again.

I have an idea. Reaching into his pocket, I grasp the marble. I press it to his palm and manipulate it under his thumb in a circular motion, demonstrating how I use it to calm my nerves.

It seems to work because the tightness in my gut unwinds as he rolls it around.

Hanging his head, Kirian admits, "I've played right into Gia's games. At this point, she might've gained loyalty among our people. She could be building an army for all I know. Control is what she wanted all along, and I handed it to her on a silver platter."

He looks at the table, and somehow I know he's thinking about flipping it over. Probably wouldn't be the best thing to wreck Astrid's home after she's done so much for us.

I take his hands in mine. Gazing up at his face, I place gentle kisses on his knuckles. Pain swims in his eyes as he looks back at me. His tumultuous emotions turn into a deep hurt, crashing into my heart with a different kind of pain.

It isn't physical. I feel the betrayal.

I'm not sure if it'll help, but I try to send strength and sympathy to him.

"Don't be too hard on yourself." Astrid pats his forearm. "Like I said before, this was bound to happen. You and I will see each other again soon, but don't delay. I'm afraid this home might not be safe for me much longer."

Kirian seems lost for words, so I take it upon myself to ask, "You said something about witches to Kirian? Are they involved?"

"Yes." She glances into the bowl again before shaking her head. "But it's all murky. They found out about me and cast a distortion spell."

"Why would they team up with Gia?" I wonder. "More importantly, why would Gia agree to something like that?"

"She was the perfect person to exploit." It isn't a detailed answer, but it's something. "Some witches think they're more powerful than the royals."

"Are they?"

She glances at Kirian. "Would it be treason to say yes?"

His strong arms go around me, and he pulls me in for a hug. "Not if it's true."

"Then, yes. Many of us could wipe you off the map," she

states plainly. "But it's not in our nature to rule. We don't want the spotlight. We like our privacy. However, that doesn't mean the coven isn't attracted to power. They'd rather be puppet masters, controlling the outcome behind the scenes."

"And the future?" I ask. "Can you be more specific about anything? Any detail could help."

"I see nothing." Rubbing her temples, Astrid seems tired and frustrated, and I get the feeling she's not used to being out of the loop. "The answers you seek are near. You'll find out soon enough."

Kirian tilts his head. "You're much more forthcoming than usual. No hair bargains this time?"

She sighs. "It would benefit me if you prevail. If you win, I'll consider that my reward."

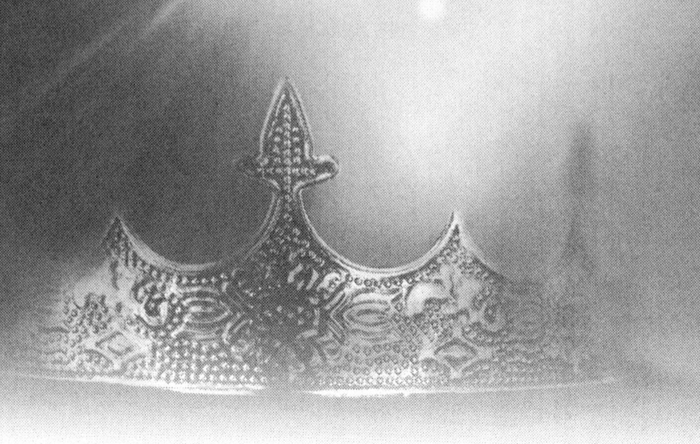

CHAPTER 33

Quinn

GETTING OUT OF THE SHADOWLANDS ISN'T AS SCARY as going in the first time. Probably because I'm too busy worrying about the man carrying me. We don't have the carrier this time. He's just got both his arms under me, and I prefer it this way.

I like being held by him, even if it does occupy his arms. He's running like our lives depend on it, and maybe they do. Or maybe he just wants to exert some of his anger.

Now that Kirian's gotten over the initial shock, he grapples with his rage. It's bubbling just below the surface like lava, ready to spew out any second.

He keeps dropping kisses to the top of my head, and I can tell it's more for him than it is for me. Staying focused on me pushes his temper down.

Soon, the rock walls start to narrow, and the rough surface grazes the toe of my shoe as it closes in.

Then, we're out.

We go from complete darkness to the dim pink glow on the horizon. As we adjust to the sudden change of light, Kirian and I both blink as he sets me on the ground.

I try to stay focused on him. I don't want to miss the expression on his face when he sees the sky here for the first time since he was a kid.

When he finally looks up, breath whooshes out of him as his jaw goes slack. His knees give out and he falls to his butt on a patch of grass.

I sit beside him and he promptly pulls me onto his lap. We don't talk. I don't ask questions or try to make conversation. I just let him take it all in.

At least three minutes pass before he says, "It's bittersweet. I always imagined this moment would be the best of my life, but how can I be happy when my sister—" His voice cracks, and he lowers his gaze to the ground.

Pinching a weed, he bends the stem, watching the way the fuzzy yellow top bounces up when he lets it go.

"It's okay to feel a mix of emotions right now," I say softly. "You've been through a lot. Even if you want to be pissed, go ahead. I can handle it."

"I won't hurt you." Toying with the marble, he mimics what I showed him earlier. "Damon's castle is just on the other side of the hill." He points down the road, and I welcome the change of subject. A distraction is good. "It's in a town called Cassia. Just a short walk, or an even shorter flight."

"The Dream Realm is pretty." My head whips around. Now that I'm searching for the differences in the landscape, I see them. The Dream Realm still has the same purple trees, but the grass has a blue tint to it and the land isn't as flat. A shimmering light between two hills in the distance catches my attention, and I realize it's the moons reflecting on water. "Is that a lake?"

"Issika Lake," he confirms. "Mermaids live there."

I gasp. "No way."

Kirian grins, and it's nice to see him smile. "Yes way. I'll take you there when we have time."

"I'd love that." Sighing, I rest my head on his shoulder. "I'm looking forward to our life together here. As long as no one's trying to murder me." My joke falls flat. Way, way flat, like if a monster truck ran over a pancake. "I'm sorry, Kirian."

"Nothing will ever be the same again. When we were kids, Gia followed me everywhere. She'd beg me to play with her, and I did, even though I was too old to be participating in childish games." He works his jaw. "I don't want to end her, but isn't that what I promised?"

"Do you have to follow through? Is that a fae thing?"

"Yes. You know we don't say things we don't mean. I'm bound to the promise the same way I'm tied to our vow."

"Maybe there's another way. A different bargain you can make."

He caresses my cheek. "But how can I let her live after what she did to you?"

I place my hand over his. "If killing Gia means hurting yourself, then find another solution."

"Don't you want vengeance?"

"Not if it comes at the cost of your happiness."

Briefly closing his eyes, Kirian leans over to bump his forehead against mine. "Just a few hours on the job, and you're already the best queen this kingdom has ever seen."

I give him a doubtful smirk. "Let's see what the nobles have to say about that."

"They'll learn to love you. It's impossible not to."

The sun fades away, draining the pink wisps and the yellow light in the sky, and Kirian stands before helping me up.

"Was that dawn or dusk?" I ask, completely unaware of the time here.

"Dawn."

Gazing up at the constellations and the moons, I remember Astrid's demonstration; the way they clicked into place as if someone had stamped the sky right onto my face. "If you'd been able to see me, would you have recognized the patterns?"

I don't have to explain what I mean, because Kirian answers, "Absolutely. In fact, I don't understand how no one else here noticed it."

His observation makes me pause. "Maybe someone did."

Kirian and I lock eyes as we both come to the same conclusion. "Gia."

CHAPTER 34

Kirian

To save time, Quinn and I decide to fly to Cassia. Seeing the world from above is thrilling, and I'm not the only one who thinks so. As Quinn clings to me, she doesn't hide her face by my neck. She glances over her shoulder, looking down on the lands that are now her home.

I haven't told her yet, but Damon and I plan to merge the Dream Realm and the Night Realm once again. He'll still be king, but our people will be free to pass from one place to the next as citizens of both. Our resources will be pooled instead of traded. Together, we'll be stronger.

As we soar over a gnome district, Quinn smiles at me. I can't help smiling back.

"Yes, we'll go there someday," I say before she can request it. "I think a celebratory tour will be needed once we've set everything straight."

She beams, her eyes becoming wider and her grin stretching as wide as possible. "I'd love that."

Happiness bursts from her heart to mine, and for a second, our problems dim. Right now, I'm with my mate. She's alive and well, and we're going to have a future together.

"I love you," I breathe out, our eyes locked.

"And I love you." Pulling herself up, she closes the distance between us to press her lips to mine.

Did I think seeing the landscape was important? It isn't anymore.

Nothing is better than the feel of my mate wrapped around me.

Shutting my eyes, I go on autopilot, kissing her while paying attention to the direction we're going.

I know we're close when I hear the Dream Realm flag flapping in the breeze. Reluctantly, I separate my mouth from Quinn's.

"Damon's palace is quite a bit smaller than yours," she observes as we swoop down to the bridge.

"Don't let the size fool you," I tell her, unable to look away from her expression of awe. I like watching her face as she sees my world. Our world. "This place is more valuable than the castle in Delaveria. Damon and his parents have expensive taste. The entire thing is built with stone from the meteors."

Quinn's mouth pops open. "Is that why it's glowing?"

I glance at it, realizing the light I followed here wasn't from lamps, lanterns, or chandeliers.

It's the castle itself.

Every rectangular stone is illuminated from within, and I'm taken aback by the beauty of it. I've been on this bridge countless times, stayed hundreds of nights here. I've felt the rough texture of the walls on my hands and the cool floors under my feet.

But I never pictured it like this in my mind. Like a faded star.

The inside is probably the same, and I can't wait to see it.

Guards outside the front door blow their horns in a familiar tune, alerting Damon of my arrival. They add a couple notes at the end to signal I'm not alone.

"Kirian." Damon rushes over as soon as we step through the main entrance.

I recognize his voice, but seeing him is surreal. His dark blond hair reaches just under his shoulders. He has a build like mine, but he's just a couple inches shorter than me. No tattoos visible on his shirtless torso.

I've never asked him what he looks like. Both of us have always considered ourselves too manly to play a game of feel-my-face.

The women call him pretty boy, and they aren't wrong. His features are softer than his father's.

"We need to talk." Sniffing the air, Damon tilts his ear toward us. "Hi, Quinn. Glad you're back."

"Likewise. I'm sure all of Valora missed me terribly," Quinn says sarcastically.

Damon's face is serious when he replies, "You have no idea. Kirian was unbearable at times. Terrible company."

"Hey, I wasn't that bad," I defend, even though I know he's right.

"You trashed my throne room. Broke a table, six chairs, and two mirrors."

Quinn gapes at me. "Seriously, Kirian?"

I can't answer her because my mind is stuck on the word *mirrors*. Up until now, I hadn't even thought about what *I* look like. But I've never seen myself in adult form. Quinn tells me I'm attractive, but I need to see it.

"A mirror," I blurt out, suddenly desperate to see my reflection. "I need one."

"Before you go breaking shit, you need to know we have a big problem." Damon chases after me as I sprint through the dining hall.

Scanning the walls, I search for a reflective surface. There are paintings and tapestries, but no mirrors. I stop at a silver tea pot, but when I bend down, my face is distorted in the round shape.

I continue on through the kitchen to the servants' stairs.

I've got Quinn's hand in mine, and I'm practically dragging her behind me. She doesn't protest. She knows this is important.

"Aha!" I spy a full-length mirror at the end of the hallway on the second floor.

"Kirian!" Damon shouts. "This is serious. I've got news. Zella sent a sprite, but since the message is for you, she won't say anything without you present."

I raise a finger. "Hold that thought for just two minutes."

Releasing Quinn's hand, I approach the glass. I don't recognize myself. I almost expected to see a child on the other side. Last time I was face-to-face with a mirror, I was a boy. I was thinner. Shorter. Younger. Smoother.

Running a hand over my jaw, I feel the rough stubble and watch the way my skin stretches. I note the higher cheekbones, sharper jaw, and how my nose has grown.

I puff out my chest and flex my muscles. I turn so I can see how my butt looks in leather.

Quinn's right. By regular standards, I'm a stud.

"Whatever you're doing, we don't have time for it," Damon snips impatiently, interrupting my self-appreciation.

"All right." I face him. "What's going on?"

"I'll let Gemma tell you herself."

Suddenly, a sprite flies in front of my face, and she's a blur of sparkles. Wings, hair, clothes—all blue. I'm surprised, and a bit alarmed, to realize I had no idea she was trailing us. I didn't hear her wings flapping. Didn't sense her movement in the air.

I've been so consumed by what I'm seeing, I'm not paying attention to what's going on around me. Not good. I can't let my other senses fall to the wayside. They've protected me, guided me, kept me alive.

Quinn gawks at the little sprite.

On our road trip, we'd passed by a couple sprite forests, but they couldn't be bothered with our presence. Many sprites consider themselves separate from the kingdom. They don't do our bidding without hefty rewards, usually requesting gold or jewels for their tiny treehouses. And we pay them well for their ability to send word across the entire realm within hours.

"She's so pretty," Quinn says with amazement. "I've never seen one up close. Her wings move so fast, like a hummingbird."

"I'm right here," the sprite harrumphs, her voice high and reedy. "You don't have to talk about me like I'm not in the room."

"Sorry," Quinn responds, adequately chastised.

Sprites are known for their saucy attitudes, but I won't let Quinn get lectured for simply making an observation.

I bristle, shooting daggers at the little troublemaker. "If I didn't need your message so badly, I'd send you away for being rude to my mate." Shocked, the sprite flies back a little when she realizes I can see her. Raising an eyebrow, I nod. "That's right."

"Forgive me, night king." She bows her head. "I was told your mate had perished."

"Still—" I start to argue with her, but Quinn cuts me off.

"What's your name again?"

"Gemma."

"You must be exhausted after flying for so many hours."

"Yes." Gemma pouts, milking Quinn's compassion.

"If you need a place to rest, I've got two good shoulders." Quinn looks at me and whispers, "Or is that offensive to offer?"

"No," Gemma answers with a tinkling giggle. "I'll get to tell everyone I sat on the queen."

She isn't shy about taking Quinn up on it. Flying around us twice, she lands on Quinn's right shoulder, primly crossing one leg over the other as she looks in my direction.

"I need you to promise no harm will come to me. If I'm found out, she'll kill me."

"Who?" I ask. "Princess Gia?"

"Yes."

"Of course we'll keep you safe here," I offer up Damon's castle, knowing he wouldn't refuse. "Your risk won't go unrewarded, either."

"And my family?"

"Refuge will be available to all who need it," Damon interjects. "Now, for the love of the constellations, tell us."

"I have a message from Queen Zella," Gemma states formally, before her voice changes and becomes an exact replica of my mother's. "Come home quickly, my son. Gia's out of control. She made trade deals with the Day Realm. Some of our females have been sent away for breeding against their will. Gnomes and trolls have been sent to harvest Day water. Some of them... they're children, Kirian." There's a sob, then she continues, "Your father has gone to retrieve them. The treaty will be no more, and I fear war will be in our future. Be careful when you enter Delaveria. Gia's powers are... unleashed."

Well, strike it all. It's been a long time since I heard my mother sound so shaken.

Quinn grips my forearm and looks up at me with concern. I know how much our people mean to her. Especially the gnomes.

I have to make this right. Fast. "Gemma, do you have the energy to deliver another message to the citadel in Aelustria?"

"I'll require four rubies."

"All right."

"And twelve emeralds."

I growl, because she's pushing it. "Fine. Go to Torius. Give him this message: Torius and Kai, I owe you an apology. If you're not already aware of what's going on in Delaveria, just know I need you to meet me there as soon as possible. Bring reinforcements."

As soon as I give Gemma a nod, letting her know I'm finished, she takes off, zipping away so quickly I almost can't see her.

Whistling, Damon rakes a hand through his hair. "This is low, even for Gia."

"It gets worse." Needing comfort, I hug my mate from behind. "Gia's the one who tried to kill Quinn."

"Your own sister," Damon mutters, shaking his head. "I should've suspected. It's not like this hasn't happened before."

I know he's referring to the rift between our own fathers or the deadly altercation between Zarid and Zed. The royal fae families of Valora don't have the best history when it comes to greed and the pursuit of power.

"I wonder what resource she traded for." Damon's face is pinched with a thoughtful expression as he paces away before turning back. "King Zarid's been gunning for this for a long time. Our females would go at a high price."

A couple tidbits from Gemma's message stand out to me—harvesting Day water and unleashed powers.

"I'd bet my best axe it's distilled Day water." Grabbing Quinn's hand, I start walking down the hall. "Damon, are you coming with us to Delaveria?"

Running up beside me, he grins. "Wouldn't miss it for all the stars in the sky. Besides, this means you'll owe me. You know I love it when someone racks up a debt." His smile falls away. "But how are we getting there?"

"Be a lot faster to fly," I say. "If we push hard, we could be there by dusk." Giving Quinn's fingers a reassuring squeeze, I pat my chest as we descend the stairs. "We can use the carrier. Strap you to me for the ride."

"Won't it be difficult for you to go that far with the extra weight, though?" She sounds worried for my well-being, and it's cute.

"You're not that heavy."

"Still, I'm going to slow you down and you'll be worn out by the time we get there."

She's right, but what other choice do we have?

We're walking through the large kitchen when Damon says, "She can ride my pet griffin."

Whipping toward him, I cock my head to the side. "You don't have a griffin."

"Yes, I do. Had him since he was a baby."

A cook stirring a steaming pot of soup on the stove lifts her head long enough to back up his statement, while a baker kneading bread on the butcher block countertops nods.

"How did I not know this?" I ask, thinking of all the time I've spent here without a clue.

Damon shrugs. "You've never been to my stables. Listen, Talon's totally safe. My parents used to ride him often, and he's never dropped anyone."

I steal a glance at Quinn's comically wide eyes. "What do you say?"

Swallowing hard, she looks a little pale when she squeaks, "Sure. His name is Talon and he's never dropped anyone. Sounds great."

Noting the sarcasm, I smirk. "At any point, if you want to ride with me, just say so."

"And if I fall?"

"I'll catch you, love. Always."

Quinn melts at my words, and the affection and trust shining from her eyes is something I'll never tire of.

"All right." Damon claps his hands once. "Let's go. I've been looking for a reason to kick Gia's ass ever since she chopped off my hair in my sleep."

"That happened when you were seventeen." I follow him out the rear entrance nearest to the stables. "You're not over it yet?"

"You know how important my hair is to me."

I roll my eyes at Quinn, and she cups her mouth, stifling a laugh.

"I heard that," Damon mumbles, irritated.

The guy really is touchy about his hair.

When we get outside, the air is cool but there's hardly any wind. It'll be a nice night to fly.

As a kid, my wings were underdeveloped and I didn't have the strength to go far. This'll be the first time I've ever seen the entire Night Realm from above. The mountains, the villages, the sprite forests.

My body hums with excitement as we stop at the stone outbuilding. "Oh, Damon, by the way... it's great to finally *see* you."

"See me?" The color drains from his face when he catches my meaning. "I knew something was different about you! Why? How?"

"Quinn," I explain, unable to keep the pride out of my voice. "She's more than just the girl I fell in love with. She's my fated mate."

"A human?" Damon seems as baffled as we were when we found out.

"Mostly human," Quinn informs him. "Turns out, one of my ancestors got it on with a fae dude."

Blowing out a breath, Damon rubs his jaw. "And I thought my parents were so foolish."

I turn to Quinn. "King Silas and Queen Tehya left for the human realm about six hundred years ago in search of Damon's mate. They were sure they'd find her there and swore they wouldn't return until they did."

Her lips turn down as she looks at my cousin. "That must be really hard for you, Damon. Being all alone here."

"It is," he agrees, opening the wooden stable door. The smell of hay and animal feces assaults my nose, but it isn't as strong as it normally would be without my sight. "My staff is great. They've been loyal, but it's not the same as having family around. I worry about my parents every day. There was no talking them out of it, but maybe they were onto something." He gives me a hearty slap on the shoulder. "Having this guy around has been nice, even if he was a broody asshole the whole time."

We're interrupted by a huff, some scraping sounds, and a screech.

Quinn jumps.

Damon smiles. "That would be Talon."

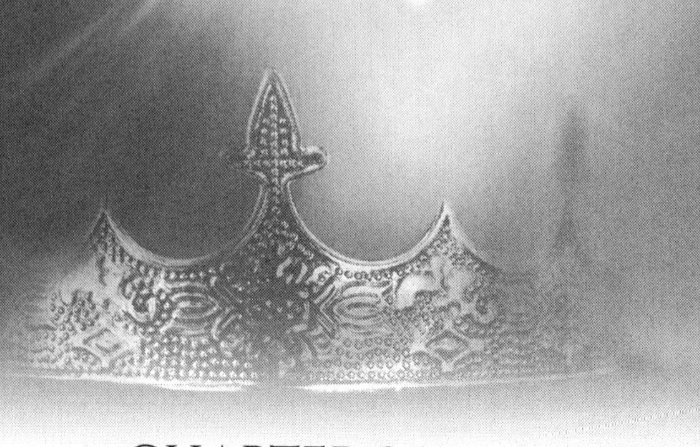

CHAPTER 35

Quinn

YOU'D THINK RIDING ON A MYSTICAL CREATURE would be really cool.

It's not.

I've been holding in a scream for hours.

Talon came by his name honestly. Each of his claws are as long as one of my arms. His beak looks like it could snap me in half with one bite. Long white-feathered wings flap in time with the fae kings on either side of me.

Kirian shouts a question at me, but it's hard to hear it above the wind rushing past my ears. I just give him a quick thumbs up before going back to holding on for dear life. The saddle is secured to Talon's lion-like rear end, and the fluffy brown puff on the tip of his tail occasionally whips around and smacks me on the back.

A gust of wind hits us, and the ride gets rough for a few seconds.

After this is over, I think I'm going to take a break from riding anything requiring reins.

Shutting my eyes, I try to imagine I'm on a horse, but it's not the same. I miss the bumpy carriage, because that's nothing compared to the turbulence up here.

It doesn't help that I'm sore from my time with Kirian. Not

sore in the sense that I'm in pain. There's a hollow ache deep inside. A craving. I can feel that he was inside me and now he's not. Every time I shift, it causes a twinge of yearning between my legs. Like phantom pains, but in my vagina.

A wave of exhaustion hits me, and my eyes droop. I shake my head to keep myself alert.

Adrenaline combined with the lack of sleep is taking a toll on me. My body wants to sleep, but my nerves are ramped up.

I need a nap. With Kirian. Some downtime and snacks.

I think of Kirian's soft mattress and—*holy shit!*

My stomach drops when we suddenly go higher, plunging through a cloud and stealing my fantasy of being safe in bed. The cool mist kisses my skin, and the hazy fog is too thick to see more than two feet in front of my face.

Don't panic.

I hold my breath until we break through to clear skies. When I look down, I'm pretty sure I see flashes in the dark mist below.

As we've gotten closer to Delaveria, the weather's changed for the worse. The normally clear skies are thick with storm clouds.

I don't miss the concerned glances Kirian keeps sending my way.

"Is that lightning?" I yell.

He nods.

That's just great. I could've been electrocuted. According to Kirian, getting struck by lightning isn't a big deal to faeries. It's a nuisance because it causes temporary paralysis, which makes them fall from the sky. The result is usually some bruises and broken bones when they hit the ground. It's the origin of their 'striking' cuss words, because it can really mess a person up.

Well, the fae might be able to survive it, but I sure as hell can't.

Another blast of wind rocks us, and Talon lets out a sound between a roar and a squawk as he rights himself. Thunder rumbles beneath us, and a second layer of clouds form above. The stars disappear as the sky darkens.

We're being closed in.

My heart pounds as rain begins pelting us. At least it isn't cold anymore. I'm still wearing the coat, and I'm so sweaty I'm not sure getting wet will make a difference.

"Not much farther!" Kirian shouts. "Let's get down to land. Quickly."

Both guys do a nosedive, and this time I really do scream when Talon trails right behind them.

This is it. I'm going to die. Death by griffin, of all things.

I should close my eyes, but I can't.

Frozen with fear, I watch as the ground approaches at the speed of falling. Right before we crash, Talon swoops so he's level with the road.

The landing is jarring as he trots to a stop, but I don't care that I'm being jostled around.

I'm still alive.

Before I have a chance to dismount, Kirian is picking me up. "I'm sorry. That was much rougher than I thought it'd be. Are you okay?"

Now that I'm not moving, I realize I'm shaking. My teeth are chattering so much I can barely answer him. "I—I think s—so."

I'm hot and cold at the same time, and I can't feel my fingers. I might be in shock, but I have enough sense to look around and realize we're on the outskirts of Delaveria. I recognize this road as the one we left on.

"This storm isn't right, Kirian," Damon says as the wind whips through his hair.

Kirian nods. "It's Gia. It has to be."

"I didn't know she can manipulate the weather."

"Under normal circumstances, she can't." Kirian rubs my upper arms, like he's trying to massage some sense back into me. Lightning flashes behind the palace. When Kirian follows the light, his eyes go wide. "Oh, fucking shit."

"What?" Alarmed by his outburst, I look in the same direction. It's darker than normal, but when another bright bolt slices through the sky, I see what he sees.

And he's not wrong. *Fucking shit* is right. The entire perimeter of the palace is blocked by brown thorny vines. The walls go all the way up and around like a dome, and the only part of the castle sticking out is the highest tower. Black billowy clouds circle right above it, as if that's the eye of the storm.

It's our only way in.

"Obviously, that's a trap," I say, even though I'm sure Kirian's already figured that out.

"I might be able to break through the vines or make them move. Maybe not. Gia's never been as strong as me, but if she's hopped up on distilled Day water, her power might outweigh mine."

"What about Torius and Kai?" I suggest. "Will they be here soon?"

"This can't wait. We have to go ahead without them."

"Agreed." Damon nods. "Let's get this over with."

I figured they'd say that.

I'm also not surprised when Kirian adds, "And you'll stay here."

He motions to a nearby home with a barn. I see a few faces peering out through the windows. I'm not sure if they're looking at us, or whatever the hell is happening to Delaveria.

But I know I'm not game for staying behind. "No."

"Yes."

"You said you're stronger when we're together," I point out. "Your powers will be better if I'm near you."

"And you're also my greatest weakness. Gia knows that. She could use you to get to me."

I throw my arms up. "She doesn't even know I'm here. The whole kingdom thinks I died."

"But you didn't." Kirian's tone is patronizing, like he's talking to a kid. "And it's going to stay that way."

Going behind me, he takes me by the shoulders and starts leading me forward to the two-story stone house. The people inside scatter when they see us coming, and a tall fae woman opens the door.

Nobles.

Well, isn't this the icing on the cake.

But the face staring at us isn't one filled with pride or snootiness. She's devastated, on the verge of tears.

"King Kirian, thank the stars you're back." Wringing her hands, the woman's chin trembles. "My youngest daughter was taken and sent to auction in the Day Realm." She falls to her knees on the front stoop, clinging to Kirian's pants as she sobs. "The princess's soldiers came into our home and dragged her out. Please, I beg of you, bring her home. She's only fifteen. She's not yet of breeding age."

Kirian clumsily gropes around until he finds the woman's head, and when I look at his eyes, I realize he's not focusing on anything. For a second, I'm afraid he's lost his sight again, but then I realize he's pretending to be blind.

He doesn't want anyone to know he can see. Clever.

Facing straight ahead, he gives the woman a few comforting pats. "I assure you, I'll make this right."

As soon as he utters the promise, she lets out a sob of relief. "Thank you, Your Majesty, thank you."

Before she can start kissing his feet, he steps back. "My mate has been found. I need you to keep her and the griffin safe while I tend to business at the palace."

"Of course. Anything you need." Glancing over her shoulder, the fae woman doles out a couple orders to a female in servants' clothing, telling her to put Talon in the stables and heat up some soup for me.

"Kirian, please," I beg quietly. "I want to go with you."

All my instincts are yelling that we need to stay together, but from the stubborn set of his jaw, I can tell he won't budge on this.

My unbendable king.

Kirian plants a swift kiss on my mouth before backing away. "Don't let Quinn out of your sight and protect her with your life if need be."

He sends me a heat-filled glance and mouths, "I love you."

I mouth it back.

Then he takes off with Damon, flying straight for the castle. I want to stand here and make sure they get inside, but there's a small fae boy pulling me into the house while babbling about wanting to show me his toys.

The door shuts behind me, and our greeter takes my soaked coat. "Hello, Quinn, I'm Nalia, and this is my mate Garryn." The dark-haired woman gestures to the blond man who's still peering out the window.

He seems way more interested in what's happening out there than having a houseguest. I'm not insulted. I'm just glad they're being friendlier now than they were at the ball. I recognize them. They were amongst the fae whispering about my unappealing appearance.

Guess dealing with a stolen family member really puts things into perspective. Who has time to gossip about my freckles when their daughter is missing?

I feel a tug on my hand, and I glance down at the boy. He's like a little clone of his mother, with his inky hair and yellow eyes. "I have a griffin, too. Wanna see?"

"Gerris, stop hounding the future queen." Nalia shoots him an unhappy look.

"It's okay," I say with a smile. "I like kids."

"You'll play with me?" Gerris bounces, still holding onto my fingers.

"Sure. If that's okay with your mom." I glance at Nalia, and her mouth is hanging open.

She seems surprised, and I'm guessing a member of the royal family has never offered to babysit before.

"All right," she says pleasantly, recovering quickly. "Are you hungry?"

"No, thank you." Although I haven't eaten since the spaghetti and meatballs last night, my worry is overshadowing my appetite right now.

I hate being away from Kirian. It feels wrong.

At least I have entertainment to distract me. Leading me in front of a stone hearth with a blazing fire, Gerris dumps a wicker basket full of carved wooden animals. One of them is a griffin.

While Nalia watches us from a rocking chair in the corner, he runs circles around me, pretending to fly it through the air. When he asks me to help him line all the animals up, I do, although my fingers are still trembling from the scary ride here.

Thunder rumbles, and I glance outside. I didn't think it was possible for the sky to get darker, but somehow it does. Hail starts pinging against the window and hitting the house.

"Nalia," Garryn says, his breath fogging up the glass. "Take cover in the cellar."

"Is that necessary?" she asks, her clasped hands tightening with concern.

Lightning flashes three times, and much to my horror, it illuminates the clouds. They're circling faster now, like it could turn into a tornado any second. Suddenly, a bright bolt shoots straight down into the castle.

I feel a sizzle in my chest and dizziness makes my head sway from side to side.

Kirian.

Something happened to him. I know it.

Fear jolts through my heart as the burning heat continues. Sweat breaks out on my forehead, and my vision temporarily blurs.

I don't know what's going on, but it's bad.

Kirian needs me, and I can't just sit here and do nothing.

"I'm gonna go check on Talon," I announce, rising on wobbly legs.

Nalia stands so abruptly she almost knocks the chair over. "But we're not to let you out of our sight."

Moving in front of the door, she appears to be ready to physically stop me from leaving, and from the knowing press of her lips, I'd say she can read through my bullshit.

We both know I'm not stopping at the stables.

Stiffening my spine, I try to sound as royal as I can. "I'm going to be queen. It's my duty to take care of Valora. If I have to venture to the Day Realm myself to get your daughter, I will." I'm surprised to realize I mean it. I care about these people, even if they haven't always respected me. "But I won't be able to do that if the king is dead."

Nalia must hear the truth in my statement, because she slowly shuffles out of the way, sending a resigned look to her husband.

I don't waste any time. My shoes are still wet from the ride here, and they squish when I fit my feet inside. Deciding to leave the heavy coat behind, I reach for the doorknob. A soft touch to my shoulder makes me pause. I glance to my left.

Garryn's towering over me, and for a second, I think he might toss me over his shoulder and restrain me.

Instead, he presses a sheathed dagger into my palm. "It isn't much, but it's better than being unarmed."

Gulping, I nod. I've never used a weapon before. Hell, I've never even punched anyone. I'm not sure if I'd have the balls to stab someone, but it does make me feel better to have it.

As I sprint to the stables, I get soaked all over again. The rain comes down in heavy sheets, and I wipe my eyes as I pull the stable door open. Inside, it smells musty and damp. It's too dark for me to see well, but I don't have to search for Talon. He must be sensing the danger, because he's scraping at one of the doors and letting out a series of pitiful moans.

"Yeah, there's trouble," I say, sliding the metal bolt on his stall to let him out. "I need you to take me up to the tower, okay?"

Surprisingly, he nods as if he understands me. Maybe he does. Thankfully, he's still wearing the saddle.

I pet his beak. "Let's go kick some Princess Gia butt."

I don't know why she didn't kill me when she had the chance. Was sending me back home a small mercy? Maybe she just wanted me out of the way long enough to gain control.

Of course, she couldn't have planned on Kirian having my marble or Astrid's help. If it wasn't for that, he might not have been able to get to me at all.

And since she knew we were soul mates, she thought separating us would make Kirian lose his mind. Eventually, he would've.

Boy, she'll be happy to see me.

CHAPTER 36

Kirian

"It's too solid." Using my axe, I chop at the thick vines around the base of the dome. Every time I cut through them, they grow right back. "Fuck. Gia's never been able to do anything this big before."

Damon puts his sword away. "We'll have to go up."

"I know."

It isn't ideal. Falling into her trap is probably the dumbest decision I could make, but we need to act quickly. I don't know how far her powers can go. If she loses control, she could decimate Delaveria. As it is, the sky looks like a cyclone could form.

And my mother is in there. I don't know if Gia would hurt her, but I won't underestimate my sister. Not ever again.

Deciding it's now or never, I put my axe away and leap into the sky. Damon isn't far behind, and strong wind blows us off course a few times.

When we make it to the bell tower, lightning shoots down, striking the highest point.

We narrowly miss getting struck, taking cover on the stone floor under the rows of bells just in time. Several of them knock against each other, chiming out an eerie tune. Even after the lightning retreats, heat crackles along my back and my hairs stand on end.

"This is fucking wild," Damon says, crawling to the trap door leading to the stairwell. "Distilled Day water should be illegal."

He has a point. No one should be this powerful. It's dangerous, and the secret is definitely out. Once the fae of Valora learn their powers could be this intense, they'll stop at nothing to get their hands on the substance.

When I shut the door above our heads, we're cloaked in darkness. None of the lanterns along the walls are lit, and I can't see a thing. It's oddly comforting. These are the conditions in which I've honed every skill I have.

Reverting back to my days of blindness, I place my feet on each stair with confidence. "Once we get to the hallway, we'll check the guest quarters for anyone hoping to get a jump on us."

"Good call," Damon says behind me. "I'm officially freaked out. Do you hear that?"

"Hear what?"

"Exactly. It's too damn quiet."

Agreed. The palace is always bustling with activity. Between council members, noble guests, maids, and other staff, noise is constant.

Right now, aside from the wind whistling above us, there's nothing.

As I descend the winding staircase, I see a faint glow coming from the bottom. Lights are on in the hallway on the other side of the door. This wing of the castle was built after the curse, and believe it or not, it's fancier than my quarters. I'm excited to see the rooms, even if it's just to check for ambushers. They're reserved for the guests of honor, and no expense was spared when they were designed. Plus, they have the best view of Dawn and Dusk.

Quinn would love it.

A strange sensation swirls inside my chest at the thought of her. It feels like something is tugging at my heart. A persistent yearning that's almost painful.

It's the bond rebelling against being separated from her so soon after our first mating. Weird to think a third party is butting into our relationship, but the bond is its own entity.

And it wants Quinn.

Well, it's going to have to wait. I have important business to—

"Kirian, look out for the—"

I feel the wire against my ankle just as Damon shouts the warning. But it's too late.

As I flap my wings to propel backward, arrows shoot from somewhere ahead. One nicks my thigh, and I recognize the sting of iron. Dozens of others ping against the stone steps, falling uselessly to the floor with a clatter.

Gia's not playing around. If it wasn't for Damon's warning, I could've been speared through the heart.

I didn't sense the tripwire. Damon felt the frequency in the air—the way the draft bounced off the metal that was strung tight.

Damn.

As glad as I am to have my sight back, I probably regained it at the worst possible time. I feel like I've lost a superpower I took for granted.

"Maybe you should go first," I suggest to Damon, ignoring the burning pain in my quadricep.

"Oh, no. I'm here as back up. I'll make you a deal, though. If Gia kills you, I'll take her down and run your kingdom for you."

Coming from anyone else, I'd perceive that as a threat, but I know he's not serious.

For one, I'm not sure he could defeat Gia if his life depended on it. Sure, he's a decent fighter, but physical violence has never been his strong suit. Sparring usually ends with me pinning him to the ground and him promising buckets of my favorite ale in exchange for letting him up and not bragging about the victory later.

"Just swear an oath to me," I say, avoiding the wire along the bottom step while kicking arrows out of the way. "If I die, take Quinn back to Astrid. Have the witch create another portal so she can get home."

So she can move on. Go to college like she'd planned. Build a life.

Without me.

The mere idea of it hurts me a thousand times more than iron ever could.

"Stop talking like that." The previous playfulness in Damon's voice is gone. "You're not going to die."

I wish I had the same confidence, but a bad feeling nags at me. I'm not sure if it's intuition or the bond throwing a tantrum, but something is very wrong.

Dim light streams through a crack as I open the door a few inches. I peer into the empty hallway, only to be greeted by the same eerie silence.

The storm still rages outside, but in here, there's no movement. Not a breath from anyone on the whole floor.

Cautiously, I move forward. Damon guards my back as I peek into the rooms.

The walls are made from white marble with golden swirls, and crystals drip from the chandeliers. Some of the beds are made and the floors are clean. Others, though… the linens are tossed back, and clothes are littered about the space, as if someone left in a hurry.

"Do you sense anyone?" I mutter quietly.

"No," Damon replies. "Maybe Gia evacuated the castle?"

I shake my head. "I doubt it. She's always liked an audience during our challenges."

"I remember. Shall we go to the throne room, then?"

I make an affirmative noise. "Let's just hope she hasn't set booby traps the entire way down."

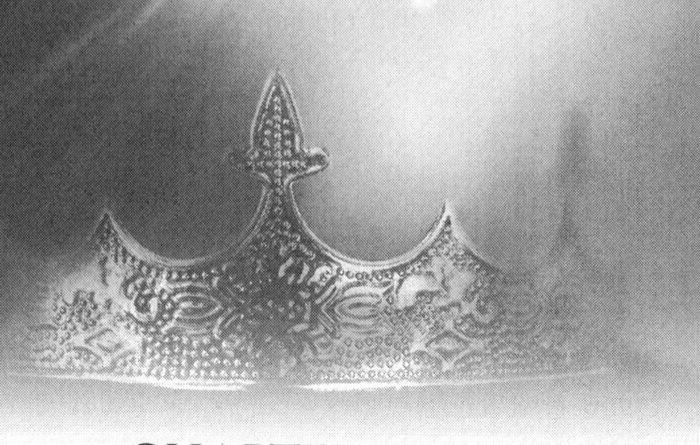

CHAPTER 37

Kirian

WE ENCOUNTER THREE MORE TRIPWIRES, ALL OF which I set off on purpose by throwing my axe toward the string. At least they seem to be a one-and-done. After the first round of weapons has been released, there isn't a second. It's a poor attempt to avoid a fight.

"The palace has undergone some renovations since the last time I was here," I deadpan, kicking a few arrows out of the way while eyeing the ornate double doors ahead.

"I'd say so," Damon quips. "Arrows shooting from the walls is definitely new."

"You should stay out of sight until I need you," I tell him quietly. "It's better if Gia doesn't realize I have backup."

He gives me a solemn nod.

Voices carry to my ears as we near the great hall. I catch a few worried murmurs about the weather, and some whispered concerns about the insane princess.

Damon and I pause just outside, listening for clues as to what we're about to walk in on.

From the impatient tones of the nobles, I predict Gia's been waiting for me for a while.

Let the showdown begin.

Giving her the dramatics she wants, I kick the doors open, busting the hinges and splintering the wood.

Terrified shrieks and screams ripple through the crowd. And I do mean crowd. There has to be at least seventy-five fae huddled together at the opposite end of the hall. Some I recognize from our events, but others are new, and from the looks of their ragged clothing, Gia decided to round up some of our farmers.

Scanning the faces, I realize she gathered fae from every station. Probably wanting to strike fear into the hearts of every social class in the kingdom.

It's hard to keep up the farce of being blind, but I force my gaze to go blank as I look in the direction of my sister.

She's in my peripheral vision, and I feel like I'm seeing her through new eyes—no pun intended.

She's sitting in my seat. My crown is upon her head, and it looks too heavy for her small frame. Dressed to impress, she's wearing a fancy white gown. It glitters, as if it's made from stardust. And maybe it is.

On the way through the castle, I saw a painting of her. The artist did a good job, because he captured her devious smile perfectly.

"Kirian," she calls, and I don't miss how she intentionally leaves 'king' off my title. "I was wondering when you'd make it back this way."

I stare at a spot somewhere above her head. "Gia, we need to have a serious talk. Privately." My words echo off the tall ceilings, and I turn to address the crowd. "Anyone who isn't a member of the royal family needs to leave."

I don't want someone getting caught in the crossfire. Blood will be spilled today, and I'd like to limit it to mine and Gia's.

I catch a few relieved sighs and grateful glances as the fae hustle toward the exits.

"No!" Gia's command makes everyone halt.

"Yes."

They glance from me to her, and it pisses me off that they don't know who to obey.

"You left me in charge," Gia protests. "I've been doing the job you were too weak for, dear brother."

"I was under the impression you could handle the position. I was wrong. I also thought you were loyal, but that was a mistake. I know what you did, Gia. You've committed the highest crime against me and the kingdom."

A few gasps float up through the air, because everyone knows what that means. Killing a fae's fated mate is the ultimate offense. To kill one is to kill both.

Which means Gia's a traitor.

Farrel is probably her accomplice.

Speaking of him, he sits at her side in my father's place, and I don't miss the way he squirms uncomfortably. He keeps looking down at his fidgeting hands with a morose expression. The two chairs on either side of them are unoccupied, and when I covertly search the crowd, I don't see Mother anywhere.

No one speaks, but their eyes nervously volley back and forth between us. They're not sure who to pledge loyalty to. I'll fix that right now.

"Go!" I roar. "Go to the safety of your homes. Tell your families I'll fix the mess Princess Gia has made."

"Stay." Huffing, Gia stands, gesturing to the frozen figures. "These are my witnesses. I hereby issue an official challenge for the throne."

Fine. If she wants a fight, she'll get one.

I palm my axe as I come down the stairs. My power stores are high right now, thanks to Quinn and the mating bond. I just hope it's enough to beat Gia.

The thought of truly harming her makes my stomach churn.

In all the other matches we've had, I went easy on her. She didn't know it, but I held back because I didn't want to hurt her.

But there's no trace of the little girl I once knew.

There's a wild glint in Gia's eyes, and her fingers twitch at her sides as she sizes me up.

With a flick of her wrist, a gust of wind opens the window across the room. The glass panes shatter against the walls.

Just as my foot makes it off the last step, a lightning bolt shoots inside, heading straight for me.

Everything goes white.

My muscles seize and I fall to the floor. The back of my skull smacks hard against the marble, and pain radiates through every cell of my body.

Everyone is screaming, but I barely hear it over the ringing in my ears.

My head throbs. My skin sizzles. My heart beats in an odd, unstable rhythm. I try to move, but I can't.

I've been hit by lightning many times before. Just a hazard of flying. No big deal. It usually stuns me for a few minutes, but I can't afford to be immobile right now.

I blink up at the ceiling as Gia struts over to me.

I hate to admit it, but if the beginning of our fight is any indication, I'm no match for someone with enhanced powers.

Wielding lightning? My father's the only person I've ever known who can do that.

I try to call on the birds, the vines, insects—anything that might be able to create a diversion. But they're all under Gia's command. If our abilities were different from each other, I might have a chance, but right now, we're pulling on the same rope.

I'll lose this tug of war because she has more influence than I do.

All I have is my wits and physical strength, both of which are extremely hindered at the moment.

As if being completely incapacitated wasn't already enough, roots break through the floor underneath me. The marble cracks as brown ropes twist around my torso, arms, and legs. Some of them have thorns that scrape and stab me.

Gia circles my body, and I spy an iron spike in her hand. It's unlike a knife or a spear. The tip is needle-sharp, and it becomes thicker toward the base.

My sister doesn't want a challenge.

She wants an execution.

I've always had respect for her, but memories of her cowardly attempts to claim the crown bubble to the surface. The way she tried to take advantage of my disability. The times she pretended to be finished, only to jump up and strike me in the back. Her use of iron weapons; even after we'd agreed to leave the dangerous metal out of it, she always found a clever loophole in her wording.

Nothing was too low for Gia.

I used to think her smart and resourceful.

Now, I see her for what she truly is—ruthless and deceitful.

"I'm doing this to help you." Frowning down at me, she grips the wooden handle of the spike. "What sort of existence could you possibly have now? Your fated mate is gone. You're blind. You won't be a ruler. I'm simply putting you out of your misery."

She actually sounds sincere. It's so ridiculous that I laugh.

"You knew Quinn was my fated mate," I croak out, trying to keep her talking. "How?"

I mentally will my body to pull against the binding roots, but I barely manage a twitch because of the electricity still numbing my limbs. If I was at full strength, I might be able to break them. But right now, it's no use.

Gia snickers. "Oh, poor Kirian. The fact that you were too much of a moron to realize it is proof I should be queen. It was obvious the second I saw you together in the dining hall. The way you had to touch her all the time and how you angled your body in front of hers, protecting her. Even when there was no threat, you were willing to die for her. Besides, you ran off to the human realm all that time for no reason? I don't think so. You were drawn to her and couldn't stay away."

"Just another reason to be jealous of me, eh?" I probably shouldn't try to piss her off right now, but I can't hold in the low blow.

"Yes," she hisses, then throws a quick glance at Farrel. "No offense, dear."

"None taken," he grits out. "But, darling, I think you should take a moment to reconsider your actions. This isn't you."

"This is me! For the first time in my life, I feel right."

"Where's Mother?" Tingles are replacing the numbness in my fingers, and I successfully make a fist.

Slowly, I try to get to the handle of my axe. It's just a few inches away, and Gia doesn't seem to notice my movement.

"In the dungeon, along with the rest of the council and anyone who dared to defy my orders." She grimaces, looking somewhat ashamed. "I had to use iron shackles. It was the only way to keep her from interfering. She'll forgive me someday."

"She won't," I say with certainty. "Don't do this."

She ignores me. "Goodbye, brother. I'll see you someday on the other side of the stars."

As she raises her weapon, my grip closes around the handle of my axe.

But it's too heavy.

Fear strikes me harder than the lightning did. This might actually be the end for me.

My life flashes before my eyes, and the whole thing is a culmination of Quinn.

She's pulling me out of the river. She offers her coat when I know she's colder than I am. She gives me her marble. Years pass, and everything is a blur but her. She reads to me. She hums while she helps me harvest the honeysuckle. She cries because her peers at her school are mean to her. We fish. We eat butter-scotch pudding. We dance.

More than anything, we love.

I almost think I can smell her sweet scent. My mind must be playing tricks on me, because my veins buzz as if she's near, and I swear I can feel her strength flowing into my body.

What I wouldn't give to kiss her one more time.

My eyes zero in on the sharp tip of the spike.

And then it comes down.

CHAPTER 38

Quinn

I'M WINDED FROM SPRINTING THROUGH THE CASTLE. I got lost a couple times, but the arrow traps led the way.

Nausea from fear—not my fear, Kirian's—makes my stomach flip. My muscles burn as I pump my legs faster down a familiar corridor. I've only come through here once before, but I recognize the portraits of all the royals as I get closer to the great hall.

Splintered wood is hanging where the doors once were, and the howling wind inside is unnerving. When I run through to the balcony, I see Gia standing over Kirian on the first floor below.

She's about to stab him.

"Stop!" I scream, and Gia pauses mid-crouch, the tip of the spike just a couple inches from Kirian's chest.

Her lavender eyes are angry slits when she looks over her shoulder at me.

"She isn't supposed to be here!" She aims her rage-filled voice at Farrel. "You didn't snap her neck before you pushed her through the portal? You defied me."

He stays silent, smoldering at her with a hateful look. Yikes. I'd say there's trouble in paradise.

At least now I know who was manhandling me in the Shadowlands, and I'm thankful my spinal cord is still intact. But I don't have time to contemplate Farrel's reasoning for letting me live.

My hands splay on the smooth railing as I lean forward and try to figure out how badly Kirian's hurt. He's bleeding in several places and his clothes are ripped. The vines restraining him have long thorns, and one is buried deep in his right shoulder.

My hand goes to my upper arm in the same spot. I ache there. His pain affects me.

Our eyes lock, and I almost expect him to scold me for coming here or tell me to run.

Instead, a grin spreads over his face. It's not the kind of smile where he's happy to see me. It's mischievous, like he has a secret.

I feel a strange tingling in my veins, and the pain I'd been experiencing gets replaced with an essence of power.

Before I can ask Kirian if he's okay, Damon is suddenly dragging me back and trying to push me behind him.

I struggle, because I'm losing sight of what's happening.

I don't know if it'll help, but I toss Garryn's dagger over the balcony, hoping my aim is good enough for it to land where Kirian can reach it.

A second later, I hear some loud snapping sounds and then a high-pitched scream of agony.

Managing to break away from Damon's hold, I crane my neck to see what's going on down there.

Kirian's upper half is free from his restraints, and Gia's on the floor with the dagger sticking out of her kneecap. Her silky gown is pinned to her leg and a red stain spreads over the white fabric.

In a quick move, Kirian grabs his axe and swings it down on her foot, slicing the metatarsals longways.

Revolted by the gruesome sight, I cover my mouth.

Gia lets out a guttural howl as she drops her weapon and blood pools around her. Kirian rips the rest of the vines off, sending dirt and debris flying as he stands.

He spins his axe around in a practiced motion and kicks the spike across the floor, away from Gia. "By the way, my fated mate is alive. The curse is broken. I can see, and I'll rule this kingdom until the day I die—which will be a long time from now."

Taking advantage of Gia's momentary distraction, he calls on his powers. Vines spill through the open window, crawling over to her. They wrap around her arms and legs, binding her hands behind her back.

Now that she's restrained, I think it's over.

But I'm wrong.

All the windows fly open, and a lightning bolt dances into the room. It's moving sluggishly, as if Gia's weakened. At first, I'm worried she's going to use it on Kirian, but it's not headed toward him.

It's going straight for me.

As I back up, Damon puts himself in front of me, and I hear the flap of Kirian's wings before he lands on the stairs. He's blocking us, planning to take the strike.

Both of these men are willing to endure a lightning bolt for me.

But Kirian and self-preservation are one in the same. If he gets hurt, so do I.

I'm about to shout to him to get out of the way when, suddenly, the electricity begins slowly draining away, leaving the room the same way it came in.

Everything gets quiet when the wind dies down. The rain stops, clouds recede, and I see a few stars twinkling in the night sky outside.

"What happened?" My adrenaline is at an all-time high, and I'm panting like I just ran a marathon.

Peeking around Damon, I glance down at Gia. Her eyes are closed, and her breathing is slow. She's unconscious.

"Asleep," Damon explains. Walking down the stairs, he claps Kirian on the back. "Did I ever mention I can lull people into slumber?"

"You've got to be kidding me," Kirian says flatly, following him. "Why didn't you tell me that earlier, say, I dunno, two thousand years ago?"

Damon shrugs. "We've all got secrets."

Pissed, Kirian narrows his eyes. "A shit ton of conflict could've been avoided if you'd used your power earlier."

"I was waiting to reveal it at the right time."

"The right time would've been before Gia kicked my ass." Kirian spits some blood onto the floor at the bottom of the stairs, and I'm concerned about all his injuries.

My tongue hurts, which means he must've bit his at some point. He's got a gash running down the back of his skull, and countless cuts from the thorns.

But before I check him over, I just need to touch him.

He turns and opens his arms to me. Jumping from the second step up, I leap onto his body. I squeeze him tight, my legs wrapped around his waist.

I kiss him, and the metallic taste of blood hits my tongue. "You jackass. You almost died. Don't do that again."

"But I didn't, thanks to you." He kisses me again before nuzzling my cheek. "I appreciate the dagger, my queen. You're my hero."

"Hey, what about me?" Damon complains. "I'm the one who knocked Gia out."

We ignore him. Our hair and clothes are damp from rain, sweat, and blood, but relief makes me feel light.

The danger is over.

Kirian presses his nose to my hair and inhales. "How did you get in?"

"Talon flew me up to the tower. Don't worry." I throw a look at Damon. "He's safe. He went back to the stables after dropping me off."

"You should've stayed in the nobles' house," Kirian says, but there's no bark behind his words.

I twist my lips to the side. "I just saved your life."

He lets out a resigned sigh. "That you did. As soon as I saw you, my strength increased, and I was able to get free."

"I would've put Gia to sleep before she ran you through," Damon huffs, insulted he's not getting more credit. All that earns him is a scowl from both Kirian and me. At least he has the decency to look guilty. "I just wanted to find out how powerful this distilled Day water really is. Now I know."

"When will she wake?" Kirian asks him, setting me down.

"Whenever I allow it, but I'll have to stay near her. If I get more than fifty feet away, my influence will wear off in a matter of minutes."

I start to fuss over Kirian's wounds while he continues his conversation with Damon.

"She needs to stay asleep until the water leaves her system." He raises his right arm so I can inspect a cut on his ribs. It isn't deep, and the bleeding has already stopped.

In fact, all his injuries seem to be healing quickly. My finger goes over a scrape on his arm that's already closed.

"How long will that be?" Damon wonders.

Kirian looks to Farrel. "If anyone would know the answer, it's you."

As Gia's chosen mate gets up from King Keryth's chair, he's visibly trembling. "King Kirian, I can explain many things, if you'll allow me."

Kirian holds up a hand to silence him.

"First things first." Tucking me close to his side, he turns to the frozen, wide-eyed fae still lingering in the hall. "I am your king, and this is your new queen. That isn't changing anytime soon. It's true that Quinn is my fated mate and the curse is broken. Spread the word: traitors who took advantage of my absence will be dealt with harshly." When no one makes a move to leave, he shouts, "Go!"

After everyone has shuffled out, Kirian motions for Farrel to continue.

The dark-haired fae lowers himself to both knees, bowing his head while linking his hands behind his back.

"You take the position of someone who's up for a beheading." Kirian's shocked by Farrel's submission. "Why? You don't want to fight me?"

"I don't want to fight anyone," he replies to the floor. "Not you, not your sister. I'm tired, my lord. Gia has made me do so many terrible things."

Am I supposed to feel bad for this guy? "You pushed me through the portal."

He nods. "I apologize. I never wanted to hurt you. Truly."

"How did you manage to navigate the darkness?" I ask.

"A seeing spell Gia got from the witches," Farrel replies, stealing a quick glance at Kirian. "The coven that cursed you, King Kirian—they contacted her about a year ago. They wanted to join forces with her. They said they would help her gain control of the Night Realm."

"In exchange for what?" Kirian's voice is hard.

"At first, it was information they were after. They wanted her to tell them right away if you found your mate, and she did as they asked."

"What was their end goal? To hurt Quinn?"

Farrel grimaces. "I suppose. Gia wouldn't tell me specifics. All she did was give me orders."

"The first night in my room?" I persist, wanting all the answers. "That was you, too?"

"Yes. As I said, I couldn't harm you. I could've killed you if I wanted to, but it's not in my nature. I've never taken a life before."

I start tapping my foot. "But the explosion and the poisoning? I could've died then."

"That wasn't my doing. A witch named Merina set up those catastrophes. When they failed, Gia sent me to end you before putting you back in your home world."

A strange prickly sensation crawls up my neck, but it's not a bad feeling. It's the same one I've gotten before when I know someone's being honest. I don't know how I know Farrel's telling the truth—I just do.

"You had mercy on my mate," Kirian says, his tone unreadable. "You went against Gia. She was your superior and your mate, yet you defied her."

Farrel gives a nod as he glances at the woman sprawled on the floor a few feet away. "Over these past several months, I've grown to hate her. As of now, I revoke our mating vows. I am no longer hers and she is not mine. As for how much of the water Gia ingested, it was a lot. I don't know the exact amount, but she's been like this before. It'll be at least three days before she's back to normal. The Glow—it's addictive and dangerous."

Kirian tilts his head. "Glow?"

"That's what people have been calling it. If my powers were more useful, I might've become just as lost as Gia. I drank a few sips once. I could hear animals communicating as far as the Day Realm. I couldn't sleep for two nights because it was so loud." His dark-blue eyes swim with shame. "Your Majesty, I've brought harm to your kingdom and I willingly accept any punishment you deem fit."

Swallowing hard, I look away from him, wondering if he'll be executed soon. I might be witnessing my first beheading today. Possibly two, depending on what Kirian decides to do with Gia.

"I need a moment to consult with the queen." Kirian leads me away, and it takes me a second to realize he's referring to me.

I'm the queen.

Damon stays put, silently towering over the kneeling fae.

When we get a good distance away, Kirian lovingly strokes my face and whispers, "What do you think we should do?"

"You're asking me?" I say it a little louder than I intended, and Kirian puts a finger to his lips.

But seriously. As if I'd know what to do in this situation?

We enter a staring contest, and I realize he's not going to move forward without my input.

I sigh. "Tell me about Farrel. What kind of person is he?"

"He and I have never been close, but I've always thought him to be a decent man," Kirian replies. "He's quite a bit younger than me—born about seven hundred years ago. Because of his ability to communicate with animals, he was hired on as a stable boy here when he was a child. He was orphaned and young, and we gave him a home at the palace. Unfortunately, he was easy prey for Gia. He had no family, no assets. When he came of age, she seduced him with the hopes that having a mate would make her seem more worthy of the crown." He scratches his jaw. "Farrel always treated her well. He was willing to marry her, despite the fact that she was too old to have children and she wasn't his fated mate."

"So, he got tangled up with the wrong person," I conclude. "But he didn't kill me when he had the opportunity. I think we should give him a chance to redeem himself."

I really don't want to see anyone's head roll, especially not because of my order.

Kirian gazes at me with affection as he runs a hand through my hair. "My merciful mate."

"Is that a bad thing? Am I too soft?"

"No," he answers before adding, "your kind heart is exactly what our kingdom needs right now."

I sigh with relief. Maybe I won't be bad at this.

Taking my hands, Kirian squares his shoulders and says, "I hereby transfer my vow of punishment to you. The decision is yours now, if you accept."

My eyebrows go up. "You can do that?"

He nods. "Giving it to someone of equal power is the only way to rescind my original promise."

"Oh," I breathe out. Kirian found the loophole he needed to have compassion for his sister and the others involved in her crimes. I can take this burden from him. "Then, yes, I accept."

I feel the flutter of the oath in my chest, and I swallow hard.

Because, wow, this is a lot for me. It's probably the first of many verdicts I'll deal with as queen, but this one's a doozy.

"Okay." Steely resolve flows through me. I'll make this right. "I don't know how I can tell—call it intuition or whatever—but Farrel's remorse seems genuine. I suggest a kind of probation and community service. After some jail time, that is."

"This is a custom from your world, yes?"

"Yeah. It works for some people, if they want to do better. I think Farrel should be given the chance to do something good with his life."

Kirian inclines his head. "Then it will be as you say."

With his arm around my shoulders, we walk back to the men.

"Stand, Farrel," Kirian says, and the fae scrambles to his feet. "My mate lives because of you. I'll show you the same courtesy, but you're still in my debt. A mess has been made here. You were part of creating it, so you'll be part of fixing it."

"Seriously?" Farrel rubs his neck, like he can't believe his head is still attached to his body.

"Seriously," I say. "Don't fuck it up."

"Yes, my queen," he rushes out, bowing repeatedly. "You have my word. I'm forever at your service."

Seeming pleased with Farrel's fervent loyalty toward me, Kirian commands, "Release my mother and the rest from the dungeon. You need to help the council confiscate all the Glow from the castle and dispose of it properly. Then, have them lock you up until I can figure out what to do with you. I need your word that you'll do as I say."

"You have it." Without hesitation, Farrel runs off to carry out the tasks.

Then there's the matter of Gia.

As the vines unwind from her limp body, they crackle and snap, slithering away. I watch as they disappear out the windows.

A pained expression paints Kirian's face as he stares down at his sister. Her mangled foot is bleeding, and the dagger is still sticking out of her knee.

"I could kill her right now," Kirian says quietly. "I could use my axe to sever her head. It would be painless for her."

"But not for you." I slide an arm around his waist and give him a squeeze.

"I can see the pulse in her neck," he goes on. "I'm disgusted at the thought of ending her life. Even after everything she's done, there's still a part of me that cares for her. I'm sorry, Quinn. You deserve better from your mate."

Tugging on his arm, I turn him to me. I frame his face with my hands, loving that his eyes can connect with mine. "You don't have to apologize, and you don't have to do anything you don't want to do. Besides, it's not up to you anymore. This is on me."

He places a hand over mine, holding my touch to his cheek. "The way you love me is humbling."

Damon makes a noise close to a gag. "I thought we were going to battle today. All this mushy stuff is giving me the willies. I'll just be over here. Alone. Without a mate. By myself."

An amused smile tugs at my lips as Damon goes to sulk on the stairs, and Kirian shakes his head.

Before I can think too hard about what to do with Gia, an anguished cry rings through the great hall.

"Don't do it, Kirian!" Zella yells. "Don't kill her." Running over to Gia, she falls to her knees, weeping. "Why do families do this to each other? I've seen too much of it. I can't take it anymore."

The yellow gown she wears is dirty from being in the dungeon, and it reeks of sweat, urine, and mildew. Although I've never been down there, I'm willing to bet it's pretty disgusting.

Red bands of blisters and open sores decorate her wrists where she was restrained by iron shackles. Judging by the streaks of dried blood on her arms, she was chained up for a while.

Even after this, she begs for her daughter's life.

I know my mom would do the same for me. Not that I'd ever do what Gia did, but still. The unconditional love of a parent is endless.

"She might not be right in the heart, but I can't imagine a world without her in it." Tears drip down Zella's cheeks as she takes Gia's hand. "Is there anything you can do to change your vow, Kirian? Anything I can give you to reverse this?"

Zella's so consumed by grief she doesn't realize I'm standing here next to Kirian. She doesn't know her son has already given her what she begs for.

"Mother—"

"Kirian, I have a confession to make." Without looking up, she interrupts him. She takes a deep breath, as if what she's about to say is difficult. Prolonging the suspense, she combs Gia's hair away from her face, fixing the messy strands before continuing, "About ten years after the curse, we found the witches."

Shocked, Kirian jerks back. "What?"

"They wanted Gia. They said they'd lift the curse if we gave them our daughter, but she was just a child. They wanted us to choose between the two of you, and I couldn't. I couldn't do it then, and I can't do it now. Forgive me."

"Why didn't you tell me about this?" he rasps. "Why did you continue to let me search for them when you already knew what they wanted?"

"Your father and I hoped you could persuade them. Maybe you had something else to bargain with. After all this time, I thought Gia was safe, but they got to her anyway. Before she locked me up, she admitted she'd been working with them. I'm not trying to defend her—she's at fault. But they saw an evil in her and took advantage of it. Don't end her. I'll do anything you ask."

"It isn't my decision anymore," Kirian tells her.

She looks up at him, and that's when she notices me. Her eyes go wide. "Oh, Quinn. You're alive!" Smiling through her tears, she reaches up to grab my hand. "You have no idea how glad I am to see you."

"It's good to see you, too," I tell her honestly.

Kirian's arm goes around my shoulders, and his gaze flits to me. "My fated mate will make a choice here, and it will be final."

"Did you just say fated?" Zella glances back and forth between us a few times before finally settling on Kirian's focused eyes. "You can see."

A grin stretches over both their faces, and I blink back tears when I see mother and son looking into each other's eyes for the first time in thousands of years.

Temporarily forgetting about Gia's predicament, Zella jumps up and grabs his hands. Bouncing, she chants, "You can see, you can see!" Then, she pulls me into a tight hug. "You did it. It was you all along."

Her affection makes me happy, and I giggle.

"Yep. And don't worry—no one's dying here today. I've got

a better solution. If Gia likes being evil and hanging out with witches, I know a place where she can go." I share a look with Kirian, and I know he's thinking the same thing. "But we'll need a spell to keep her from leaving."

"Banishment?" Zella asks, hope in her voice. "That would be preferable to death."

Nodding, I lightly touch her long blond locks. "This sounds weird, but I'm going to need some hair to make it happen."

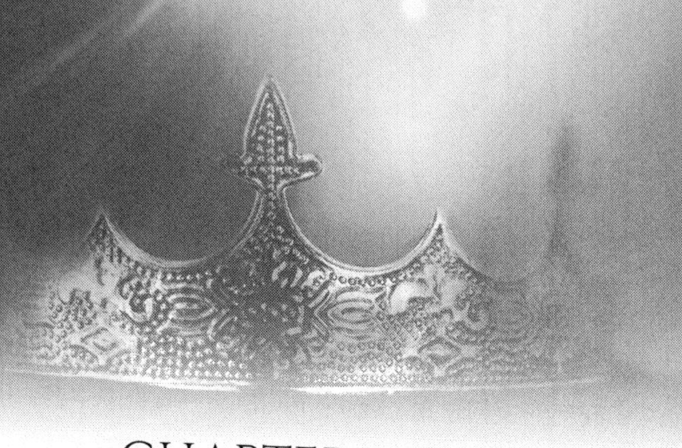

CHAPTER 39

Quinn

Kirian cups my ass while we walk through the seemingly endless darkness. It isn't necessary for him to hold me up; I'm securely strapped into the carrier.

But I like that he wants to touch me. That he can't keep his hands off me.

The feeling is mutual.

Sliding my arms around his neck, I press my nose to the skin at the hollow of his throat and inhale.

This time, our trip to the Shadowlands was a bit different. We traveled by carriage—the non-explosive kind—and got here in a record-breaking three days.

We didn't sleep at any of the inns and we didn't stop to eat. Kirian personally packed up our food supplies and we slept for short periods of time inside the carriage. It was a little weird with an unconscious Gia in tow, but I knew Damon wouldn't let her wake up.

On our way through the villages, we made time for the announcement that I'm very much alive, but not much else. To celebrate, the gnomes broke out the sugar beet vodka, but the mood was subdued. After all, some of their children are still missing. Fiona, the girl who gave me my midnight rose, is among the taken.

I tried not to let my tears show as I promised I'd get every one of them back.

A day into our journey, we ran into Torius and Kai. Or rather, they flew over us and stopped to talk. Instead of heading to Delaveria, they insisted on coming with us to make sure we had a safe journey.

Ever the faithful soldiers, there were no hard feelings on their part. They were just happy to be back in Kirian's good graces. They're currently waiting for us back in Aelustria.

"Almost there," Kirian says, low.

I shiver, and it's not from the cold.

His gravelly voice triggers sexy memories from this morning. The way he growled dirty somethings while he pounded into me from behind. The way he pulled my hair and smacked my ass. The way he rubbed and pinched my clit until I screamed his name.

Countless times over the past few days, Kirian sent the guys a good distance away and had his way with me in this carriage. In the twenty-five thousand-ish years we'll have together, I don't think I'll ever get enough of him. There's a hollow ache between my legs, and I want more.

I'm tired, hungry, horny, and ready to go home. Delaveria home. With my palace, my bed, and my people.

Like Kirian said—they'll learn to love me.

"We're here," he murmurs into my ear.

Sudden light makes me wince, and I recognize the inside of Astrid's cave.

"Oh, good. You're all here." She gets up from her rocking chair as Damon comes through the door with Gia in his arms.

She's lifeless and unresponsive, just as she has been ever since the Dream Realm king put her in that state. Pretty impressive. Gotta say, when I first heard about Damon's ability, I felt kind of bad for the guy. I mean, dream walking is cool and all. I'm sure it's entertaining, but how useful can that be?

Being able to make people go to sleep on a whim is seriously badass.

As Kirian helps me out of the sling, I hold onto our precious payment. Astrid will be thrilled with the new material for her rugs. Zella didn't hesitate to take scissors to her own hair when I told her the price for the spell.

"We need a favor," Kirian tells Astrid, bypassing formalities like the bossy king he is.

Before the witch can go on about how much it will cost us, I hold up the long braid and run my fingers over the silky strands.

She gasps, snatching it from my hand. Bringing it close to her nose, she smells the length of it before rubbing it on her cheek. "Queen Zella. This is beyond my wildest hopes."

"Good," Kirian grunts. "Because we need a big spell. Something that will entrap Gia in the Shadowlands for the remainder of her life."

"And let me guess." Astrid thoughtfully taps her chin. "You want Princess Gia to have my home."

"You knew this part was coming," I pipe up, remembering the way she'd muttered something about her house no longer being safe.

"I suspected. Where am I to live?"

"With me," Damon supplies. "There's a room in my palace for you."

"Well, this works out nicely for you, doesn't it?" Astrid affectionately pats him on the cheek, then motions to the cot on the floor where he can set Gia. "You've been trying to get me to move in with you for years."

"Seriously?" Kirian asks his cousin.

"What? It'd be pretty awesome to have a resident witch."

"And the boy gets lonely without his parents," Astrid adds.

"I'm not a boy," Damon says defensively. "But yeah, it'd be nice to have a friend. Now that Kirian has Quinn back, I doubt I'll see much of them for a while."

Kirian and I exchange a troubled look, because he's not wrong. We've got a lot of crap to straighten out. Not to mention, I want a honeymoon.

Although he tries to hide his loneliness with comic relief and funny quips, Damon can't fool me. He's pretty secluded. No mate. His parents have been away for over half a millennium. Obviously, he's not dating. The Dream Realm is a lot smaller than the Night Realm, so he has fewer people to look after.

"All right." Astrid crouches on the floor and begins rolling up her rugs. One by one, she dumps the hefty logs in Damon's arms. "We'll have to do this fast. I don't want Princess Gia waking up before we get out of the Shadowlands." She levels all of us with a serious look. "You'll have to tell your people not to pass through here—ever. The coven might follow the princess, taking refuge in her domain. The Shadowlands will be more dangerous than ever."

"Understood." Kirian rubs his jaw thoughtfully.

"You have a question, my king?" Astrid surmises, a sly smile spreading over her face as she reads his mind. "I'm feeling generous today. Go ahead."

"I don't get why the witches would pursue Gia after so many years of silence and inactivity. Why now?"

"The timing was not a coincidence." Astrid goes to her empty bowl on the table and sprinkles a chalky substance inside. "All curses have a shelf life, and yours was expiring. Once the curse is broken, they no longer have control over you. They got desperate to intervene before the bond could be completed."

It all becomes clear when I remember what Astrid said about witches being puppet masters. "Holy shit, it totally makes sense now. Kill the fated mate, eliminate the way out of the curse. Gia was their way to infiltrate the royal family to get to me. She was their vessel. Basically their puppet."

Astrid points in my direction. "Exactly."

"But they didn't succeed. They lost. Does that mean they'll stop coming after me?" I ask hopefully.

She nods. "They'll focus their efforts elsewhere. You're both free to live your lives."

A burst of satisfaction and a feeling of security come at me through the bond. Kirian and I exchange a glance, complete with relieved smiles. Mystery solved, and no one had to die. We can get on with our plans.

A wedding. Ruling the kingdom. Maybe some babies.

"What about mine?" Damon interjects eagerly, his face hidden behind the pile of rugs in his arms. "Is my curse expiring?"

"Yes."

He waits several seconds, and when he realizes Astrid's not going to give him more information, he makes an impatient sound. "Well, when?"

"Soon."

Frustrated, he groans. "Soon in fae time could mean tomorrow or a thousand years from now."

Unfazed by Damon's dramatics, Astrid begins stirring the contents in her bowl. She recites a few words I can't understand, and mist floats up before snaking around the room like it's alive. When it gets to Gia, it settles around her like a heavy fog before the gray stuff absorbs into her.

"It's done." Astrid packs up her dishes and a few books, dumping them into a burlap sack as she bustles around the room. "Princess Gia will be tied to the Shadowlands for as long as she lives."

Walking over to Kirian and me, she scoops a handful of nothing out of her pocket. She blows whatever it is onto our faces before sprinkling it on herself.

"This will make it so you can see through the darkness. We'll have to hurry to the Dream Realm." Hoisting her bag of belongings over one shoulder, Astrid glances back at her rocking chair. "I guess I can leave that for the princess." As she walks by Damon, she adds, "You better have a nice room for me."

"You can have your own suite," he says, following behind her as he adjusts his hold on the rugs. "Take my parents' room. It's not like they're using it."

Continuing to discuss the details of Astrid's new living situation, they disappear through the rock wall.

Right before we're about to duck through the doorway, Kirian turns back to look at Gia one last time.

I squeeze his hand. "Does it help to know she didn't seek out the witches? That they came to her?"

"No. It doesn't matter how it started. The end result is still the same. Gia cared for power more than anything. More than her kingdom, more than her family. Now she has nothing." Shaking his head, he quietly adds, "May the shadows be merciful on you, sister."

Not bothering with the carrier, he picks me up. One arm supports my back and the other is under my knees. Looping my arms around his neck, I hide my face against his chest as he surges forward into the darkness.

And then we're running.

Well, *he's* running. I'm just hanging on for dear life while being jostled around. My eyes are shut, but then I remember we're supposed to be able to see with Astrid's help.

I'm not sure if I should look. Maybe I don't want to know what dangers lurk here.

Oh, hell. Who am I kidding? I can't resist.

I peek through one eye.

Everything is illuminated around us, but it's not a natural kind of light. There's a murky green tint to everything, as if we're wearing night vision goggles.

The cavern is bigger than I thought it'd be. It's probably the width of a football field, and every fifty feet or so, there are wide cracks in the walls. Slitted eyes glow from the shadows inside, and I see the glint of sharp teeth.

When we pass a dead tree with bats hanging from the branches, Kirian's legs pump faster. The creatures take flight, swarming overhead.

Peering over his shoulder, I look behind us. A scream lodges in my throat when I see a man with a boar's head standing in the middle of the cavern. Watching us, his tusks glisten with saliva and his eyes are an unnatural yellow.

Welp. There's a reason why people can't see in the Shadowlands—because it's fucking terrifying.

Deciding I've had enough, I close my eyes and bury my face by Kirian's neck while silently praying we make it out alive.

Thankfully, it doesn't take long.

Kirian dodges to the left, probably avoiding something awful, and the toe of my shoe scrapes against something rough. The canal is narrowing toward the exit.

The air changes, going from oppressively stagnant to a refreshingly cool breeze.

I breathe out a sigh of relief when I look up and see the night sky.

We're in the Dream Realm.

Just as Kirian sets me on my feet, we hear a blood curdling scream full of rage from inside the Shadowlands. The ground shakes and a flock of birds squawk as they take flight from a nearby tree.

Gia's awake.

"Right on time," Damon announces. Panting from exertion, he sets the load he was carrying on the ground.

"Well, what now?" I ask Kirian.

"Back to Delaveria," he replies, urgency in his tone.

Damon faces us. "Kirian, I'll need to get Astrid settled. I want to help you with everything that's going on, but…"

"Your mate," Kirian finishes for him. "You want to find her."

He nods. "The sooner, the better. After what Astrid said… my mate could be in danger. I want to search the human realm. Now that I know it's possible to find her there, that's where I'll look."

"I wish you luck." Kirian holds out a hand, and Damon shakes it.

"You'll still come to our wedding, right?" Hopeful, I clasp my hands together. "It probably won't be for a while. We can't have the ceremony until the Night Realm is back to normal."

Damon grins. "I wouldn't miss it."

"Me either," Astrid chimes in.

I smile at my friends. And that's what they are. Real friends.

We say our goodbyes to the Dream Realm king and the witch, and they walk leisurely together on the path to Damon's castle. Astrid laughs at something he says.

Those two have an odd dynamic, but it works. I'm glad they have each other.

My gaze moves to Kirian, and I catch him staring at me. "You okay?"

Blinking, he shakes his head, like he hadn't even realized he was gawking.

I love it when he does that.

"How could I not be? You're safe and we're together." His arms circle me. "Do you have any idea how gorgeous you are? I'll never get tired of looking at you."

"Even when I'm old and wrinkly? It'll happen someday, you know."

"And I'll be right there with you. Fae age, too—just very slowly. But now that you're here, your ears will get pointy and you might grow wings. In time, you'll become fae just like the rest of us."

I tilt my head to the side. "Will I develop powers?"

Kirian pauses. "You know, usually, the humans who change into fae don't. But since you have fae blood in you, maybe."

"I could be like a superhero." I grin. "How cool is that?"

"Well, if the hairs on the back of your neck start to stand for no reason, let me know. Fae children often feel that when they're honing their abilities."

Oh my God. That's happened to me. A few times.

"Is it normal for people to be able to sense truth or dishonesty here?" I ask, wondering if that's a common power.

Kirian's lips twist. "Like they can tell when someone's lying?"

"Yeah."

"Not that I know of. We have clairvoyants, but they're more into connecting with spirits or telling fortunes. Why?"

"Well, this might sound crazy, but I swear I can tell if someone's being honest or not."

Touching my blue silk scarf, I think back to the first time it was noticeable. I remember being so sure Fallon was telling the truth about his motives behind throwing it at me.

I quickly explain that particular instance, and what I felt when Farrel was spilling his past with Gia. Come to think of it, I also experienced the same sensation when Torius and Kai denied any involvement in trying to hurt me.

"It's definitely a possibility," Kirian says, stroking my cheek. "The longer you're here, the stronger it will get. Let's test it out once we get back home."

Home. This time, instead of feeling dread at the word, I'm relieved. It feels right. I couldn't care less about what the fae think of me—I have a purpose.

Getting the women and gnomes back from the Day Realm is priority number one.

There's a teeny tiny worry in the back of my mind about what my parents will think in the morning when they wake up and I'm not in my bed. They'll probably just assume I spent the night in my treehouse. It wouldn't be the first time I've disappeared into the woods at night.

And then on Kirian's birthday, we'll use his portal to go back. I'll be able to visit with my parents one last time before I "leave" for my new adventure.

It's going to take some time for me to get used to the new time conversion. To my parents, only a day will have passed. But for me, so much is going to happen.

Kirian and I already talked about it, and we decided the best plan is for me to not return for a while after that. After all, Mom and Dad will think I'm off working somewhere. We can use Kirian's portals to go other places in the world where I can make a phone call, but I won't see them until Thanksgiving. Which, in Valora, is like ninety-some years from now.

I'll miss them, but I'll be okay as long as I have Kirian.

His wings bust out, and it's seriously sexy when he does that.

"You ready to go back to the shit storm we left behind?" His expression is serious as he lifts me up. "Our people will need extra care and time to recover. I don't think anyone will be better at mending their hearts than you."

"You really mean that." It's not a question. That hair-raising thing happens again, and I know he has a hundred percent faith in me. "Let's hurry back. The sooner we get there, the sooner we can get married."

A growl rumbles in his chest as we leap into the air, and his response is almost lost in the wind. "I can't wait."

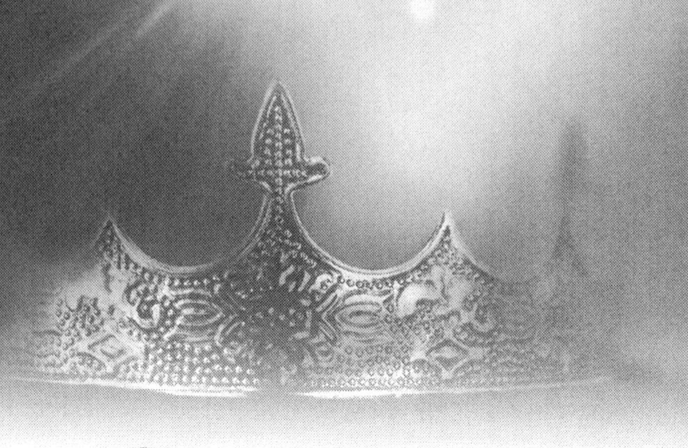

CHAPTER 40

Kirian

THE CARRIAGE ROCKS AND SWAYS ON THE UNEVEN PATH as we enter the city. Quinn dozes peacefully with her head on my lap. Kai is at the reins and Torius rides behind us.

Gia's betrayal still stings but having Quinn and my best men with me dulls the pain.

Soon, all will be right again in the Night Realm. We'll retrieve our people from the Day Realm, we'll outlaw distilled Day water, and Quinn and I will have the best wedding Valora has ever seen.

The love I feel for her is overwhelming. It grows with every passing minute, and I wonder if there's a limit. Will it ever stop or plateau? Or will it keep expanding until I can no longer stand to be apart from her for even a few seconds?

My pleasant thoughts are interrupted by the distant sounds of rioting, and my mood plummets.

Fuck.

Riots don't happen often, but when they do, the fae take it to dangerous levels. Think of a normal angry crowd, then add in special powers and the ability to fly. Cities can be burned to the ground and reduced to rubble in minutes.

Kai snaps the reins and we speed up. I carefully move Quinn, trying to slyly slide a pillow under her face, but her eyes pop open.

"What's going on?" Sitting up, she blinks sleepily. "What's that noise?"

"Stay inside." I hate to leave her in here without an explanation, but whatever's happening out there needs to be stopped, and I don't want her involved.

The carriage is still barreling down the road when I open the door. With my hand on my axe, I hop out. My boots land on the familiar cobblestone, and as my wings unfurl, I break into a run, getting ahead of our caravan.

But what I see has me stopping in my tracks.

Smiling faces. Flailing arms. Dozens of Night Realm flags waving through the air.

The streets are filled with people, and they're not yelling or fighting—they're cheering.

Having spotted us, Delaveria guards are already approaching. Kai stops the carriage and jumps down beside me, and Torius joins us after dismounting his horse.

"The women and children have been brought home," one of my newest guards says, smiling. I can't remember his name. He's young, just turned twenty-five last spring, and he hasn't experienced a true battle yet.

"All of them?" I ask skeptically.

"Yes, Your Majesty. Every single one."

"Unharmed?"

His grin falters. "Queen Zella is assessing the damage herself as we speak."

That's a no. "And my father?"

"He is well."

"My soldiers?"

"Six dead and thirty-nine injured."

We've had worse outcomes. I'm actually surprised we fared so well. I feel like there has to be a catch somewhere.

"Kirian?" My mate's voice causes chills to sweep through my body, and I turn to see her leaning out the window. "Can we go to the people? Now? I'm worried."

I couldn't have asked for a better partner. "Yes, love."

I move to get Quinn out of the carriage, but the soldier stops me. "Uh… One more thing you should know. The Day Realm king is here."

My eyebrows furrow. My uncle has always refused to step foot on Night Realm territory. Whenever matters needed to be discussed, he sent a council member in his place.

"King Zarid is in Delaveria?"

"No. King Zander," a drunk fae pipes up, stumbling over with ale dripping from his beard. "The pipsqueak finally got the crown."

"Zander is king now?" I ask slowly.

Something isn't right. I'm not unhappy to get a visit from my other cousin. Zander and I have only met a handful of times, but he's a good man. From our talks, I know he wants more than just peace for our kingdoms—he wants prosperity.

Needless to say, he isn't like his father.

But King Zarid wouldn't just step down. I'm sure of it. In so many words, he's told us we'd have to pry the crown from his cold dead hands.

"This is good news for Valora," I say cordially. "Tell my men they've done well. There will be a banquet in their honor within a fortnight."

"Yes, Your Majesty." The soldier jogs away, taking up his post on the street again.

Extending my hand to Quinn, I help her down before scooping her into my arms.

She knows the drill. Wrapping both legs around my waist, she hangs onto my neck as we take flight.

Within minutes, we're landing in front of the palace doors. Two soldiers open them for us, and when I acknowledge them with eye contact, they still seem taken aback by the fact that I can see.

Takes some getting used to.

Hand in hand, Quinn and I hurry to the great hall. Since it's the largest room, I have to assume that's where everyone's being assessed.

And I'm right.

As soon as we walk through the doors on the lower level, we're greeted with mayhem.

At least two hundred Night Realm residents take up the space. Young fae females and gnomes are huddled by the stairs. Several are weeping on the floor or sitting on the steps. Others stand still, staring off into space as if they're dazed. They look dirty and tired, but otherwise uninjured.

I can't say the same for my soldiers.

Makeshift cots are set up along one wall, and palace nurses are tending to the wounded men. Bandages are wrapped around deep gashes and missing limbs.

Quinn covers a gasp when she sees one who lost a leg.

"Fuck." Even I'm overwhelmed by the sight of so much blood. "I should've ordered Kai here right away."

"I'm on it." He marches past me, his wings still out, approaching the ones who seem to be the worst off.

I can't believe I ever doubted him. Or Torius. I make a silent vow to make it up to them somehow.

When my mother sees us, she runs over to hug me, then turns to my mate. "Quinn, will you tend to the gnomes? Some of the children have been asking for you."

"Of course." Quinn puts a hand to her chest while emotional tears fill her eyes.

She leaves me with a quick caress to my forearm, and when

she makes it to the group of little people, she kneels down and they swarm her. There's got to be thirty of them. It's the biggest group hug I've ever seen.

When Quinn stands, she's hefting Fiona in her arms. "I bet you're all hungry. Let's go find some pudding, huh?"

The gnomes' excited chattering fades away as she leads them through the door that goes to the kitchen.

"They love her," Mother says, affection in her voice.

"And she loves them back. Are they okay?"

"Overworked and exhausted, but yes."

"The females?" I'm almost afraid to hear the answer.

Mother confirms my fear when she frowns and looks down at the floor. "Some are untouched. Others weren't so lucky."

Father comes over, his dark hair still a tangled mess from battle. Blood is smeared and splattered on his body from head to toe. I'm not sure if any of it is his, but I don't see wounds on him.

"You look well." I embrace him with a few manly claps on the back.

"That's because I am. Not a scratch, my son." His confidence could be mistaken as cockiness, but my father is one of the best warriors I've ever known. He's just being honest. "We were victorious today."

"So I heard." When we separate, my eyes find Zander.

He's sitting on my father's throne. His head is hanging down and inky black hair hides his face. The shirt he has on is dark blue with gold buttons and his pants are black leather.

I cock my head to the side. I find it odd that he wears Night Realm clothing.

A crown is in his grasp, and he turns it in his hands. Memorizing it by touch, he bumps his fingers over the light jewels and the designs etched into the gold.

I wonder if he wants to be king, or if this is a burden to him. He could let his mother rule as a lone queen, but I'm not sure if their people would respect a human fae. Discrimination is still very much an issue in the Day Realm, and having special powers is a deciding factor in social status there. As far as I know, Rowan has none.

Come to think of it, I don't know what Zander's fae ability is. Maybe he doesn't have one either. After all, he inherited his mother's olive skin and dark hair. Lack of power would explain why his father didn't want him involved in physical altercations.

"A victory for us is a loss for them." My father tosses a concerned glance at Zander. "A very big loss."

"Care to elaborate?"

"I couldn't have won without Zander's help."

"History repeats itself," my mother interjects sadly, pressing close to my father's side. "My brother suffered the same fate as my father. Zarid was killed by his own son."

Surprised, my eyebrows shoot up. "Zander killed Zarid?"

Father makes a sound of confirmation. "Zander wasn't even supposed to be there today. You know Zarid never let him fight."

I do know. It's one of the reasons I've seen so little of my cousin. Zarid ruled his kingdom with an iron fist, and that included his own wife and son. They were like his captives, always under his thumb.

"A griffin swooped down out of nowhere," my father continues, his light-blue eyes wide with horror. "Everyone was so busy fighting they didn't see him until it was too late. He went straight for Zarid. He—he snapped his head off with one bite. Completely decapitated."

I couldn't be more confused.

"Talon?" I ask, a little disturbed by how shaken my father is by this. Not much phases him, so it must've been bad.

His eyes narrow. "Who?"

"Damon's griffin," I clarify. "It's the only one I know of. Large beak, white wings, lion ass."

"No. This one had black wings, and it was no pet. It was Zander."

Stunned, I cough. "Excuse me?"

"Zander. After it was done, he shifted to human form, naked as the day he was born, covered in his father's blood."

As Quinn would say, *holy shit*. "He can shift?"

"Into a griffin, apparently." Father nods. "I've never heard of a fae being able to do that."

"Me neither."

"After Zander appeared, he ordered all his men to retreat. He helped us find our people. He's the real hero here."

"And that's why he's wearing borrowed clothes," I conclude, looking at my cousin with new appreciation. "I'll go have a word with him."

As I approach Zander, I study him. Most of his father's blood has been cleaned off, but there are remnants left on his neck and ears. His shoulders are slumped, and I have sympathy for him. No matter how strained his relationship with his father was, it couldn't have been easy to do what he did.

That could've been me sitting alone with my guilt and sorrow. It would've been, if it wasn't for Quinn.

"King Zander," I greet my cousin formally, taking a seat next to him on my throne. "I can't thank you enough for what you've done for my kingdom. We're in your debt."

"No, King Kirian," he responds flatly, void of emotion. "You don't owe me anything."

"I do," I insist. "I'm grateful for your bravery and your sacrifice."

"No offense, but I didn't murder my father for you." He finally looks in my direction, his golden eyes unfocused, just like mine used to be.

But I see relief there.

I mistook his posture for remorse, and now I understand the reality. "You hated him that much, huh?"

"Yes. But it wasn't for myself either. I did this for my mother."

"Queen Rowan asked you to do this?"

"No." Letting out a humorless chuckle, Zander runs a hand over the side of his head where his hair is buzzed. Since it's so hot in the Day Realm, shorter hair styles are common. Men typically keep a few inches on top, and he spears his fingers through the dark strands there. "She hated him, but she's too tender-hearted to wish death on anyone. I made the decision on my own. That bastard kidnapped her from the human realm, threw her in a harem full of other unwilling women, and the only reason he picked her as his mate is because she's the one who got pregnant first."

"I'm aware of the history." If there's one thing I hate hearing about, it's a man forcing himself on a woman.

I glance over at the females on the stairs. Intermittently, their families are being ushered in to retrieve them. The reunions are tear-filled and bittersweet. While the girls are happy to be reunited with their loved ones, their haunted eyes tell of unspeakable crimes against them.

When I hunt down the men who bought them like merchandise, they'll pay with their lives.

"I felt his spine sever." Zander makes a slicing motion across his neck. "You know the resistance and the crack of bone?"

"Yes, I do." I've beheaded enough people to know exactly what he's talking about. But none of the people I've killed were family and I didn't do it with my own teeth. Or beak, in his case.

"I enjoyed it," he adds, sounding surprised by his own bloodlust. "That's sick, isn't it?"

I'm not sure how to answer him. King Zarid was a different level of evil. If someone as good-natured as Zander felt the need to end him, then his death was earned.

"You did what you had to do. It's as simple as that." I lean back, relaxing in the seat. "Why take action now, though? Because of all the Night Realm people he took?"

Zander shakes his head. "Because of you."

"Me?"

"Well, you and your mate. I heard the curse is broken. It gave me hope for myself. I can't tell you how many times I've thought of ending my own life, of leaving this cruel world behind. At least if I was dead, I wouldn't have to watch my mother suffer or exist as a useless prince. But now… there's a chance I could be happy."

"Zander," I start, not sure what to say.

I don't know what it's like to have nothing to live for. I've always had Quinn. Even when I didn't know she was my soul mate, she was the best aspect of my life. She gave me something to look forward to. Honestly, I don't know what my mental state might've been if I didn't have her all these years.

Zander holds up a hand to stop me. "I don't want your pity. I'm going to be fine." Sighing, he places the crown on his head. "Let's get down to business, shall we? I've come here in seek of your aid, King Kirian. Though I wouldn't blame you if you turn me down."

"Just Kirian," I request. "We're family. If we can end this rift between our realms, I'll do it. You're not your father, Zander. You'll be a good ruler."

"I wish I had as much faith in myself as you do, but I'm afraid we've got more than one mess on our hands. The distilled Day water—it was my invention." He grimaces. "When all the other men were out training and fighting, I was in the library, studying history and alchemy. I had good intentions, amplifying the concentration of Day water. There are healing powers in it, and with the plague starting up again—"

"The plague is back?" Shit. Shit, shit, shit. "It's the coven. They've been causing trouble."

He gives a curt nod. "The first case popped up over a year ago. It's affected about a hundred females in the southern part of the realm. Ninety-five deaths—the same mortality rate as last time. We've tried to contain it by quarantine. While that's helped to slow it down, it hasn't stopped the spread. Yet another village got hit last month. All those mothers, sisters, wives… lost."

"The water—this Glow—does it heal them?"

"No. That's the worst of it. It doesn't work. I created a dangerous concoction that doesn't even help for the reason which it was created. Word has gotten out now. Everyone wants some. Secret distilleries are popping up every day. There's an underground network of distributors."

"So you have an incurable plague, a widespread addiction problem, and witches who are after your fated mate," I sum it up.

"My fated mate?" He turns a pointy ear toward me, as if he didn't hear me correctly. "She's in danger?"

"I have reason to believe so. You wouldn't happen to know who she is? Where she is?"

"Not a clue."

"Well, there's a chance the witches don't either. I can't say for sure. But when they find out… Let's just say it'd be best if you got to her first."

"Strike," he mutters under his breath, scratching the dark scruff on his jaw. The static electricity from his profanity sparks against my shoulder, and he sends me an apologetic look. "Sorry. And on top of everything, the female auctions still continue. I assume they'll only get worse now that the sickness is back."

"How can we assist you?"

"Soldiers and doctors would be a start. But no female fae. It's too dangerous for them to be around the disease."

"I know a troll who might be able to lend his medical services. He was already knowledgeable about the distilled Day water. I'll have Torius round up a team. You'll get what you need."

"Thank you." Zander heaves out a breath, seeming lighter as he sits up straight.

"I want to help." Quinn's soft voice comes from behind me, and I roll my eyes to the ceiling.

This infuriating girl. I knew she was near. I felt the vibrations in my soul, but I simply assumed she wanted to listen to our conversation, not offer herself up as a sacrifice. Although she isn't fae yet, there's no guarantee she wouldn't catch this illness.

I grit my teeth. "I forbid it, Quinn."

Coming closer, she places her hand on my shoulder and levels me with those chocolate eyes. "I'm queen now, right?"

I know where she's going with this, and I won't have it. "Yes, but my answer is still no."

"I didn't come to start a lovers' quarrel," Zander interrupts, holding his hands out in a placating gesture as he gets to his feet. "Besides, the Day Realm might be too dangerous for you anyway. There will be backlash for my father's death. He had many faithful followers who enjoyed his lack of law enforcement. They'll likely retaliate."

His discouraging speech seems to instill doubt in Quinn.

Frowning, she asks, "Will there be a civil war?"

"Possibly. While I appreciate your offer, the soldiers and doctors are all we require for now." A half-smile ticks up on his face. "Just enjoy each other. I know I would if I'd found my mate."

As he walks away, I pull Quinn onto my lap and nuzzle her neck. Inhaling her sweet scent, I practically purr as my hands roam her thighs.

"Kirian. People are looking at us," she scolds lightly.

"Let them watch. Let them see how much I love my mate."

Giggling, she leans back, giving me a view of her beautiful face. I brush a thumb over her freckled cheek before tracing a pattern over the bridge of her nose.

When I touch a few spots above her mouth, she licks her lips. Her tongue grazes my finger, and my cock roars to life.

"The gnomes," she starts, trying to distract me. "They're asleep in the kitchen. After finishing off three gallons of butterscotch pudding and some scones, they couldn't keep their eyes open."

"Good." I decide to stop torturing us both and keep my hands still, because she's right—we have serious matters to discuss.

"The girls." Quinn anxiously chews her lip. "Should I go talk to them? I don't know what to say."

We both look over to see the noble family who sheltered Quinn while I tried to defeat Gia. They collect their daughter, who seems to be the youngest of the bunch.

"Her name is Isla," my mate tells me, her eyes filled with worry. "She needs therapy or something. They all do."

Anger flares in me again, but I push it down. I need to be calm and rational right now.

Strategic.

"Let's let their families take them home first," I murmur. "We'll call a council meeting to discuss how we should proceed. Above all else, our kingdom needs justice."

"Our kingdom," she repeats, giving me a soft smile. "I like the sound of that."

I plant a swift kiss on her lips. "Get used to it, my queen."

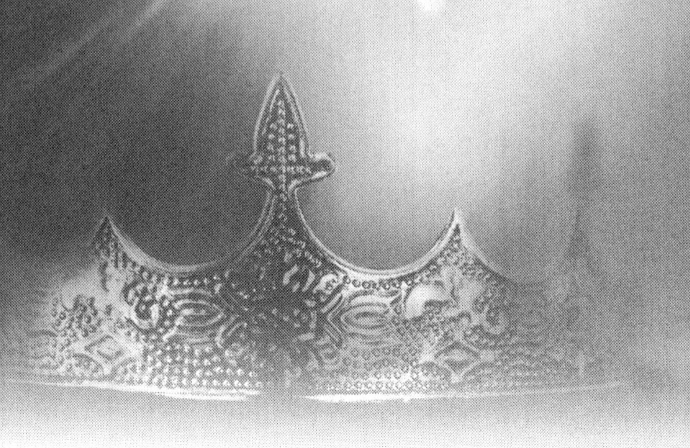

EPILOGUE

Quinn

Three weeks later

"YOUR MAJESTY, STOP PEEKING," ISLA HISSES, fussing over my hair. "Someone might see you."

Quirking an eyebrow, I shoot her an amused look. "Are you sure no one's allowed to see me in my dress before the ceremony? Where I come from, it's just the groom."

"I'm sure. The groom has to see you before anyone else. Or the union could be jinxed."

"Except for you," I tease. "You saw me."

Wrinkling her nose, she doesn't seem to catch my playful tone. "I'm your lady in waiting. That's different."

Kirian and I are fated mates. Our relationship is the epitome of good luck and fortune, and I highly doubt it would change simply because a guest caught a premature glimpse of me.

But I decide to humor my attendant, dropping the curtain as she goes back to placing honeysuckle flowers in my half-updo.

The wedding traditions here are similar to the human realm, but some of them are just slightly off. It's almost like someone played a game of telephone, and certain details got lost in translation.

As Isla concentrates on getting every strand of hair on my head just right, I study her youthful face. Her porcelain skin is framed by long blond hair, and she's so serious. I wonder if she was like that before the Day Realm clusterfuck, or if she's been irrevocably changed because of it.

During the council meeting we had about the victims the day after their return, I'd suggested everyone get two special requests. One for justice and one for personal gain.

I quickly learned fae justice is very different than where I come from.

Not pulling any punches, Isla had asked that her rapist be publicly executed—beheaded, not spiked, which was a mercy on her part. Wish granted. And she wasn't the only one who chose that fate for her attacker. Many of the men who bought the females didn't waste any time trying to impregnate them. They had to be punished.

Although I was happy those bastards got what they deserved and the women got closure, I stayed inside on that bloody day. I just can't stomach such gory scenes.

Isla's second request was to be given a high position in the castle, and Kirian suggested a personal companion for me. At fifteen, she's old enough to be hired by the palace. I'll admit I was skeptical in the beginning. I wasn't sure if she'd stare at my freckles or judge me for not having pointy ears. But she's been nothing but respectful, and now I honestly don't know how I could go a day without her assistance. She knows I hate dresses with corsets, how I like my tea, and all my favorite foods. Although we have cultural differences, I've been enjoying her company.

"It's just so pretty out there," I say, turning so she can stick one more pin in the braids at the back of my head. "It's hard not to look."

"Believe me, I want to peek, too. Dawn and Dusk is beyond my wildest imagination. But we have three more minutes, so we'll just have to wait. Sorry, Queen Quinn."

"Just Quinn," I remind her.

I can't get used to people calling me Queen. I still think the title plus my name sounds ridiculous. Maybe someday it won't bother me, but for now, I prefer something less formal.

"One last thing." Isla's yellow eyes glitter with excitement as she wiggles her fingers in the air.

A small box lifts from a stool in our canvas tent. I gawk as it floats over to us. Seriously, I'm not sure when I'll stop being shocked by her power to move objects.

It lands gently in my hands. When I open the wooden lid, I gasp when I see the necklace nestled on a bed of dark-blue velvet. "My marble."

Golden prongs hold onto the sphere, and it dangles from a shiny chain. I pick it up, pressing the smooth glass to my palm. I roll it back and forth against my skin and smile.

Grinning, Isla claps her hands. "Surprise! It was my idea. King Kirian has one, too. You match. Isn't that great? These will be your objects of commitment."

Kirian had explained to me that we wouldn't exchange rings. Instead, we'd have something more meaningful. Something totally personal to us.

"Thank you," I breathe out, touched. "I couldn't have thought of anything better than this."

My compliment makes Isla do a happy jig, and I'm glad to see her smiling. Maybe we're good for each other. She's told me before that I give her motivation to keep going, and I admire her determination to move on. If I'd gone through what she did, I'm not sure I'd be able to bounce back so quickly.

She's resilient, creative, and *oh my God*.

I think I have a friend. A real, female friend, close to my age.

When I jump forward to hug her, she squeaks with surprise, but it only takes her a second to return the embrace.

I never thought I'd be the kind of person who cries on my wedding day, but I sniffle as my nose begins to sting.

A barrage of emotions suddenly hit me. I'm incredibly happy. I have the love of my life, all the luxury I could ask for, and people who are becoming important to me.

But I'm also a little sad. This is such a big moment, and my parents aren't here to witness it. It's only been a month since the spaghetti and meatball dinner, and I already miss them so much.

"There, there." Isla pats my back. As if she can read my mind, she adds, "We all think of you as part of us. You belong here. Your kingdom is your family."

The neck prickle happens, and I can feel the truth to her words.

Turns out, I really do have a power and it's extremely useful.

I'm a living lie-detector test.

Kirian's had me sit in on several interrogations already. Instead of torturing the truth out of someone, he looks to me. I can just give a nod or a shake of my head, and he decides what to do from there.

People have been calling me the Queen of Honesty, and I gotta say—I kinda like the nickname.

In the distance, a harp and a flute begin playing music, signaling the start of the ceremony.

I pull away from Isla as I wipe the wetness from under my eyes. I'm not wearing much makeup, but I don't want to ruin the little I have on.

"One last check. Everything has to be perfect." Isla flits around me, smoothing the white silk of my gown and fluffing the short train. She makes sure the pearl buttons in the back are secured, she runs her fingers over where the waist is cinched with a stardust belt, and she adjusts the gauzy shoulder straps.

"This is really happening," I mutter to myself as she clasps the new necklace on me.

"Yes, it is." A honeysuckle bouquet is shoved into my hands, and then Isla grasps my shoulders, turning me so I can see myself in a full-length mirror.

Well. I'm stunning. Shimmery stardust acts as my eyeshadow. My lashes are coated with mascara. I chose a dusky rose pink for my lips. My freckles aren't covered, and I wear them proudly now.

"Beautiful and ready," Isla announces, partly for me but mostly for the guards standing outside the tent. She gives my shoulder a pat. "Smash a leg."

Biting my lip to hide a smile, I don't tell her the saying is actually "break a leg" and it's meant for show business, not weddings.

The canvas flaps part to reveal my entourage of a dozen soldiers, including Torius and Kai. They all have their backs turned and their eyes averted, because Kirian's walking toward me to get the first look.

And boy, does he look.

His heated gaze roams my body from head to toe as he licks his lips.

My nipples pucker beneath the smooth fabric, and I know he can see them because I'm not wearing a bra. As his eyes zero in on that part of me, his pupils dilate until the lavender is almost completely black.

I like that he's out of his battle clothes. With his white button-up shirt and light-colored pants, it reminds me of what he used to wear when he'd come visit me in my forest. His hair is still short on the sides, and he has tight braids along his scalp. Probably Astrid's doing. I wouldn't be surprised if she coaxed him in to playing beauty salon.

"Are you ready?" He offers his elbow, and I slide my hand through the crook of his arm.

"Never been readier."

The music changes when he leads me out of the tent, but the new melody isn't coming from the instruments. As the insects join in with our song, I give Kirian a knowing smile.

Of course he'd play our own music.

We pass the serious soldiers, and I can't help but give Kai a little crap. He might look grumpy as fuck, but he's actually pretty cool. "Hey, Kai. Ever heard of resting bitch face?"

A thoughtful expression replaces his frown. "No, I don't know this bitch. Who is she?"

I laugh. "Never mind."

We'll have to work on his human lingo another time.

Smirking, Kirian covers my hand and draws me closer. I rest my head on his bicep while we walk on a deserted path between rows of trees blooming with turquoise flowers.

This part is just for us. Our quiet moment. Aside from Isla and the soldiers standing back at the tent, we're alone.

Up ahead, there's a stone staircase built into the incline of the ground. It's tradition for fated couples to climb it together, and I swear I can feel some kind of power in the air as we place our feet on the first step.

"Is Dawn and Dusk as beautiful as you remember it to be?" I ask, looking up at the sky through the trees above.

Half of it is day and half is night. The place down the middle where the two merge is a clash of light and color, making it look like a rainbow Aurora Borealis.

The light here has a pinkish hue, casting a warm glow over everything.

Mist floats in the forest around us, and Kirian already told me it comes from one of the many waterfalls. The air has a sweet smell to it, and unique colorful flowers I've never seen before are sprouting up everywhere—from the ground, out of the tree bark, even the rocks.

Later, we'll be staying in a special cave. It's a place just for the royals on their honeymoon. Since it's behind a waterfall, we'll have mist to drink. Exotic fruit and leafy vegetables grow from the rocks, so we'll have plenty to eat. We won't have to leave for days.

No visitors. No servants. Just us, uninterrupted.

"Yes." Kirian's gaze darts around us, unable to stay focused on one thing for long. "I was worried this place wouldn't look the same. Maybe I'd built it up in my mind to be something it isn't. But it's actually better this time around. I appreciate it more because you're here with me."

Grinning, I press a kiss to his arm. A silent thanks for loving me. For always coming back to me. For just being him.

When we get to the top of the stairs, I see a trellis at the end of the aisle. The archway is covered in ivy and midnight roses—a wedding gift from the gnomes. Speaking of my little friends, they're among our guests, along with our family and friends.

When everyone notices us, they get up from their chairs and I'm incredibly happy to see all the familiar faces.

Even Zander decided to come as a show of peace between our kingdoms. It's selfless of him, considering the turmoil going on in the Day Realm. He's taking time away from his people to be here for us.

Although, his problems are our problems, too.

The Glow addiction is getting out of control. Just last week, Kirian's soldiers busted a distillery in the Night Realm, and there've been reports of volatile incidents involving amplified fae powers in Delaveria and Aelustria.

For the first time in thousands of years, there's actually a shortage of soldiers. They're just spread too thin.

Damon even mentioned putting his mission to find his mate on hold. Poor guy. He's standing at the front, fulfilling his role as Kirian's best man, and Astrid is on the other side as my maid of honor. I've never seen her look so happy. Or colorful. There's a big smile on her face and she's traded out her drab gray dress for a neon pink gown with bright yellow trim. I don't know if she's trying to upstage me—I wouldn't put it past her—but I'd told her I didn't care what she wore as long as it wasn't made out of hair.

The whimsical song comes to an end, and a new tune begins for our wedding march. My nerves kick in full force. Everyone's staring at me, and I hate being the center of attention.

Needing something to calm me, I glance up at Kirian to find him staring at my face.

A grin tugs at my lips. I keep my gaze locked with his, blocking everyone else out as we move forward.

I like that Kirian's the one to walk me down the aisle.

Here, that's what mates do.

There's no one to 'give me away' because I'm already his. I've always been his, and he's mine.

We'll take this walk *together*, because this is how we intend to live our lives—side by side.

And, apparently, we don't need a flower girl, because Kirian's got this. Pink petals shower down from the trees, sprinkling us with his magic.

My new in-laws are the officiators. When we get to them, Zella tells us to clasp hands. I barely listen to Keryth reciting the ancient words in a language I can't understand, and I'm still gazing into Kirian's eyes when the crown is placed on my head.

All hail me as queen.

That was fast. I didn't realize the ceremony was going to be so quick, but I'm glad. Now we're getting to the good part.

Kirian steps closer because it's time for us to kiss. It's a little backward to do this before the vows, but whatever.

Cupping my cheek, Kirian leans down and rests his

forehead against mine, like he wants to savor this moment. His shirt parts, and his marble necklace catches a glint of light right before he presses a light kiss to my lips.

Compared to all our other kisses, it's chaste and innocent, but from the way his teeth graze my bottom lip, I can tell there's more to come. Much more, once we're in the privacy of our cave.

He nips my mouth one more time before straightening to his full height.

Then we say the promise we've already made to each other—the one that will last for all eternity.

"From dawn 'til dusk, from dusk 'til dawn, I'll never love another."

THE END

Well… sort of. While Kirian and Quinn get their HEA, there are still issues to be resolved in Valora, and two kings who need to find their fated mates before the coven does. Damon's story is coming later this year! To get updates on my books, please sign up for my newsletter.

OTHER BOOKS BY JAMIE SCHLOSSER

Good Guys Series:

TRUCKER

A Trucker Christmas (Short Story)

DANCER

DROPOUT

OUTCAST

MAGIC MAN

The Good Guys Box Set

The Night Time Television Series:

Untamable

Untrainable

Unattainable

Standalone Novellas:

His Mimosa

Sweet Dreams

Between Dawn and Dusk Series:

Between Dawn and Dusk

The Fae King's Curse

ABOUT THE AUTHOR

Jamie Schlosser writes steamy new adult romance and romantic comedy. When she isn't creating perfect book boyfriends, she's a stay-at-home mom to her two wonderful kids. She believes reading is a great escape, otters are the best animal, and nothing is more satisfying than a happily-ever-after ending. You can find out more about Jamie and her books by visiting these links:

Facebook: www.facebook.com/authorjamieschlosser
Amazon: amzn.to/2mzCQkQ
Bookbub: www.bookbub.com/authors/jamie-schlosser
Newsletter: eepurl.com/cANmI9
Website: www.jamieschlosser.com

Also, do you like being the first to get sneak peeks on upcoming books? Do you like exclusive giveaways? Most importantly, do you like otters?

If you answered yes to any of these questions, you should consider joining Jamie Schlosser's Significant Otters!
www.facebook.com/groups/1738944743038479

Printed in Great Britain
by Amazon

79891421R00192